Charlotte Pass

In 2009, former corporate trainer Lee Christine decided to turn her writing hobby into a serious day job. *Charlotte Pass* is her first crime novel. She lives in Newcastle, New South Wales, with her husband and her Irish Wheaten Terrier. To read more about Lee Christine visit leechristine.com.au.

LEE CHRISTINE

Charlotte Pass

ALLEN&UNWIN
SYDNEY · MELBOURNE · AUCKLAND · LONDON

First published in 2020

Allen & Unwin
83 Alexander Street
Crows Nest NSW 2065
Australia
Phone: (61 2) 8425 0100
Email: info@allenandunwin.com
Web: www.allenandunwin.com

 A catalogue record for this book is available from the National Library of Australia

ISBN 978 1 76087 729 3

Set in 11/15 pt Sabon by Midland Typesetters, Australia
Printed and bound in Australia by Griffin Press, part of Ovato

10 9 8 7 6 5 4 3 2

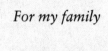

For my family

Prologue

July 1964
Charlotte Pass, Australia

They had to jump, or die.

For it to all end like this, suspended in the pitch dark above the unforgiving terrain, hands gripping the safety bar as the chair bounced up and down on the cable—it wasn't an ending he had ever imagined. He and Celia, their dead bodies frozen together like two ice carvings, only discovered once the blizzard had subsided.

Fucking chairlift.

He loosened his grip on the safety bar as the wind died down and the rattling of the protective canopy lessened. The unusually designed chairlift had been an engineering failure from the beginning, a poorly designed mess of metal plagued by one problem after another. He should have foreseen this, should never have taken the risk that the chair would get them into Thredbo before the storm came rolling in. But Celia had been desperate to get out of Charlotte Pass.

He tugged his scarf higher to cover the lower half of his face and inhaled some warm carbon dioxide. He could barely make Celia out under the protective canopy that was fitted over the chair, much less see out through the small rectangular viewing pane. But he could feel her beside him, and he could hear her voice in the lull between gusts.

1

Teeth chattering, her body shaking, she was reciting Hail Marys with the piety of the blindly devout. That's what happened when people lost all hope. They prayed.

'We have to jump!' he shouted as another burst of wind rocked the tiny capsule. 'We stay up here, we die.'

'No . . . I can't.'

'You can, Celia. You will. You have to.' He groped in the dark, his ski goggles bumping hers before he found her arm and curled his fingers around her wrist until she cried out. 'That crash we just heard—it was a chair up front falling off the cable.'

He waited for her to speak, staring into the tomb-like darkness.

'I want to stay here,' she whimpered. 'Someone might come.'

She started praying again. The Lord's Prayer this time.

He edged away from the freezing steel framework of the chair and sat in a tight tuck to preserve his body heat. Chin resting on his chest, hands shoved beneath his thighs, he contemplated the drop. Twenty feet, maybe twenty-five, judging by the seconds he'd counted when he'd unbuckled his skis a while back and let them fall to the ground.

His bowels moved as he pictured the giant boulders and twisted snow gums beneath them. Landing on Mount Stillwell would be brutal, the odds of survival slim. But the alternative . . .

He wriggled his feet inside his ski boots and counted how many toes he could feel. None. Pain speared through his fingers like a hundred needles. His throat burned with every breath.

Celia's rosary turned into a cry as another sub-Antarctic air mass built around the peaks of Mount Kosciuszko, arriving in a freezing squall of snow and sleet, howling through Charlotte Pass with a roar that sent the hapless chair swinging sideways in the darkness. Celia whimpered as her body fell against his, pushing him against the side of the chair. All around, the steel pylons of this, the so-called longest chairlift in the world, swayed and groaned.

And then the wind dropped suddenly, just enough for the chair to right itself momentarily, but Celia clawed at the front of his ski jacket, begging him to do something, or not do something—he couldn't tell.

'I'm going to raise the canopy,' he shouted. 'We'll go together.'

'No! Wait—'

But before she could say anything more, he raised the steel canopy against the onslaught. The blizzard slammed into him, ice pellets stinging his cheeks and forehead. He blinked away the freezing water seeping inside his goggles, until finally he tore them from his head, his beanie going with them. As they fell away into the blackness, he hauled Celia towards him and dragged her, kicking, punching and screaming onto his lap before pinning her against his torso with his arms. She went quiet, paralysed by fear and the inevitability of what was about to happen.

He raised the safety bar and gritted his teeth, shifted onto the edge of the seat and pictured the rocky slope in his mind's eye. When the chair tipped forward he launched their bodies as one into the blackness.

And he prayed.

Prayed Celia's body would break his fall.

One

Detective Sergeant Pierce Ryder strode into the meeting room on the first floor of the Queanbeyan Police Station, his newly appointed partner of three days, Detective Constable Mitchell Flowers, right behind him. They'd had a good run down the Hume Highway from Sydney, though the tension in the car had made the drive seem longer than it was.

To Ryder's way of thinking, Flowers should have been a woman. Ryder knew of at least three female Detective Constables whose insight and intuition would have been an asset to Sydney's Homicide Squad. Unfortunately, the women had been placed elsewhere, so Ryder was now teamed with a millennial who ate activated charcoal gluten-free bread, and whose main ambition was to become a police prosecutor.

The decision still irked Ryder.

Inside the meeting room, a group of local officers and detectives were standing close to the windows, drawn to the weak fingers of sunlight slanting through the glass. Flowers closed the door firmly behind him, and the buzz of conversation began to wane.

Ryder took his place at the front of the room and waited while the men of various age, size and rank settled themselves into chairs.

'Morning everyone,' he said as he placed his laptop on the front table.

'It's afternoon, Sarge.'

Ryder suppressed a sigh. That'd be right. The country cops sticking it to the city boys before he'd even started the briefing. Ryder looked up, ready to tick off whichever smartarse was getting stuck into him—only to see the twinkling eyes of Detective David Benson. Ryder had first met Benson at the academy and they'd been stationed in Newcastle together before Benson transferred down here.

Ryder smiled. 'Good to see you again, Benson,' he said, checking his watch. 'You're right. It is indeed past midday.' Reaching for the laser pointer, he scanned the other faces, but only Benson's was familiar. 'For those of you who don't know me, I'm Detective Sergeant Ryder from Sydney Homicide, and sitting behind you is my partner, Detective Constable Flowers.'

Ryder shot a look at Flowers while the men glanced over their shoulders. Homicide's latest recruit was slouching in his chair looking unimpressed despite the briefing being as much for his benefit as for the others. He was probably annoyed at having to leave the metropolitan area and his smashed avo breakfasts. Doubting he would ever share the same camaraderie he'd had with his former partner, Macca, Ryder launched into their reason for being at Monaro Local Area Command.

'Gavin Hutton.' He clicked on the first slide, and a head shot of a man appeared on the pull-down screen. 'According to our sketch software, Hutton could look like this.' The fugitive had a long face partly covered by limp, dishevelled hair and an unshaven jaw. 'A former member of the Australian army, Hutton is wanted in Sydney in connection with the murder of a homeless man. He's also our main suspect in the murder of another man whose body was found in a Goulburn park. Despite extensive manhunts following both murders, our investigations have stalled.' Ryder looked at the photo. 'To date, Hutton's been a ghost. There's no trail, paper or electronic—at least none we've managed to uncover.'

He waited for a few seconds before clicking to the next slide.

It was a map covering the area between Jindabyne in New South Wales and Mount Beauty in Victoria's high country.

'In the past month, Jindabyne Police have received several reports of a man sleeping rough. He was glimpsed running from a machine shed on a property here in Khancoban.' Ryder used his laser pointer to mark the spot. 'Another owner found a makeshift bed of straw and old blankets inside a disused barn on his property. That was down here around Tom Groggin Station.'

Ryder clicked over to the next slide. It was another map, this time of the narrow Alpine Way. 'Then, yesterday, four snowboarders set off from their campsite at Dead Horse Gap. They hiked up to Eagles Nest and took the chairlift from the summit down into the village. The group ate lunch and then walked back along the Alpine Way to their campsite. They found two sleeping bags were missing, along with their food, matches and the vehicle's first-aid kit. Inside the ute were wallets and other valuable items. They were untouched.'

The detectives exchanged sideways glances. Even Flowers lost his bored expression and straightened in his chair.

'This is consistent with what we know of Hutton. If it's him, he's not purchasing anything. He's not showing his face. He's taking what he needs to survive.'

A sudden gust of wind rattled the aluminium-framed windows. Ryder moved to check out the weather. Ominous clouds hung low in the sky and, down on the street, dried leaves from the trees surrounding Brad Haddin Oval scuttled along the gutter like cockroaches. A hamburger wrapper, tossed into the air on a gust of wind, snagged on a hanging street banner advertising Winterfest.

Ryder's stomach gave a hungry growl. Or was it another pang of nicotine withdrawal? After ten weeks he still had trouble distinguishing between the two.

He turned back to face the men. 'It's been a slow start to the ski season but the weather's coming in now. That's good news for Winterfest, but snow will make our job harder. I want a thorough check of all properties along the Alpine Way. Question the owners.

I'll need evidence of more camps or a guaranteed sighting before I can throw all our resources behind this.'

'That's a lot of ground to cover,' Benson said, his eyes on the map. 'Will the uniform boys up in Jindy be giving us a hand?'

'No. They'll be out on the roads in force.'

A loud knock silenced the conversation and the door swung open to admit a slightly built, grey-haired man with silver spectacles. The man beckoned for Ryder to step outside.

Leaving the laser pointer on the table, Ryder spoke to Flowers. 'Run off the image of Hutton so the boys can take it with them.' He headed for the door, towards the unexpected visitor. 'I want all freestanding garages, work sheds and barns scoured and searched. And don't forget treehouses and cubbyhouses.'

A chair scraped across the floor, someone stretched and yawned, others reached for their mobile phones.

'Lew, what the hell are you doing here?' Ryder said as he stepped into the corridor and closed the door behind him, turning to face his one-time mentor and long-time friend, former Inspector Roman Lewicki. 'How's Annie?'

'Nice to see you too,' Lewicki retorted, gesturing for Ryder to accompany him down the corridor. 'Annie's fine. Coming down here got me out of the grocery shopping, and that's a good thing. Bores me shitless, it does.'

Ryder matched his pace to Lewicki's slower one. 'Does she know how much you hate it?'

'She doesn't care. I trail after her with a trolley like a brain-dead puppy. Then I wait while she studies ten different types of olive oil. Olive oil! I swear, one day I'll kick the bucket in that aisle.'

'You're an ungrateful bastard. Annie deserves a medal for putting up with you. You realise it's her good cooking that's keeping you alive?'

'Which reminds me, she said to get your arse over to our place for dinner one night while you're gracing the alps with your presence.'

'Annie wouldn't say "arse".'

'She misses you.'

'I bet she does, having only you for company.' Ryder had often wondered how Lewicki would manage if anything happened to Annie. There'd only ever been the two of them. He glanced at his friend. 'You're not regretting your decision to retire and move back here, are you?'

'Not a chance. Sydney never felt like home to us. I miss the thrill of the chase sometimes, though.' He shot Ryder a glance. 'What's been happening in the big smoke since I left?'

'Enough to keep us flat out.' Ryder frowned. 'Why are you here, Lew?'

Lewicki pointed a bony finger towards a hallway branching off to the right. 'We're going to Hendo's office.'

Ryder smiled. Even to his face, Lewicki called Senior Sergeant Gil Henderson 'Hendo' knowing full well the lack of respect would get up Henderson's nose. Lewicki had never approved of Henderson's fast-track promotion through Monaro Local Area Command after Lew had vacated the position a dozen years ago to take an Inspector's job in Sydney.

They halted as a young Constable came rushing out of the ladies' bathroom. 'Oh, excuse me,' she said, straightening her jacket and flashing a smile at Ryder.

Lewicki stepped aside. 'After you, my dear.'

The woman flushed, and with another glance at Ryder continued on her way.

'I think she likes you,' Lew said as they approached Henderson's door.

'Yeah? Well, she can keep dreamin'.'

Lewicki stopped in his tracks, a frown creasing his forehead. 'When are you going to settle down again? You're two years off forty.'

For fuck's sake. 'When are you going to tell me what's going on?' Ryder growled, glancing around and making sure no one was in earshot. 'And who are you, my mother?'

Lewicki smirked and hitched his thumb over his shoulder. 'What's your new partner like?'

'He's twenty-six, drinks turmeric lattes and lives with his parents.'

'Give the bloke a chance.'

'You go talk to him. He'll tell you how your generation screwed the country over.'

With a wry smile Lewicki rapped on Henderson's door. He pointed at Ryder. 'Don't go back to Sydney without seeing Annie. She wants to make you a cake for your birthday.' Then without waiting for an invitation, Lewicki stepped into the Senior Sergeant's office.

Henderson looked up from his desk, his arctic, blue-eyed gaze singling Ryder out as he followed Lewicki. 'Pierce, have a seat. Good of you to join us.'

'Sir.' Ryder couldn't remember Lew ever greeting him in such a way for turning up when summoned. But Henderson came from police royalty, whereas Lewicki's father had been a Polish immigrant recruited to build the Snowy Hydro Electric Scheme after World War Two.

'Sorry, I was in a rush when you arrived. We've had a busy morning.'

Ryder studied the Senior Sergeant across the expanse of desk. Henderson wore his air of entitlement as easily as he wore his well-tailored uniform. He was known for pressing the flesh with the fat cats in Canberra, and Ryder, along with everyone on the Force, had heard the talk about Henderson having his eye on a political career following his retirement.

Turning in his swivel chair, Henderson picked up a bulky file from the credenza behind him and put it on the desk. 'This morning, bones believed to be human were discovered up at Charlotte Pass.' He glanced at Ryder. 'I phoned Roman right away.'

Charlotte Pass. A shiver ran up Ryder's spine. So, that was why Lew was here.

Henderson cleared his throat as though he were about to make a speech. 'A ski patroller working on the mountain discovered them. They're high up on the slope of Mount Stillwell.'

'Did he cordon off the area?' Ryder asked.

'*She.* Vanessa Bell.' Henderson scanned a report sheet. 'According to this, she roped off the area with hazard fencing, then radioed it in to the mountain manager. He called the village doctor, who phoned us.'

'The ski patroller must have known they were human to do that.' Ryder rubbed a hand across his jaw and looked at Lewicki, but his friend's eyes were trained on the file.

'There's no skull, so she couldn't be sure,' Henderson said. 'One bone looks like a femur and there's some smaller ones that could be ribs.'

'Who formally identified the bones as human, then—the village doctor?'

'That's right.' Henderson closed the file and began tying it up with the coloured ribbon. 'The uniform boys from Jindabyne are there now. They'll stand by until you get there.'

'Until *I* get there?' Ryder needed a smoke, or to press the nicotine patch harder into the skin of his upper arm. In the end, he settled for raking a hand through his hair. 'I'm here to hunt for Gavin Hutton. We think he's crawled out from whatever hole he's been hiding in and is collecting supplies for winter.'

'How many people have gone missing from Charlotte Pass over the decades?' Lewicki barked the question at Ryder.

'Over the decades? I could probably count them on one hand.'

'Five. And three of those bodies were recovered.'

Ryder paused. He knew exactly where this conversation was going. 'You really think it could be her?'

'Yes, or that bushwalker who disappeared a few years back.'

'But that's *her* file, right there, on the desk.'

There was a determined spark in Lewicki's eye. Ryder pulled in a deep breath and huffed it out again. He knew that Lew wouldn't let go of this, not while there was a chance the bones were those of Celia Delaney. This was the man who'd returned to Charlotte Pass after the winter melt in 1964 to tramp all over the mountains searching for her body, the man determined to give her parents closure and himself some peace of mind. Lew had never believed that Celia had lost her way in those mountains. He was haunted by a case that had cast a long shadow over his career. And his life.

'Sixty-four's a long time ago, Lew. If I were a betting man, my money would be on the missing bushwalker. There's no evidence that Celia—'

'You could be right,' Lewicki snapped. 'But I was the one who had to tell Celia's parents time and again that there was no trace of their daughter. It destroyed their lives, and I had to watch that happen. You of all people should understand that.'

Ryder's chest contracted. Hardly able to breathe, he fought to absorb the blow his friend had just delivered. Was this how far, how personal, Lew would go if learning the truth about Celia Delaney was at stake?

'Get yourself organised as soon as possible, Pierce,' Henderson barked, oblivious to the tension between the two men in front of him. 'I've spoken to Sydney. You and Flowers are to go up to Charlotte's. Benson can lead the search for signs of Hutton. You're the best man to take over Roman's old case.'

Ryder opened his mouth to argue, then shut it again. He knew he was the logical choice. Apart from Lew, Ryder knew more about Celia Delaney's disappearance than anyone. How many times had he heard the story—sitting on Lew's back verandah in Castle Hill, drinking Galway Pipe long after Annie had gone to bed? Lost in his own agony, Ryder had absorbed every last investigative detail without even trying.

He stood up and pressed his fingertips into his forehead. How could he refuse this case? He wasn't sure who was issuing the order, Henderson or Sydney Homicide, but it may as well have been Lewicki, the man who'd hauled him up by the shirt collar, backed him against a wall and told him in no uncertain terms that he wasn't special—that everyone had their own horror story to tell and to get the hell on with it.

Ryder leaned forward and spread his fingers over Henderson's perfectly polished desk. With luck they would leave smudge marks. 'What about Hutton? He's killed twice already, and he won't hesitate to do it again if he's cornered.' As much as Ryder owed Lewicki, he was a Homicide detective and Hutton a wanted man—a serious threat to the community. 'Even if Lew's right, and Celia Delaney *was* the victim of foul play, that case is fifty-five years old. The perpetrator's probably dead and no threat to anyone.'

'That's a big assumption, Ryder,' said Lewicki.

Ryder closed his eyes briefly and shook his head. 'Hutton's the biggest case of my career. What if something's missed while I'm up at Charlotte Pass chasing a bunch of bones that could belong to a hiker who didn't take a satellite phone?'

'Then you'll pick up where you left off,' replied Henderson. 'At least we'll know it's not her.'

Lew stood up quickly. 'Unless it is.'

Two

The Rambling Wombat's Kids' Club didn't look at all like the other buildings at Charlotte Pass village. The octagonal windows were adorned with metres of butcher's paper boasting the children's latest crayon masterpieces. Inside the colourful space, twinkling fairy lights dangled from a high raked ceiling.

Vanessa Bell smiled as she watched four-year-old Jake spoon mouthfuls of wobbly green jelly from his Frog-in-a-Pond dessert into his mouth. He was seated at the end of the table closest to where Libby Marken stood, a noticeable gap between him and the other children.

'He has a life-threatening nut allergy,' Libby whispered to Vanessa, turning away and taking an EpiPen from her pocket.

Vanessa looked at the curly-haired little boy with a Harry Potter scarf looped around his neck. 'Must be hard for the parents to relax,' she said in a hushed voice. 'I got lost on the farm once—it trauma-tised my mother for life. She'd still be checking up on me every day if she could, and I'm thirty-three.'

Libby opened a cupboard and took a plastic box labelled 'Medicines' off the top shelf. 'They're confident he'll be well looked after here,' she said, putting Jake's EpiPen inside before returning the box to its place.

'Oh, I'm sure they know. You do a fantastic job running this place, Libby, everyone says so.' Vanessa checked her watch for the umpteenth time. 'How long do you think it will be before those detectives want to talk to me?'

'I have no idea.' Libby gave a shudder. 'You poor thing. It's enough to give anyone nightmares.'

Like Vanessa needed any more of those after what she'd found in the snow.

'You can put the presentation off until tomorrow if you like,' Libby offered. 'It's been an awful shock for you.'

'Thanks, but I need something to distract me.' She reached for the silver snowflake around her neck and ran it up and down the chain. 'I keep wondering who it was. And how did they die—was it quick, or slow and agonising? And what about their poor family?'

'I know. Why don't you give your sister a call when you're done here? She's close by, isn't she?'

Vanessa nodded. 'Thredbo.'

They turned back to the tables and began clearing away the used paper plates, soggy napkins and plastic glasses. 'I really don't want to burden Eva this late,' Vanessa said a few minutes later as they dumped the scraps in the garbage bin. 'She has her hands full with Poppy and running the lodge. How about we go to the bar when you finish here? The instructors are always up for a fishbowl cocktail.'

Libby grinned. 'That's a hangover, not a distraction.'

'Doesn't matter. The thought of going to sleep tonight is freaking me out.'

'The kids will take your mind off it for a bit,' said Libby, leading the way out of the kitchen. 'Listen up, guys,' she called out, clapping loudly as they walked back into the main room. 'We have a very special guest this evening. Everybody, say hello to Vanessa.' Libby waited until the chorus of hellos had died down before proceeding. 'You might have seen Vanessa out on the mountain, or maybe the other ski patroller she works with. You'll recognise them from the super-cool red jackets they wear.'

'Like Santa!' yelled one of the kids.

As the group erupted in laughter, Libby moved aside so Vanessa could take centre stage. Because this was her first season working at Charlotte Pass it was her job to give the safety talk to the kids' club while the other staff headed to the bar at the Charlotte Mountain Inn. Not that she minded. She enjoyed spending time with the kids, and Libby had become a good friend.

'It *is* the same colour as Santa's!' Vanessa feigned surprise, as if it were the first time she'd heard that comment. 'But mine has this symbol on the front and back.' She spun around so the kids could see the white cross on her red zip-up fleece. 'This cross is the medic symbol. It's also on my ski parka. If you or someone you're with gets sick or injured while you're out on the slopes, or maybe you don't know where to go, just look for me or my co-worker Johan in our red jackets. We're always around.'

'And if you can't find a ski patroller, ask a ski instructor or, failing that, an adult,' said Libby.

'Are you a policewoman?' asked a little girl with huge blue eyes and blonde pigtails.

Vanessa smiled. 'Not exactly. But I'm the next best thing.'

'You're the boss?' the little girl persisted.

'Out on the mountain I am. My job is to make sure the resort is safe for you to have fun in, and to help people who might be injured or in trouble.'

'Or lost!' a boy yelled from up the back.

'That's right. You won't get lost if you stay inside the boundary fence.' Vanessa looked around the group of children ranging in age from five to twelve. 'As we all know, skiing and snowboarding are *major* fun, but there are safety rules we need to follow when we're out on the mountain. Does anybody know of a rule from the Skier's Code of Conduct? It's on the back of every bathroom door and on the back of your lift passes. We have lollies if you get one right.'

A young girl in a pink tracksuit put up her hand. 'Give way to people below you.'

'Correct.' Vanessa smiled. 'What's your name, sweetheart?'

'Audrey.'

'As Audrey says, you must give way to people further down the slope than you. They don't have eyes in the back of their heads.' Vanessa curled her hands into fists as though she were holding her stocks and made an exaggerated skiing movement with her hips. 'There you are, skiing away, minding your own business, then *boom*, someone below you on the slope turns right into your path. *Carnage!* Blood and guts everywhere.' She paused, waiting for the excited giggles to die down. You could always count on the kids to laugh at the gruesome stuff. 'That's when I get a call on this,' she said holding up her radio. 'So, it's *very* important to keep an eye on the people below you, and to give them plenty of space. Well done, Audrey. Anyone else know a ski rule?' Vanessa looked around the group as Libby handed a lolly to Audrey. The sweets usually won the kids over. Pretty soon the boys would be making up all sorts of stuff.

'Don't jump off the poma lift halfway up!' yelled a boy who looked to be about eight.

'Woohoo! Good answer. You must never jump off the poma until you reach the unloading area. If a piece of loose clothing gets caught—' she laid her hand lightly on Jake's shoulder '—like this super-cool Harry Potter scarf, it will drag you up the hill. And you can imagine what might happen.'

One of the boys put a hand to his throat and made a choking sound.

'Exactly.' Vanessa pointed at the boy. 'If something horrible like that happens in the unloading area, the lift operator can hit the emergency switch and stop the lift. But if you jump off where no one can see you, you could be in all sorts of trouble.' Vanessa leaned over and high-fived the young boy. 'Give this handsome dude a Freddo, Libby, and—'

'Excuse me.'

Vanessa wheeled around at the sound of a deep voice. A man— tall, wearing a suit, which was definitely not the standard look at Charlotte Pass—was standing inside the door, flecks of snow speckling his dark hair. The wind had blown his tie over his shoulder, but he hadn't noticed or didn't seem to care.

He slid his hands into the pockets of his overcoat, his dark eyes on her face. 'I knocked. You couldn't hear me over the din.'

Heat warmed Vanessa's face. 'I'm sorry.'

'No need to apologise. Vanessa Bell?'

She nodded. He was here, finally.

'Detective Sergeant Pierce Ryder.'

There was a collective intake of breath from the children. The detective glanced at them briefly but didn't come any further into the room, nor did he whip out his badge like they did in the movies. 'I'm sorry to interrupt, but would you be able to come down to the inn, please?'

'Go—you're needed.' Libby shooed Vanessa away, her gaze never leaving the detective. His attention had shifted to two boys who'd lost interest in the conversation and were now wrestling on the floor.

'Guys, listen up.' Vanessa smiled at the kids. 'I'll come back and finish our talk another time, okay? In the meantime, study the rules for the chance to win more treats. And if you're nice and quiet, I'm sure Libby will let you watch *Frozen*.'

Chair legs scraped across the linoleum floor as the kids fell over each other in their haste to secure prime position in front of the flat screen.

'See you, Jake,' Vanessa leaned over and ruffled the little boy's hair before walking over to the detective.

'Is Jake your son?' he asked when they were out in the corridor.

'No.' Vanessa took her ski parka from a hook on the wall. 'He's one of the kids in Libby's care.' She pushed an arm into one sleeve, then felt her face flame when the detective reached for the jacket and held it for her so she could slip her other arm into the sleeve. 'He has a serious nut allergy,' she went on as she shrugged the jacket onto her shoulders and turned up her collar. When she turned around, he was already waiting at the door.

Not bothering with the zip, she pulled her parka across her chest and hurried towards him. It was a short walk to the Charlotte Mountain Inn. If he could do it in a business suit and overcoat, she could do it with her ski jacket open.

18

'Does he have an EpiPen?' he asked, holding the door open.

'Of course.'

Ryder nodded. 'Shouldn't be a problem, then.'

Vanessa looked around the familiar suite while Detective Ryder hung his overcoat in a closet by the door. A tarpaulin was spread over the carpet beneath a wall half-painted with undercoat, and wooden planks and trestles were stacked neatly into a far corner.

'Sorry for the paint smell,' he said. 'This was the best they could do at short notice.'

'You're lucky this was available. A section of roof blew off in a storm a while back. This suite was water damaged.'

'So the owner said.' The detective dragged his tie from his shoulder and made a cursory attempt at straightening it. 'My partner's downstairs in the staff quarters. Normally, we'd like somewhere more private, but the place is booked out for Winterfest.'

'I like this suite.' She pointed to the heavy drapes. 'In the morning you'll have an awesome view over the mountain, and there are only one or two suites here that have two bedrooms and a kitchenette like this one.'

'You seem to know the place well?'

'I helped them out with some cleaning at the start of the season. They were having trouble getting staff.'

'I see.'

'They were hoping it would be fixed up and ready for guests in time for Winterfest, but I heard on the grapevine the plasterer held things up—'

'Christ, it's hot in here,' Detective Ryder said suddenly, shrugging off his suit coat and tossing it over the back of a sofa. 'Do you think it's hot? That's the thing I hate about the snow. It's freezing outside and then you come inside and roast in the central heating.'

So, the detective wasn't a fan of the snow—or small talk. Vanessa doubted he'd even registered her comment about the plasterer.

'They turned the second bedroom into an office for me.' He strode across the suite, beckoning for her to follow. A brown leather holster criss-crossed his back emphasising the width of his shoulders. 'Come on in and take a seat.'

He waved a hand towards a straight-backed chair that Vanessa recognised from the hotel dining room. 'I've read the report you gave to the uniformed police, but I'd like to hear in your own words how you came to discover the bones.' He rolled out a wonky-looking typist's chair for himself.

'Where would you like me to start?' she asked, slipping off her jacket and draping it over the back of the chair. She sat down, her gaze drawn to the handgun hugging his left side. She hadn't been this close to a firearm since she'd left the farm.

He turned the swivel chair a little so that he was sitting at an angle to her, hiding the pistol from view. 'Anywhere you like. I'll interrupt or ask for clarification if I need to.'

Vanessa took a deep breath. 'Well, given the slow start to the season, we only have a thin cover, so it's patchy in a lot of areas. That makes the groomer's job difficult. He has to shift snow around. Mostly, he's been putting it into the loading areas, so people can get up the mountain.'

He leaned on an elbow, thumb under his jaw, one long index finger resting beneath a full lower lip. Vanessa stared at the deep vertical crease between the detective's brows. He'd spent a lot of time concentrating. Or worried. Or in pain.

She waited a couple of beats. When he didn't comment, she went on. 'So, the groomer asked Terry Harrison, the mountain manager, if ski patrol could build some snow fences up on Mount Stillwell. I've worked a lot of seasons in the northern hemisphere but it's my rookie year here, so of course I got the job. Terry told a couple of the lift operators who weren't rostered on to give me a hand. We went out early, before the first lifts.'

'What are snow fences?'

'Oh, they're just posts with plastic mesh hung between them. The snow builds up behind them, so it's easy for the groomer to pick it up and distribute the snow where it's needed. The mesh lets a little bit of snow through, though, so the weight doesn't push the fences over.' She paused, realising that most of what she'd just said couldn't possibly be relevant to what he was interested in.

The detective didn't seem to mind, though. He nodded, then asked, 'And while you were doing this, you found the bones?'

'Yes. I was rolling out the plastic fencing. It got away from me and rolled down the slope a bit. I called for one of the young lifties to come and help me roll it back up. That's when I saw them. The liftie said they were probably animal bones, but I knew they were human. I radioed Terry, and he called the village doctor.'

'The doctor said you were adamant they were human bones. And he did confirm that to be the case.'

'Yes,' she replied, watching the detective. He hadn't written anything down. Maybe he was one of those people who committed everything to memory.

'Was it because of your training that you were able to identify them as human?'

Vanessa shook her head. 'We only need first aid. Our most important skill is being able to ski all over the mountain in any sort of weather. We have to be able to reach people and bring them down safely so they can get proper medical attention.'

He frowned. 'So, despite limited medical knowledge and the absence of a skull, you were convinced they were human?' He quirked an eyebrow. 'Lucky guess?'

Vanessa smiled. He was smart. Perceptive, too. 'This is going to sound ridiculous. But I grew up on a farm, and our family doctor in town had one of those full skeletons in the corner of his surgery. I was fascinated by it as a kid. Every time I went in there, I'd study it. He appreciated my interest and began showing me parts of the skeletal system. It went on for years. Sometimes he'd quiz me to see if I remembered.' She shrugged. 'Maybe he hoped I'd go into the medical field.'

The detective leaned back. The typist chair groaned under his weight. 'I've heard a lot of ridiculous things in my time but that isn't one of them.'

Warmth crept back into Vanessa's face. Serious he might be, but the detective had a nice way about him. She liked his old-fashioned manners, too, though he was probably only half a dozen years older than her. He was nothing like the guys she had dated. 'Do you have any idea who it is, Detective?' she asked, forcing her mind back to the subject at hand.

He sighed. 'A couple of people have gone missing over the years and never been found. We'll know more once the pathologist gets here in the morning.'

He consulted what looked like a police report. 'Tell me one thing . . .' He looked up. 'Earlier, I had to walk up the slope to get to the site. It's steep and treacherous. If you're carrying fence posts and rolls of fencing, do you take it all up on the triple chairlift and come down that way? How on earth do you get down there?'

The detective's words dragged her back in time and brought her wailing six-year-old self into sharp focus. *'How did you get all the way down here, Vanessa?' Strong arms reached for her and she clutched her Jemima doll closer to her chest. The man had a kind face and wore a uniform. Her arms went around his neck as he settled her on his hip and brushed leaves and twigs from her hair and cardigan.*

Strange—usually it was the subtle scent of eucalypt or the faint aroma of a dried-up creek bed that awakened her earliest childhood memories.

A gust of wind slammed against the inn's windows and she jumped. The detective glanced at the creaking roof like he feared it might be torn off again. His eyes returned to her face. 'How did you get down there?' he asked again.

'Normally, if I was going up there without any extra gear, I'd take the triple chair up to Kangaroo Ridge and then hike across the top towards Mount Stillwell and ski down. But this morning the groomer took the posts, fencing and us as far up the hill as he could, and we carried them the rest of the way.'

'Was anyone else around?'

'I don't remember anyone in particular.'

'Just the groomer?'

'Yes. He was smoothing out the section of hill underneath where the old chairlift used to be, not far from where the fencing was going in.'

'Old chairlift? There was another one here at some stage?'

Vanessa nodded. 'It used to run at right angles to the present one. The trees are sparser under where it used to be. It's the perfect place for the new inflatable tube run to go in.' She and Libby were looking forward to having a go in the giant inner tubes that would shoot them down the slope. The instructors were already placing bets on who would make it to the bottom first.

The detective's frown deepened, and his gaze moved to the file on his desk. 'When did the old chairlift operate?'

Vanessa shrugged. 'Ages ago.'

'How close is the run under the old lift to the site where you found the bones?'

'About fifty metres, I guess.'

'Can you take me?'

Vanessa blinked. 'I'm sorry . . . what?'

'Can you take me up there, I mean, in the morning? Show me where the tube run's going in.'

'Oh, sure.' Vanessa swallowed. 'I'm probably not the best person to help you, though. I think the Alpine Ski Club have lots of historical information on the area and a ton of old photographs. They've put together a display for Aidan Smythe's return.'

Aidan Smythe needed no explanation. The skiing legend's return to Charlotte Pass after his incredible European season fifty-something years ago was bigger news than Eddie the Eagle returning to Calgary thirty years after his famous ski jump. The detective might not be a fan of snow sports, but he would have to have been living under a rock not to have heard of the celebrations.

'I'll speak to the alpine club,' he said, his gaze lingering on her face.

'There is one thing I can show you.' Vanessa stood and moved to the window. Drawing aside the heavy drapes, she listened to the sound of him sliding his firearm into one of the desk drawers. She tapped a fingernail on the window as he joined her. 'That building over there, where the lights are on, it's called "Long Bay" because the rooms are the size of jail cells. It's staff housing for ski instructors, ski patrol and mountain operations.'

'Is that where you're living?'

'Yes, if you could call it living. It's more like boarding-school accommodation. Shared bathrooms, claustrophobic and overcrowded. Anyway, that's not the reason I'm showing you. See how it's the only building on that side of the creek? All the lodges and hotels are on this side. That's because Long Bay was originally the bottom station for the old chairlift that went up Mount Stillwell. I don't know when it operated, but there are people here who still remember it. I can write their names down for you if you like?'

'Okay. That would save me time. Thanks.'

'Of course.' Vanessa took a deep breath. The anxiety that had kept her on edge all day was slowly seeping away. The wait was over, and now she could do something to help. 'I want you to find out who the bones belong to, Detective. Their family's torment . . .'

His eyes cut to hers and he gave a brief nod. 'I understand.'

Vanessa watched his reflection in the glass as she closed the drapes. He was turning back to the desk, where he picked up a pen and finally jotted something down.

'He's arriving tomorrow, right?' he asked when she turned to face him.

'Who?'

'Smythe.'

'He's already here, at the inn.' And then the words slipped out before she could stop them. 'Going to ask for his autograph?'

He shook his head. 'No. I'm worried about the media. I don't want them reporting anything about the case. We may have relatives to contact.'

Heat crept up Vanessa's face, and she silently berated herself for her silly remark. 'Of course. It would be awful for them to hear something on the news.'

'That's right.'

He didn't say anything more or sit down again.

'Well, if that's all . . .' she said, taking that as her cue to leave.

'Yes, you've had an eventful day. You should try to get some sleep.' He stood aside so she could lead the way out of the makeshift office.

As Vanessa stepped into the living room, she couldn't help but glance into the main bedroom, where a black overnight bag and zip-up suit bag sat on the end of the bed.

'Where should I meet you in the morning?' she asked, turning to face him. 'There's patchy mobile reception in the village. They're working on improving it, though.'

'Hmm. Quaint.'

'You can thank the National Parks and Wildlife. Still, a lot of guests like it. They come here to unwind. Part of that is unplugging for a week.'

He nodded. 'I'm sure they do. What's the earliest you can meet up?'

'Around seven-thirty, after I've had a look at the mountain. The bridge over the creek is a good place to meet.'

'That suits me. I'm sorry I had to interrupt your presentation.'

'Oh, the kids will keep,' she said, surprised he'd given her safety talk a second thought. 'And one other thing. I don't know if anyone's mentioned this but the wi-fi has a habit of crashing around four when everyone comes inside and logs on. If you need to use the internet, do it while everyone's out on the hill.'

'Thanks for the heads-up.'

She smiled. 'See you bright and early at the bridge, Detective.'

'You will indeed.'

Three

In the freezing hour before dawn, Ryder and Flowers waited on the uneven slope above Stillwell Lodge and watched the pathologist at work. Harriet Ono, recently arrived from Canberra, was crouched beneath a set of portable lights that illuminated the cordoned-off area brighter than Circular Quay during the Vivid Sydney festival. Beyond the police fencing, snow gums clung to the hillside, their trunks smooth and streaked from shedding their bark, their boughs twisted into eerily ghostlike shapes.

Harriet took hold of the final bone from where it lay partially entangled in strawy snow grass. She held it aloft, turning it this way and that in her gloved hand until she was satisfied, then she put it down next to the others, lowered her protective face mask and spoke to Ryder over her shoulder. 'I'd say it's the body of a small, adult female.'

He knelt beside Harriet on the rubber matting, his heavy duty police gear keeping out the cold, though the frigid air pierced his cheeks like a hundred needles. He stared at the bones. The femur, pelvis and three-quarters of a rib cage were laid out on a strip of felt fabric like pieces of jewellery on a counter top.

'It's the shape of the pelvis.' Harriet ran a latex-covered index finger around a curve in the bone. 'Female.'

'How old?'

26

'It's impossible to say with what I have here. There's no evidence of osteoporosis but that doesn't prove anything. It's not present in all older people, and young people can have juvenile osteoporosis.'

Ryder thought of the smiling young woman in the black-and-white photograph on file. Celia Delaney had been twenty-one when she'd disappeared without a trace in 1964.

'So, it's not the male hiker you hoped it would be.' Flowers stamped his feet, folded his arms and stuck his hands under his armpits. 'That sucks. I was hoping we'd wrap this one up quick and get back on the Hutton case.'

Ryder got to his feet. 'Personally, I was hoping they were animal bones. Whoever this person is, they lost their life up here, so show a little respect.' He gestured over his shoulder. 'Go and look through the file. Find out Celia Delaney's height.'

Harriet lifted her camera and took a photograph of the bones. 'Still your charming self, I see,' she said as Flowers trudged off in the darkness.

'He's a self-absorbed pain in the arse, most of the time.'

'Go easy, he might surprise you. Then you'd have to eat your words.'

'If Flowers picks up his game, I'll gladly eat my words.' He looked at Harriet, her bulky layers covered in protective overalls. She was one of the best pathologists in the business, and he'd been pleased she'd agreed to come to Charlotte Pass. 'How long do you think she's been up here?'

'Hard to say.'

'Take a guess—an educated one.'

'Decades.' Harriet lowered the camera. 'Do you think it's her?'

Ryder nodded slowly. 'It's looking that way. She went missing in a storm back in 1964 when the Australian ski industry was in its infancy. Strange, though, isn't it, how the bones were just lying there?' To Ryder, it looked like someone had put them there. Or maybe an animal had interfered with them.

'Yeah, I don't know,' Harriet said. 'We're on a pretty steep slope. Soil erosion over time could have exposed some of the bones. These ones could have been washed away during a storm.'

'So, the rest of the skeleton could be further up the slope?'

'Not much further up. There's another possibility: the bones could be those of an indigenous woman.'

'Can you tell if it is?'

'Nope. I need a skull.'

'So, what are you saying, Harriet? That you suspect an Aboriginal woman died right here sometime in the last, what, forty or fifty years?'

Harriet blew out an exasperated breath. 'I'm not saying anything, Pierce. You're the detective. You work it out.'

Work it out? What he should be working on was the manhunt for Gavin Hutton. Where was that bastard now, anyway? Probably as warm as toast, tucked up inside the two sleeping bags he'd pilfered from the hikers. Still, Harriet had a point. The mountains were sacred to many clans. For thousands of years they had trekked from the east coast of New South Wales to the Snowy Mountains to set up camp at Dead Horse Gap, where they held ceremonial rituals and feasted upon the protein-rich Bogong moths. It was a possibility he hadn't considered.

Ryder looked to the horizon where the sun was beginning to lighten the sky with a gentle glow. Despite what Harriet said, his gut was telling him this was Celia Delaney. The Traditional Owners had extensive knowledge of the land and how to survive the seasons. Celia Delaney had no such knowledge. She was a dental nurse who'd gone missing during one of the biggest snow dumps in Australian alpine history. Seven years after her disappearance, the Coroner's Court found she had left Charlotte Pass on foot after an argument with her musician husband. Taking into consideration the extreme weather conditions and the balance of probabilities, the court had found that Celia had perished. They concluded she had most likely become disoriented and wandered off the roadway between Charlotte Pass and Perisher Valley. Lost in the back country in that weather, she would have frozen to death within hours. Only Detective Constable Roman Lewicki had been convinced otherwise. He'd always suspected that Celia's husband had played a hand in her disappearance.

Ryder shivered as icy air seeped inside his jacket. Across the valley, he could just make out the spot where the road into Perisher met the driveway winding down into Charlotte Pass village. If this was Celia Delaney, how the hell had she ended up here?

'Go back to what you said before, Harriet. What makes you think she's been up here for decades?'

Harriet unzipped the plastic evidence bag and took out the femur that she had carefully packed away. 'It's interesting. There are no signs of bleaching. That tells me the bones haven't been exposed to the sun. Water does a massive amount of damage, as does ice, but unlike the rest of the world our alpine areas don't have glaciers.' She pointed to patches of discolouration on the femur. 'See these differential patterns of staining? That happens over time. The green ones could be from sphagnum moss. The brown ones are probably from the bones interacting with broken-down plant and animal matter in the soil.'

'Soil?' Ryder's heart kicked against his ribs. 'She was buried?'

'These bones were. I don't know about the rest of her.'

Sweat broke out on the back of his neck and he groped in his pocket for the nicotine gum. This was the first solid indication that what Lewicki had been saying for decades might be right—Celia's death wasn't an accident.

Craving the sensation of flimsy cigarette paper clinging to his lower lip, and the peppery taste of smoke hitting the back of his throat, he put a piece of gum in his mouth and chewed hard. Was this isolated mountainside the final resting place for Celia Delaney? He hoped so, for Lewicki's sake. And for her parents, who were still alive and had never recovered from their only child's disappearance.

Turning up his collar, Ryder adjusted his stance on the rocky slope and waited for the horrible stuff to work. Relief came quickly, the nicotine flooding his bloodstream via the lining of his mouth. He blew out a breath. *Jesus Christ*. His addiction never waned, stalking him like a jilted lover, keeping him edgy during the day and awake at night. He looked at the bones again. Who had left her here, all alone and buried in the dark?

He watched as the small, white coffin covered in baby's breath was lowered into a black hole in the earth. Teary mourners clutching flowers between their fingers moved forward as he retreated. Someone touched his shoulder—

'Pierce?' Harriet was standing beside him, her hand on his shoulder.

'What?'

'I spoke your name three times. Are you all right?'

'Apart from freezing my arse off?' He took another deep breath. As he blew it out he watched the small cloud of mist form and wondered if he could still blow smoke rings. Anything to distract himself. 'I'm fine,' he said.

Harriet raised a sceptical eyebrow.

'I said I'm fine.'

'Okay, keep your hair on. I'm just about done.' She set about packing the individual evidence bags inside a large Rossignol ski bag, the canvas emblazoned with a red 'R' on the side.

'Pierce? Are you ready?'

'Give me the bag, you take the torch,' he said when all the bones were safely inside. He pulled the zipper closed and picked it up. There was something sad about the lightness of it.

They concentrated on the perilous descent, glad of their sturdy mountain boots as they skirted around granite boulders and picked their way to the bottom. In the gloomy dawn, ravens swooped and called overhead, their mournful cries cutting through the steady rumble of the grooming machine.

As Ryder turned towards the sound, Vanessa Bell's voice rang in his head. The groomer was the only person in the vicinity when she discovered the remains. But not this morning. The groomer was on the other side of the valley smoothing out the snow that had fallen overnight.

'Can you give this top priority?' Ryder asked as the gradient began to level out. Up ahead, the village emerged through the murky dawn like an old-fashioned photograph developing in a dark room.

'A skull would expedite things.'

'What's the chance of dental records from 1964 existing today?'

'Good. Many practices have only changed hands a couple of times. Her records are probably archived.'

'With luck there'll be a copy in the file.' A movement up ahead caught Ryder's eye. The two uniformed police officers who'd been first on the scene, and who'd done an excellent job keeping the site dry and secure overnight, were waiting on the footbridge that crossed Spencers Creek. The same footbridge where he would meet Vanessa Bell. After he'd spoken to Flowers.

'Are you heading back to Perisher on the snowcat?' Harriet asked.

Ryder's gaze shifted to the accommodation Vanessa had called Long Bay—still shrouded in semi-darkness. He shook his head. 'I have a feeling I'm just getting started.'

Four

Ryder walked into his makeshift office and set a takeaway coffee on the desk in front of Flowers. 'Those bones have been in soil.'

The coffee wasn't a peace offering. Ryder had needed a caffeine hit, and though he might have been a lot of things, stingy wasn't one of them.

'Thanks,' Flowers said, surprise showing in his tone. 'What do you think happened?'

'I don't know what to think.' Ryder gestured to the takeaway cup. 'Bring it with you. Harriet said there's a possibility erosion has occurred further up the slope and washed some of the bones downhill. We need to find the rest of them before it starts snowing again. Oh, and how tall was Celia Delaney?'

'Tiny. Five foot one.'

Ryder took a breath and nodded as they left the suite.

In the foyer, the inn's owner, Di Gordon, was unlocking the hotel shop. 'Morning,' she said without a smile. 'I saw lights out on the hill earlier. Are you finished up there now?'

'Not yet,' Ryder replied, matching her brusqueness. He had been entirely unimpressed when he met her at check-in the previous day; her lack of concern about the human remains found was only equalled by her evident worry that the police presence would disrupt the planned festivities for Aidan Smythe. 'We were speaking to Terry

Harrison yesterday.' He pointed to the doors that led outside. 'His quarters are in Long Bay, right?'

She nodded, looking none too pleased. The woman had the kind of thin-lipped, unsmiling mouth Ryder didn't like.

Outside, the first oversnow transport of the day had arrived from Perisher to deposit the entertainment at the front door. Instrument cases and a PA system were being unloaded by a handful of retirement-aged men. Dressed in denim and adorned with silver jewellery and black hats, their faces boasted more stress lines than their well-worn leather jackets. A white sticker on a battered musical case revealed they were 'The Other Miller Band'.

'I've seen those old guys play—at Marble Bar in Sydney,' Flowers said as they tramped across the bridge. 'Their style's kind of a jazz–rock fusion.'

'Huh. I wouldn't have picked you for a jazz buff.'

'There're a lot of things you don't know about me. Have you seen them? They've been around forever.'

'Nope. The Chili Peppers are more my style.'

'No shit?'

'Yep.'

Vanessa Bell opened the door to Long Bay, a piece of Vegemite toast in her hand. Her hazel eyes widened. 'You're early. I haven't checked the mountain yet.'

'There's been a change of plans.'

She gave a faint nod, her gaze direct. 'Okay.'

Ryder took her in with a single glance. She wore a long-sleeved, black thermal top, black leggings and thick ski socks. The stretch material clung to her body, and her dark hair fell in tousled waves past her shoulders. One long piece of hair had caught in the neck warmer that was looped around her throat. Her gaze shifted beyond Ryder's shoulder to where Flowers stood behind him.

'We're here to see Terry,' Ryder said, a little more gruffly than he'd intended.

Her eyes flicked back to his. 'Sure, I'll get him.'

He watched her spin around, appreciating the urgency with which she moved. Vanessa Bell wasn't a time waster. Ryder got the feeling she knew what was important in life. He watched her saunter off down the hallway past a row of jackets hanging on the wall. Overcrowded and claustrophobic was how she had described Long Bay. A bit like boarding school.

'Close the bloody door!' someone hollered from a room off to the right. 'Were you brought up in a cave?' Loud shrieks and laughter followed.

Ryder turned and raised an eyebrow at Flowers. 'Sounds like a fun place.'

Terry appeared within a minute, 'Charlotte Pass' embroidered on the breast of his hoodie. Thickset with uncombed, sun-bleached hair sticking out in every direction, his uneven gait suggested arthritic knees as he came towards them.

'Morning,' he said, stopping for a few seconds to push an empty ski bag against the wall.

'Morning, Terry,' said Ryder. 'We need to search a section of the mountain. Are ski patrol able to rope it off for us?'

'Yeah, no problem at all.' He turned and shouted over his shoulder for Vanessa.

She reappeared with a rustle of clothing. She'd slipped on her ski-patrol uniform and was fixing her hair in a ponytail. A few steps behind her was a broad-shouldered bloke with a tanned face, a messy man bun and a short-cropped beard. Dressed in long johns and a fleecy top, he was holding a glass of milk and listening to their conversation.

Terry turned to look at them. 'Okay, so you're rostered on, Vanessa?'

'I am,' she said, slinging a wide leather tool belt around her hips and buckling it up.

'What's the snow report say, Johan?' Terry asked the bloke with the milk.

'Ah. Twenty centimetres fallen up top.' Johan spoke with a heavy European accent Ryder couldn't pinpoint. 'There's a quarter of that on the lower elevations, and a fifty-centimetre dump forecast for mid to late afternoon.'

'Right.' Terry turned back to Vanessa. 'Vee, you go with the detectives. I'll come up shortly and give you a hand. Johan can do your sweep this morning.' Then to the European: 'Go and get dressed.'

Johan sighed and turned around, muttering that it was supposed to be his morning off.

'Thanks for this,' Ryder said to Terry, stepping back so Vanessa could slide past him.

'No dramas. We'll get it roped off. You don't want punters coming down through the trees while you're trying to work.'

The estimate Vanessa had given Ryder turned out to be spot on. In the daylight, he could see where the groomer had worked the day before, smoothing out the snow for the tube run some fifty metres from where she had discovered the bones, down the slope from the snow fences. Ryder considered the space, looking up and down the hill, wondering whether the vibrations from the grooming machine could have disturbed the soil in the area and caused some slippage. Harriet's explanation of soil erosion over time seemed more likely but, even so, Ryder extended the search area past the snow fences and left to the boundary of trees.

Now, he could see Flowers' police issue heavy weather jacket as he combed through the terrain higher up. Terry had joined them, and he and Vanessa had rolled out more orange fencing and hammered it into place.

He looked skywards at the angry black clouds weighed down with moisture. The wind was picking up, and across the valley ski instructors were setting flags in place for a downhill race taking place after lunch. Aidan Smythe would do the honours and fire the starting gun.

'Sergeant!'

Ryder swung around to see Flowers beckoning him. He headed up the slope, his boots sliding on stones slick with ice, clumps of snow clinging stubbornly around tree roots. It was probably another false alarm. So far, they'd found the matted pelt of a dead pygmy possum, or a rat—Ryder wasn't sure which one—a kid's teddy-bear beanie and a rotting bird carcass.

'What have you got?' he asked, drawing level with his partner.

Flowers led the way into a tight space between the trunk of a snow gum and a huge, overhanging boulder. He was holding up an item for Ryder to see: small, pink, about two inches long. 'It's one of those plastic-coated wire twist ties.'

Ryder looked from it to Flowers. 'Like the thing you wrap around bread? Jesus, Flowers, you brought me up here for this?'

'It's not much on its own,' Flowers countered, 'but look around— they're scattered all over the place. They're different colours, too. You can't see them unless you brush away the layer of snow. They're caught in the strawy grass. Look at this one further up.'

Ryder moved around Flowers to where he was gesturing and went further into the narrow area between the tree trunk and the boulder.

'It's close to the roots,' Flowers said from behind him. 'It's pink. I can see it from here.'

Ryder leaned over and scrutinised the area around the tree roots. It took a few seconds of hunting to locate the pink wire tie, but there it was, its plastic coating corroded in parts to expose the rusty wire inside.

'Weird, hey, how they're twisted into small circles?' called Flowers.

Ryder shrugged. 'People tramp all over the mountains in spring and summer.' Tilting back his head, he peered at the boulder towering above them. 'Hikers could have sat up there and tossed their rubbish down here. It's probably a popular resting place. I'll ask Terry or Vanessa.'

'Ask us what?'

Ryder swung around at the sound of Vanessa's voice. They'd followed him up the slope, and were standing further down, their hands resting on their hips.

'Flowers, can you speak to them, please? I want to check this out a bit more.' Leaving his partner to question Vanessa and Terry about hikers in the area, Ryder pushed further into the narrow space between the snow gum and the boulder. This section of the slope was slushy, with tufts of grass poking through the snow where the overhanging rock and tree branches had sheltered it from the weather. Ryder spotted a tiny speck of blue caught in a tuft close to the bottom of the boulder.

Pulling off his gloves, he squatted low to the ground. It was a tight fit, the space so narrow he could barely rotate his shoulders. He reached for the circle of blue wire and froze, his scalp crawling inside his woollen beanie. Something very small was caught in this one. Careful not to disturb the area around him, he extracted the wire tie from the damp ground matter and held it aloft. A tiny, dried-up flower hung limply from the circle of wire.

Ryder patted down the wet grass, his fingers digging into the freezing soil as he felt for any anomaly. He was close. He sensed it. Felt it in his guts with the same certainty as when he'd flung open the driver's door that terrible day. He shifted onto his knees, searching the area around the tree and under the boulder. Within minutes he'd pulled more wire ties from the semi-frozen soil.

'Here!' he called over his shoulder. 'There's something here.'

'Use this,' said Vanessa, slipping into the crevice. She unclipped a spade from her tool belt and passed it to him; it was the one she had used to dig shallow post holes before she hammered the orange fencing into the ground. Terry wore a similar belt.

Ryder took hold of the handle and drove the spade into the earth. The frigid air stung his nose, and the terrain beneath his knees was cold and sharp.

'Vanessa, let me in there,' he heard Terry say. 'I'll help.'

Vanessa retreated out of the narrow space and then Terry was there.

Ryder looked up at the mountain manager. 'It's pretty frozen where you are, but here where I'm feeling with my fingers, it's looser, like it's been disturbed.'

They worked together, excavating the area as best they could with the tools they had on hand. Every now and then they would stop digging to wrench away handfuls of tufty grass or to prise stubborn stones from the partially frozen soil.

With one eye on the deteriorating weather, Ryder unzipped his ski jacket and flirted with the idea of calling in the experts. But they were racing against the storm, the barometer falling like a stone. Any damage he might cause by going in heavy-handed—well, he'd cop that criticism if and when it came.

'Detective.' Terry tapped something with the tip of his spade. Ryder sat back on his haunches, watching as the mountain manager put his spade aside and worked his fingers into the soil. 'I feel something long and hard.' He looked at Ryder with wide eyes. 'I dunno, it *could* be a bone.'

A chill shot down Ryder's spine.

'Sergeant?'

He looked up at the urgency in Flowers' voice. His partner had been sifting through the pile of loose soil. White-faced, Flowers held up a small, narrow object covered in dirt. 'Is this a . . . rib?'

'May I?' Vanessa reached for the object. She ran her fingertips over it for a few moments, feeling the shape, then peered around Flowers to look at Ryder. 'Phalanges.'

Ryder moved forward, calculating dimensions in his head. Terry had touched what he thought was a long bone. Flowers had found a finger. Had they discovered the rest of the skeleton?

'Give me some space.' Ryder wiped the sweat from his forehead with his parka sleeve and started to dig. When the tip of his spade struck something hard, he cast it aside.

'Here.' Terry handed him a three-blade ice pick with a wooden handle.

Ryder worked alone, making a crater around a bulbous object buried in the earth. Dirt caked beneath his fingernails as he chipped away the half-frozen soil until finally he cast aside the ice pick. Gently, he laid his hands on the object, feeling its ridges and contours with the pads of his frozen fingers. Then slowly and carefully, he coaxed it from the soil.

He stood awkwardly and followed Terry out of the claustrophobic space. He placed the object on a tuft of snowgrass beside the finger and long bone. Squatting, he stared at the skull. One side of the cranium had caved in, and two chilling hollows stared blindly at the daylight for the first time in God only knew how long. Ryder had only set foot in a church a few times in his life but, in this moment, he had an unbearable urge to make the sign of the cross.

Vanessa drew level and for the briefest moment laid a light hand on his shoulder. When he looked up, she was staring at what he had uncovered, her eyes glistening. Terry's face was devoid of colour. Flowers was coughing like he might start retching any second.

Ryder pushed himself to his feet. The mountain manager looked like he was going to fall over. The sooner Ryder got him talking the better. 'The old chairlift, Terry. When did it operate?'

Terry sucked in a deep breath, blinked hard then shifted his gaze to Ryder. 'The one over there? It opened in 1963, I'm pretty sure, and was dismantled the following year.'

1964.

The year Celia had gone missing from Charlotte Pass.

'Detective Flowers,' Ryder said, 'we need a forensic pathologist up here right away. Call Harriet and tell her to turn around. Find out what extra personnel she needs. Then call Queanbeyan. We'll need to chopper the extra help in from Canberra.'

'Yes, Sergeant.'

Finally, Ryder looked at Vanessa. Calm. Competent. Compassionate, too, judging by the tears she was still trying to blink away. He softened his voice, remembering how she'd touched his shoulder moments earlier. 'Those plastic wire ties Flowers found, they weren't for holding someone's sandwich bag together. They were for holding posies of flowers.' He reached into his pocket and displayed them in the palm of his hand for Vanessa and Terry to see. 'Some are in worse shape than others because they've been exposed to the elements for different amounts of time.' He picked out the blue one and held it up for them to see. 'This would be the most recent. It still has a dried flower attached to it. They look like they've come out of the same packet.'

LEE CHRISTINE

'What are you saying?' asked Terry.

Ryder glanced at the mountainside grave wedged between the granite boulder and the roots of the snow gum, then looked to the village far below.

'I'm saying somebody's been coming up here and leaving posies on her grave. I'm saying that someone has known exactly where she's been all this time.'

Five

Ryder turned off the audio book when he reached Kooragang Island. The narrator's well-modulated voice had drawn him into the music biography during the seven-hour drive from Jindabyne. Coffee and the riveting memoir had kept him alert, filling his head with the crazy exploits of the Red Hot Chili Pepper's lead singer, and distracting him from the unpleasant task ahead.

He glanced at the dash and checked the time. Twelve minutes past eight. Taking a deep breath, he loosened his grip on the wheel and flexed his fingers. To his left, a long row of coal heaps destined for China and farther afield loomed over the narrow road like small black mountains in the darkness. On his right were the loaders, giant pieces of robotic machinery that lit up the night sky brighter than a theme park. And, up ahead, the Stockton Bridge was a sharp arc of lights spanning the Hunter River.

Ryder recalled one of the old coppers he'd worked with telling him about Stockton's inaccessibility before the bridge was built. 'It's the only suburb on the other side of the river, so it was hard to get to in the old days. A punt used to take the cars and trucks across.'

Ryder made a right-hand turn at the hospital, then pulled off the road as a call came through from Flowers.

'Did we get DNA?' Ryder asked.

'Yes, from the teeth. We searched the familial database hoping to get a match with her parents, but nothing came up.'

'Was there a file note saying swabs were taken from the Delaneys?'

'Not that I remember.'

Ryder frowned. That was odd. Surely Lewicki would have arranged for Celia's parents to give DNA samples in case her body was discovered after their deaths. It was standard practice for families in missing person cases to come forward.

'What about cause of death?'

'Still working on it. It's complicated. There are multiple injuries.'

Ryder rested his head on the back of the seat. He wanted to speak to Lew, but it was getting late and he was minutes away from Eunice Delaney's home. He didn't want her to retire for the night before he could speak with her.

'Sarge?'

'I'm here.' He pulled onto the road, his mind racing. Going by the age, gender and size of the remains, there was little doubt they were Celia's. He could tell her mother it was highly likely they had found her daughter's body, but he would need a positive familial DNA match before he could confirm it one hundred percent. 'Where are you now, Flowers?'

'Still in Canberra.'

'Tell Harriet to keep working on the cause of death then head back to Charlotte Pass. Vanessa Bell has offered to make a list of people who've lived in the village for a long time. Get that list and start making appointments for me to interview them. Someone paid their respects to Celia up there on Mount Stillwell, and we need to find out who.'

'What do I tell the media?'

'A body's been found, that's all.' Ryder flicked on his indicator and turned left. 'I'll update Homicide.' He'd speak to Lewicki, too.

'Any chance of the Coroner re-opening the case, Sarge, if we find out there was foul play?'

Flowers was already thinking like a future police prosecutor. 'Don't worry about that now. Our priority is coming up with compelling evidence that we can show Inspector Gray. Homicide won't throw resources at a case if they think there's little chance of us getting a conviction.'

'Right.'

'I spoke to Benson, too. The search along the Alpine Way turned up zip. The Hutton case is on ice, for now.'

'Got it, Sarge.'

'And, Flowers, make sure you copy Monaro in with everything. We need to keep Senior Sergeant Henderson on our side in case we need extra resources. I think that's it.'

'I'm all over it, Sarge, and I'll take pleasure telling Di Gordon we'll be needing our rooms for a few more days. I don't know—there's something about that woman I don't like.'

Ryder smiled. Maybe there was hope for Flowers yet. His partner might be a pain sometimes but he was showing he had good instincts about people. 'Ask if they can finish the work in my suite before I get back. Tell them the paint's giving me a headache.'

There was a pause, like Flowers couldn't decide if Ryder was joking. Then an amused chuckle reverberated around the cabin, temporarily lifting Ryder's spirits. 'Too easy, Sarge.'

Five minutes later, a feeling of dread settled on Ryder's shoulders as he parked the unmarked car in front of Eunice Delaney's brick home. The police file stated that Celia's parents' marriage had broken down a few years after their daughter's disappearance. A further file note written in Lewicki's careful handwriting noted that Arnold Delaney had re-married, though Ryder had been unable to find a current address. So, Ryder would start here, with Eunice. He only hoped the ninety-year-old was cognisant enough to understand what he was about to tell her.

He needn't have worried.

'Come in,' she said, unlocking the security door after he'd shown his badge and identified himself. The woman was tiny but sure on her feet. She swung her walker around, and Ryder followed her down a long hallway, passing a print of the Virgin Mary and a silver crucifix hanging on the wall. In the sitting room, a skeletal man was propped up in a recliner rocker, a multi-coloured crocheted blanket covering him to the waist. A television with the sound blaring flickered in one corner, and a gold picture frame holding a black-and-white photograph of Celia sat on the mantelpiece above a large oil heater.

'I apologise for calling unannounced.'

'You might have to speak up a bit, Detective.'

'I said I'm sorry for dropping in unannounced, Mrs Delaney.'

She smiled. 'Call me Eunice. And that—' she waved a hand towards the elderly man, who picked up a remote and muted the TV '—that's Arnold, Celia's father.'

The man lifted an electrolarynx to his throat and spoke in a strange, metallic voice. 'It's been a long time since the police have been here.'

Ryder nodded and gently shook the old man's frail hand. He had been fearful of finding Eunice Delaney not of sound mind. Breaking news of her long-lost daughter to an impaired nonagenarian mother was something Ryder hadn't been able to bring himself to do over the phone. So, as frail as the old man was, Ryder was relieved to find him here with Celia's mother. 'I'm pleased to meet you.'

'I took him back after his second wife died.' Eunice peered at Ryder through her magnified lenses as though expecting praise for her selflessness. 'Couldn't depend on the two layabout children he had with her to look after him.'

When Ryder didn't say anything, she waved him towards a green velour lounge with lace covers draped over the arms. 'I refused to move from this house.' She pressed down the brakes on her walker then slowly sat on the flat, black seat. 'At first, I told myself that Celia had run away. I thought she wouldn't be able to find us if she decided to come home. Then later, after the Coroner's hearing—' the old woman's voice cracked '—I wanted to stay here in case you found her. This is where she lived for twenty years, Detective. I remember her in these rooms.'

Ryder inhaled a deep breath, his heart an ache behind his ribs. 'I understand.'

They nodded, as though his words were a token statement they had heard many times. But he did understand. More than they would ever know.

Arnold stared at him through rheumy eyes. 'Have you found her?'

'We may have.'

He gave them a minute, watching as they groped for each other's hands—this former husband and wife, reunited in their dotage by the same tragedy that had torn them apart in their younger years.

Ryder watched them, not knowing what kind of a life they had led. What good things they might have done or what mistakes they had made. He only knew that he wanted to give them answers, so they could die in peace.

'The remains of a body was found at Charlotte Pass. An initial examination of the remains has taken place in Canberra today. DNA has been extracted. We're hoping to keep it out of the press for as long as we can, but it's going to be hard. There's a crowd down there right now.'

'They searched that place for years and turned up nothing,' Arnold said.

'Who found her?' asked Eunice.

'A ski patroller. She was working on the mountain at the time.' A fleeting image of Vanessa came into Ryder's mind. Efficient. Natural. Effortless.

'Where . . . where was Celia?'

'On Mount Stillwell, above the village.'

A faraway expression came into the old woman's eyes, as though she were picturing Charlotte Pass in her mind. 'Oh . . . she was high up?'

'Yes. Is there anyone you'd like me to call? Someone who could come and stay with you?'

Eunice shook her head. 'There's no one, but we're all right on our own, aren't we, Arnie?'

Arnold nodded, and Ryder gave them a few more moments to come to terms with the news. When neither of them said anything, he went on. 'I'd like to have a detective from Newcastle arrange for you to give DNA samples. It's a simple mouth swab, nothing intrusive. It will help us with identification.'

'Again?' Arnold asked.

Ryder blinked in surprise. 'You've already done it?'

'Roman arranged it.' Arnold looked at his former wife. 'When was that?'

'Oh, I can't remember. Sometime in the nineties, when that new testing came in.'

Ryder frowned, confused. So Lewicki *had* organised mouth swabs, but the Delaneys' details weren't in the database. And why was there no documentation on file? Ryder cleared his throat. 'Look, anything could have happened to the DNA results. It's probably something simple, like the search didn't pick it up first time round.'

'Maybe they got lost,' Eunice offered.

Maybe they had. It had been known to happen. 'It's unlikely, but it's not a problem, we'll just take another swab.' He pointed to the photograph of Celia. 'May I take a look?'

The old woman nodded. 'I'm lucky it's black-and-white. The coloured photos fade.'

Ryder picked up the tarnished gold frame and studied the photograph. Dressed in a light-coloured sleeveless shift and white gloves that came to her elbows, Celia stood smiling at the camera. Her eyebrows were darkened, her eyeliner heavy, her hair piled on top of her head in keeping with the fashion of the day. 'She looks a bit like Priscilla Presley.'

'A lot of people used to say that, and Celia did marry a musician, like Priscilla.' Eunice gave a sad smile. 'That was taken the day she moved to Sydney. We were just about to take her to The Flyer.'

Ryder smiled at the old-fashioned name used for the train linking Newcastle and Sydney. 'Can you tell me anything about Nigel Miller?'

The Delaneys exchanged glances. Arnold was the first to speak. He raised the metallic voice box to his throat. 'He was okay.'

'*You* thought he was okay,' Eunice countered. 'He was a philanderer.'

The venom in Eunice's tone made Ryder wonder if Arnie might have been a bit of a philanderer in his day, too.

'You didn't tell me that, Eunice, until years later.'

'Celia didn't want you to know. She swore me to secrecy.'

'You should have told me. I could have done something, and she mightn't have run off in the snow like that.'

The silence was laden with mutual blame. Despite the passage of time, emotions were close to the surface.

'Have you had any contact with Nigel Miller?'

Eunice shook her head. 'I haven't seen him since the inquest. Only in the paper, when The Other Miller Band are playing up this way.'

Ryder blinked as his brain made the jump. 'The Other Miller Band?'

She nodded. 'That's what he calls it now. I don't know how many name changes they've had.'

Ryder's mind raced. He and Flowers had watched the band unload musical equipment off the snowcat this morning. What were the odds of the band arriving at the inn the very day Celia's body was discovered? Slim to negligible, at best.

He looked again at the photograph of Celia. Had she been murdered and buried, this beautiful girl with the trendy sixties hairstyle? And who was the person who cared enough to leave flowers on her grave?

The murderer?

Unlikely.

In Ryder's experience, it was only arsonists who returned to the scene of the crime, though it had been documented on occasion in crimes of passion. Was this one of those times? If so, was the perpetrator local, or an occasional visitor like the members of The Other Miller Band?

Of course, there was another possibility. What if she was killed unintentionally, and the person responsible buried her to cover it up?

Ryder knew all about manslaughter.

'Mrs Delaney, Eunice, how long was Celia's hair?'

She stopped briefly, looking surprised by the question. 'How long? Oh, well, up until she was sixteen it was down to the middle of her back. But later she cut it to her shoulders, so she could flip up the ends.

'So, this "nesty" style she has in this photo,' he asked. 'Did she need a hairpiece to get that look?'

'You can't do that style without one. She had the hairpiece made from her own hair, when she cut it.'

Ryder's heart was pumping harder. 'Do you still have it?'

'The hairpiece? It's in her wardrobe.'

'Do you mind if I take a look?'

'I don't mind.'

Celia Delaney's room was a 1960s time capsule. Blue curtains with scattered images of kittens hung at the window, and a fluffy-dog pyjama bag with spaniel ears sat on the pink ruffled quilt. Faded posters covered two walls, their edges torn and curled where they had been pinned with thumbtacks. Elvis, Bobby Darin and The Everly Brothers covered one wall. Roy Orbison and Johnny Cash the other.

'She had good taste in music, your daughter,' he said, watching as Eunice dipped her fingers into an angel-shaped holy water font on Celia's dresser before making the sign of the cross. 'Some of the best are up there.'

'She was boy mad when she was a teenager.' Eunice pointed to a small poster of The Beatles stuck to the inside door of the lowboy, an advertisement for their Melbourne concert in June 1964. 'She was at that concert. I was so pleased she got to go, because a month later she was gone.'

'Did Nigel go with her?'

'Yes, he went. And a couple of Celia's girlfriends, too. They were at school together and they all turned twenty-one that year. One of them had a birthday around then—Pam, I think. I remember them being very excited.'

Ryder took his notepad from the breast pocket of his shirt. 'Do you remember the names of Celia's friends?'

'Of course I remember,' she said with a scornful snort. 'They grew up here in Stockton. Pamela MacAuley and Gail Williams.'

Ryder jotted down their names. 'Did they change their names when they married?'

'Oh, I couldn't be sure of that.'

'Do you know if they still live here?'

'No, they both moved away.' Celia's mother shook her head and reached inside the lowboy. Taking out a wig stand, she set it down on a dressing table beside another small china statue of the Virgin Mary. 'It's the only part of her I have left,' she said, stroking a dark piece of hair hanging from the Styrofoam head. 'I didn't have any other children. My mother said it was punishment for marrying a Protestant.'

A lump formed in Ryder's throat preventing him from speaking, so he busied himself putting his notepad and pen back inside his suit coat.

'Eunice,' he said after a while, 'when we do familial DNA checks, sometimes they are only seventy-five percent positive. That's usually enough for us to identify a person. I know Celia's hairpiece is precious to you, but would you entrust it to me for a short while?'

'Would it help to identify her?'

'It could. It's cut hair, which means there's no follicle, so we can't extract nuclear DNA. But provided there's enough of it, it's sometimes possible to extract mitochondrial DNA from the hair shaft. People inherit their mitochondrial DNA from their mother.'

'Does that mean we don't have to do mouth swabs again? Arnie's not well . . . and with his throat?'

'I understand. Look, there's every chance the old ones will show up when they do another search, so how about we just take yours for now? You're the most important parent in the identification process.'

Mrs Delaney looked up at him, her faded blue eyes glimmering. 'Just as well I'm still alive, then.'

Ryder held her stare, knowing she didn't understand the science behind what he'd just said. Not that it mattered. The most important thing for Eunice was learning whether or not it was her beloved daughter who'd been found on that lonely mountainside.

Ryder ignored the headache lurking behind his eyes that reminded him he should eat. Bittersweet memories resided in this city, and they were more important to him than a hastily consumed hamburger and coffee. In his darkest hour, when his life had turned to shit, he'd clung to the happy memories, revisiting them time and time again. Later, he read that it was normal practice to do that when life became unbearable. People comforted themselves by looking back to earlier times when they'd been happy.

Deciding to do a circuit of Newcastle's beaches, he drove along the harbour foreshore towards Nobbys Lighthouse. The place had changed in recent times. Cranes hovered above the skyline, testament to the boom taking place as the city went about reinventing itself. Whiskey bars and cafes had sprung up. Even the bitumen beneath his wheels was as smooth as a European autobahn thanks to the track laid down for the V8 supercar street race.

Ryder glanced at the briefcase in the passenger footwell and thought about the valuable contents inside. If he dropped the hairpiece at the station in Queanbeyan tonight, one of the boys could deliver it to Harriet in Canberra in the morning. Hopefully by then he would be back at Charlotte Pass.

He accelerated up Watt Street, passing the police station where he had worked a decade ago, before skirting around the perimeter of King Edward Park. At the top of High Street, he turned right into Memorial Drive then began the winding descent into Bar Beach. In a nod to the city's steel-making history, the Anzac Walk towered above the headland, an ambitious monument dedicated to the memory of fallen World War One soldiers.

He pulled into the beach carpark and killed the engine. As he lowered the window, memories rushed in on a breeze, tangy with the scent of salt and seaweed. He'd taught Scarlett to swim here, in the toddler pool between the rocks. He could feel the fabric of her pink-and-white–checked sunhat against his cheek, the softness of her arms around his neck as he carried her across the sand. Ryder held the happy memory in his heart, sustaining himself with the love he'd shared with his child, the sweet memories rarer than the nightmares that left him shattered. Stark flashes of him throwing open the car door. Scarlett's lifeless body in the driveway, beneath the wheels of his car.

Before his grief could swamp him, he dragged his mind back to his work. Picking up his phone, he set up a playlist: The Beatles, The Everly Brothers and the others Celia had worshipped enough to display on her wall. Finally, there was only one thing left to do before he headed south, accompanied by the soundtrack to Celia's life.

Ten minutes later, Ryder turned into a quiet tree-lined street and pulled up across the road from his parents' house. After three rings his mother picked up.

'Hello, Mum.'

'Pierce! Oh, it's so good to hear your voice. How are you, sweetheart? Where are you?'

Ryder's eyes stung as he gazed across the street to the neat front garden and the soft lamp shining from the lounge-room window. 'I'm good, Mum. I'm working.'

'You're always working.' His mother's voice turned muffled and he heard her call out, 'Bill, it's Pierce.' Then she was back, clear as a bell again. 'Your father's coming. I'm putting you on speaker.'

'Okay.' Ryder took a deep breath. He was steps away from two of the three people he loved most in the world, and yet he couldn't bring himself to get out of the car and go inside, knowing he was responsible for the excitement in his mother's voice. And the anxiety.

'Hello, Pierce?' His father's calm voice washed over him, the voice of reason during his childhood and teenage years.

'G'day, Dad. What have you been up to?' Ryder closed his eyes and leaned back against the headrest.

'Not a lot. Every day's pretty much the same when you're retired.'

Ryder smiled at the droll response. Knowing his father, he would be keeping himself busy walking the dog, working in the yard and playing golf. It weighed on Ryder's conscience that his parents had uprooted themselves from the family home in Forresters Beach and moved to Newcastle so they could give him and Tania a hand and be closer to their granddaughter. They'd been filled with optimism for the next stage of their life. But he'd wrenched it all away when he'd reversed out of the driveway that day.

He took a steadying breath. 'I'm sure Mum's keeping you busy enough, mate. And what about you, Mum?'

'I'm fine, Pierce. There's no need for you to worry about us.'

'I do, though.' He bit out the words, hating himself for causing them so much loss.

'I know, I know. It's been so long since we've seen you, when are you coming home?' His mother rushed the words as though he might hang up at any second.

He'd done that, too.

'Soon, Mum. I promise. I'm working on a cold case of Lew's. One that's important to him.'

'As long as you're looking after yourself, son,' put in his father.

'I am. I gave up the smokes thirteen weeks ago. I'm fitter than I was at eighteen.'

'That's great news, mate.'

'You're so precious to us, Pierce.' Ryder gritted his teeth at the quaver in his mother's voice. 'We miss you.'

'I know. I miss you guys, too.'

A dog barked. Ryder opened his eyes and looked at the house. In the weak glow of the streetlight, he could just make out Bentley, the family beagle. He was looking at the car and jumping around behind the front gate.

'I have to go. I promise I'll be home soon.'

'We'll be here. Bye, darling.'

'Bye, Mum. See ya, Dad.'

'Take care, son.'

Mouthing a silent apology to Bentley, Ryder hit the ignition button, shifted the car into gear and moved off. Only when he reached the corner did he switch on his headlights.

Six

Vanessa stood amid the crowd, her beanie pulled low on her forehead so the flaps covered her ears. Her gloved hands were wrapped around a steaming mug of glühwein from the ice bar, her second for the night.

The temperature had fallen to four below zero, and for the past seven hours snowflakes the size of twenty-cent coins had drifted from the sky. Mountain operations had switched on the snow cannons, adding more snow to the existing cover. Not that any were pointed at the front valley where she and Libby waited, along with other members of staff and resort guests, beneath the powerful night skiing lights. But if she listened hard enough, she could make out the hum from the motors, and the whoosh of the cannons as they shot streams of ice particles onto the ski runs further out.

Libby stamped her feet and looked towards Kangaroo Ridge where a ring of fire could be seen at the summit. 'Come on! Let's get this show on the road. I'm friggin' freezing. How hard is it to work out how many seconds to leave between each skier?'

The flare run was to mark the official opening of Winterfest, and Aidan Smythe was doing the honours leading the way down.

'There's a bit more to it than that,' Vanessa explained. 'The other skiers have to be given the right length broom handle, so when the flares are raised in the air, they're all a similar height. Then there's a

53

safety talk on how to hold the flare away from you as you're skiing. The top of the broom handle is dipped in something like napalm and lit. If the liquid drips onto your clothing, it'll burn right through.'

Libby screwed up her nose and looked towards the summit again.

'We should do it before the end of the season, Lib. It'll be fun. I haven't been in a flare run for a while.'

'Have you ever done one here?'

'Eva and I did a couple way back in our teens, when Mum and Dad used to bring us here. I've done lots overseas, though.'

'Hmm. I'll think about it. Right now, I want them to hurry the hell up because I can't feel my toes.'

Vanessa pointed at the media scrum gathered at the base of the home run. 'Maybe they're the hold-up.' Sound booms hovered over the group while the photographers fiddled with their telephoto lenses, desperate to capture every moment of Aidan Smythe's return to the ski fields where it had all started. 'They'll want to film Aidan as he skis into the light.'

'Meanwhile, I'm freezing my arse off out here.'

'That's the thing I hate about the snow. It's freezing outside and then you come inside and roast in the central heating.'

Vanessa smiled. Libby and Detective Ryder were of the same mind when it came to the snow. Libby wasn't here because of her love of the mountains. She'd followed a boyfriend to Charlotte Pass. A week after she'd taken the job at the kids' club, he'd broken up with her. Libby now spent most of her free time trying to avoid him.

Vanessa sighed and looked across to the silent shadow of darkness that was Mount Stillwell. The skeleton had been fully unearthed, and police tape now roped off the area, along with the hazard fencing. Terry had gone even further, erecting signage warning people to keep away.

'I'm sorry, Vee,' Libby said, following Vanessa's line of sight. 'Here I am whinging about the cold when you've had another shit day.'

'Shit morning.' Vanessa took another gulp of her glühwein. The mulled wine was going down easily—a bit too easily. 'Terry gave me the afternoon off.'

'So he should have. Only a callous bastard would make you work after the detectives left for Canberra. Do you know if they're coming back?'

'I have no idea.' She'd already told Libby she wasn't allowed to talk about what had been discovered, but word had got out that a body had been found.

Libby's gaze moved beyond Vanessa's shoulder. 'Well, speak of the devil. Here comes one of them now.'

Vanessa turned to see whom Libby was dissolving into sweet smiles for. Detective Flowers was coming towards them, picking his way through the throng, skirting around excited children, skiers and boarders, all of them in high spirits as they waited for the flare run to begin. Dressed in his regulation heavy weather gear which added weight to his slim frame, his short-cropped, dark auburn hair was completely hidden under a blue and grey beanie. Vanessa scanned the crowd beyond the Detective Constable, but stilled as unexpected disappointment caught her by surprise.

Disappointed? *Seriously?*

Detective Ryder might be taller, darker and hotter than his junior partner, but she met tall, dark, hot men all the time. Half the ski-school instructors fitted that description.

The lights went out.

Libby swung around and squealed so loudly Vanessa covered one of her already muffled ears with a gloved hand. Detective Flowers had clearly been relegated to Libby's mental backburner for now, at least until the light show was over.

Vanessa trained her eyes on the summit and the first flicker of a flare. Aidan Smythe began his descent. Despite his age, Smythe's impeccable timing and smooth, wide radius turns were executed with the finesse of a prima ballerina. One by one the other skiers followed, their flares glittering and shimmering in illuminated formation, like an enormous sparkling serpent sliding down the face of the mountain. Vanessa sighed with pleasure. After an upsetting couple of days, it felt good to witness something so beautiful. And the glühwein settling into her nerve endings wasn't doing her any harm either.

As the skiers neared the bottom of the mountain the night skiing lights came back on, bathing the lower part of the run in daytime brilliance. An expectant hush fell over the gathering before Smythe skied out of the darkness and into the light, arms extended above his head, a flare in each hand.

The crowd cheered. Vanessa drained the remainder of her glühwein before the jostling crowd could knock it out of her hands. Holding her phone aloft, she edged forward, keen to capture footage of Australian skiing royalty.

'Ms Bell?'

She swung around to find Detective Flowers standing next to her. He'd made it up the slope quicker than she'd expected him to. 'Oh, hello.'

'Sergeant Ryder said you had something for him.'

'Yes, I do.' Ignoring Libby's raised eyebrow, Vanessa dug in the pocket of her jacket for the folded piece of paper. 'We don't have wi-fi where we're staying, and I couldn't send a text. Anyway, I thought it would be safer writing it down.' Now, she wasn't so sure. She'd imagined handing the list of Charlotte's long-term residents to Detective Ryder privately. Instead, she was standing under floodlights surrounded by hundreds of people who may or may not be watching her exchange with the visiting policeman. Hoping it would go unnoticed, she slipped the piece of paper into the detective's hand, like a schoolgirl passing notes in class. 'Those are the only people I know of.'

'That's okay, we'll track down the others. Thanks very much.' The detective nodded to Libby. 'Enjoy the rest of your evening, ladies.'

Libby peered over Vanessa's shoulder, watching as Detective Flowers descended the slope. 'How old do you think he is?'

'Too young.'

'I like them young.'

Vanessa grinned. 'I know you do.'

Another cheer went up as the last of the skiers reached the bottom. Vanessa barely had time to take photographs before the lights were extinguished again. And then the first pyrotechnic sliced through the air with a high-pitched whine. It detonated overhead before burning itself out like a hundred shooting stars trailing back to earth.

Rock music blared from the speakers, and for the next few minutes Vanessa forgot everything and enjoyed the fireworks display. The finale came in a flurry of multi-coloured starbursts that left revellers clapping and cheering—and a few toddlers crying.

Eventually the lights came on again. A pall of gunpowder smoke hung over the village as the crowd gathered up their possessions and began to head home to the warmth of their fireplaces.

Vanessa pulled her neck warmer over her nose to block out the charcoal smell, and shivering a little inside her jacket, trudged down the hill behind Libby.

Winterfest was well and truly open.

Standing in the hallway and peering through the glass pane in the centre of the heavy wooden door, Vanessa saw that the bottom bar was alive with people, most of them resort staff. She smiled when one of the instructors tipped a packet of gummy fish lollies into a fishbowl cocktail. The girls in the group laughed loudly when the drink slopped over the rim, their drinking straws at the ready. Meanwhile, another larrikin instructor was heading back from the bar, a jug of beer in each hand as he shouted to his mates over the eighties glam-rock music blaring from the sound system. Just inside the door, the resort's entire maintenance team, their football beanies pulled low over their brows, had commandeered the pool table. Every now and then a few brave guests would venture past Vanessa and into the bar, but they didn't last long. They soon sensed the revelry spiralling around them before turning on their heels and heading to the cocktail bar upstairs with its cosy lounges, crackling fire and peaceful ambience.

Vanessa hesitated, in two minds whether to join the party. Libby had left for her lodging, declaring only a hot shower would warm her up. If Vanessa joined the ski school in the bar, there was a good chance she would have to fend off a barrage of questions she couldn't answer about why she'd been crawling around on the mountain with police officers that morning. It would be a lot simpler to just head back to her room and listen to music.

Outside in the freezing air, she gripped the edge of her hood and headed across the narrow wooden bridge towards Long Bay. The temperature had dropped again, and the wind was coming in intermittent gusts strong enough to stop Vanessa in her tracks. Water gushed between rocks in the creek and she kept her gaze trained on the few lights shining from the windows of the old timber building just ahead.

She was almost at the bottom of the slated wooden stairs when a dark figure materialised in front of her. 'Hey!' Vanessa shrieked and recoiled, rolling on her right foot. She regained her balance, staring hard through the darkness as she tried to make out who it was. 'Back off!' Fear constricted her throat, and though she'd yelled at the dark shape the words had come out as little more than a croak.

There was a spark, then a flame split the darkness. Vanessa's heart beat wildly as she stared into the sunken eyes of a man.

'Bruno! What the hell are you doing? You scared the shit out of me.'

The groomer made no apology. The old man never did. A lifelong employee of Charlotte Pass, he'd never been one to bother with social niceties. The raised scar that ended at the corner of his eye was clearly visible in the light from the flame. Legend had it that a steel disc from a surface lift had struck him in the head years ago.

He bent his head and the cigarette tip flared as he inhaled smoke deep into his lungs, holding it there for a few seconds before letting it go.

'What do you want?' Vanessa flexed her smarting foot inside her boot and waved away his smoke.

He opened his jacket and slipped the lighter into the pocket of the checked, flannelette shirt he wore underneath. Bringing the smoke to his lips again, he cocked his head in the direction of Mount Stillwell. 'What's the story up there?'

Vanessa dragged in a breath. 'Why are you asking me?'

'You're ski patrol, aren't you?' He took another drag and blew it out the side of his mouth.

'You know I am.'

'I have a problem, you see.' The burning tip of the cigarette arced through the air as he lowered it to his side. 'I have to get the grooming machine into that area so I can get to the snow behind the fences. If I can't do my job, nothin' else happens.'

She couldn't deny that, but she hated his self-importance as much as she hated the way he'd accosted her in the dark. 'I don't have the authority to tell you anything. You'll have to ask the police, or Terry.'

Vanessa reached for the metal railing, but he shot out a hand and grabbed her wrist, fingers digging into her flesh through layers of clothing.

'Let me *go*!' She rounded on him, striking his forearm with the side of her hand in a move a self-defence instructor would have been proud of. His fingers loosened, and Vanessa wrenched her hand free. She fled up the stairs, relieved to be able to put her full weight on her ankle. Breathless, she flung open the door and slammed it behind her. She paused for a few beats, holding her breath and listening. Outside, the timber steps creaked beneath Bruno's weight as he climbed the stairs.

Vanessa ran down the corridor, ears pricked for the sound of voices coming from the bedrooms. Silence. She checked the common areas. The TV room was in darkness, its lounges empty, and only the cold glint of stainless steel shone from the darkened kitchen.

Behind her, the outside door opened with a scrape then slammed closed.

Vanessa's heart pounded so hard she could feel the blood pulsing in her temples. She hurried towards her room, taking note of the missing jackets that normally hung from hooks in the corridor. Most of the others, if not all of them, were still in the pub celebrating Winterfest. When she reached her door, she looked back the way she'd come, past the men's and women's bathrooms, towards the kitchen. Bruno's dark silhouette appeared at the end of the corridor.

Vanessa fumbled with the door handle then burst inside. Closing the door quickly, she cursed the non-existent locks and the lack of mobile phone coverage. Heart thundering, she stood with her back to the door and listened. Bruno's room was on the floor above. He would need to pass her door to go to the stairs. He came slowly, deliberately, his footsteps stilling outside her door.

'Vanessa?' he said quietly.

Vanessa pressed her full weight against the door and stared down at the handle, watching for any movement. A shudder ran through her body as she heard the click of his lighter. Once. Twice.

Please. For the love of God, move on.

Long seconds passed. And then there was a rustle of clothing as he began moving away, clearing his throat as he tried to shift fifty years of tar built up in his lungs.

Vanessa moved towards the moon lamp and switched it on with a shaky hand. A creamy glow lit the shabby room, sending light into the dark corners and chasing away the claustrophobic blackness. Grabbing hold of a straight-backed, wooden chair that lived in the corner, she wedged it under the door handle. Not satisfied it would keep Bruno out if he came back, she dragged her ski bag out from the bottom of the wardrobe and dumped it on top of the chair together with her tool belt. If he tried to get in, he'd make a hell of a noise doing it.

Laying a hand over her pounding heart, she wondered why he'd waited in the dark rather than speak to her in the open. Had he been afraid of being overheard? He'd purposely tried to intimidate her by grabbing her wrist then loitering outside her room, but why? Up until now, she'd barely exchanged more than two words with him.

Feeling better now she could see properly, Vanessa sat on the bed and pulled the duvet around her shoulders. There was no way she was getting into her pyjamas—not until a few of the others had straggled in from the pub and she was no longer alone in the building with Bruno. She didn't care if she had to stay in her bulky ski gear for another two hours.

Just as her breathing felt normal again, something thumped against the wall.

Vanessa shot to her feet, nerves jangling, heart jumping in and out of time.

A soft snore travelled through the plaster from the room next door, and relief turned her body weak. She slumped down hard on the bed. How often had she cursed that oversnow driver when he'd woken her up? Not tonight. Tonight, she almost laughed aloud. She could have gone in there and kissed him for his habit of bumping the wall with his knee when he turned over.

She laid her head on the pillow, massaging her sore wrist and flexing her foot to make sure it was fine. She would need to report Bruno to Terry, even though there was every chance he could walk off the job in a huff. He had it in him to do that. And if it happened, Winterfest would lose some of its shine. He was one of the most experienced groomers in the Snowy Mountains, and he wasn't afraid of using it as leverage to get what he wanted.

And his name was on the list she'd given to Detective Flowers.

Seven

Day 3

Detective Sergeant Ryder had arrived in Charlotte Pass at first light, the pilot setting the police chopper down on the helipad behind the inn.

'Looks like you're in for a bluebird day, Sergeant,' the pilot had said cheerfully, as though Ryder had flown in for a ski holiday. 'We had a serious dump of snow last night.'

Ryder nodded, his mind already back on the crime scene and what state it was in. He'd made good time on the return trip from Newcastle, only stopping in Queanbeyan to drop the hairpiece in at the station. Then he'd woken Inspector Gray and updated him on the case. When Gray learned of Ryder's lack of sleep over the previous twenty-four hours, he made a call and arranged for a chopper to fly him up to the mountains.

Now, Ryder stood at the window, sipping his mid-morning coffee, and looking out over the front valley. The pilot had been right. It was a bluebird day, and skiers and boarders were making the most of it. Some were racing down the slopes while others picked their way to the bottom. Directly below Ryder's window, a ski instructor in a royal blue uniform was demonstrating a stop manoeuvre to a group of beginner adults. Further down the slope, a snowboarder lost control, cartwheeled and stacked it hard on the way to the T-bar.

Ryder winced, then turned away as the sat phone rang.

'We have enough mitochondrial DNA to conclude that it's a perfect match,' said Harriet. 'There's no doubting the identity of the body.'

Ryder closed his eyes briefly against the mix of emotions. Sadness, relief and satisfaction that Celia had finally been found. 'What about Eunice Delaney's mouth swab?'

'It will be processed in Newcastle, but it's unnecessary now as far as the identification process is concerned.'

'I'd still like it done.'

'Okay . . . noted.'

'And the autopsy results?'

'We have a broken femur, broken ribs and numerous fractured vertebrae. Multiple skeletal injuries like this happen when there's been a sudden deceleration.'

'Like in car accidents?'

'Yes. And falling from heights. We see a lot of workplace injuries like this when tradies fall from construction sites.'

An image of a woman falling flashed into Ryder's mind, her arms flailing, her lips parted in a scream. 'An old chairlift used to go up the mountain back then, close to where she was found.'

There was a pause, then Harriet spoke again. 'Falling from a chairlift would do it.'

'What about hitting a tree at speed?' He needed to cover every scenario.

'Possibly,' Harriet said slowly, 'but this is where it gets tricky. Her skull sustained a depressed bone fracture consistent with being kicked in the head or hit with something hard, like a hammer or a rock. The pieces of broken bone get pushed inwards when that happens. The impact would have been forceful enough to cause trauma to the brain and surrounding tissue.'

Ryder picked up a pen and made some dot points. 'So, we have deceleration injuries *and* a blunt force trauma to the head?'

'Yes. This will all be in the report I send through, but my conclusion is that she was struck on the head first, then thrown from a substantial height. This woman didn't wander off and die from exposure, Pierce. She met with a violent death.'

'And then someone put her in the ground.'

There was a pause before Harriet went on. 'We also found small pieces of leather and rubber, probably from her boots. There's some kind of small case, too, with a clasp. It could have been a change purse she carried in her coat pocket. We're cleaning it up. Sorry, I can't tell you when it will be ready.'

'Thanks, Harriet. I owe you.'

'You're buying me lunch the next time you're in Canberra.'

'It's a date.'

'It's lunch. I have a girlfriend.'

'Huh. News to me.'

After Harriet rang off, Ryder stared at the phone in his hand. Nigel Miller, the band's lead singer and Lew's major suspect back in 1964, was Celia's husband and next of kin. And he had arrived at Charlotte Pass the same day his wife's body was discovered decades after her disappearance.

Ryder rang the front desk. Now that he had the confirmation he needed, it was time to set up some interviews.

'Mrs Gordon, could you confirm that Nigel Miller is staying in the village or in one of the surrounding lodges? I saw the band unpacking their equipment early yesterday morning.'

There was a pause. 'Mr Miller always stays at the inn when the band's in residence.'

'I'd like his room number, please.'

'We're not supposed to give out that information . . .'

'We're the police, Mrs Gordon. If you'd prefer I go door to door—'

'That won't be necessary,' she interrupted crisply. 'We're in the middle of a very busy week, that's all.'

'I'm aware of that,' Ryder replied, trying to keep the derision out of this voice.

'His room is along the corridor from my office. If he's in, I'll send him up to you.'

Ryder frowned, taken aback by the woman's sudden U-turn. 'That would be helpful.'

'No problem. How do you like your room?'

It had come as a surprise to find the painters had finished, the planks and trestles nowhere to be seen. It was unlikely Flowers had hurried them on; more likely Di Gordon wanted the room ready for her next guests. It was clear she had wanted him out of the inn since the day he arrived. Maybe she thought a cop—even a plain-clothes one—snooping around was bad for business. Other than that, there seemed no good reason for her lack of hospitality.

'The room's very nice, thank you,' he replied, and killed the call.

He'd spent the morning listening to Roman Lewicki's old interview tapes with Celia's husband. The musician had an airtight alibi. The band had been playing in the lounge at the time Celia was believed to have gone missing. Miller said he had spoken to his wife in their room before the band started their warm-up. He had no idea what her movements had been after that.

Ryder called Lewicki's mobile phone for the third time that morning, and for the third time the call went to voicemail. He asked his friend to call him back, then debated whether he should ring the house. Chances were Annie would answer, and she wouldn't be thrilled to hear that the Delaney case had resurfaced. Plus, she would try to pin Ryder down for his birthday dinner, and right now he didn't have anything to celebrate.

Sipping his coffee, he looked towards Mount Stillwell where the police tape fluttered in the wind. Celia had been murdered in these mountains that cast such a powerful spell over snow enthusiasts, drawing them back year after year. He could understand why. They came here to ski and unplug for a week or two. But what of the people who had moved out of the mainstream and decided to stay here long term? The ones on Vanessa's list.

A flash of red halfway down the home run snagged his attention. An enviable skier in black pants and a red jacket, her dark ponytail streaming out behind her, cut across the mountain at speed heading for the fallen snowboarder. She dug in her edges and, with a light spray of snow, came to a graceful stop a metre or so from the snowboarder who'd cartwheeled earlier. In one movement she clicked out of her skis, picked them up and drove them into the snow in a cross formation to warn skiers approaching from above to keep clear. Then she squatted, the medic cross on her back clearly visible, and spoke to the snowboarder who was hunched over and cradling a wrist.

Vanessa.

He'd been thinking about her and suddenly there she was, as if—

A soft tap at the door intruded into his thoughts. Ryder turned away from the drama on the hill.

'Mr Miller, come in,' he said as he opened the door, taking stock of the man who stepped inside with his grey hair closely cropped in a modern style, and a perfectly manscaped goatee. The musician was about five ten and so slightly built even his straight-legged jeans hung loose on him. 'Apologies for the paint odour.'

Ryder waved him towards his makeshift office, standing aside so Miller could go in first. 'Have a seat,' Ryder said, pointing to the dining chair.

Miller hitched up the legs of his jeans and sat down, eyeing Ryder warily.

'Firstly, I'm Detective Sergeant Pierce Ryder from Sydney Homicide.'

Miller's eyes widened. 'Homicide?'

Ryder nodded. 'Our headquarters are in Parramatta but we work all over the state.'

'Okay.'

'I need you to confirm that you are Nigel Anthony Miller, husband of Celia Miller née Delaney who disappeared from Charlotte Pass in July 1964.'

Miller cleared his throat. 'Yes. I'm Nigel Miller.'

The man was fidgety, tapping one leg up and down as though in time to some imaginary beat.

'Look, Mr Miller, I realise it's been a very long time, and you wouldn't be expecting this but, as you're Celia's next of kin, I have to inform you that two days ago her remains were found within the bounds of Charlotte Pass Snow Resort.'

'Oh, dear God,' Miller whispered, his voice husky. 'So, it is true what people are saying?'

Ryder had no idea what people were saying, so he stayed silent.

'Do her family know?'

'They've been advised that the body is likely to be Celia's. We'll confirm it shortly.'

'Oh, dear God,' he said again, covering his face with his hands. An opal dress ring on his third finger caught the light and made patterns on the wall. 'I can't believe it. Poor Celia. After all these years.' He lowered his hands and stared at Ryder, his expression puzzled. 'I know where you found her. Everyone can see the police tape up on the mountain.'

'Yes, it's been upsetting for a lot of people.' Ryder paused briefly before going on. 'Mr Miller, I need you to answer some questions.' He held up the portable recording device he'd brought with him. 'I'm going to record our conversation because I want to hear your version of the events surrounding the night your wife disappeared, and this is the most accurate way of capturing it. If you prefer, you can give me a written statement, or I can type it directly into the computer. Believe me, this way is quicker.' He looked at Miller, knowing it was unlikely he'd object.

Miller sighed loudly and gave Ryder a pained look. 'I told that prick Lewicki everything I knew back then, numerous times.' Fifty-five years later, and the anger and resentment were still palpable in Miller's voice. 'Yes, okay.' Miller raised a hand to shield his eyes as if he had suddenly developed a headache.

Ryder started the recording device and tried to wipe his mind clean of everything Lewicki had told him about this man.

'The previous file notes state that you and Celia were heard arguing late in the afternoon on the day she disappeared. Is that true?'

Miller lowered his hand. 'Yes.'

'Do you remember what you were you arguing about?'

'Yes. Look. You need to understand: Celia had a jealous nature.'

Ryder raised his eyebrows, wondering if Lew had known about this personality trait. 'Did you give her reason to be jealous?'

Miller spread his hands, palms up. 'It was the sixties, man. If you were lucky enough to escape conscription, it was sex, drugs and rock 'n' roll for the rest of us.'

'What did you argue about?' Ryder asked. According to Lew's file notes, Miller had previously said he and Celia had quarrelled about his fondness for alcohol.

'We were arguing about Di Gordon.'

Ryder blinked and tried not to show his surprise. The only mention of Di Gordon in Lewicki's file was a note that she and her husband owned the lease on Charlotte Pass. 'Why were you arguing over Di Gordon?'

'I was sleeping with her back then—periodically.'

'Periodically?'

'We had an arrangement.'

'Was Celia aware of this . . . arrangement?'

He nodded. 'I was straight with Celia before we got married. She knew the deal.'

'And what was the deal?'

'The band had a standing two-week gig here every season. During that time, Di and I took the opportunity to . . . be together. We'd been doing it for four years before I met Celia. I wasn't going to give it up.'

'And Celia accepted this?' Ryder asked, trying not to show the rising contempt he felt for this man.

'No. She gave me hell about it. In the end she got her own back, though.'

'By dying?' He hoped the question would throw Miller. He wasn't disappointed. The musician's mouth fell open and he stared at Ryder, visibly shaken.

'That wasn't what I meant.'

Ryder pictured the smiling girl in the black-and-white photograph at her parents' home in Newcastle. 'How did Celia get her own back? By taking a lover for herself?'

'I think so.' He shook his head slowly, his eyes narrowing as though he were still angry about it all these years later. 'I don't know who he was. Somebody down here.'

Ryder considered the musician. Without rushing, he took a plastic sleeve from the old file and slid it across the desk in front of Miller. 'You'll recognise this photograph of the village back then. The inn and ski club were the only available accommodation. The rest of the buildings were garages and machinery sheds. It would have been difficult to keep an affair under wraps, don't you think?'

Miller shrugged. 'I have no idea who she was seeing. It crossed my mind that she might have invented someone just to get back at me.'

'Tell me in your own words what was said during the argument.'

Miller looked nervously around the room before turning back to Ryder. 'Basically, she said that when we got back to the city she'd be filing for divorce. She hated life on the road with the band, and she also hated being home alone. She said that even when we came down here, I made a fool of her by sleeping with Di.'

'How did you react? Did you threaten her?'

'Of course not. I reminded her that she knew what the deal was before she married me. She said that she'd thought she could handle it, but it turned out she couldn't. I tried to reassure her that Di was just an interlude for two weeks a year. That it was nothing serious.'

'Did you get angry?'

'Sure, I got angry. She sprung this on me shortly before we had to go on stage and play. I told her we'd talk about it after the gig. That's when she said she was meeting someone else that night, and she was done talking about it.'

'What time was this?'

'It was the pre-dinner set. So, before five.'

'Did you see your wife after that? Did she come down to watch the band?'

He shook his head. 'No. I never saw her again—ever.'

'Did you have your suspicions as to who she might have been meeting?'

'I had no idea.'

69

'Did you try to find out?'

'No, I just told the police what happened.'

'You told them you'd argued about your drinking, not about Di Gordon. Did you lie?'

'No.' Miller shifted in his chair. 'Celia and I argued about everything.'

'Tell me, Mr Miller, was your wife a good skier?' asked Ryder, noting the changes in Miller's story. 'Would she have been tempted to go out skiing that day?'

Miller gave him an incredulous look. 'Celia was a nervous skier. She stuck to the lower slopes that were accessed from the T-bar and poma. There's no way she would have gone out skiing in that blizzard, no matter how pissed she was at me.'

That sounded reasonable to Ryder. So, where *had* Celia gone after their argument? 'What do you think happened?' he asked.

'Up until now I agreed with the Coroner's findings. That she got the shits and decided to walk into Perisher, believing she'd get to Jindabyne and then make her way home from there. But, now . . .' He swallowed, then cleared his throat again. 'How do you think she ended up all the way up there—on that mountain?'

'She might have got on the old chairlift, the one that went up Mount Stillwell back then.'

Miller shook his head. 'Celia wouldn't get on that chairlift. There was a restaurant at top station—on the peak of the mountain before the chairlift went down into Thredbo. Beautiful spot. Magnificent views. I was always trying to convince her to go up there with me and have lunch, but she wouldn't have a bar of it.'

'Afraid of heights?'

'No, she was afraid of that chairlift. It was a lemon. There'd been reports of chairs falling off and stranded riders having to be rescued.'

Ryder nodded slowly. 'Did you realise Celia was missing later that night?'

'No. I didn't go back to our room after she'd chewed me out. I stayed with Di.'

'When did you raise the alarm?'

'The next day—sometime during the afternoon. The power was out. The village was in chaos. The inn was buried up to its roof in snow. We had to dig our way outside from the front door. The road was totally inaccessible, and they couldn't groom it because the snowploughs were all buried. The guests had to help dig them out.' Miller shook his head, a faraway expression in his eyes as though he'd travelled back through time. 'In all the years I've been coming here, I've never seen weather like that, before or since. There was so much snow, people were skiing off the roof of the inn. It was something else.'

According to the reports Ryder had read from back then, the blizzard blew on and off for thirty days. 'So, you don't mind coming back here, to the place where your wife disappeared?'

'To Charlotte's? No, I dig this place. I never did a thing to harm Celia.'

'Someone harmed her. Your wife was murdered, Mr Miller, we're certain of that now. We know she was hit with a blunt object and thrown from a height. Then someone buried her up on that mountain to conceal their crime.'

Miller's complexion turned a sickly shade of grey as he absorbed Ryder's words. 'Murdered?' he whispered, his voice hitching.

'You look shocked, and yet you were interviewed rigorously back then over her disappearance.'

'It wasn't *me*. I swear to God! Why would someone want to murder Celia?'

'That's what we're trying to find out. Tell me, does this arrangement with Di Gordon still exist?'

'Of course not! Christ, man, we're in our seventies. Most of us are lucky to get it up. But I still play the two-week gig.'

'But you're still friends?'

Miller swallowed hard then nodded. 'We're still friends.'

Ryder leaned back in his chair and let the musician sweat for a minute. When he spoke again, he adopted a conversational tone. 'Did you ever remarry, Mr Miller?'

'No. I got close once, but . . . When women find out my first wife disappeared—well, you can imagine.'

Ryder nodded slowly. 'How did Celia get along with Di? I mean, you were happy with your *arrangement*, you were kicking goals everywhere. Maybe Di wanted more from you.'

Miller shook his head. 'She didn't.'

'What about her husband?'

'Henry's a man of few words. Keeps to himself, mostly.'

Ryder wondered if Lewicki had known about this unconventional arrangement between the Gordons and the Millers. There was definitely nothing in the file about it. 'Okay, Mr Miller. That'll be all for now.' He switched off the machine and stood up. 'We would appreciate it if you didn't leave the village,' he said as he opened the door for the musician to leave.

Satisfied with the progress he'd made, Ryder wandered over to the window looking towards Charlotte's front slope and immediately saw a flash of red zigzagging down the mountain. Ryder squinted against the brilliant sunlight reflecting off the snow as his gaze followed the skier as they bypassed the queue, the lift operator beckoning them forward and giving them priority up the mountain. It was then Ryder realised that the ski patroller was too tall and broad to be Vanessa. It was Johan.

He scooped up his room key and left the suite, irritated at himself for seeking out every red jacket with a white cross. He'd had zero sleep, and he hadn't eaten since he'd stopped at the servo near Goulburn around midnight. No wonder his thinking was skewed, he was running on empty. He grabbed his coat and headed for the cafe downstairs; a couple of takeaway sandwiches and a strong coffee was what he needed. He wanted to be sharp when Flowers came back so they could work on their strategy for interrogating Henry and Di Gordon later today.

Ryder spotted the red jacket the instant he stepped inside the cafe. Vanessa was sitting at a table with Terry. Her long hair was windswept, her cheeks pink from fresh air and exercise. The two of them were hunched over a table devouring their lunch. Vanessa was dipping a sweet-potato fry in aioli when she looked up and snagged his gaze. She stilled as he passed the table, a ghost of a smile on her lips, the chip caught between her thumb and forefinger.

With a faint nod in her direction, Ryder stepped up to the counter.

'What can I get you?' the young woman asked in a sing-song voice.

'Two cheese salad sandwiches and a strong flat white, thanks.'

Ryder glanced around the cafe as he absorbed the rich aroma of espresso coffee. Jackets were hung over the chairs, while goggles, gloves and beanies were shoved inside helmets rocking precariously on the Formica tables. Laughter reverberated off the walls, drowning out the hiss of the coffee machine. A flat screen mounted high in one corner was showing a Warren Miller film.

Ryder reached into his pocket for his wallet as the woman calculated his order.

'Have here or take away?'

He tapped his card on the machine and waited for the beep. 'I'll have it here.'

Eight

Ryder looked up as Flowers came into the office, a half-eaten pie clutched in one hand, a white paper bag in the other.

'What happened to your healthy diet?' Ryder asked.

'It's a bit hard down here. Too cold. I'll pick it up again when I get back to Sydney.'

'Right. How'd you go at the alpine club?' Ryder asked.

Flowers sprawled in the chair like he'd completed a marathon. 'For someone with little information, that bloke certainly can talk. He couldn't tell me much about the chairlift, but he did give me some info about the people on Vanessa's list. There are four of them.'

Ryder frowned and put down his pen. 'Vanessa said there were others.'

'Yeah, but there aren't many who stay here year-round. There are Henry and Di Gordon, Burt Crofts and Bruno Lombardi. The Gordons keep the inn open—it's busy in the off season with people hiking up to Kosciuszko, and mountain biking's growing bigger, too. The bushwalkers and bikers have to use the triple chair to get up the mountain, so Lombardi and Crofts look after the maintenance over summer. They take their holidays then, too. Crofts especially is a highly experienced lift mechanic. Lombardi's a jack of all trades. Crofts was here until a week ago. He got called back to Sydney for something urgent, apparently.'

'Lombardi—I recognise that name.' Ryder opened the file and flicked through the documents until he found the statement Lewicki had taken. 'Here it is. Bruno Lombardi. He might be the groomer now, but he was the lift operator back then. He told Lewicki he was on duty at bottom station around four-thirty when a ski patroller told him the weather was too bad for the lift to keep operating. He was told to put the chain across and go inside. He did that, and by quarter to five he had a beer in his hand back at his lodgings.' Ryder mulled over the information for a minute. 'Nigel Miller told me Celia broke the news that she wanted a divorce just before the band were due to play their set at five pm.'

'Which means if Lombardi shut the lift at four-thirty, Sarge, she couldn't have been on it.'

Ryder cocked an eyebrow. 'If the times are correct, and if everyone's telling the truth.'

'Which they aren't. You think Lombardi lied?'

'I don't know. If he did, he must have convinced Lewicki, and that's not easy. Go through the file, Flowers. See if you can find the name of the ski patroller who gave Lombardi the order. Anything else?'

'I couldn't find out much about the chairlift. But—' Flowers took a huge bite of his pie, concentrated on chewing it for a few moments, swallowed, then licked the tomato sauce from his lips '—I did get the name of a lady in Thredbo. She belongs to the historical society up there. Apparently, there's a museum in the village that has a heap of information on the old chairlift.'

'Well, give her a ring and set up an appointment.'

'Already done.' Flowers screwed up the paper bag. 'It's open today between one and five.' Speaking with his mouth half-full, he lobbed his rubbish into Ryder's bin. 'We can drop in any time. Want me to go?'

Ryder pushed back his chair. 'I'll come. I'm getting more and more curious about this chairlift.'

An hour and a half later, they turned off the Alpine Way and began the winding descent into Thredbo.

'It's somewhere in the Village Square,' Flowers said to the highway patrol officer who'd picked them up from the Bullocks Flat ski tube station.

The officer nodded. 'I know where it is.'

A short while later they were standing in front the museum. 'Well, that was bad timing,' Flowers said, staring at the *'Back in 10 mins'* note pinned to the front door.

'Let's hope she's not too long.' Ryder turned up his collar and gazed at the towering peaks of Thredbo Mountain. 'When you look at this, you can see how they thought the chairlift was a good idea. It's probably twenty minutes as the crow flies.'

'Oh, I do apologise.'

Ryder swung around at the French accent. A woman was hurrying down the steps, keys in one hand, a coffee cup in the other. 'I'm usually never more than five minutes, but I put ten on the sign in case there's a queue at the cafe.' She smiled at Ryder as she slid past him and went to open the door.

'Don't hurry. We've only just arrived,' he said.

They followed her into the museum, where she switched on the lights and dumped her keys and coffee on a small desk. She was dressed in a long black jumper and black leggings tucked inside fur-lined boots. A black, military-style cap with a shiny gold brim was perched at a jaunty angle on her head, and covered most of her lolly-pink hair. 'I'm Chloe Cambron,' she said, peeling off a fur-lined glove and thrusting her hand at Ryder. 'You must be Detective Flowers.'

'Actually, I'm Detective Ryder. This is Detective Flowers.'

'Oh. Pleased to meet you,' she said, shaking Ryder's hand before turning to Flowers. 'We spoke on the phone earlier,' she said warmly.

'Yes.' Flowers shook Chloe's hand, his face blushing a beetroot red. 'Pleased to meet you. I noticed your French accent.'

Ryder looked away, feigning a sudden interest in a pair of old-fashioned, wooden skis propped against the counter.

'Well, I came out with my husband. He went back to Toulouse after two years. I stayed.' Chloe took off her other glove and laid them beside the rest of her things. 'Just so you're clear about the situation here, Dorothy Reynolds is the museum's main volunteer. She knows more about the history of this area than anyone else. I've been filling in for her for a couple of years now while I'm doing my PhD, so . . . I *should* be able to help you.'

'I'm sure you can,' said Ryder.

'Good, then if you'll just come over here.' She led them to where three large display folders, the size of art portfolios, sat side by side on top of a glass display cabinet.

'Some of the old photographs and newspaper articles are printed on A5 paper.' She slid several pages out of the plastic sleeves and put them side by side on top of the cabinet. 'Copying them can be problematic because the print is so faint.'

'I imagine it would be,' said Flowers.

'Let's start with this one.' She pointed to a cartoon-like advertisement from the sixties with a call-to-action heading inviting the reader to '*Take this Cab to Australia's Highest Restaurant—Up Kosciuszko Way*'. 'This chairlift was marketed as the longest in the world because it ran for over three miles, but that wasn't quite true. It was really made up of two separate lifts, so in a way it was a false claim to fame.'

Chloe pointed an orange-painted fingernail at the second picture. 'The first chairlift started at the Alpine Way in Thredbo and ran to the top of the Ramshead Range. In this photograph you can see the chairlift towers built across a series of shallow bowls. You'll notice that the chairlift was fairly standard except for these covers, which came down over the passengers. They were sometimes called "cabs". They were to protect the passengers from the wind. Each chair had a brightly coloured cover, or canopy, and there was a small window at face level, so passengers could look out.'

'It's an unusual-looking chairlift,' observed Ryder.

'Oh, this chairlift was unique in more ways than one.' She tapped a nail on the next image. 'This is the Stillwell Restaurant.'

Ryder studied the picture of the restaurant, a substantial structure of wood and stone. The photograph showed skiers from the 1960s, dressed in Fair Isle jumpers, enjoying drinks and lunch on a sunny verandah.

'Some of the ruins are still up there,' said Chloe. 'Years ago, the army used parts of the structure for target practice, so unfortunately they're riddled with bullet holes.'

Ryder looked up. 'I bet that pleased the National Parks and Wildlife?'

'Oh, yes. For many people, it's still a bit of a sore point.'

'So, the chairlift from Thredbo terminated at this restaurant, Chloe?' asked Ryder. The restaurant Celia refused to visit, according to Nigel Miller.

'There were a series of stations along the way but, essentially, yes.' And now look at this final photograph.' She slid another image from the folder and put it on top of the others. 'This one shows the second chairlift. It ran from the restaurant down into Charlotte Pass. This photograph is taken looking back down into the village.'

Ryder peered at the photograph. Sure enough, there was the line of cabs swinging their way down to Charlotte Pass and terminating in the building now known as Long Bay. In this photograph, the inn and ticket office were surrounded by a cluster of buildings, one octagonal in shape that now served as the kids' club. The lodges that presently dotted the surrounding landscape hadn't been built yet.

Ryder traced an index finger across the grainy image. Taken from such a height, it was impossible to pick out the spot where Celia's body had been found. The trees were too dense, and the large boulders like the one beside Celia's grave couldn't be seen. 'So, there were two chairlifts and they both terminated at the restaurant at the top,' he mused aloud.

'That's right.'

'Who built the chairlift?' asked Flowers.

'It was one of those public/private arrangements between banks, companies and the government. Oh, and interested individuals. Thredbo and Perisher were being developed at the time, and both those resorts could be reached by road. It was feared the competition would send Charlotte Pass bankrupt.'

Ryder nodded. 'So, this ambitious piece of infrastructure was thought to be the answer to Charlotte's isolation problem?'

'Yes, and the engineers were full of confidence back then. They were riding high on the success of building the Snowy Hydro Electric Scheme. This chairlift even had special luggage containers so people could leave their cars at Thredbo. When the wind was bad, which was a lot of the time, luggage ended up strewn all over the mountains. The entire thing was a disaster. One of the banks pulled out, and then the engineering firm handed it over to another company, but no one could make it work. They were still running safety checks the day before the 1964 ski season opened.'

Ryder shook his head. 'How could a team of structural engineers get it so wrong?'

'By building it at the wrong angle to the cross-winds. It was a wonderful idea, Detective Ryder, but it didn't work. The cabs would swing like crazy and slam into the towers. Some fell right off the cable. It was a miracle no one was killed.'

Celia was killed. And then someone put her in the ground.

Flowers cleared his throat. 'I read a report that said people were at risk of death from exposure. The defenders of the chairlift say it was bad timing. It was built in 1963, and 1964 holds the record for being one of the wildest weather seasons ever.'

Chloe gave a dramatic sigh. 'The thing was plagued with problems from the beginning. In the end, they dismantled it. The longest chairlift in the world existed for only two years.'

'I bet the investors weren't happy,' Flowers said with a shake of his head. 'All that money down the gurgler.'

'I feel sorry for the workers,' said Chloe. 'A lot of blood, sweat and tears were spent on its construction.'

While Flowers took shots of the photographs on his phone, Ryder looked around the museum. A male mannequin stood in one corner, dressed in 1970s ski apparels, while nearby a wooden rack held a display of old lace-up ski boots. One wall was entirely covered with skis and poles dating back almost a century.

'And now, I have something special to show you,' Chloe said when Flowers had finished. She beckoned them towards the back of the room, where it doglegged to the right. 'I think you're going to love this,' she said to Ryder, her eyes flashing with excitement.

He saw it the moment he stepped through the archway. Bright red in colour, the Number 94 cab from the doomed Kosciuszko chairlift, complete with its intact framework and small viewing window, sat resplendent in the back corner of the room.

Ryder gave a low whistle and moved towards the cab, trying to imagine the people who'd ridden it and repaired it over half a century ago. Had Di and Henry Gordon sat side by side in this very chair? What about Nigel Miller and the other band members? Ryder laid a hand on the shiny metal paintwork, the steel hard and cold under his palm. He could imagine the band lunching together at the restaurant while Celia entertained herself back at the Charlotte Mountain Inn. And what of the revered Aidan Smythe? How many times had he taken advantage of the vast terrain on the other side of the mountain while training for his events?

'So, these were the hoods?' he said, lifting back the metal cover. 'Geez, there's some weight in that.'

'You can sit in it,' urged Chloe.

Ryder ducked his head and climbed into the metal seat, bringing his feet up to rest on the thin metal footrest. Despite the central heating in the museum, the cold steel seeped through the layers of his clothing until he could feel it chilling his spine. 'It must have been freezing on these things.'

Chloe nodded. 'Very uncomfortable.'

'I'll put the cover down,' said Flowers. 'Watch your head.'

The space was so confined, Ryder needed to hunch over. 'I feel like I'm taking a ride in one of those kids' Ferris wheels,' he said, looking at Chloe and Flowers through the rectangular gap. 'The wind must have been ferocious that year, to blow these things into the pylons.' He grabbed a metal handle that was welded to the inside of the hood and raised the cover. 'I wouldn't like to be trying to push that up in a blizzard.' He straightened up. 'It's heavy enough as it is.'

Chloe watched as he carefully lowered the cover. 'Well, now you've seen the infamous chairlift, detectives, what do you think?'

'I think when it went down, it took many secrets with it,' said Ryder.

'The story of the old chairlift is a fascinating one,' Chloe said as Flowers took photos of the red cab. 'Not many people know about it, even those who come to ski in the mountains year after year. Some locals think the entire thing should be erased from the landscape. Others feel the ruins should remain part of our history, the way silos and water reservoirs are preserved.'

Ryder nodded. 'It seems this chairlift has always been contentious.'

'Oh, there's no doubt about that.'

At the front desk, Chloe wrote her contact details on a white card, the silver ring she wore on her thumb gleaming in the light of the fluorescents. Ryder pocketed the card without looking at it.

'Do you live in the village?' Flowers asked as they walked back to the entrance.

'No, in Jindabyne. I have two dogs. They aren't allowed in the National Park.'

'French bulldogs?' asked Ryder.

'Yes. How did you know?'

Ryder merely smiled and raised a hand in farewell.

Nine

'Nigel Miller told me Celia refused to get on that lift,' Ryder said from where they sat in the back row of the oversnow. This late in the afternoon, the vehicle was empty. It trundled along the winding road, flicking snow into the air from beneath its caterpillar treads.

'Was Celia afraid of heights?' asked Flowers.

'Not according to her husband. He said she didn't trust the lift not to break down. She wouldn't even get on it to go up to the restaurant.'

'Smart girl,' said Flowers. 'So, if she wouldn't get on it in fine weather, why would she get on it during a snowstorm?'

'I've been wondering about that, too.' Ryder could understand why the chairlift hadn't figured prominently in Lew's investigation. The chairlift was supposed to have been closed at 4.30 pm. Celia was heard arguing with Nigel right before his 5 pm set. And Lew had been searching for a missing person. With the chairlift closed before Celia had even left the inn, any copper would have discounted it and concentrated the search along the road between Charlotte Pass and Perisher Valley. The road they were travelling along now.

'Okay,' Ryder went on, 'who had the most to lose when everything started going wrong with the chairlift?'

'Well, Charlotte Pass, obviously.'

'That's Henry and Di Gordon. I'm assuming they were the

"interested parties" Chloe spoke of. They're the holders of the ninety-nine–year lease.'

Flowers' eyebrows shot up. 'Is that the set-up at Charlotte's?'

'Yep. It's Crown land.'

'Well, people get desperate when their livelihoods are threatened,' Flowers mused. 'Maybe they tried to hush up the problems with the chairlift. If Celia knew there was a risk to the public, she could have threatened to blow the whistle.'

Ryder shook his head. 'The ski community's small. News spreads fast, especially bad news. The operational problems would have been all over the newspapers. Celia wouldn't have been telling them anything they didn't already know.' He told Flowers about the ongoing affair between Nigel and Di Gordon.

Flowers gave a disgusted snort. 'Miller sounds like a real stand-up kinda guy. No wonder she was going to leave him.'

'So, who had motive?'

'Well, Di Gordon for one.'

Ryder nodded. 'With Celia out of the way, Di could have ditched her husband and had Nigel for herself. If she wanted him, that is.'

'But why murder Celia and go to the trouble of burying her up on Mount Stillwell? Would Di be physically capable of doing that, even back then? If they wanted to be together, why not just get a divorce?'

'It was the sixties, Flowers. No-fault divorce didn't become law until 1975. In most cases, the party who could prove the marriage breakdown was the fault of their spouse got awarded more money from the property settlement. And there were two marriages at stake here. We know Celia and Nigel argued, and she told him she was going to get a divorce. These things don't happen overnight. Back then, she would have needed proof of his infidelity. Maybe she'd been waiting for an opportunity to get a photograph of the two of them in bed together.'

'Nigel could have killed her after she revealed she was leaving him,' Flowers suggested.

'Lewicki always suspected he did, and he didn't know Miller was having an affair with Di at the time. It's not in the file.'

'So, why do you think Miller's admitted to it now? It shows motive.'

Ryder shook his head. 'I don't know. Maybe because the affair's been over for decades. Perhaps he's trying to cast suspicion onto Di Gordon and away from himself. I suspect his relationship with her husband isn't good. When I asked about that, he was pretty tight-lipped.'

The oversnow ground to a halt, giving way to a sister vehicle rumbling past in the other direction. In the glow from its interior light, Ryder could see it was packed with day trippers returning home, as well as the media contingent who had been reporting on Winterfest. The Gordons might be saddled with providing lodging to the police, but the media had no choice but to base themselves in Perisher. Charlotte's signal was too weak to upload the news footage they had taken during the day.

'Okay, let's keep going,' said Ryder, as the oversnow set off again.

Flowers reached for the grab handle, steadying himself against the vehicle's body roll.

'Henry would have had motive, too. All he needed for proof of infidelity was a photo of his wife and Nigel Miller in bed.'

'And with that, he could have got the lion's share of the property settlement, which included the lease on Charlotte Pass.'

Flowers snorted. 'That would be the lion's share of nothing, Sarge, if they were going to end up bankrupt.'

'Or the lion's share of a fortune, Flowers, if it all worked out.'

'Lewicki always suspected that relationship issues were at the centre of the investigation,' Ryder said when they were back at the inn. 'Damn. I wish we had a whiteboard.' He made a circuit of the desk, trying to pull the threads together in his mind. He glanced at Flowers, who was perched on the side of the desk. 'So . . . Celia decides her marriage is over—she tells Nigel. That brings things to a head and she wants to get away. Leave aside for a minute the time the chairlift was supposed to have been shut down. Celia is so upset and desperate to get out of the village that she puts her fear aside and somehow manages to get on that lift. The rest is simple. The chair slams into a tower fracturing her skull. A pylon is blown over. She goes down with the chair, coming to a sudden stop when she hits the ground. There's the deceleration injuries Harriet told us about.' Ryder stopped pacing and looked at Flowers, who'd slumped into the dining room chair. 'What do you think?'

'Impossible, Sarge.'

'Why?' asked Ryder, surprised at Flowers' quick comeback.

'She was too light to travel in that cab on her own.' Flowers leaned across the desk and dragged the Delaney file towards him. 'That safety report I read . . . ' he said, turning over the pages on the spike. 'Here it is, it's from the Department of Labour and Industry. It states that every cab needed to carry a certain weight to stabilise it. They needed two people to do that. Celia weighed seven stone six pounds back then, that's about forty-eight kilos. There's no way the liftie would have let her get on that lift on her own, not if he wanted to keep his job. If he did, he's culpable.'

Ryder stared at Flowers for a moment before nodding slowly. 'Bruno Lombardi. Good work, Flowers. Could she have slipped past the liftie without him seeing her?'

'She could have. Passengers were able to self-load onto that chairlift. But if she'd done that, then who the hell buried her?'

Ryder smiled and clapped his partner on the shoulder. 'Well done. You might have ambitions of becoming a police prosecutor but you're beginning to think like a detective. Okay, so we've established that the Gordons had motive and so did Nigel Miller—'

A rustling sound coming from the sitting room had Ryder turning around. 'What was that?'

In the other room, they found a large, white envelope lying on the carpet just in front of the door. Ryder picked it up and turned it over in his hands. Blank, and sealed. He opened the door and looked down the corridor towards the top of the staircase.

'Is anyone out there?' asked Flowers from behind.

Ryder shook his head. 'No.' He tore open the envelope and took out a large black-and-white photograph framed by a white border. A 'With Compliments' slip pinned to the corner showed the photograph had been left by Flowers' contact at the alpine club.

Ryder studied the photograph. A young Aidan Smythe was seated on a lounge with a woman perched on his knee. Di Gordon flanked one side of the group, Henry the other. Nigel Miller and his bandmates stood, holding their instruments and laughing—except the drummer, who held his drumsticks and poked out his tongue. Celia stood next to Nigel, a wooden smile on her face. Ryder recognised the fireplace and the arched windows in the background. 'This was taken here at the inn. Downstairs.'

'Who's the woman sitting on Aidan Smythe's knee?' Flowers asked, leaning in for a closer look.

'I'm guessing it's his wife, Carmel. She was his fiancée back then.' Ryder turned the photograph over. Sure enough, the names and date were written on the back. 'This photo was taken a couple of days before Celia's death and, yes, it says here the woman is Carmel, and apparently the band was called "Trippin" back then.'

'That's so weird, Sarge. Every person in that photo is here for Winterfest, except for Celia. It's like some reunion in an Agatha Christie novel.' Flowers glanced at him, excitement flashing in his eyes. 'You know, where all the people who were here back then have returned to the scene of the crime years later.'

'That makes for good fiction, Flowers, but let's try to stick to the facts.' Ryder slid the photograph back into the envelope. 'The groomer asked for snow fences to be built close to the grave site. That put people up in that area. They discovered the bones, which led to us finding the grave. And we know that grave had been interfered with. Someone's been leaving flowers up there, among the trees and away from the groomed runs where most people ski. So, how and when did this all start? When the groomer asked for the snow fences to be built. The odds are decreasing by the minute, don't you think?'

'So, you believe Lombardi's the key to all this?'

Ryder nodded. 'Bring him in after I've interviewed the Gordons.

And I want to talk to Aidan Smythe as well. The timing of this can't be a coincidence.'

'Do you think Lombardi did it so the body would be discovered during Winterfest, when the place is crawling with media?'

Ryder walked towards the windows and gazed out at the darkening mountain. 'I think whoever's been leaving posies on Celia's grave thinks she should be here, at the reunion.'

Ten

Day 4

The former ski champion had kept himself in good shape, the only sign of his prosperous lifestyle a small paunch visible when he sat down.

'Thanks for agreeing to talk to us, Mr Smythe,' said Ryder.

'I'm happy to help in any way I can.'

Ryder held up the portable recording device. 'I'm going to record our conversation because my handwriting is really crappy,' he said ruefully. 'Sometimes when I go back, I can't read it.'

Smythe gave a brief nod. 'Fair enough.'

'I'll start by noting a few details. Where is your place of residence?'

'I live in Whistler, British Columbia, Canada.'

'When did you move to Whistler?'

'In 1970.'

'And prior to that?'

'Prior to that I lived in Jindabyne, and then in the Dolomites in Italy for five years.'

'You lived there while you were skiing professionally?'

'Yes. Back then, Europe was the grail. Now it's the US.'

'Why Italy?'

'My wife preferred it to France, and I preferred the food. Races

88

are held all over Europe—Switzerland, Italy, France. The choice was ours to make.'

'What prompted the move to Whistler?'

'They offered me a job,' he said with a smile. 'Very important because we were about to start a family. We jumped at it. We loved living in Europe, but the language barrier was difficult in those days. It's much easier now.'

'Did you need a job?'

'Sure, I did.' Smythe's accent was a pleasant fusion of Canadian and Australian. 'Professional racing was a lifestyle—it didn't really pay. When I see what the racers earn today, I think I was born too early.'

'Your wife's family are wealthy?'

Smythe's smile died. 'I don't see how that has any bearing on anything.'

'It's true though, isn't it?' Ryder pushed. 'Your father-in-law built a lot of the infrastructure around here, including the ski tube?'

'Yes, the company he started are involved in a lot of projects. They bore out tunnels for underground motorways and things.'

'You never considered joining the family business?'

Smythe hesitated for a few moments, as though he resented the further probing into his in-law's affairs. 'Carmel was keen for me to join the company,' he said reluctantly, 'but it meant coming back to Australia permanently, and . . . skiing's my thing, you know. The terrain in the northern hemisphere is so much more expansive, and the mountains a hell of a lot steeper. Our children were born in Canada, too. It's home to them.'

'Do you get back here often?'

'To Australia? Not as often as I'd like.'

'Rarely?'

'We've been back a few times over the years, for special birthdays and family weddings and the like. My parents died long ago but Carmel's parents are still alive. They're in aged care and very frail, so we'll be coming back more often.'

'You've never been back here, to Charlotte Pass?'

'No. A visit is long overdue.'

'I want to ask you about the weekend in July 1964. You were here, weren't you, when the old chairlift that went up Mount Still-well was buried?'

'I was.' Smythe leaned forward, at ease again now the emphasis was off his family. 'It was one of those natural disasters you never forget.'

'Tell me about that weekend.'

'There's not much to tell. It was a simple matter of survival.'

'How so?'

'For a start, the weather was a threat to everyone's physical survival. The power was out. People were freezing. Emergency supplies couldn't get through. I'll never forget that morning when we woke up. The chairlift was torn apart and buried by huge snow-drifts. There was this awful feeling that the place was doomed. It was very sad.'

'When did you learn that Celia Delaney was missing?'

Smythe frowned. 'Nigel's Celia? Celia Miller?'

'Yes, though she went by her maiden name.' According to Lew's file notes, Celia had grown tired of her husband's fans, and their insatiable appetite to know everything about him.

Ryder took out the photograph of the group taken in the bar. 'That's her, standing behind you in the photo.'

'Yes, I know who she is. I'm just trying to think back to when I heard she was missing. That was your question, wasn't it? You'll have to forgive me, Detective, it's been a long time. Mostly what I remember is working until we dropped. Everyone was bone weary.'

'How well did you know Celia?'

He hesitated. 'Not well. I knew her as Nigel's wife.'

'The four of you didn't socialise together, away from Charlotte Pass?'

Smythe shook his head. 'No. Charlotte's was a bit like that. People met up here every year for a week or two, and then left and went about their lives until the following year.'

Ryder nodded. 'Do you remember a lift operator who worked here back then—Bruno Lombardi?'

Smythe hesitated. 'No. I don't remember anyone by that name.'

'What about Burt Crofts, a lift mechanic?'

Smythe shook his head. 'I don't remember him either. I'm sorry.'

'The afternoon before the storm—the storm that hit with ferocity that night . . .'

'Hmm.' Smythe's gaze was direct as he concentrated on the question.

'The chairlift was shut down around four-thirty that afternoon. Do you remember where you were at the time?'

'Not specifically, but I would have been out on the hill. That was a bumper season, Sergeant, and I was just about to leave for Europe. I was taking advantage of the conditions every single minute, I know that.'

'That makes sense,' said Ryder, switching off the recorder and pushing back his chair. 'Well, I guess that's all I need for now. It's a shame this had to happen during your week of celebrations.'

'Oh, it can't be helped,' Smythe said, getting to his feet.

'So, what have they got lined up for you today?' asked Ryder as they walked into the sitting room.

Smythe checked his watch. 'Di has me on a pretty tight schedule. I've got about half an hour until I have to be at the top of the mountain. Do you ski, Detective?'

'Me? No.' Ryder shook his head and opened the door. 'Give me the surf any day.'

Eleven

Vanessa raised the safety bar and wriggled to the edge of the seat. As the moving chair descended over the safety net, she tucked the two orange PVC poles and the CLOSED sign under her arm. When the chair skimmed over the platform, she touched her skis onto the compacted snow and, keeping her weight forward, glided down the unloading ramp. The empty chair swung around the bull wheel with a rattle and continued on its way downhill.

She came to a stop near the boundary rope that separated the resort's terrain from the ungroomed back country. The weather had cleared during her lunch break, typical of how quickly it could change in the mountains. In the distance, Kosciuszko's flat-ish peak nestled towards the back of the main range.

A scrape of edges behind her made her turn. Vanessa blinked in surprise. Aidan Smythe had come to a stop beside her. 'I'd forgotten how spectacular the view is from up here.' He used his stocks to draw level with her. 'You're practically standing on top of Australia.'

'I love it,' she said, admiring his blingy gold jacket and matching wraparound sunglasses. Up close, his freckled complexion and uneven skin tone spoke of decades of UV exposure and wind burn.

'Back in the day, I used to hike out there to Kosciuszko. We used to stop for lunch at the Blue Lake. I loved skiing off-piste.'

Vanessa rested the sign and posts on the snow. 'I never ski out of bounds. The worry would kill my mother.'

He chuckled. 'Very sensible. I'm afraid my mind might be willing, but the old legs wouldn't stand up to it these days, especially in these boots.' He tapped the shell of his ski boot with his stock. 'The leather ones we used to wear were easier to hike in than these rigid things.'

'Are you enjoying being back in Australia?' she asked, trying not to look too star struck.

'Very much so. Everyone's gone to a lot of trouble arranging things. I'm looking forward to a fun time.' He glanced over his shoulder to where a small group of people had gathered.

'I hope you brought a pen. It looks like you have autographs to sign.'

Aidan Smythe's eyes twinkled mischievously. 'They're my students. I'm taking a masterclass this week.'

'Of course.' Heat warmed Vanessa's face despite the cold breeze. With everything that had happened over the past few days, she'd forgotten all about his special ski class.

'Well, I won't keep you. It's looks like you have an important job to do.' He gave her a friendly nod. 'Nice chatting with you, dear.'

'Yes. Enjoy your stay.'

Vanessa watched him push off. Aidan Smythe was a tall, fit seventy-odd with a physique many younger men would envy. Whatever he said to the group must have been funny, because within seconds of him joining them they broke into laughter. He pointed with his stock for them to take the back track. A winding road high on the ridge, it had intermittent falls and a few steep rises that required the skier to work up a good amount of speed so they weren't reduced to walking up the hills sideways.

'So, what's the king like?'

Vanessa turned around to see Sam, the liftie, leaning on his shovel and smiling at her.

'He's charming,' she said, a little irritated. Sam's job was to keep an eye on the people getting off the chairlift, not to watch her and Smythe. 'Hand me the drill from inside the hut, will you?'

'I love a woman who knows her way around power tools,' Sam said with a cocky grin as he handed her the heavy snow drill.

Shaking her head, Vanessa hoisted the posts and sign onto one shoulder and hung the drill over the other. She pushed off, taking the back track, but in the opposite direction to where Aidan Smythe and his students had gone. With a skating action, she headed up the slight rise, making for a spot thirty metres away where two large boulders sat either side of the track. Earlier, Terry had spotted half a dozen dare-devil snowboarders riding the fresh powder close to Celia's grave. Despite having already roped off the immediate area around the site, he'd now decided to cut off access to the entire side of the mountain. At least until the police had given them the go-ahead to remove everything.

The police. Vanessa smiled, her thoughts shifting to Detective Pierce Ryder. Her heart had skipped a beat when he'd walked into the cafe, though he'd arrived at an awkward time when she was telling Terry about her run-in with Bruno.

'It's just not on,' Terry had said of Bruno's intimidating behaviour. 'I'll give him a warning, and hopefully you'll have no further problems. If you do, come and see me straightaway.'

'I will,' she'd promised, with a sideways glance at the detective sitting a couple of tables away. She'd been surprised to find him looking right at her. Their gazes had held for an intense second or two before he'd looked away to focus on the flat screen in the corner. He went still, staring unblinkingly at the film as though he'd developed a sudden interest in skiing Valdez in Alaska.

Vanessa had stared at her coffee, ridiculously pleased that she'd sprung him checking her out. Or had she imagined that? Maybe he'd just been wondering what she and Terry had been discussing so seriously.

Pushing all thoughts of the detective to the back of her mind, she snowploughed to a stop as the boulders came into view. Clicking out of her skis, she let everything bar the drill drop to the ground. Choosing an appropriate spot, she set the heavy-duty bit to the hard-packed snow. The high-pitched whir from the motor shattered the silence as she bored a hole on either side of the track. Once the posts were firmly jammed in, she strung a florescent orange CLOSED sign between them.

'That should do it,' she said to herself, surveying her handiwork. Anyone who chose to disobey that signage would get a ticking off from the closest person in uniform and their lift pass confiscated.

Back at the lifties' hut, she left her skis with Sam and gave him strict instructions that no one other than ski patrol was to go beyond the CLOSED sign. Then she traded him the drill for the keys to the snowmobile that was always parked beneath the platform.

After making sure her path was clear of guests, she drove in a direct line across the side of the mountain she'd just closed, easing off the throttle only when she reached the trees. For the next few minutes, she manoeuvred the machine though the gnarled snow gums, the furrowed snow evidence of the few adventurous guests Terry had spotted earlier. When the fences and police tape came into view, she parked the snowmobile a safe distance away and walked to the fences to do the check she had promised Terry. The posts were on a lean, the weight of the built-up snow forcing them downhill.

Vanessa took out her two-way radio. 'Vanessa to Terry.'

'Go ahead, Vee.'

'I'm at the snow fences. Any more tonight and they'll collapse.'

Vanessa grimaced as static crackled in her ear. Then Terry's voice came through loud and clear. 'I'll talk to the detectives. We'll need to get Bruno in there. Did you close the trail up top?'

'All done.'

'Righto, thanks.'

She pocketed the radio, unwilling to leave without pausing for a few seconds as a mark of respect to Celia. It had started to snow again, large flakes clinging to the branches of the snow gum that stood by the grave site like a sentinel. Vanessa watched the snow settle on the leaves, hoping that the young woman who'd lost her life up here would be transferred to a heavenly garden somewhere, her final resting place surrounded by flowers rather than crime-scene tape.

She was turning away when a tell-tale build-up of snow near the base of the tree caught her eye. Pushing her goggles onto her forehead, she edged closer to the police tape for a better view. A dangerous hollow, a tree well had begun to form around the roots of the snow gum. Vanessa lowered her goggles, her body suddenly chilled despite the thermal layers she wore beneath her jacket. She'd pulled dead people out of tree wells in north America and France. How deep would that void have been back in 1964, when the snow had reached the eaves of the inn, and people had been skiing off the roof?

Back on the snowmobile, she opened up the throttle and headed straight for the village. She made a beeline for the run under the old chairlift and exited the trees at speed, a whiff of diesel in her nostrils, eyes watering behind her goggles.

At the inn, she parked at the side of the building and walked around to the entrance. An outdoor cafe had been set up a little way down the hill, where people were huddled close together, warming their hands around steaming mugs of coffee and hot chocolate.

Terry emerged through the front swing doors.

'Hey. Have you seen Detective Ryder?' she asked.

'He's in the foyer, on his phone,' he said without stopping.

'Vanessa!'

She wheeled around to see Libby tramping down the slope followed by a group of children pulling plastic toboggans.

'Hey. What's up?'

Libby came closer and whispered in her ear. 'I might have to crash on your trundle again soon.'

Vanessa grinned. 'Are you being sexcluded from your room again?'

'Shh!' Libby glanced around but nobody was paying attention, least of all the kids. 'Just my luck I get stuck with a horny roommate. I swear, she's working her way through every guy in the hotel staff accommodation.'

'Well, you can crash on my trundle anytime.'

'Thanks, Vee. You're a lifesaver. I wish I lived at Long Bay. You don't know how lucky you are having a room to yourself.'

'It's a ski-patrol perk.' Vanessa turned at the sound of an oversnow transport vehicle. It was trundling up the hill towards the inn, snow flying from beneath its caterpillar treads.

'Stand over here, kids,' Libby called as the vehicle drew level with the cafe patrons.

'Are you up for a drink tonight?' Vanessa asked. 'The more I hang around Long Bay, the more chance I have of running into Bruno.'

'Oh, my God. What a loser that guy is. Of course I'm up for a drink. And it's my shout.' Libby raised her voice over the rumble of the diesel engine. 'Does six work for—'

'Get those kids out of here!'

Vanessa swung around at Detective Ryder's furious voice. His brows were drawn together, his eyes sparking with anger as he marched towards them, the inn doors swinging to a close behind him. 'What the hell do you think you're doing?'

Vanessa blinked. 'What?'

'Tell me you can see that.' He stabbed a finger at the approaching oversnow.

Vanessa glanced over her shoulder then looked at Libby, who was herding the children into a tight group. 'It always pulls up here. People ski around it and stand out here all the time. Nothing's ever happened.'

He leaned in close and practically growled the words. 'I don't know what kind of a show you're running here, but *that* practice is unsafe.'

'I'm sorry,' Libby said, her pale complexion turning a fierce red. She leaned over and scooped up a little girl who'd burst into tears and settled her on her hip. 'I'll take the kids away now.'

Her words seemed to appease him a little. He gave a brief nod, watching as Libby made her escape, shooing the kids away in front of her. The driver had cut the engine and a couple of porters looked on in amusement as they came outside to unload the guests' luggage.

'You were *talking*, and not taking any notice of the children,' he hissed, hustling Vanessa to one side of the entrance as incoming guests began to scramble down from the vehicle's specially modified cabin.

'There's a law against talking, is there?' Vanessa bristled, her cheeks burning with embarrassment from the public dressing down.

'Libby is in charge of the children. Not that I'm blaming her. It's just the way things work around here.'

'Well, it needs to change,' Ryder retorted. 'Kids are unpredictable. They shove one another. They chase one another. If one had darted away from the group they could have ended up under those caterpillar treads.'

'I get your point, but I think you're over-reacting.'

His eyebrows shot up and his lips parted.

'What I mean is,' she said quickly before he could continue his tirade, 'the oversnow moves very slowly. We've never had a problem.'

'There's always a first time. Believe me, Vanessa, that's something you don't want to see.'

Vanessa stared at him, curling her fingers inside her gloves, too angry to speak. He held her gaze for a few seconds of loaded silence before turning and striding back into the inn.

Face flaming, Vanessa kicked at the snow. She needed to tell him about that friggin' tree well, but as for chasing after him, the . . . She didn't know what to think of him now.

She looked up. The people from the oversnow were milling around, most of them too busy admiring the gorgeous vista to have noticed their heated exchange. Only one elderly man was watching with keen interest.

Oh, to hell with it.

Vanessa weaved her way around the luggage, and with a pointed look at the man, followed Ryder into the inn. Confrontation might be unpleasant, but if she could ward off creepy Bruno, she could handle angry Pierce Ryder. It was important he learn about the tree well; more important than any embarrassment she might suffer.

She took off her ski boots and shoved them under the bench seat in the foyer. She couldn't handle Di Gordon going ballistic right now. Even her paying guests were subjected to death stares for failing to remove their ski boots. A patroller wouldn't escape so lightly.

Upstairs, she rapped loudly on the door of Ryder's suite.

She waited, steeling her mind. There was the sound of movement from inside, and she bit her lip wondering if Detective Flowers was with him. Then Ryder flung open the door, his face pale, his dark hair dishevelled like he'd been running a hand through it.

He stared at her, disbelief in his eyes. 'Have you come back for more, or are you going to give me a piece of your mind?'

She didn't answer, just pushed past him and walked into the sitting room.

'Come in,' he said dryly, though he didn't order her out. He closed the door and turned to face her.

'You're right.' She spoke first, her voice shaking with renewed anger. 'I don't ever want to see a child, or an adult, go under those caterpillar treads. I'll raise the issue of oversnow safety at the next meeting. What I do object to is you treating me like I'm personally responsible for some horrific thing that hasn't even happened.'

He moved past her and sat on the edge of the sofa. Elbows resting on his knees, he clasped his hands together and stared across the room.

'I was waiting to see you when you let loose down there,' she said.

He raised a shaky hand and rubbed at his forehead with his fingers.

What was going on with him? Vanessa frowned, her anger cooling. 'You're shaken up. I can see that. You remind me of . . .'

'An addict?' He bit out the words.

'Someone who's had a shock, actually.' She walked over and sat at arm's length from him. 'Are you an addict?' She asked him quietly, desperately wanting him to say no.

He shook his head. 'Not unless you count the cigarettes I gave up three months ago.'

'Nicotine doesn't stay that long in your system.'

'And yet I'd kill for a smoke.'

'That's stress.'

'Post-traumatic—so they tell me.' He glanced at her, a weary smile tugging at the corners of his lips.

'Have you spoken to any—'

'Yes. It's not unusual. Half the Force has it.'

'That's a sad statistic.'

He gave a curt nod as though the subject were closed.

She smiled, her anger gone. 'My mother suffered from it, too.' The tree well could wait a few minutes. 'I caused it. Seems I have a knack for triggering post-traumatic stress.'

'What happened downstairs had nothing to do with you. You were in the wrong place at the wrong time. I'm sorry.'

He gave her a half-smile and reached for the glass jug on the coffee table. He poured water into two tumblers. 'I'd prefer something stronger, but not while I'm on duty.' He handed her a glass, cool fingers brushing hers for a nanosecond. 'Tell me about your mother,' he said, clearly in need of a distraction. 'Were you a disorderly teenager?'

Vanessa watched him through her glass as she drank the water, feeling a sudden desire to distract him another way, whether he was on duty or not. Bothered by her thoughts, and hoping her emotions didn't show on her face, she gulped down the rest of her water and put her glass back on the table. Something stronger would have been good.

'It's kind of a long story.'

'I'd like to hear it.'

'Okay,' she said, pleased that he seemed to be calmer now. 'I was five. My older sister, Eva, was at school. Dad had gone to pick her up, and Mum was on the verandah busy making presents for the school's Mother's Day stall. I was riding around on my bike. The verandah wraps around three sides of the house. There's a vegetable garden down one side. I remember feeling hungry, but I knew Mum was busy, so I got off my bike and went into the garden. We had strawberries growing. I loved them so much I would eat them when they were only half-ripened. I'd given myself an awful stomach ache a few times, and Mum had warned me not to eat them while they were still green. She said I would be in all sorts of trouble if I did. Of course, she meant I'd get ill, but I imagined she'd get really angry with me. I remember hearing her calling me. I had pink juice all over my hands and clothes. I knew she'd know what I'd been doing, so I ran out of the garden and onto the property. I was lost all night before they found me the next morning.'

'Your poor mother. She would have been blaming herself for taking her eyes off you, and fearing the worst the whole time.'

'She was. We have a few dams on the farm. I avoided them, though, and dossed down beside a creek with my trusty Jemima doll.' She left out the bit about the impenetrable fog, and the terror she'd experienced at not being able to see.

The colour had come back into his face, but he was looking at her with so much pain in his eyes that she kept talking. 'My mother became over-protective after that. She did her best to wrap me in cotton wool.'

'So, you pushed back and became a ski patroller?'

Vanessa laughed. 'Something like that.'

She waited for him to speak, though she got the impression Ryder wasn't an over-sharer. She could almost feel sorry for his counsellor.

'I'm glad things turned out well for your family,' he said eventually. 'You were all very lucky.' He set his glass down on the table. 'Now, what did you want to talk to me about?'

'Okay.' Vanessa took a breath. 'At lunchtime, Terry asked me to close off access to Mount Stillwell, which I did. While I was up there, I noticed that a tree well was starting to form around the roots of that big snow gum right by the gravesite. I couldn't get a closer look because of the police tape.'

Ryder stared at her. 'What's a tree well?'

'It's a void that forms around the lower part of the trunk. Snow falls on the boughs and branches. That stops the snow around the trunk from becoming hard-packed. Of course, snow still collects there, but it's softer. I think it's got something to do with the warmer temperature around the roots too. If you took my ski pole and prodded the snow around the roots, it would probably disappear right into the well. They're dangerous traps for skiers, deadly sometimes, particularly in the back country. I've had to dig a few people out in the northern hemisphere.'

He nodded, the furrow between his brows deepening. 'Keep going.'

'Well, people tend to fall in head first. When their skis or boards hit the slushy stuff, it stops their momentum. They pitch forward into the well and suffocate.'

'Suffocate?'

Vanessa nodded. 'Usually they're upside down, their skis or board stuck in the snow above them. The more they struggle to get out, the more the snow caves in around them. It's like being buried head first in sand at the beach.'

'Christ, it sounds bloody awful. Were they okay, these people you had to dig out?'

'Not all of them. Tree wells are the leading cause of death in the snowfields.'

Ryder paused, considering her words. 'In that case, why wouldn't that tree have been roped off? I know it's your first season here, but surely the people who've been here for years would know it's a hazard?'

'It's in the ungroomed part of the resort. We can't rope off every tree.' But he had a point. People like Bruno, who knew every inch of Charlotte Pass, would know the regular spots where tree wells formed. 'It hadn't begun to form the other day when you dug up the skeleton, but it's been snowing non-stop since then and you can see the beginnings of it.'

'Okay.' Ryder pushed himself to his feet. 'Well, thank you for this. It looks like I'll have to go up there.'

Vanessa stood in her socked feet. 'I'd better get back to work, too. If you want to read more about it, search up SIS—snow immersion suffocation—from tree wells.'

He smiled a little. 'Why would I do that when you can show me?'

Vanessa blinked. 'I'm not an expert. I assumed you'd want to do more research.'

'The wi-fi's crap. You said it yourself.' He snatched up his parka from the back of the sofa and shrugged it on. 'Come on.'

'But . . .'

'You've dug people out of tree wells. You can't beat firsthand experience.' He pulled on a pair of leather gloves, his eyes on her face. 'How do we get up there?'

'Snowmobile. It's parked around the corner of the inn.'

'Then let's go.'

A loud rap on the door pulled them up.

'It's probably Flowers, or the cleaners,' he said, taking two quick strides before flinging open the door.

A few seconds of silence followed.

Vanessa moved from behind Ryder to see who it was. The elderly man who'd arrived on the oversnow, the one who had witnessed their altercation and watched her follow Ryder inside.

'Lew. What are you doing here?' Ryder asked, the surprise evident in his voice.

'I'm taking a ski holiday.'

'Like hell you are. I've been trying to call you.'

'The reception's bad.' There was another silence, then the man spoke again. 'Well, are you going to let me in? My room's not ready yet.'

'Where are you staying?'

'Here. A teenager broke his arm. His parents took him home so I got their room.'

Ryder stood aside so the man could enter. 'Did you get a short-term contract to work on the case?'

'They offered to keep my bags behind the front desk, but I told them we were friends and you wouldn't mind me waiting up here.'

'Annie always said you had selective deafness,' Ryder muttered. 'Come in, Lew. I could do with your help. Are you here to help solve the case?'

'Someone has to.' The man called Lew dumped his bag on the floor and looked at Vanessa with interest. 'All you seem to be doing so far is shouting at the staff.'

Twelve

Ryder loosened his fingers on the rear grab handles, enjoying the surge of adrenaline as the snowmobile roared up Mount Stillwell. The late afternoon sun cast long shadows over the ski runs, but it was the view inches in front of Ryder that held his interest. Vanessa was leaning forward, the medic symbol emblazoned across her back, her upper body constantly in motion. There was a graceful physicality to the way she manoeuvred the snowmobile through the wooded terrain, avoiding the areas of loose deep snow where the machine was at risk of getting stuck.

The gradient increased as they neared the site and Vanessa slid back on the seat. She wriggled forward, putting an inch or two between them, only to slide back again as they climbed higher. With his spine pressed into the snowmobile's backrest, Ryder had no room to move. Not that he wanted to. Eventually, she gave up fighting gravity and stayed put, her bottom resting snugly between his thighs.

Ryder smiled at his good fortune but forced himself to focus on something other than the woman pressed against him. Instead, he inhaled a deep breath of freezing air and thought about Lewicki's unexpected arrival. Ryder had been relieved to see his friend. Lew's historical knowledge of the case would be invaluable, though he'd have to be prepared to take a back seat, which would be hard for someone with Lew's temperament. Flowers had been doing some decent work, and Ryder didn't want Lew upsetting their fledgling partnership because he was so invested in Celia Delaney's case.

Ryder caught sight of the granite boulder through the trees and then the police tape came into view.

'I hope this doesn't prove to be a waste of time,' Vanessa said, unclipping her helmet as they climbed off the snowmobile a few minutes later.

Ryder tried to keep his expression neutral. But—a waste? Never. Riding pillion behind her had been worth every damn second in the freezing cold. His body hummed with nervous anticipation, and it wasn't because he was about to look at something called a tree well. He managed a casual shrug as they walked towards the tape. 'It's always best to check things out.'

He lifted the tape so she could duck underneath, then followed her into the cordoned-off area. The snow was deeper away from the trails, and despite his calf-length hiking boots, Ryder sank to his knees in the snow.

'Be careful here.' She moved tentatively towards the base of the ancient gum. Snow weighed down its foliage, the lower boughs resting on the ground. Ryder watched as Vanessa squatted and took hold of one of the smaller branches. Even before she'd pushed it aside, he could see the circular void that had formed around its trunk.

'Let me hold that.' He squatted beside her and she let him take the weight of the branch. Pushing it out of the way, he leaned forward and peered down into a wide, deep hole. 'Jesus. Ski too close to that and you could find yourself buried in a matter of seconds.'

'That's why you should never ski alone. If you fall into one of these, you have little chance of digging yourself out.'

Ryder reached into his pocket for his point-and-click camera. Vanessa held the branch again while he took photographs for the file.

As they straightened up, the branch flew back in place with a shower of snow. Ryder took a couple of steps back and looked up at the crown of the tree. He had no idea how high it would have been in 1964, but even if it had been half the height, the bottom of the tree well would have been much farther down because the snow had been so much deeper back then.

Vanessa was looking at him wide-eyed, like he might suddenly have an answer, and he wished he did.

'Thank you for showing me this. Unfortunately, it raises more questions than it answers.' He couldn't discuss the case with her, but his mind was racing. Could Celia have fallen into the tree well and suffocated? Was that how she'd suffered the deceleration injuries? The area was isolated, even more so back then. No one would have heard her cries for help. Ryder banished the disturbing image from his mind, his gut telling him she hadn't been on skis. The area was hostile, and she'd been a tentative skier. The fact that no ski fragments had been recovered near the bones added weight to the theory that she had been on foot. Ryder slipped the camera back into his pocket. The more he mulled it over, the more he suspected she had gone down with the chairlift. Could she have survived the fall, only to tumble into the tree well? It was significant that the hazard was only steps from her grave. But it didn't explain how she had sustained the repeated blows to her head.

He lifted the tape for Vanessa, certain of one thing: the person who had been leaving posies on Celia's grave had to be the same person who'd found her body in the spring melt, and who'd made the decision to put her in the ground.

And that raised the question of why.

The clink of keys brought Ryder back to the present. He glanced sideways at Vanessa.

'Do you mind if I drive?' he asked, watching as she put on her helmet and fastened the strap. 'It's been a while.'

She pointed at the snowmobile. 'You've driven one of these before?'

'An older model than that one.'

'Well . . . since you're pulling rank, Detective.' She grinned and lobbed the keys in his direction.

Ryder shot out a hand and caught them. 'You'll need to show me the way.' Feeling more twenty-eight than thirty-eight, he tossed the keys in the air, snatched them back again and swung his leg over the snowmobile. With luck, she would move up nice and securely behind him, her head close to his as she directed him.

'The newer models work the same way as the older ones,' she said. 'The throttle's still on the right, the brake on the left. It's a push-button start now. The biggest difference is in the power. Take it easy until you get the feel of it.'

He slipped the key into the ignition and pressed the start button, enjoying the light pressure of her hands on his shoulders and the brush of her body as she slipped in behind him. With the sun sinking fast, he switched on the headlights. When she gave him the thumbs up, he opened the throttle and headed back the way they'd come.

Vanessa leaned easily with the machine, her knees brushing his hips as she waved him away from the deeper snow drifts and pointed out places where partially submerged rocks could cause a problem.

'Can we go via the old chairlift?' he shouted over his shoulder.

'What?' She wriggled closer up behind him.

'The old chairlift?'

'That way.' She pointed past his shoulder. 'Keep to the higher track.'

When they reached the smoothed-out area being prepared for the tube run, Ryder let the snowmobile idle. Lights were coming on inside the Charlotte Mountain Inn, the jewel in the crown and the centre of village life. In his mind's eye he pictured the chairlift, the colourful cabs soaring higher than the trees on their way to the Stillwell Restaurant. Then his mind shifted gear and he imagined Celia cowering, hands raised to ward off whatever or whoever was coming towards her. Blood and brain matter, leaking from her fractured skull to congeal in her hair. Her lifeblood, seeping from her tiny, twisted body to form a black stain in the virgin snow.

A sudden gust of wind sent the top layer of snow swirling around the snowmobile.

'We'd better keep going,' Ryder said, with a quick glance at Vanessa.

She nodded, but didn't say anything. That was one of the things he liked about her: she was comfortable with the silences.

For Ryder, the trip back was over all too soon.

He parked the snowmobile in the same spot, away from the busy entrance with its rows of ski racks lined up out front. With a pang of regret he hit the ignition button and waited as the engine petered out. For long seconds neither of them moved, and then he slid forward giving her room to swing her leg over the seat.

'Oh!'

He swung around, lunging towards her the same instant she grabbed his shoulder. A buckle on her ski boot had snagged on the padded seat and she jolted backwards, the leg on which she was standing beginning to twist at the knee.

'Steady.' He wrapped an arm around her slim waist, supporting her until she'd righted herself. Then he reached out and gently unhooked the black boot with the orange flame design on the side.

'Oh, my God, thank you.'

Only when she had both feet firmly planted on the ground did he let her go. 'That could have been nasty. Are you all right?'

'I am.' She unclipped her helmet then bent down to rub a hand over her knee. 'Sorry about that. I could have pulled you off the damn thing.'

'Who knew skidoos could be so dangerous?'

'It was my fault. I undo my buckles when I'm walking around. I should have done them up again.'

'That's why I never took to skiing. Too much equipment involved. With football, you pull on a jersey and run onto the field.'

'Have you ever tried it?'

'Oh, sure. I went on a couple of school trips, and a group of us came down when we were younger.' He smiled. 'I was playing football back then. There was a clause in my contract saying I wasn't allowed to ski or bungee jump, so I spent the weekend drinking schnapps in the hot tub. The ultimate skiing experience.'

'What code did you play?' she asked, continuing to massage her knee.

'League. Not for long, though. I retired when I kept dislocating the same shoulder.'

'Ouch,' she said, straightening up. 'I don't blame you for giving it up.' She went to say something more, then hesitated, as though she'd had second thoughts.

He held out the keys to the snowmobile. 'Take these, or you'll be looking everywhere for them.'

She took the keys from him, and dropped them inside her helmet. 'When did you learn to drive a snowmobile?'

'Oh, on a Contiki tour I did with a few mates. I was about nineteen, I think.'

She smiled. 'Sounds like fun.'

They hadn't moved from the spot where they'd parked. Ryder hoped it wasn't wishful thinking on his part, but she seemed as reluctant as he was to leave.

'So, is there an end in sight for your day, Detective?' she asked eventually.

He sighed. 'It's not looking good, especially now that I have a visitor.'

She nodded. 'Oh, yes, Mr Lewicki.'

Ryder smiled. 'Lew and I go way back.' He might still be smarting from Lew's harsh words in Henderson's office, but it would take more than that to damage their relationship.

She nodded. 'So, do you get time off when you're working on a case, or are you expected to be on duty twenty-four–seven?' She held his gaze for a few long seconds then began loosening the fingers of her other glove. 'Don't worry. Forget I said—'

'I get time off.'

She stilled, two pink spots forming on her cheekbones.

'What did you have in mind?' he asked.

'Coffee, or a drink. In Jindabyne—if our days off coincide.' She looked down and pushed her gloves inside the helmet on top of the keys, then looked up as though ready to hear his answer.

He nodded. 'I'd like that.'

She smiled, then ever so slowly ran her eyes over him, like he'd finally given her permission to do so.

'It's not risky for you, is it?' she asked, as they finally began to make their way towards the corner of the building.

'Only if you're a felon, or there's a warrant out for your arrest.'

'Oh, no. I'm clean, Detective.' She smoothed her hair back from her face, her hazel eyes twinkling, a satisfied smile curving her full lips.

'No problem then,' said Ryder. He needed to let her know, right now, just how keen he was. 'So, when's your next day off?'

She laughed, and his skin turned to gooseflesh the way it did when he heard the first notes of his favourite song.

'I'll check my roster, but I'm sure I have one owing.'

Lewicki wasn't in the suite.

Ryder walked into the room that served as his office and stared at the file in the centre of the desk. It looked much as it had when he'd left. He flipped open the file cover and stared at the stack of documents held together by a metal split pin. There were no signs of Lew having gone through it, though Ryder secretly hoped he had. He'd already made up his mind to use Lew regardless of whether he had a short-term contract. Lew's knowledge of the original investigation was a valuable police resource you couldn't put a price on.

Ryder closed the file as the sat phone rang. 'Harriet.'

'You getting cabin fever up there yet?'

Ryder smiled. 'I'm doing okay. We've had an interesting development this afternoon.'

'Okay, you go.'

He told her about the tree well. 'Do you think Celia could have sustained those injuries by falling into one?'

'The deceleration injuries for sure. The injury to her skull was more consistent with being struck repeatedly with a heavy object.'

Ryder shook his head, the possibilities percolating in his mind. 'Okay. What have you got for me?'

'Well, remember I said we'd found a small object with a clasp?'

'Yep.'

'Turns out it wasn't a purse. It's a cigarette case.'

'Okay, not so unusual for the time.'

'No, but Tiffany is unusual. We don't see many of those.'

'Any inscription?'

'No.'

Ryder frowned. A Tiffany cigarette case wouldn't have been an easy thing to get your hands on back in 1964, especially for a young dental nurse from Newcastle and her musician husband. They hadn't exactly been rolling in money, according to a statement Lewicki had taken from Nigel. If not for his gigs, they wouldn't have even been at Charlotte Pass.

'Any kind of identification number?' he asked.

'Only the jeweller's trademark number, but we're still working on it. I'll take a photo and send it to you.'

'Thanks, Harriet.'

He'd just hung up when Inspector Gray called for an update. At the end of his summary, Ryder added: 'I believe someone has interfered with the burial site. They've put the bones in a place where they were certain to be found. In my mind, it's the same person who's been leaving flowers on the grave. That shows remorse. Whoever this person is, they wanted Celia Delaney found.'

'Looks like it.' Gray's gravelly voice was so clear he could have been in the next room. 'But if their aim was to confess before they shuffled off to meet their maker, why not walk into the nearest police station?'

'We think they're looking to expose someone else. Now, during Winterfest, while the place is crawling with media. They're after maximum exposure.'

'They've set the stage?'

'I think so. This plan has been a long time in the making.'

Ryder could imagine the Inspector, his craggy face close to the window glass as he peered at the Parramatta foot traffic below.

'So, this Aidan Smythe? Where does he fit in?'

'He was here the weekend Celia went missing. He's back for a superannuation tour. Detective Flowers has spent all morning keeping the media at bay, so I've given him a half day's break.

He's been doing an excellent job, doling out the "We're carrying out further investigations" line. But once I start pulling in the locals for questioning tomorrow . . .'

'Who are you talking to?'

'All of them. There's a groomer who asked for snow fences to be built in the area. There's a lift mechanic, too. Both know the mountains better than anyone. And the couple who owned the lease back then, Henry and Di Gordon—they're still the proprietors. We're also keeping Senior Sergeant Henderson at Monaro copied in.'

'Good idea. What about the pathologist's report?'

Ryder outlined Celia's multiple fractures. 'She sustained massive injuries. She didn't wander off and die of exposure. And her body was found close to where an old chairlift used to run into Thredbo. It's turned the logistics of the prior investigation on its head, though I have to agree with Roman Lewicki's view that this was a crime of passion.'

There was silence at the other end of the phone.

Ryder wandered over to the window while the Inspector mulled over the facts. Lights were beginning to come on inside Long Bay, and Ryder wondered if Vanessa was out doing a last sweep of the mountain, or whether she'd clocked off and gone inside.

'What are the chances of us getting a conviction?'

'Reasonable. The suspects are in their seventies, but they're all still holding down jobs.'

'Okay.' There was the sound of Gray shuffling papers. 'I have a note here that Newcastle Police Station have made contact with Celia Delaney's parents. You can go through them for anything you need. Other than that, it's the status quo.'

Ryder smiled. He'd deliberately not mentioned the tree well and cigarette case. He might need them for his next progress report.

'Has Gavin Hutton resurfaced, Inspector?' Ryder held his breath. He'd put up a fight not to be sent to Charlotte Pass. Now, he hoped Gavin Hutton would lie low until he could get back on the investigation team.

'The search along the Alpine Way turned up nothing, as you've probably heard. We went ahead and released a facial sketch, and a few people have come forward. I'll call you if we get any traction.'

'I'd appreciate that, sir.'

'Well, let me know if you need more manpower up there, will you? Oh, and Pierce, don't forget to put in your overtime.'

'Will do. Thank you, Inspector.' Ryder killed the call and took a deep breath. Gray wasn't ready to pull the plug on the Delaney case yet but, if Gavin Hutton resurfaced, that could change quickly.

Ryder stared at the phone in his hand. He hadn't said anything about Lewicki turning up. Strictly speaking, Lew was on a ski holiday, which meant it was no one else's business. But tell that to Gray, and he'd know it was bullshit.

Ryder switched off the light and grabbed his leather jacket.

It was time he found his friend.

Ryder opened the door to the bar, the pulse of the bass guitar hitting him in the chest. Dimly lit with a low ceiling, the space resembled an underground cavern. He ordered a beer at a well-stocked bar with colourful bottles displayed on glass shelving, and cast his eyes around the room. To his right, a dish-shaped light hung low over a billiard table where two men were engrossed in a game of pool. Ahead of him, a wooden dance floor led to where The Other Miller Band were playing against the rear wall. Tables of assorted sizes were arranged on a carpeted area around the dance floor's perimeter.

Ryder collected his beer then weaved his way through the crowd. 'Hangin' out with all your friends?' he asked, sliding onto the high stool next to Lewicki.

'I'm sitting here having a quiet drink and making a few people nervous. Miller's played a couple of wrong notes already.'

Ryder smothered a smirk by taking a long pull on his beer. He welcomed the cool slide of liquid down his throat along with the music that drowned out their conversation to anyone who might be listening. Every now and then one of the band members would glance in their direction then look away when Lewicki made eye contact.

'You must have aged well. They recognise you.'

'Oh, they remember me, as I remember them.'

'Do you want a short-term contract to work on the case? I'm sure Gray will have no qualms giving you one.'

'Are you crazy? Annie would have my balls.'

'That what I thought. Does she even know you're here?'

Lewicki nodded. 'She doesn't mind if I'm helping you.' Lewicki turned to look at him, his eyes sliding down to Ryder's beer. 'You clocked off for the night?'

'Yep.'

'Where's your sidekick?'

'Just about to come back on duty.'

Ryder looked up as an external door beside the stage opened and a group of people piled in from outside, bringing a blast of icy air with them. Laughing and kidding around, they hung their jackets on hooks inside the door then headed across the dance floor in the direction of the bar. One girl stopped in front of the band. She struck a pose, then busted out a few dance moves before chasing after her mates.

Staff from Long Bay.

'How's your new partner turning out?' asked Lewicki.

'He's getting there.'

'See that table at ten-to-two?'

'Yep. The Gordons. I'm interviewing them tomorrow. I've spoken to her a few times, but he seems to keep a low profile.'

'For a Vietnam vet, he's a gutless bastard, and not too bright. He wouldn't confront anyone himself if they had any sort of a problem. But he'd be right behind her, though, stirring her up and egging her on. She always had more nous than him, but she's difficult to work with. It was like a revolving door at their office back in the day.'

'I'm getting the feeling you don't like the bloke.'

'There are a lot of people down here I don't like.'

Ryder smirked. That's what was great about having Lew here.

He was able to remember things about people that could never be picked up from a file.

'I talked to Smythe today,' Ryder said. 'I'm guessing that's his wife next to Di. Carmel, right?'

'Yep. Rolling in money. Her family own a tunnel boring company. I think her brother and nephew run it now. They did the tube up here, and the Sydney Harbour Tunnel.'

'So he said. He married well.'

'Yep. Pro skiing didn't pay much back then.'

'He got a bit sensitive when I asked him about her family money.'

'Yeah?'

Ryder shrugged. 'He's spent a lifetime in the spotlight. Most celebrities try and keep their family life private.'

Lew sniggered. 'Yeah, I do the same.'

Ryder smirked and took a pull on his beer. 'He told me he was here that weekend.'

'He was. Worked like a Trojan. He was flying to Europe a few days later to compete in the downhill.'

Ryder studied the guest of honour. Every so often his gaze would shift from table to table as though he were scrutinising each patron. On more than one occasion Ryder caught him staring at Lewicki as though trying to place him.

'There are questions I need answered, Lew. Like, what happened to the DNA samples you took from the Delaneys back in the nineties? There's nothing on the file and they weren't entered into the familial database.'

Lewicki tipped back his head and blew out a breath as though he'd suddenly developed an interest in the popcorn ceiling. 'You know how it is.'

'How's that?'

Lew brought his chin down and reached for a beer coaster lying on the table. Ryder frowned at the age spots speckling the back of his friend's hand, a physical reminder of Lew's advancing age.

'We do our best to abide by the rules, but we're human. Some-times we step over the boundaries.'

Ryder stayed silent, waiting while Lew tapped the coaster on the table.

'After I'd taken the mouth swabs, Eunice followed me out to the car. She told me that she wasn't certain Arnold was Celia's father. She was Catholic, he was Protestant. They married against their families' wishes, and they were still copping all kinds of grief. During this period, Eunice had an extra-marital affair. I'll never forget the day she told me. Decades later, and the shame was still evident in her face.'

The band had finished playing. Miller was speaking into the microphone, telling the crowd they were taking a short break.

Lewicki lowered his voice. 'She was scared stiff that if Celia's body was found, the DNA might reveal that Arnold wasn't her father. Eunice was terrified he'd leave again, or the shock would kill him. He was all she had left. And he'd loved Celia as much as she had. He'd mourned for her. More importantly, he'd been the only father she'd ever known.'

Ryder stared at the coaster, endeavouring to swallow the painful lump building in his throat. Would he have loved Scarlett any less if he'd found out she hadn't been his?

Not a chance.

Ryder shook his head and tore his eyes away from the coaster to focus on Lewicki. 'Did you call Inspector Gray and ask for me to be put on the case?'

'Course I did.'

'Jesus. It was all set up before I walked into Henderson's office. And it wasn't because we'd talked about it all those times either, was it? You knew I'd find the discrepancies in the file.'

'I knew you'd understand.' Lewicki drained his glass as he slid off the stool. 'Celia had already been missing for thirty years when DNA testing first came in. At that time, I doubted her body would ever be found. In the unlikely event it was, why ruin her parents' lives all over again?' He put his glass on the table with a snap and gave a resigned sigh. 'Arnold and Eunice had reunited. They found some kind of happiness. So, I got rid of the samples.'

Thirteen

Day 5

Ryder's day began with an improvised exercise routine of stomach crunches until he was buggered. In Sydney, he'd pound the pavement for forty minutes then tune into the news while the endorphins continued to work their magic. But running wasn't an option in Charlotte Pass, and with the room devoid of a television he hit the shower with twenty minutes to spare. He shaved and donned his suit, which now felt odd in his snowy surrounds, ate a quick breakfast, and was ready by the time Flowers and Lewicki walked in at eight.

Ryder made the introductions, registering Flowers' surprise to find the man dressed in corduroy trousers, a roll-neck skivvy and a knitted jumper was a former high-ranking member of the Force. And Ryder had no intention of telling Flowers that Lew had disposed of the DNA samples back in the nineties, not unless Flowers somehow found out and put it to him. All Flowers needed to know was that Lew was here to share his knowledge. Unofficially.

'So, where are you dossing down?' Lewicki asked, looking at Flowers with interest.

'In the staff quarters out the back. It's full of hospitality staff. It's hard to sleep with the usual antics going on. The walls are paper thin.'

Ryder checked his watch. 'Okay, listen up. Flowers, you and I will conduct the interviews on the lounge like we're having an informal conversation. Lewicki will sit at the desk in the other room, as though he's working. We'll leave the office door open so they'll see him as they come in and realise he can hear what's being said. If they've lied in the past, they'll be on edge as they try to remember details. Hopefully, some will slip up.'

There was a soft knock at the door. Ryder looked from Flowers to Lewicki and back again. 'All set?'

They nodded.

Lewicki rubbed his hands together as he headed into the make-shift office. 'Let's go.'

Ryder watched as Di Gordon sat on the lounge and crossed her legs. She was dressed in the formal skirt and jacket she wore while working in the hotel office, and he could tell now she was one of the women in the photograph from the 1960s. Her dark-brown hair was styled in the same chin-length bob, only her hair was thinner, her face harder, and her mouth sloped down at the corners like she was disappointed at how her life had turned out.

Ryder sat opposite her while Flowers stood and offered a glass of water.

'No, thanks,' she said with a quick glance at the office door. She hadn't missed Lew on the way in.

Ryder ran through the preliminaries. When he mentioned that he was recording the interview, she gave an impatient nod. 'Yes. Is this going to take long? I have a busy day ahead of me.'

It was the green light for Ryder to go in hard. 'Nigel Miller said he was having an affair with you at the time his wife went missing in 1964. Is that true?'

Her eyes widened, and then her mouth pulled into an unattractive sneer that Ryder would have liked to capture on camera if they'd been doing this at the station.

'How is that relevant now, more than half a century later?'

'Because with the discovery of Celia Delaney's body, the Coroner's finding that she went missing in bad weather will be set aside.

Detective Flowers advised the media half an hour ago that we've opened a formal murder investigation.'

'Murder?' Suddenly Di Gordon looked her age, despite the carefully pencilled eyebrows and heavy make-up. 'How?'

'According to the autopsy, she was bludgeoned to death and buried,' Ryder said bluntly. He leaned forward, his elbows propped on his knees. 'I'll ask you again. Were you having an affair with Nigel Miller?'

'It was hardly an affair, more like a bit on the side.' She pressed her lips into a line and challenged Ryder with her eyes.

'How did you keep it from becoming common knowledge?'

'I run a hotel. I kept a room free. It wasn't difficult.'

Ryder changed tack. 'It says on the file that you inherited the lease of Charlotte Pass village.'

'Yes, from my uncle. He didn't have any children. I used to come down here and ski as a child. We shared a great love of this place.'

'It must have been tough when you almost lost it?'

She frowned. 'Lost it?'

'That awful weekend when Celia went missing, and the chairlift all but disappeared in the snowdrift. It was supposed to save this place—connect it to the outside world. It failed.'

Di Gordon gave a reluctant nod. 'Yes, it was tough, but we've had lots of difficult times in the past. Surviving one year to the next is a challenge.'

'Do you remember which ski patroller was on duty the night Celia Delaney went missing?'

Di Gordon stared at him in disbelief. 'It's over fifty years ago.'

Ryder didn't reply, just waited for the growing silence to make her so uncomfortable she'd talk again to fill the gap. He didn't have to wait long.

'We used to have all the records going right back to when my uncle first took over the lease, but there was a fire in the storeroom one year. Everything was lost.'

Ryder made a mental note to check her story and decided not to question her whereabouts in the early evening on the day in question.

It was all there in Lewicki's notes. Multiple witnesses had seen Di and Henry working in the hotel and serving glühwein to the guests. But that didn't mean she hadn't arranged the whole thing.

'Mrs Gordon,' he began, adopting a more conversational tone, 'the way I see it, you had motive—'

'You've got to be joking!'

'You were sleeping with her husband.'

She gave a harsh laugh that dripped with self-righteous sarcasm. 'You think I wanted Celia out of the way because I wanted *Nigel*?'

'Did you?'

'No. Nigel was a convenience for a few years, like all the men I've slept with since.'

'How would you describe your relationship with your husband?' Ryder asked, refusing to break eye contact.

She shifted in her seat, then glanced at Flowers as though wondering if he was going to speak. 'My relationship with my husband is workable. I run the hotel, the front desk, and the cleaning staff. I oversee the restaurants, take care of the hiring and the firing and look after our guests. Henry retrained as an accountant after he came home from Vietnam. He keeps to himself in his office. He does all our ordering, pays the bills, attends to the payroll, oversees our taxation obligations, that sort of thing.'

'You just don't sleep with him.'

'Henry is impotent, Detective Ryder.' Di Gordon gave him a withering look. 'He has been since he came home from the war.'

'I see. So, did your husband know about Nigel?'

'He would have, though I always tried to be as discreet as possible. The situation was painful for Henry.'

Ryder studied Di Gordon, and the lines of disappointment he'd noticed earlier. Maybe it had been painful for her, too. 'You were never tempted to get out of this place and take off with your lover?'

'Never. If you haven't noticed, Charlotte Pass is my life. Do you really think I'd do something to Celia, just so I could have Nigel?'

'You said yourself it's tough down here.'

'If I wanted to bump anyone off it would be Henry.' She swept a hand around the room. 'Why would I give up all this for a struggling musician?'

'Were you and Celia friends?'

She frowned at this sudden shift. 'No. She was an acquaintance, that's all. She was naïve. Needy. They had a troubled marriage because Nigel's music always came first. In the beginning, I got the impression she liked being married to a musician. But I think in time the sheen wore off, probably the nights spent at home while he played in some seedy pub, or the groupies . . .'

'Or his lovers, which he expected her to tolerate,' added Ryder.

She gave him a poisonous look, and it struck Ryder how easily a person could get on her bad side. He suspected her relationships would last for as long as she benefited from them.

'Nigel said that you were the cause of the argument he had with Celia just before five pm the night she went missing. Did he tell you about that argument?'

She glanced towards the office door where Lewicki could be heard shifting papers around and snapping the ring binder closed. 'I can't remember. It's a long time ago.'

'Was Nigel getting tired of Celia's neediness? Did you suspect he might have wanted a more permanent relationship with you?'

'Yes, he was tired of her, but it had nothing to do with me. The band had been offered a tour of England, and there was a possible record deal in the works. Nigel was champing at the bit. He hoped it would be their big break, you know, like The Seekers. But Celia didn't want them to go.'

From the corner of his eye, Ryder saw Flowers glance at him. There had been nothing in Lewicki's file about band disunity. The musicians had been on stage when Celia had disappeared, and so had never figured prominently in the investigation. Lewicki had, however, taken statements hoping to learn something of the relationship between Nigel and Celia. In the band members' opinions, they were like any other couple. They argued occasionally, but the marriage appeared to be solid.

The band posters in Celia's bedroom came to Ryder's mind, especially the one advertising The Beatles concert she had attended in Melbourne not long before her death. Her objection to the band going to London sounded contrary to everything he'd learned about her. 'Why wasn't Celia in favour of the tour? I would have thought she'd have seen it as an amazing opportunity.'

Di snorted. 'She wanted a house in the 'burbs with a quarter-acre block and a white picket fence. Nigel was desperate for the big time. She was cramping his style. The other guys couldn't stand her.'

Ryder maintained his professional neutrality as he absorbed this new information. 'Has the band line-up changed over the years?'

'No. They're all the same guys.'

Ryder pretended to think over what she'd said. He looked at Flowers like they were exchanging some silent communication. When he sensed her growing nervousness, in the way she clasped her hands together then crossed and uncrossed her legs, he turned back. 'Why do you think Nigel chose to tell us about your affair yesterday?'

'I don't know. Why don't you ask him?'

'I'll do that.' Ryder slapped his knees and looked at Flowers. 'Is there anything you'd like to ask, Detective?'

Flowers shook his head. 'I think I've heard everything I need to know, Sergeant.'

It was a good answer, and Ryder hid his smile as he pushed himself to his feet. He could almost smell the woman's growing panic.

'Thank you, Mrs Gordon. That'll be all. For now.'

Fourteen

Henry Gordon's stooped posture told the story of a man worn down by life. Deep channels carved lines through his thickened ruddy cheeks, and the rheumy eyes he fixed on Ryder held a mixture of resignation and disappointment. A tiny mark on his left earlobe was evidence of him having worn an earring at some time in his life.

Ryder worked his way through the list of questions he had asked Di, learning little more than he had in the previous interview with the man's wife. He was an old soldier, suspicious of the police and the government, critical of people in general. He only showed his face when Di dragged him into the hotel when they were short-staffed.

'The arrangement suits me fine,' he said, shifting his gaze from Ryder to Flowers and back again. 'Is that all you want to know?'

'Not quite. Your wife tells us your marriage is . . . somewhat unconventional . . . due to your health problems.'

He sneered. 'I'm pleased she set you straight.'

'She told us you know about the lovers she's taken over the years. Is that correct?' asked Flowers.

Henry looked Flowers up and down like he was still wet behind the ears. 'I knew *of* them. I wasn't interested in getting to know them personally.'

'You knew Nigel Miller personally.' Ryder took the photograph Flowers had at the ready, and passed it onto Henry. 'That's you. It was taken not long before Celia went missing.'

Henry studied the photograph for a few seconds then passed it back to Ryder. 'He was a bit different to the others. He plays here every year with the band. Most of the other men aren't return visitors.'

'Did you ever think of leaving here?' asked Flowers.

'Nope.'

'Did you ever think she would?'

'Listen, whoever you are, I fought for this country, and we were treated like dog shit when we came home. I could have found solace in the bottom of a whiskey bottle, or done myself in like a lot of my comrades. Hell, I could have joined a bikie gang. But I'm as happy as I can be in the peace and quiet here. Doesn't mean I've forgiven the government for making us fight a war that had nothing to do with this country—and for leaving us over there for so fucking long.'

Flowers didn't respond.

Ryder resisted the urge to thank Henry for his service and went straight for the jugular instead. 'How far would you go to keep this place afloat?'

'What do you mean?'

'Celia Delaney's murder. You would have heard the news by now.'

'I know you found her body. How she died has nothing to do with me.'

'Your wife and Nigel were cosy back then. You said yourself he was different to the others. Were you aware his band had been offered a European tour and a record deal?'

Henry scratched the side of his head. 'I seem to remember something about that. I don't think anything came of it.'

'It never crossed your mind that if Celia wasn't around, Di could potentially take her place and accompany Nigel to England? You'd have had Charlotte's all to yourself.'

Henry sat back, folded his arms and gave Ryder the death stare. 'I've never heard a more ridiculous crock of shit in my life. I couldn't run this place without Di. She does everything around here.' He cocked his head towards the door leading to the office where Lewicki was sitting, and raised his voice. 'If that's the best the old codger can come up with, he should put his name down at the retirement village tomorrow.'

Ryder left Henry's words hanging in the air, and waited to see if Lew would respond.

The typist chair squeaked as Lewicki stood up. Flowers raised his eyebrows as Lew appeared in the doorway. Arms folded, he leaned one shoulder against the doorframe, looked at Henry Gordon, and said nothing.

'I heard you retired,' Henry said. 'What happened, did they recycle ya?'

Lewicki ignored the bait. 'What's with the satellite dishes on the roof of your quarters? I saw at least three of them when I came in.'

'I'm listenin' to China. Can't understand a fucking word they're saying but there's a lot of talk goin' on.' He looked at Ryder and repeated the question he'd asked ten minutes ago. 'Is that all?'

'Just one more thing. Do you remember which ski patroller was rostered on the night Celia Delaney went missing. The night the chairlift was buried?'

Henry gave a harsh laugh. 'Di told me you'd asked her that. No, I wouldn't have a clue.'

Ryder nodded. 'Okay, I think that's all for now, unless Detective Flowers has any further questions.'

Flowers shook his head. 'No, I'm done.'

'Flowers,' Henry said as he stood up from the lounge. 'Pansy name for a cop.'

'Watch your manners,' Ryder eyeballed him as he opened the door, 'or I'll be down to check out those satellites.'

'What do you think?' Ryder asked, handing Flowers and Lew a mug of instant coffee each.

'I don't like him,' said Flowers, 'and not because he called me a pussy.'

'A pansy.'

'A pansy, then. He's got a chip on his shoulder, and a them-and-us attitude.'

'He's a conspiracy theorist,' put in Lewicki. 'He was never high on my list of suspects.'

'Contrary to his wife, he wasn't nervous.' Ryder stirred milk into his coffee. 'Makes me think he's got nothing to hide.'

'They're a strange couple,' Flowers went on. 'She's screwing the guests while he's sitting with his headphones thinking China's hacking into Canberra.'

'China *is* hacking into Canberra,' said Lewicki.

'I know. But, still, he's a bit of a nut job.'

'Okay,' Ryder said. 'Nigel Miller admitted to the affair with Di. Why?'

'Because now you have a body,' said Lewicki. 'I wasn't here for that interview, but it wouldn't surprise me if Nigel tried to cast suspicion on Di to deflect it away from himself.'

Ryder nodded. 'My thoughts exactly. So, tell me, Lew, why was Nigel your main suspect?'

Lewicki spread his hands. 'The stats were the same back then as they are now. The majority of crimes against women are committed by a close family member, often the husband, and Nigel admitted to them having had a heated argument.'

'He was probably covering his arse in case they'd been overheard,' said Flowers.

'That was my suspicion but, without a body, I couldn't prove anything. And he was a cagey bastard. I couldn't shake the feeling he was hiding something. Now I know he and Di were getting it on . . . maybe that's what he was trying to cover up.'

'Makes sense,' said Ryder. 'And let's not forget about the other band members. They had a lot to lose if Celia stood in their way. Flowers, make a note to round them up as soon as you can.'

'Too easy, Sarge.'

'Lew,' he continued, turning to Lewicki. 'There was nothing about the band in the file.'

'They weren't suspects. They were playing when she was supposed to have gone missing. The last one to see her was her husband right before five o'clock.'

'Hmm. From the location of the remains, I think Celia got on the old chairlift, and her injuries support that theory. The liftie back then, Bruno Lombardi, he said in his statement that a ski patroller told him to put the chain across and go inside around four-thirty. Do you remember getting the name of the patroller, Lew? It's not on file.'

Lewicki shook his head. 'I can't remember. I might never have asked him.'

Ryder did his best not to look taken aback. 'Why not?'

'Because that chairlift had been shut down for one reason or another for most of the season. Bruno said he put the chain across at four-thirty, and I believed him.'

'Didn't you want to confirm what he told you with the patroller?'

'I trusted him.' Lewicki pushed his glasses higher onto the bridge of his nose. 'In hindsight, I probably shouldn't have, but I didn't have a particularly good mentor back then, and I was even younger than Daisy here.'

Flowers grinned at the nickname suddenly bestowed on him.

'Bruno and I grew up together in the Cooma migrant camp,' Lew went on. 'The Lombardis were good people. Bruno's father was killed on the Snowy Hydro build. His mum was one of those Italian widows who wore black for the rest of her life. I don't think she ever really picked up English. Anyway, Bruno became the man of the house. He was working up here supporting his mum and sister.'

'He's still here,' said Ryder.

'You're joking?'

Flowers checked his watch. 'Nope. You'll be seeing him in about half an hour.'

'Good old Bruno.' Lewicki gave a wistful smile, his eyes lost in the past. 'It'll be nice to say g'day.'

Ryder was having a hard time reconciling the man Lew had described with the one sitting opposite him. The bloke was as thin as a grey-hound, and if Ryder hadn't already given up smoking, one look at this guy's shaking hands and yellowed fingertips and he would have gone cold turkey there and then.

And that wasn't the worst of it. Half the bloke's left ear was missing, and a raised scar stretched from the crown of his bald head and ran to the corner of his right eye. Wheezing from climbing the stairs, he looked at the three detectives as he caught his breath.

Shock registered on Lewicki's face, but he managed to maintain his composure as he held out his hand to the man seated on the lounge.

'G'day, Bruno. I just learned that you were still here—it's been a long time.'

Lombardi grasped Lewicki's hand. 'It has.'

'How's your mother—is she still with us?'

The groomer released Lewicki's hand and shook his head. 'No, we lost her about three years ago.'

'And your sister?'

'Angela's good. She works in an Italian restaurant in Berridale. Mum taught her to cook, like all good Italian mamas do.'

'Neither of you moved far, then,' Lewicki said with a small laugh.

'Nah.' Bruno looked Lewicki up and down. 'You haven't changed, Roman. A bit greyer.' He touched the top of his ear. 'I lost the bottom part of me ear to melanoma.'

'Well, we didn't have sunscreen back in the day. Is your hearing okay?'

'Yeah, I can hear.' He rubbed a hand across the scar on his head. 'A poma did this.'

Lewicki gave a low whistle. 'Geez. I've never trusted those things. I've seen too many people come a cropper, even on small hills.'

'Yeah.'

Lewicki smiled. 'You're still kicking though, mate. That's the main thing.'

'Too right. Every day above ground, and all that.'

When the pleasantries were over, Ryder switched on the recording device and got straight to the point. 'Mr Lombardi, as a long-term resident of the village, you're one of a handful of people who were here the weekend Celia Delaney was murdered.'

'*Murdered?*' Lombardi recoiled, choking on the word. 'What do you mean she was murdered?'

Ryder paused for a second. 'You seem shocked by the news.'

'Bloody oath I'm shocked.' Lombardi took a few deep breaths and collected himself a little. 'How did you work out she was murdered?'

'The pathologist's report said she'd been struck in the head by a blunt object. We found her buried on Mount Stillwell between an old snow gum and a giant boulder. Do you know the spot?'

He blinked at Ryder, his eyes wide and fearful. 'Why would I know it?'

Ryder watched him closely, but kept his tone light. 'You've been here so long. I thought you'd know the place like the back of your hand.'

The groomer eyed Ryder suspiciously, then gave a vague shake of his head.

'I went up there yesterday,' Ryder continued, adopting a conversational tone. 'There's a tree well forming around the bottom of the snow gum. It must have been deep that year, when the snow was as high as the roof on this place.'

'I'd have to see it to know exactly the spot you're talking about.'

'It's right by the grave, near where you asked for the snow fences to be built. You would have seen the police tape.'

'Yeah, I know the general area, but not the exact tree and rock.'

'Why did you ask for snow fences to be built in that spot?'

'Same reason I always do. A stock of snow close by saves me time and the company diesel.'

'That sounds reasonable. Okay, I want to go back to the night in sixty-four when you were the liftie on duty. Had there been people out skiing before the lift closed down?'

'Yeah, the hardcore ones.' The groomer's skin had turned pale, and he swiped the sleeve of his sloppy joe across his forehead where beads of sweat were forming. 'The weather won't put them off when there's that much powder. They're like big-wave surfers.'

'I imagine the visibility would have been poor though. Was there concern among the mountain staff that the skiers might lose their bearings?'

'You can't get lost at Charlotte's,' he said scornfully. 'It's one big bowl. All the runs finish at the village.'

'So, despite the worsening conditions, a lift that was notorious for breaking down even in milder weather was still operating?'

He shrugged. 'People come here to ski.'

Ryder watched as the groomer reached into his breast pocket and took out a cigarette lighter. Lombardi turned it over and over in his hand, playing with it like other people play with stress balls.

'Look. I was only eighteen. I didn't ask questions. I did as I was told.'

'Do you remember anyone getting on that lift, say, during the last hour?'

'Yep. A few day trippers were trying to make it back to Thredbo. I heard later they got as far as the restaurant, but by then the second lift had been closed. They had to wait it out up there.'

'At least they wouldn't have gone hungry,' quipped Flowers.

Ryder smirked and let the comment hang in the air for a bit. 'You see, Bruno. You don't mind if I call you Bruno, do you? I have this theory that Celia got on that lift.' He spread his hands. 'How else did she wind up dead on that mountain? Did you see her, on her own, or with someone else?'

'Nope.' The groomer's eyes were fixed on the intricate carpet pattern. Every so often he'd swallow, all the while clicking the lighter.

Ryder leaned against the back of the lounge. 'Detective Flowers, get Mr Lombardi some water.'

'You all right, Bruno?' Lewicki asked as Flowers left the room.

'Yeah, I'm all right.'

Ryder caught Lewicki's eye. He'd worked with Lew long enough to know what he was thinking. Lombardi looked like a haunted man.

When Flowers came back, Ryder continued. 'Do you remember anything happening that might have taken your attention away from the people who were loading onto the lift?'

Lombardi gulped his water noisily then put the empty glass on the table. 'Nothing in particular, but there's always somethin' going on. I could have gone to help someone, or to answer the two-way.'

'We suspect Celia was a foot passenger.' The remnants of leather and rubber Harriet had recovered had been more consistent with a soft walking boot than a stiffer, supportive ski boot.

Lombardi said nothing, his gaze skittering from one side of the room to the other. 'I suppose she could have slipped by me, if I'd been distracted.'

'It's possible, then?'

'Anything's possible. It was just a standard chairlift with a special hood. People could load on themselves.'

'In your statement, you said you were told to put the chain across and go inside. Who gave you that order?'

Another vague shake of his head. 'Dunno.'

'You don't know, or you won't say?'

'It was more'n fifty years ago.'

'What did he say?'

'Somethin' like what you just said: "Put the chain across and go inside, I'll do the last run."'

'Last run?'

'Yeah, he meant he'd take a final ride on the chairlift to make sure no one was still out on the hill. It's routine. The patrollers do it as part of their final sweep before shutdown.'

Flowers leaned forward. 'Let me get this straight. Even though you put the chain across, you didn't actually stop the lift. It was still operating?'

'Yeah. The chain is to stop people from getting on. He was going to do the final run, like I said.'

'Did you actually see him get on the lift?' asked Ryder.

Lombardi shook his head. 'I went straight inside. I was freezing.'

Ryder exchanged glances with Flowers and Lewicki. This changed everything. 'Try to remember his name, Bruno,' Ryder said. 'We need to talk to him.'

'I don't like your chances. A lotta people have passed through here in the last fifty years.'

'We'll find out one way or another.' Ryder sat back, folded his arms and looked at Flowers.

'Have you ever thought of moving away from here, Mr Lombardi?' Flowers asked.

'I've had offers from everywhere. Whenever I told the Gordons I was leaving, they upped my pay. They know they're on a good thing. I'm the most experienced groomer in the mountains.'

'What do you do with all your money, Bruno?' Lewicki asked, like they were having a yarn at the local pub. 'Got any kids?'

'Nah. Angela's got three. A couple of them are in Sydney. I've helped them out with money, so they could buy a house. I don't spend much cash, only on beer and cigarettes, and an occasional trip to Thailand.' He pointed to his face. 'Girls around here don't want to get too close to this face.'

'What about Burt Crofts, the lift mechanic?' Ryder asked.

'What about him?'

'Is he a good mate of yours?'

'Sort of.'

'Detective Flowers was told he left for Sydney a couple of days before Celia Delaney's remains were found.'

Lombardi's eyebrows shot up. 'It was the same day.' He turned and looked at Flowers. 'Whoever told you that got their days mixed up.'

'It was the bloke in the alpine club.'

Lombardi snorted. 'That bloke wouldn't have a clue what was going on.'

'Do you know where we can we find Crofts?' Ryder asked.

'Luna Park. They've got a problem with one of their rides.'

'He's fixing a ride?'

'That's what he does. Check with the Gordons. He has an arrange-ment with them.' He gave a phlegmy cough without bothering to cover his mouth. 'In demand all over the place, Crofts is.'

'Okay. We'll make enquiries.' Ryder stood up. 'I guess that's all for now, Mr Lombardi. Stick around. We might need to talk to you further.'

Ryder opened the file and took his time lifting Lombardi's statement off the split pin. He'd always had the greatest respect for Lew's work, but the more he delved into the old investigation the clearer it became that mistakes had been made. Lew had neglected to get the name of the ski patroller, and to interview the other band members. He'd trusted Bruno's explanation of what had happened because of their personal connection, but all these years later it seemed that trust had been misplaced.

Ryder ran his index finger along the yellowed paper. Fortunately, the print was still clearly legible thanks to the manual typewriters of the era. 'In his original statement, Lombardi swore nothing had distracted him. He said: "There's no way she could have got past me. I never once turned away to speak to, or help, anyone. I never once left my post."' Ryder looked up at the other two men. 'Now he's saying he could have been distracted. What do you think?'

'I think he was knocked for six when you told him she was murdered,' said Flowers. 'He looked surprised then horrified. I couldn't work out if it was genuine or if he was scared shitless that he was going to be found out. And I don't like it that he's changed his story.'

'I don't either.' Ryder turned to Lewicki. 'Lew, when Bruno told you he put the chain across at four-thirty, did you take that to mean he'd shut the chairlift down?'

'Yes. As I understood it, he'd stopped the chair from operating.'

Ryder frowned. 'Now he's saying he put the chain across to stop the skiers loading on, but the chairlift itself was still operating because this unknown patroller planned on doing a final run to make sure everyone was off the hill.'

Flowers' eyes flashed with excitement. 'Which means, if there was any time gap between him leaving and this patroller getting on, Celia could have bypassed that chain and loaded onto the lift herself.'

There was a pause in the conversation as they mulled over this new information.

Lewicki was the first to speak. 'Bruno knows more than he's letting on but, remember, Nigel Miller has also changed his story. He didn't admit to an affair with Di Gordon back then, so why bring it up now if not to cast suspicion on her, and away from himself?'

'Lew, it's hardly surprising he kept it a secret. Adultery was a much bigger deal back then.'

'That's true, but Miller's still my number one suspect.'

'I can see that.' Ryder held up a hand to stop Lew continuing. 'Just indulge me for a minute. And, Lew, please put the Bruno of old out of your head.'

Ryder began pacing. 'I'm imagining Celia, intent on getting out of Charlotte Pass irrespective of the weather. She turns up at the lift loading area, on foot. Only the hardcore skiers are out, and most of them are sticking to the T-bar and poma because visibility is bad.' He paused and leaned both hands on the back of the sofa. 'A few have gone up on the chairlift, trying to get back to Thredbo, but it's very quiet in the building across the creek—now known as Long Bay. Only the liftie, Lombardi, is there, working his shift.' Ryder pushed off the sofa and resumed pacing, punctuating each point with a series of hand gestures. 'Lombardi stops Celia, tells her it's dangerous and the cab needs extra weight. But she's an attractive woman, only a handful of years older than him. She's upset and vulnerable, fleeing from her husband. She begs him to let her get on, otherwise she's going to walk into Perisher.' Ryder stopped pacing and spread his hands. 'What does Lombardi do? He can't order her back to the inn. Does he leave his post and accompany her on the lift? It's nearly closing time and there's no one else around.'

'Maybe he was going to take her as far as the restaurant and come back down, when everything went pear-shaped,' said Flowers.

'Maybe he took her up knowing she'd never make it to Perisher if she went through with her threat to walk,' added Lewicki. 'Maybe he was trying to do the right thing.'

Ryder nodded. 'Maybe. We have no way of knowing yet exactly what happened up on Mount Stillwell, but Lombardi definitely looks like a man hiding something.' He turned away and went to stand at the window. 'Have you thought about this? Perhaps the reason he can't give us the name of the ski patroller who supposedly told him to put the chain across and go inside is because there never was one.'

Fifteen

'I reckon this low-pressure system is coming in quicker than they've predicted.' Terry jabbed a finger at the weather forecast pinned to the noticeboard in the inn. 'I thnk we'll start getting snow overnight.'

'We'd better put together a shovel squad for first thing in the morning, then,' Vanessa replied. Many on the ski-school staff thought Terry was a frustrated meteorologist, but more often than not he was right.

'Anyone you know need a kick in the pants?' Terry asked.

Vanessa shook her head.

'I can't think of anyone in particular,' said Johan, 'but I just walked through the pub and a group of lifties have been in there for a while. They don't look like they're slowing down anytime soon either.'

Terry gleefully rubbed his hands together. 'Then I'll go down and give them the good news. They can look forward to being the first out of bed in the morning.'

'Excuse me, Vanessa,' someone said from behind them.

It was one of the young women who worked behind the reception desk. Vanessa had spoken to her a few times earlier in the season but now she searched her mind for a name—but it remained just out of reach. 'Hi,' she said with a smile.

'That was lucky. I thought I was going to have to go over to Long Bay to get you.'

Vanessa frowned. 'Is anything the matter?'

'I don't think so. Mrs Gordon just asked to see you. She's down-stairs in Mr Gordon's office.'

Vanessa raised her eyebrows and looked at Terry.

'Do you know where the office is?' the woman asked.

'Yes, I do,' Vanessa said. 'Thank you for telling me.'

'What's all that about?' asked Terry when the woman was out of earshot.

'I have no idea. Only one way to find out, though.' Vanessa sat on the bench and pulled off her ski boots. 'Can you save me some dinner please, Johan? I'm starving.' Long Bay's first-in-best-dressed policy left those who were late at a disadvantage.

'Sure. I'll put a plate in the oven for you.'

The Gordons' personal suite of rooms was tucked away in an isolated corner of the inn, rarely frequented by employees. The noise from the common areas faded as the dimly lit hallway stretched ahead of her. Vanessa approached the door tentatively, her socked feet silent on the plush pile carpet.

Di's angry voice filtered towards her through the door that was ajar. Vanessa hesitated, unsure whether to go back or to knock and make her presence known.

'This is the last time you'll work down here,' Di hissed. 'As soon as your gig is over, pack up your gear and get the hell out.'

Vanessa froze, her heart beginning to pound. Was she next in line to be laid off?

'It was a stupid thing to do, telling them what we did back then.' Di was almost shouting now. 'Why would you do that? We were only young. It's over fifty years ago, for fuck's sake.'

Stomach churning, Vanessa retreated a few steps. She wasn't supposed to hear this. Better that she leave now and come back.

She turned around and came face to face with Henry Gordon. She gasped, a hand flying to her mouth, her skin crawling at his close proximity. 'I . . . I got a message that Di wanted to see me,' she stammered, taking a step back. 'But she has someone else in with her. I'm happy to come back later.' She went to brush past him, but he stepped in her way.

'No need to come back. All we wanted to do was to remind you of your priorities.'

Vanessa hesitated. 'I'm sorry. I don't know what you mean.'

'Your priorities regarding your work. You're employed by the village as a ski patroller and, as we own the lease, that's us. It's come to our notice that you've been spending a lot of time with the police.'

An indignant heat warmed Vanessa's face. She took a deep breath. 'I have never neglected my duties as a patroller. Everything I've done has been at the direction of the mountain manager, or has been in response to a direct request from the police. I can't refuse to co-operate with them.'

That wasn't entirely true. She'd followed Detective Ryder into the inn so she could tell him about the tree well. And she'd offered to write down the names of the long-term residents at Charlotte Pass. Any number of people could have seen her passing the note to Detective Flowers the night of the flare run. The floodlights had lit up the hill like daytime.

'Well,' Henry said, 'as long as you remember who's paying your wages.'

Vanessa nodded. Like she'd forget. 'Of course.'

He stepped aside, allowing her to make her escape, and though she didn't look back she had the uneasy feeling he was still watching her when she reached the end of the corridor.

Relieved to be back in the communal part of the inn, Vanessa yanked her boots on and stepped out into the darkness. Her unexpected meeting with Henry Gordon had left her more chilled than the freezing night air. With snow crunching underfoot, she looked left and right, blinking at the blackness, searching out the shadows that could be Bruno lying in wait. Thankfully, it wasn't too long before the distinctive sound of water trickling over rocks told her she had reached the bridge.

Safely on the other side, she pulled her jacket more tightly around her and hurried towards the faint glow at the top of the stairs.

Sixteen

Day 6

'Have you seen him today?' Libby asked.

They were standing at the top of the new tube run, waiting for the guest of honour to arrive and formally declare it open. Vanessa was the ski patroller on duty, and Libby's charges were lined up behind them, the first group to put the tube run to the test.

Vanessa raised her eyebrows. 'Who, Aidan Smythe?'

Libby snorted. 'Not him. The hot detective who put us in our place the other day.'

'He apologised to me for that.' Vanessa looked downhill to the inn nestled beside the creek. She could just make out the windows of the corner suite from where Ryder was conducting the investigation. 'The kids being close to that snowcat seemed to trigger something horrible that he'd seen, probably on the job. He said we were in the wrong place at the wrong time.' She smiled at her friend. 'And, no, I haven't seen him since yesterday, when I took him up to the grave on the snowmobile.'

'Oh, my God! You took Ryder for a ride?'

'*Libby.*' Vanessa glanced around, but the kids were too busy crawling over their giant inner tubes to notice. She lowered her voice. 'I'm telling you this because you're my friend. We're

139

going to meet for coffee, or possibly a drink, very soon. I actually asked him.'

Libby's eyes glowed with admiration. 'You dark horse. How did you pull that off?'

Vanessa shrugged. 'I didn't want to waste an opportunity to let him know I fancied him. I'm thirty-three, Lib. People are always saying, "You'll meet the right one when you least expect it," but for all the dates I've been on, so far it hasn't happened. Anyway, I think he's worth the embarrassment I suffered.'

'Did he say if he has a girlfriend?'

'He would have told me if he did. I don't know, he's . . .'

'Hot?'

Vanessa laughed. 'Yes, but that's not what I was going to say. He's different. He seems like the kind of guy you could rely on.'

'Well, I want to hear all about it when it happens.'

'It's only coffee.' Vanessa turned at the sound of a snowmobile roaring towards them. The rider kept to the centre of the run, away from the rope tow that had been installed off to one side to drag the inner tubes up the hill.

The rider parked the machine close to where Vanessa and Libby stood with the children. The group who'd been waiting, many of them parents, gathered around, their cameras at the ready as Aidan Smythe climbed from the snowmobile, dazzling in his signature gold ski jacket and sunglasses.

'Well, hi there, everyone,' he said, waving to the crowd before turning to look back down the slope that stretched all the way to the bridge over Spencers Creek. 'What a beautiful day we have to christen this fabulous new ride. I know it's going to be so much fun for you parents—I mean children.'

Everyone laughed, and Vanessa grinned at Libby. 'He really is a showman, isn't he?'

Libby nodded. 'It's like Santa's arrived. I love his blingy gold suit.'

'Me too. You can pick him out from anywhere on the mountain, which is the idea, isn't it? He is the guest of honour.'

'Yes, it's like the Queen always dressing in brightly coloured suits and hats—no one in the crowd can miss her.'

Before Vanessa could reply, she noticed Aidan Smythe trying to catch her eye as he walked over to join them. 'Well, hello again. I was wondering if either of you ladies had—'

Vanessa pulled scissors from her pocket like a magician. As she held them up he laughed, showing a perfect set of orthodontically straightened teeth. He leaned in towards Libby and said conspiratorially, 'Just as well someone's organised.'

Vanessa laid the scissors in his hand. Earlier, she'd strung a blood-red ribbon across the top of the slope ready for him to do the honours. 'This is my friend, Libby. Libby, our Winterfest guest of honour, Aidan Smythe.'

'Pleased to meet you.' He said graciously and then shifted his attention back to Vanessa. 'And you are? I remember us speaking at the top of the chairlift, but I don't believe I know your name.'

'Vanessa Bell.'

'Well, Vanessa Bell, let's not keep this crowd waiting any longer.'

Aidan kept his speech short and friendly, expressing gratitude for his good health that had enabled him to return to Charlotte Pass and take part in the celebrations held in his honour. He thanked the Winterfest organising committee for their sustained work, and finally the crowd who had come along today—most of whom he noted were too young to know who he was.

Laughter rippled through the crowd and then, without further ado, Aidan cut the ribbon and declared the tube run open.

Vanessa gathered up the pieces then waved to Sam, who was waiting for her signal at the bottom of the slope. He switched on the engine and the rope tow started with a jerk. Libby and the kids lined up, inflatable tubes clutched to their sides.

Vanessa held a tube steady for a boy who looked about eight. 'You're first down the hill. In you go, mate.'

He settled himself inside, grinning at his friends over his shoulder. 'All set?'

When he gave her the thumbs up, Vanessa put her hands on the tyre and pushed. 'Bombs away!' she shouted as a cheer went up from the crowd.

The next half-hour was spent loading and unloading kids into tubes and sending them on their way downhill. Smaller children were accompanied by their parents, but when a parent wasn't available, it was up to Vanessa and Libby to take the littlest ones down.

Aidan mingled with the crowd, chatting to the parents and every now and then coming over to give Vanessa and Libby a hand.

'Do you have children?' Vanessa asked, catching her breath. For once, all the riders, including Libby, seemed to be at the bottom of the hill.

'A boy and a girl. They're grown up now, both married.'

'Do they live in Canada as well?'

'Yes. They live quite close to us.'

'I guess Canada's more home to you now than here?'

He grimaced. 'In some respects. I don't think you ever lose that Aussieness, for want of a better word. Here feels like home, too. Maybe because some of the old crowd are still around, which is incredible.'

'People like the Gordons?'

'Yes, they've had the lease on this place forever.'

Many thought they should have gone long ago, but Vanessa wasn't about to say that.

'The band, too,' Aidan exclaimed. 'I knew all those guys back in the day. I told them they'd improved since the last time I'd heard them.'

Vanessa laughed. 'There are a few other lifers.' She brought to mind the list of names she'd given to Detective Flowers. 'Burt Crofts, our lift mechanic, is one. I think he's on leave at the moment, so fingers crossed we don't have any major problems. And then there's our groomer, Bruno, he's been here forever as well.'

Aidan frowned and shook his head. 'Those names don't ring a bell.' He turned to look at the line of trees that shielded the gravesite from view. 'I do remember that poor girl, though, the one whose body they found recently. I met her a number of times with Nigel, her husband.'

'Yes, it's very sad.' Vanessa moved closer to the rope tow, ready to help the child who had almost reached the top. She grabbed hold of the tyre and pulled it clear of the unloading area. The last thing they needed was a pile-up. 'I hope it hasn't put a dampener on your visit.'

'Well, the Gordons are a bit on edge, having detectives on the premises. But the police seem to be keeping a low profile, which is good. And the place is booked out. I doubt they'll lose guests because of a few policemen lurking around.'

Vanessa couldn't imagine Detective Ryder 'lurking' anywhere. Whether he was sporting a business suit or mountain gear, the man had presence. And he was one hundred percent focused on his job. 'It's important they find out what happened to her, for her family's sake.'

'Oh, yes, of course it is. Don't get me wrong. I hope they do.'

'Hey, Vee! Can you help us out?'

Vanessa swung around. Libby's tyre was approaching the unloading area. She was hanging onto the rope tow handle, and had a little boy sitting in her lap.

'I'll let you get on with it, Vanessa.' Aidan gave her a friendly salute. 'Thanks for being so organised.'

'Just doing my job. See you out on the slopes.'

She leaned over, hands resting on her knees, watching as Libby came closer. When she let go of the handle, Vanessa pulled the tube clear of the unloading area. 'G'day. Was that fun?'

'It's was heaps fun,' said the little boy in a bright blue puffer jacket.

'Do you want another go?' Libby asked.

The little boy shook his head. 'Mum and Dad are over there.'

'Oh, right,' Libby said, struggling to her feet. 'Off you go then.'

They watched until the child had met up with his parents, then Libby gave a groan and stretched out her back. 'Thank God. I don't think my spine could take another jolting ride down that mountain.'

'You were ages. What were you doing?'

'That kid needed to go to the toilet. Do you know how long it takes getting all the layers undone? Then you have to sit them on the toilet, and they take forever. Half the time they don't go. Then you do all the layers up again and make sure they've washed their hands. Finally, you end up half-carrying them to the bottom of the rope tow because their little legs are just about to give out. It's bloody exhausting.'

'That's why I'm a patroller and not an instructor.'

'Smart arse. I wish I could ski like you. Hey, I saw your crush waiting for the oversnow transport. He said to tell you he's off to Sydney.'

Disappointment settled like a stone in the pit of Vanessa's stomach. 'Did he say when he'd be back?'

'Probably in the morning. He'd arranged for Detective Flowers to give you a message, but then he ran into me.'

'Oh, that was thoughtful of him.'

'I thought so, too. And me, being equally thoughtful, went and told Detective Flowers that I had run into Detective Ryder, and I'd be happy to deliver the message to you.'

Vanessa's mouth fell open. 'Libby. You just wanted to see Flowers.'

'Yep.' Libby laughed, her eyes sparkling with humour. 'Hey, you can't talk. You're the one who asked out his boss. I just delivered a message.'

Seventeen

At 11 am, Ryder stood on the edge of Sydney Harbour, his umbrella doing little to protect him from the lashing rain. Commuter ferries moved like ghost ships on the water, their lights a dull glow through the thick fog. High above him, a train rumbled across the Harbour Bridge.

Ryder headed towards the enormous laughing clown face that marked the entrance to Luna Park. A woman in a raincoat was outside a popular eatery, fiddling with a plastic blind that was flapping in the wind. Further on, a lone swimmer crawled through the water, doing laps in North Sydney Olympic Pool.

At eight this morning, the same chopper pilot had set him down in Queanbeyan, where Ryder had picked up an unmarked car. Three hours later he was walking through the clown's grinning mouth and casting his eyes around the deserted park. On his left was the function centre, on his right the Big Top concert venue. Coney Island, towards the rear of the property, looked much the same as it had during the few times Ryder had visited as a child.

'Where are you, Crofts?' he murmured, lifting his umbrella so he could get a better view. The Hair Raiser ride loomed in front of him, as tall as a mobile-phone tower. According to the park's supervisor, the lift mechanic had been working on the ride during an enforced shutdown.

'Burt Crofts is one of the best lift mechanics in the country,' the man had said. 'All the engineers want him to do their work.'

'Send the Sydney boys around,' Flowers had suggested early that morning as he'd watched Ryder getting ready to leave. 'Save yourself the time and travel.'

But Ryder wanted to talk to Crofts alone.

He walked towards the Hair Raiser, his trouser bottoms growing wet around his ankles. Clown faces were a recurring theme. The eyes in the smiling caricatures painted above the ticket office followed his every move, as did the horses on the silent carousel. But the gruesome sideshow clowns were the worst. With their elongated bald heads and high pencilled eyebrows, they were the stuff of children's night-mares. They stared at him, some through monocles, their blood-red mouths gaping.

Moving through the crowd-control rails, Ryder listened for the sounds of work being done, but only the occasional blast of a foghorn on the harbour cut through the torrent of relentless rain.

Leaving the Hair Raiser behind him, he headed towards Coney Island, dodging puddles as he searched for any sign of life.

'Come on, Crofts. Where the hell are you?' he muttered as he stopped to look at a list of safety instructions for a nearby ride.

'Ya right there, mate?'

Ryder swung around at the friendly voice. A bear of a man around Lewicki's age stood there. Bald, and naked to the waist, the man wore budgie smugglers and a pair of blue thongs. A sodden beach towel hung from his neck, partly obscuring curly grey chest hair. The man was the lone swimmer from next door.

'I'm looking for Burt Crofts,' said Ryder, closing the umbrella.

'Looks like you've found him,' the man said with a smile, stepping towards Ryder ready to shake his hand.

Ryder opened his suit coat and flashed his ID. 'Detective Sergeant Pierce Ryder, Sydney Homicide Squad.'

'Whoa.' Crofts retracted his hand, then cocked his head in the direction of the ticket office. 'You'd better come this way, seeing as you're the law.'

At the ticket office, Crofts opened the door. 'We don't lock it through the day; nothing worth taking.'

Ryder looked around the space. There was a kitchenette at the rear of the room, a door with a plastic sign on it saying 'Toilet', and a round, wooden table with four matching chairs.

'Bit cold for a swim,' said Ryder, shrugging out of his suit coat and draping it over the back of a chair.

'I figure I may as well—couldn't get any wetter.' Crofts dropped the sodden towel into a corner and, without bothering to dry himself off, pulled a faded Bathurst 1000 T-shirt over his head. 'This is balmy compared to where I come from.'

'Let's talk about that,' said Ryder.

'I have a feeling I know where this is going.'

'I'm investigating the murder of Celia Delaney in 1964.'

Crofts expression remained the same as though he'd anticipated what was coming. 'I knew Celia.'

'How well?'

'Pretty well, back in the day. They were regulars, her and Nige.'

'Have you seen the news?'

'Yes. I'm glad you found her body. I thought she was a real nice girl.'

It was an interesting change. Most of the others hadn't had a good word to say about her. 'You're aware we are now conducting a murder investigation?'

'I am.'

'Have you spoken to anyone from Charlotte Pass since you left?'

Crofts gave a definite shake of his head. 'No, no need to, it's all in the paper.' Crofts shook open a newspaper that was lying on the table, licked his thumb and turned over the pages. He pointed to a headline and read, 'Police re-open missing person case at Charlotte Pass.'

Ryder pulled the paper towards him and skimmed through the article. It recounted the facts from the original case and the Coroner's findings. The only new information was what Flowers had released to the press.

Ryder closed the paper and stilled. There on the front page was the facial sketch of Gavin Hutton that Inspector Gray had told him about. He quickly folded the paper and pushed it aside. He had to let Hutton go for now.

Pulling out the portable recording device, he gave Crofts a similar spiel as he'd given the others. 'All right, I'd like to go back to that weekend. Someone wanted Celia Delaney dead. You were there then. What do you remember about those few days?'

Crofts settled himself in the chair opposite Ryder. 'It was a long time ago, but I remember it. You don't forget the tragedies, right?'

The man locked eyes with Ryder, and Ryder's stomach clenched. It was the way Crofts said it—'*You don't forget the tragedies*'—that made him wonder if he knew about Scarlett's death. People in Newcastle remembered but, since moving to Sydney, Ryder had kept to himself. Only Lewicki had managed to break through the veneer. Still, it was all there in the old news reports if someone decided to look. They wouldn't find anything about him on social media, that's for sure.

'Did Celia Delaney have any enemies?'

'Not that I knew of.'

'Describe that weekend to me.'

Croft leaned his lumberjack-sized forearms on the table. 'It was like going fifteen rounds with mother nature. We'd land a punch, she'd give us an uppercut. Time and again we picked ourselves up off the canvas but, in the end, she delivered a knockout blow.'

'What were you doing the morning after the storm?'

Crofts' story was familiar. He'd helped carve out steps so people could enter and exit the buildings. Then he'd started digging out the buried snowploughs. 'More and more people came to help, so I left to try to find the buried electricity cable.'

'When did you hear that Celia wasn't among the head count?'

'Sometime during the day. Word was she'd had a blue with her husband and had walked into Perisher. As soon as we got the ploughs going, we cleared the road and sent out a search party.'

Frustration boiled up inside Ryder. He was hearing the same story over and over. 'See, that's what I'm having trouble understanding.

Everyone assumed she'd headed for Perisher. Why was that, when other skiers had taken the chairlift out to Thredbo?'

Crofts rubbed a massive hand across the lower half of his face. He was silent for a while, as though thinking back.

'Where was Nigel?' Ryder prompted, deciding to come at it from another angle.

'I don't know. I didn't see him.'

'Mr Crofts, you and Bruno Lombardi have worked together for a long time. How close are you?'

'Not that close. We work well together. He's a private bloke.'

'Has he always been like that?' Crofts was less cagey than the others they'd interviewed, friendlier, his memory sharper.

'Actually, he was pretty funny when he was young. He changed after that weekend.'

'How so?'

'He got really quiet. His dad had died a few years before, and he was the only breadwinner. We were all single, but he had his mum and sister to provide for.'

'I'd imagine it'd take more than a storm to change your personality to that extent, though.'

Crofts held his gaze, then eventually shrugged. 'I'm just telling you what I saw.'

'Di Gordon had reason to dislike Celia. How do you find the Gordons?'

Crofts rolled his eyes. 'This won't get back to them, will it? They've employed me for a long time and I'm on the verge of retirement.'

'It won't get back to them.'

Crofts hesitated for a few seconds. 'How can I say this? While I don't think the Gordons would *physically* harm anyone, I don't like them. They're mean, jealous people.'

It hardly surprised Ryder.

'It's the way they operate. I feel bad saying it, him being a war veteran and all, but they make their money off people who've got money, but they still resent them, if you know what I mean.'

'I've met all types.'

149

'She's a bully—likes to be queen bee—and she's terrified of getting old. If anyone outshines her, they're gone. Some of the young girls who work down here in the uni holidays, they're highly educated, sensible kids. I've seen how she treats them. And then, on the other hand, if someone's in trouble, she's the first one there, supporting them so they feel like they owe her something. She surrounds herself with people she can get something out of.'

'Sounds like you have her all worked out.' Ryder doubted Crofts was among Di's former lovers.

'In another life I almost finished a psychology degree, but I could make more money as a mechanic.' He stood up and went to fill the kettle with water. 'I do my job and stay out of Di Gordon's way.'

Ryder thought about the people in the photograph Flowers had shown him. 'Where was Aidan Smythe at this time?'

'Oh, God, I felt sorry for that poor bugger.' Crofts switched the kettle on and sat down again. 'He was set to go to Europe the following week. He got there, just. He didn't perform as well as expected, but he blitzed 'em in the downhill the following year.'

'So, you don't remember anyone acting strangely that day?'

'Strange, as in like they'd just murdered someone?'

'Strange in *any* way.' Sometimes it was the little things that led to a breakthrough.

'Well, the only thing I thought was unusual that day was Bruno telling me that the ski patroller told him to shut down the lift at four-thirty.' The man took a deep breath, his massive chest rising and falling. 'It was probably nothing, but he told me a couple of times, made a point of it, like he wanted me to remember it.'

'Who was the ski patroller?'

'God, mate, I don't know. Someone should remember who was working there that season.'

'We're asking around, but the man's a ghost.' Ryder took a card from his shirt pocket and slid it across the table to the lift mechanic. 'Give me a call if you remember.'

He stood and reached for his jacket, watching as Crofts read the print on the card. On the way out, Ryder asked how the repair to the Hair Raiser was going.

'It's finished. That's why I was having a swim. I'm waiting for the engineer to come and do a final check in an hour. I don't want to leave without making sure everything's okay. Not when people's lives are at risk.'

The bloke sounded genuine, but Ryder had met people who'd said all the right things and had then gone and massacred their family. 'Are you heading back to Charlotte Pass when you're done here?'

'Sure am,' said Crofts, following him to the door.

'Tell me something. Do you live in Long Bay, like Lombardi?'

And Vanessa. A sense of unease settled over Ryder as he imagined Vanessa living in close quarters with the groomer.

'Yep. Most of the time we're both there, unless Bruno's in Cooma.'

'What's in Cooma?'

'He inherited his mother's house when she died a few years ago.'

Ryder frowned. 'Is he there much?'

Crofts shook his head. 'Only between seasons, and the odd holiday maybe.'

Ryder opened the door and braced himself as a blast of cold, damp air rushed into the ticket office. 'Thanks, Mr Crofts. Let me know when you get back to Charlotte's.' He opened his umbrella and retraced his steps towards the giant clown face.

Ryder was halfway back to Queanbeyan when his phone rang.

'I was thinking about things after you left.' Crofts' voice boomed over the speaker. 'I don't know why it didn't cross my mind at the time.'

'Hang on a minute.' Ryder turned on his flashing lights, transforming the unmarked car into an instantly recognisable police vehicle. As he pulled onto the shoulder the cars around him slowed.

'In the old days, I was like the unofficial photographer. Small electronics were a natural progression from mechanics at that stage. But now it's all digital, I don't have the skills to keep up. Charlotte's have had a professional photographer for years now.'

'Sure,' said Ryder, wondering what the mechanic was getting at.

'I've got a storage shed in Jindabyne. There are dozens of boxes there with thirty-five–millimetre plastic slides inside. I used to take photos of the staff every year, and the visitors. I can go through them if you like, see if I can find the bloke you're looking for. Not sure if that would be helpful?'

'That would be extremely helpful. How long before you can get them?'

'I'll stop in Jindabyne on my way through. The projector's already in my room at Long Bay. I've been doing some work on it.' A couple of seconds of silence followed, and then the lift mechanic spoke again. 'Looking at the time, I'm not sure I'll make the last oversnow tonight. More likely I'll be on the first one leaving Perisher in the morning.'

'Okay, check in with me when you get back to the village.' Ryder said before killing the call. It was a long shot, but it was something. The patroller could have died already, or he could have moved to another country years ago, or even changed his name. Or, as Ryder had pointed out to Flowers and Lewicki, the patroller might only have existed in Lombardi's imagination, as a fabrication to cover up his own actions.

Ryder checked his watch then pulled onto the highway. Crofts wouldn't make the last oversnow tonight, but Ryder would if he made decent time.

Determined not to get stuck and have to spend a useless night in Perisher, he kept his police lights on, and took the Monaro Highway towards the mountains.

Eighteen

Vanessa raised the safety bar and wriggled onto the edge of the seat, ready to unload as the chair approached top station. Sam was on duty again. He was standing on the platform gazing out at Mount Stillwell, his back to the unloading passengers.

Determined to have a word to him about his inattentiveness, Vanessa stood up on her skis and glided to the edge of the platform as the chair swung around the bull wheel. The passengers' safety should be Sam's first priority—accidents could happen so easily, especially during a busy time, like now, when everyone had come out again after lunch.

Vanessa swerved to avoid a group of people spreadeagled at the bottom of the ramp like a pile-up on the expressway. 'Sam!' she yelled. 'Hit the switch.'

Seconds later, the chairlift ground to a halt.

'Are you all right?' she asked, squatting beside a woman who was lying in a tangle of skis and poles trying to pull her two boys out of the way before others crashed into them.

'The people in front got their skis tangled. They fell over and we had nowhere to go. Why didn't he stop the lift?'

'I don't know. He should have.'

The people who'd caused the fall were nowhere to be seen, which didn't improve Vanessa's temper. She helped the woman and boys to their feet then moved the family safely away from the platform.

Vanessa glared at Sam, who was watching from the spot where only the other day he'd handed her the drill. 'You can hit the start switch now,' she snapped, not bothering to hide her anger.

With a chastened nod he disappeared inside the hut. Seconds later, the chairlift cranked up again.

'He should be watching all the time,' the woman said when Vanessa apologised again, 'especially on this chairlift where the platform is steep.'

'It's unlike him. But leave it with me—I'll have a word with him.' She looked down at the two young boys who were so alike they had to be twins. 'All good?'

They nodded, and she watched them ski off down the back track with their mother bringing up the rear. They were confident skiers, and wouldn't have run into difficulties except for the unnecessary pile-up at the bottom of the ramp.

She swung around. 'Sam!'

'I'm here,' he called from outside the hut, his eyes riveted on the unloading passengers.

'You can't take your eyes—'

'I know. I'm sorry. I got distracted. Someone ducked under the rope you put across the trail. They've gone into the out-of-bounds area.'

'What!'

'I yelled at them, but they didn't stop.'

Vanessa snatched up her poles from where she'd stuck them in the snow. 'They've just lost their lift pass. What colour ski jacket?'

'Rental gear.'

'Bugger.' Vanessa pushed off and left top station behind. With wide, angry strides she skated uphill to the CLOSED sign, then slowed so she could duck under the rope. Normally, following tracks across the mountain would have been impossible, but the light snowfall they'd received overnight had covered previous skiers' tracks from days before. Thanks to Mount Stillwell now being closed, the lone skier's tracks were clearly visible in the virgin snow.

It was quieter in the trees, the canopy of snow gums muting the metallic clink of the lifts and the sound of laughter drifting across the hill. Bending her knees, her poles tucked beneath her arms, Vanessa raced along in the tracks of the skier ahead of her.

She rounded a bend, came across a fallen branch and lifted up one ski to avoid it. Hoping the branch might have slowed the other person down, she pulled her body into a tight tuck readying herself for the section ahead where the slope fell away sharply. She picked up speed, launching momentarily into the air off a mound of accumulated snow before landing safely. A flash from below where the trail turned back on itself snagged her attention. Through the trees she glimpsed the skier.

'Hey!' she shouted. 'The trail's closed.'

The skier looked around, slowed for a beat to do so, but didn't stop.

Gritting her teeth, eyes watering behind her goggles, Vanessa set herself up for the hairpin bend ahead. The tight turn was almost 360 degrees and would bring her onto the same stretch of trail as the skier she was chasing. With her weight on her downhill ski, she leaned into the turn, edges scraping across a patch of ice obscured by the shadows.

'Stop! Ski patrol!' she shouted, narrowing the gap between them. Sam had been right. Like fifty percent of guests, the skier was wearing the standard bottle-green pants and parka hired from the rental shop.

The skier rounded a bend and disappeared. Vanessa took the edge off her speed. It wouldn't be wise to pursue them in case they had a fall; better to memorise their build and technique so she could recognise them out on the hill. The resort was small—she was sure to cross paths with them at some point.

Mindful that she was nearing the snow fences, she took the next bend carefully and emerged from the trees where the area opened up. The grooming machine was parked close to the fences. Bruno looked up from where he'd been harvesting the snow. He said nothing, just pointed after the skier, a bemused expression on his face.

Hopeful she still had a chance to confiscate the skier's pass and lay down the law about disobeying signage, Vanessa headed towards the tube run. She'd have something to say about them skiing alone out here, too. With no mobile reception, and no ski buddy to help if they got into trouble, they could lose their life out here.

Like Celia Delaney.

She spotted the skier ahead, nearing the trees at the edge of the tube run. To her right was the cordoned-off area, and she couldn't help but glance at the deepening tree well with a shiver.

The skier jerked to the left, thrown off balance as their right ski tip snagged something on the ground. Losing rhythm for a few vital seconds, they regained their balance by leaning slightly into the hill, putting more weight than advisable on their uphill ski. It was usually a sign of an impending crash in amateur skiers, but the skier in front righted themselves unexpectedly, and continued skiing at top speed across the hill.

Vanessa narrowed the gap to fifteen metres. At this close range there was no doubt the skier was a man, even from the back. 'Hey!' she shouted again, right on his tail as he entered the wooded area. Breathing hard, she bent low and carved through the trees, a low-lying branch crashing against her helmet.

The skier didn't stop, flying out of the trees at the top of the rope tow and cutting across the tube run.

Vanessa stood on her edges and came to a hockey stop in a shower of snow. 'Idiot!' she hissed, watching him weave between the tubes sliding down the hill. This guy was a menace, and should be banned from skiing at the resort.

At the bottom of the hill, the skier came to a stop and stood looking back at her.

Seething, Vanessa threw her pole on the ground and pointed, hoping he'd understand her 'Stay right there, I'm coming for you' body language. She eyeballed him, trying to make out his facial features, but at a distance it was near impossible to see past his helmet and goggles.

Taking her eyes off the skier for a few seconds, she leaned over to retrieve her pole. When she straightened, he was already lost in the swarm of people milling in the heart of the village. Swearing in frustration, Vanessa had the radio halfway to her mouth before realising that putting out a call based on the man's description was pointless. He was a man in rental gear with a slight tendency to lean on his uphill ski when he got out of balance. There could be a hundred people in the village that matched that description. She wasn't even sure of his height.

'Help me!'

Vanessa swung around at the cry. A young mother with a child in her lap was waving frantically from higher up the hill. She'd let go of the rope tow handle, and the tube was beginning to slide backwards.

Vanessa clicked out of her skis and went to help.

Nineteen

Ryder found Flowers and Lewicki in the inn's Blue Lake Restaurant. The maître d' had been reserving the same table for them every night. It was through an archway in the rear wall that led to a narrow, enclosed annex. Separated from the main restaurant, the annex was a quiet space with a maximum of six small tables. Flowers and Lewicki were at the far end surrounded by walls on three sides.

Lewicki looked up and saw him first. 'Here he is.'

Flowers glanced over his shoulder and laid down his cutlery. 'Evening, Sarge.'

'Daisy, Lew,' Ryder said with a subtle nod, pleased at how these two were getting along. He dragged out a chair. 'Carry on with your dinner, I ordered something on my way in.'

As a waitress filled his water glass, Ryder stretched out the kinks in his neck and relayed his conversation with Burt Crofts.

'Makes sense Bruno's mum left him the house in Cooma,' said Lewicki, mopping up his sauce with a piece of damper. 'He probably kept up the mortgage payments after his father died.'

'What interests me most is that Lombardi made a point of telling him twice about the ski patroller ordering him to shut down the lift at four-thirty. Like he wanted Crofts to remember it.'

Flowers raised an eyebrow. 'Constructing an alibi for himself?'

Ryder nodded. 'I think so. Crofts should be back here tomorrow.

It'll be interesting to see if he turns up with anything from that storage unit in Jindabyne.'

Flowers pulled a small notepad from his pocket and relayed what he'd learned that day talking to Nigel Miller's bandmates.

'Jimmy (Jimbo) Reynolds. He's the drummer holding up his sticks in that photograph,' Flowers began. 'He admitted he was not too fond of Celia because he thought she held the band back. In his opinion she was risk averse. She wouldn't let Nigel extend their mortgage on a one-bedroom unit they owned in Kings Cross. The band were trying to raise funds to cut an LP at the time. Jimbo said, looking back now, she was only a kid, but they did have more success after she died.'

'What about the others?' asked Ryder, leaning back as the waitress put his marinara in front of him.

'Brandon Wilson (Willo). He's the bass guitarist. Back then he was a concreter. He hated his job. He admitted to being ambitious to earn a living from the band. He said he was always careful to stay on Celia's good side, because he didn't want her breaking them up.'

Flowers flipped over a page in his notebook. 'Gary (Gazza) Bennett. The guitarist.' Flowers shook his head and exchanged glances with Lewicki. 'This guy. He admitted to sleeping with Celia a couple of times.'

'Jesus.' Ryder lowered his fork onto his plate. 'Who in this joint *wasn't* sleeping around back then?'

'According to Gaz, Nigel was a womaniser who couldn't resist the groupies. Gaz felt sorry for Celia, so he gave her a bit of attention. But . . . he ended the affair because ultimately the band was more important. He's always been terrified that Nigel would find out and kick him out of the band.'

'How did Celia take Gazza's decision to end it?'

'He said she was okay about it and told him that their secret would be safe with her.'

Ryder looked from Flowers to Lewicki and back again. 'Give me your gut feelings on this.'

Flowers leaned back in his chair and stretched out his shoulders. 'I think she was this band's Yoko Ono.'

Lewicki laughed, the first real laugh Ryder had heard from him since all this had begun.

Flowers' eyes widened. 'Seriously, that's what I think. They knew this band had a shot at the big time. I don't think any of them would have actually harmed Celia Delaney, though. Nigel was the John Lennon of this band, and they were desperate to stay on his good side.'

'What about you, Lew?' Ryder asked.

'I agree with Daisy. And they were playing their set around the time she was thought to have disappeared.'

'So, you still suspect Miller?'

Lew gave a noncommittal shrug. 'I'm in two minds. Bruno's a worry.'

Ryder sighed and pushed his plate away. He was done for the day. 'How about a beer downstairs before we hit the hay?'

Flowers shook his head. 'I've already had one, so I'll leave you to it. I want to get these reports typed up.'

'I'll be in that,' said Lewicki, getting to his feet. 'I get a kick out of spoiling people's evenings.'

'I like the young bloke,' Lewicki said as they sipped their beer. 'He's smart.'

Ryder nodded. 'I had my reservations, but he's shown good instincts. He's ambitious. Loves being on the big cases like this one, and Hutton. Don't tell him I said this, but he's got the makings of a decent police prosecutor. He's a pain if he's bored, though. Need to keep him busy.'

'He makes you feel old. That's the reason you don't like him.'

'He's growing on me,' Ryder said with chuckle. 'The piccolo lattes give me the shits. Makes me miss Macca's rotating diet of fish and chips and steak sandwiches.'

'What happened to Macca?'

'He's back in uniform. Wants to become detective sergeant.'

'Huh. Good on him.'

For a while, they sipped their drinks and, to his surprise, Ryder found himself enjoying the music. The place was hopping, the band breaking into a version of Val Halen's 'Jump' that had both guests and staff hitting the dance floor. Aidan Smythe moved from group to group, chatting to the guests. Henry and Di Gordon were sitting at their usual table with Smythe's wife, Carmel, a slim, well-groomed woman who looked to be in her early seventies.

'Di Gordon's doing all the talking,' Ryder commented.

'The women usually do.'

'Henry looks like he can't wait to get back to monitoring China.'

Lewicki shook his head. 'Jesus. What a weird mob this lot turned out to be.'

The outer door near the stage opened and two women came in. Even from across the room Ryder recognised Libby from the child-care centre. She was chatting to the taller one who had turned her back to them and was searching for a spare hook on which to hang their jackets.

Ryder straightened, watching as the woman reached up and draped both jackets over a brass hook, her long, dark hair falling in waves to the middle of her back. She turned around and Ryder's breath hitched. He'd only ever seen Vanessa in her loose-fitting ski patrol suit, apart from the morning she'd opened the door to him and Flowers wearing long thermals and thick socks. Tonight, she wore a long silver jumper over stretch denim jeans that moulded to her shapely legs. Her cherry-red lipstick was a perfect match for the Doc Martens on her feet.

A young woman sitting at a table called out, and Vanessa waved and made her way towards the group with Libby. Ryder leaned back into the shadow of a square column close to their table.

'I'm happy for you.'

'What?' Ryder glanced at his friend over the rim of his glass. 'I think you're getting sentimental in your old age, Lew.' This is how it was between them. The verbal sparring was how they showed they cared. 'There's nothing between Vanessa and me. She's a ski patrol-ler and I live in Sydney. I'd be nuts to start something with her.'

So why did you agree to meet her for coffee or a drink?

'Didn't look that way to me the other day. I like the way she stood up to you. You can be a stubborn bastard.'

'That's rich, coming from you.'

Lew shook his head, his expression turning pensive. 'Why don't you give yourself permission to be happy?' he asked softly.

'You know why. And I *am* happy, sort of. She's talking to a group of ski instructors. What do you want me to do?'

Lewicki slid off the stool with a sigh. 'I'm getting us another drink.'

With Lewicki gone, Ryder watched Vanessa talk to the people at the table. Terry had moved over so she could sit beside him. An image of the two of them eating lunch in the cafe came to mind. He had sensed they had been discussing something serious. Terry had been stressing a point, his index finger jabbing the tabletop as he spoke. Vanessa had been nodding, and then she'd looked up and caught Ryder's eye for a moment.

Ryder continued to watch them now, wondering if they'd been discussing work, or if there was something personal between them. And it bothered him that he hoped they weren't involved. Surely, she wouldn't have asked him out if she had some kind of relationship with Terry?

'This'll help you sleep,' said Lewicki, putting a tumbler of whiskey on the table.

'You think I need sleep?'

'Are you getting any?'

'Not much,' he admitted, dragging his gaze away from Vanessa back to Lew. 'Tell me something. Of all the horrific cases you've worked on, why did this one get to you?'

Lew took a mouthful of whiskey, held it in his mouth for a few seconds before swallowing. 'It was a bit too close to home.'

Ryder frowned. 'Close to home?'

Lewicki sighed. 'Did you ever wonder why Annie and I didn't have kids?'

'Sure. You don't ask those kinds of questions, though.'

Lew paused as though he were having trouble knowing where to start. 'Annie had a baby before I met her. She was eighteen when she got pregnant, around Eunice Delaney's age. There were parallels. Both girls came from devoutly Catholic families.'

Of all the things Ryder had expected Lew to say, this wasn't it. Unsure of the best way to respond, he said, 'I'm sorry, Lew.'

'Don't get me wrong, Annie's not religious.'

'Right.' Unlike Eunice Delaney. Ryder thought about the holy water fonts and religious pictures on the walls. Of the way Eunice had crossed herself before entering Celia's bedroom. 'Eunice told me her parents believed God took Celia away as punishment for marrying a Protestant. Can you believe that?'

'Jesus bloody Christ!' Lew gave an angry shake of his head. 'Annie's parents made her give her baby away. They sent her to a convent as soon as she started to show, and she was forced to stay there till the birth.' He took a breath, then added with unveiled bitterness: 'And then the nuns took her baby girl away.'

Ryder shook his head, his heart sore for the gentle, compassionate Annie. She had understood his anguish. Now he understood hers.

'So much for the good old days, hey?' Lew swirled the spirit around in his glass, staring into the depths of the amber liquid. 'After Annie and I got married, we tried for a baby. It didn't happen.' He glanced sideways at Ryder. 'It was me—obviously. I suggested we adopt a baby, but Annie said no. She couldn't bear the thought of loving someone else's child when she'd given her own away.'

'Oh, God, Lew. I'm sorry.' Ryder lifted the tumbler to his lips with a shaky hand.

'I had a hard time coming to terms with Annie's decision. I was angry with her. It put pressure on our marriage. Then, Celia went missing. I threw myself into the case, determined to find Celia for the grief-stricken Delaneys.'

'It's the worst thing on earth, losing a child,' Ryder said. 'If it wasn't for you and Annie, and my family, I wouldn't have come out the other side.'

'Perspectives change over time, too. Annie now regrets not adopting, but after all the shit I've seen in this job, I'm kind of glad we didn't.'

Ryder knocked back the rest of his whiskey and set his glass on the table. 'Thanks for telling me, Lew. I appreciate it wasn't easy.'

'Yeah, well, we're getting morose tonight.' Lewicki smiled one of his rare smiles. 'Next time we'll keep Daisy with us.'

'Take it easy,' Ryder said with a chuckle. 'He'd probably order a Long Island Iced Tea.'

On stage, the rhythm guitarist began to play the intro to Pat Benatar's 'All Fired Up', and Ryder couldn't stop himself from looking around at Vanessa's table. A young bloke with surf-grommet hair was trying to coax her out of her seat and onto the dance floor. She protested, much to Ryder's pleasure, before going reluctantly. Others crowded around her. She began to move, half-heartedly at first, but it didn't take long for her to get into the spirit of things. She was the kind of dancer who gave herself over to the music. Hands raised above her head, and with her hair falling about her face, she twirled and gyrated with the best of them.

Ryder wanted to knock the drooling grommet out.

'Well, that's it for me,' he said, sliding off his stool and hooking his coat over his shoulder. He hadn't had time to change before dinner but at least he'd managed to lose the tie. 'Are you coming?'

'No, I'll have one more before turning in. You go. You're on duty tomorrow.'

Ryder clapped his friend on the shoulder and, without looking at Vanessa again, turned away.

On the dance floor, Vanessa saw Ryder stand up.

She caught her breath, excitement seeping into every molecule of her body, her racing heart now beating triple time.

How long had he been there?

Wasn't he supposed to be in Sydney?

She kept moving, watching as he stood talking to Lewicki, his suit coat casually hooked over one shoulder. The two of them had been sitting in the shadows.

As she watched, he turned and walked away. Hoping he was heading for the bar, she stopped dancing and tracked him as he shouldered his way through the crowd.

'Hey, what's the matter?'

Sam's hands landed on her waist and he spun her around.

'*Sam.*' Vanessa pushed his hands away. 'Thanks for the dance but I have to go.'

'Hey! What's up?'

Ryder was leaving—that's what was up. She ducked around a jiving couple and grabbed her jacket off the hook. Without bothering to put it on, she opened the door and stepped out into the sub-zero night.

The wind whipped her hair about her face, and she impatiently brushed it out of her eyes, determined to intercept him before he reached his suite. She struggled up the short slope towards the main entrance, her Doc Martens slipping more than once on the wind-blown ice. He needed to walk the length of the corridor then climb two flights of stairs to his suite.

With no idea of what she was going to say to him, she tramped past the ski racks outside the main entrance then pushed her way inside through the swinging double doors. At the metal grate, she stamped her feet to get the snow off her boots, then opened an internal door that led into the normally busy foyer. Tonight, it was deserted, the shop and cafe closed for the evening, the only sound the low frequency of the bass guitar reverberating through the floor.

Vanessa hurried across the foyer and swung left into the corridor.

He was about three metres away, head down, deep in thought, his suit coat still hooked over his shoulder.

He looked up and stopped, his eyebrows shooting up in surprise. 'Vanessa. Weren't you just in the bar?'

So, he had seen her, dancing with Sam.

She nodded, breathless from her impromptu sprint up the hill. Now that she'd bailed him up, she had no idea what she was going to do next. 'I didn't see you until you stood up. Libby told me you were in Sydney.'

'Libby did?'

'She spoke to Detective Flowers.'

'Oh.' He let the suit coat slide off his shoulder. Holding it by the collar, he jigged it up and down a bit. 'I'm glad you got the message.'

Oh shit! What now? She took an unsteady breath. 'There's something I need to tell you.'

He took two steps closer to her, a concerned expression on his face. 'What is it?'

She knew what he was thinking, that she was going to tell him something important about Celia Delaney.

She opened her mouth to speak, but no words came out. Before she lost her nerve completely, she let her jacket slide to the floor and closed the gap between them. Stuff Henry Gordon and his stupid warning. He could sack her for all she cared.

Taking Ryder by the shoulders, Vanessa stood on tiptoes and pressed her lips to his. For a few heady moments she stayed like that, her eyes closed to the world, her mouth on his as she breathed in his woodsy aftershave.

She broke the kiss and stepped back, licking the taste of whiskey from her lips.

He looked shocked, then pleased, a flush staining his neck above his collared shirt. He smiled, his white, even teeth a sharp contrast to the five o'clock shadow darkening his jaw. 'I'm listening.'

Vanessa's legs turned to water beneath her—from relief, or desire, or both.

He moved quickly, taking her hand and shouldering open the door of the nearby drying room. Tugging her inside, he threw his suit coat on the bench and turned to her.

'My jacket,' Vanessa gasped. 'It's outside.'

He caught the door before it swung closed, retrieved her jacket then threw it on top of his. He swore as a censor light began to flicker on, revealing rows of ski jackets hanging from hooks and boots lined up along the floor.

Vanessa laughed as he thumped the light switch, plunging the humid room into near darkness save for the filtered light from the corridor that shone through a small glass panel in the door.

They stood in the darkened room, breathing heavily, moments of blissful anticipation stretching between them. And then he was there, towering over her, warm hands cupping her face, the pads of his thumbs stroking across her cheeks. He lowered his head, blocking out the light before his lips claimed hers in a kiss so unhurriedly seductive Vanessa's body shook in a top-to-toe tremble.

She brought her hands to his chest, running her palms over the hard wall of muscle, the steady strike of his heart pulsing beneath her fingertips. She moaned softly, and he drew her closer, deepening the kiss, his jaw rough like sandpaper against her cheek.

'You're so beautiful,' he murmured when they broke for air, 'and so soft.' He pressed his lips to the side of her neck, shifting aside the neckline of her jumper so he could access the tender skin of her collarbone.

Vanessa clung to him, pressing against him in an effort to get closer. He growled low in his throat, his hands sliding downwards before splaying across her bottom and pulling her flush up against him.

'Oh . . .'

He set her away from him, breathing hard. 'We're not staying here.'

He left her to peer through the glass square, then opened the door and looked up and down the corridor. Satisfied there was no one out there, he pointed a finger at her. 'You stay here.'

She smiled. 'You just said we *weren't* staying here.'

'I have to get rid of Flowers. He's working in my rooms.'

'Oh.'

Her disappointment must have shown on her face, because he waved a hand in the air and said, 'Stuff it. Come on.'

Out in the corridor, he told her to go ahead. 'I'll follow. It'll look like I'm going to interview you.'

'That sounds like a fun game.' Vanessa headed towards the staircase on legs wobbly with excitement. 'Try and act naturally,' she whispered over her shoulder.

'Yeah, that'll be easy.'

She stifled a giggle, schooling her face into a serious expression as they passed a group of guests who were playing cards at a table close to the bottom of the stairs. Most people were in the cocktail bar or sitting on the lounge close to the open fire.

When they finally reached the door of Ryder's suite, Vanessa let out a sigh of relief.

'I'll speak to Flowers,' he said, going in ahead of her.

Vanessa followed him inside, suddenly nervous Detective Flowers would see through Ryder's explanation for her being there. Hopefully, he'd already thought of a convincing one.

She watched as he stuck his head around the doorway of the makeshift office. 'Beat it, Flowers.'

Vanessa's mouth fell open and she looked around for somewhere to hide.

'What did you say, Sarge?' came Flowers' confused reply.

'Beat it. You're off duty for the night.'

'I'm nearly finished.'

'Goddammit. How many times do you want me to—'

'All right.' The typist chair squeaked.

Vanessa glared at Ryder as he came towards her. Then Flowers appeared in the doorway, his confused expression clearing as he caught sight of Vanessa.

'Oh, hello, Vanessa.'

'Hello,' she said, trying to look serious, as though she might be there on police business.

Flowers didn't buy it for a second. He fought off a smile as he looked from her to Ryder and back again.

'Nice one, Sarge,' she heard him murmur as Ryder shut the door behind him and locked it.

Twenty

Day 7

Vanessa stirred as Ryder left the bed at 5 am. She stretched her limbs, her body deliciously sated. She propped herself up on one elbow, admiring the shape of his shadowy silhouette as he went to close the six-inch gap in the drapes. 'Can we leave them open a bit? I hate not being able to see.'

He turned and came back to the bed, sliding in beside her. 'I didn't mean to wake you.' He lay on his back, and Vanessa shifted closer so she could put her head on his shoulder.

'Lombardi's out there,' he said, wrapping an arm tightly around her.

Vanessa raised her head and listened. Sure enough, the familiar sound of the grooming machine changing gears could be heard out on the mountain. She lowered her head onto Ryder's shoulder again and closed her eyes. 'I'm used to it. I don't hear it anymore.'

A sudden flash from the machine's powerful headlights swept across the room like a searchlight. 'Did the lights wake you?' she asked.

'Hmm.' He stroked his fingers leisurely over her hip. 'What did you say about hating not being able to see?'

Vanessa snuggled closer. 'Remember how I told you I got lost on the farm once?'

169

He turned and pressed his lips against her temple. 'I'm glad they found you.'

'I was down in a gully, surrounded by fog. It was so thick I couldn't see my fingers if I stretched out my arm. My arm wasn't very long back then, either. I was only five.'

'You must have been terrified.'

'I was. Even now, I have one of those little moon lamps next to my bed. It's not as wussy as a night light. Still, people notice things when you're afraid of something.'

'Who notices?'

She nuzzled her face into his neck and ran her hand across his smooth chest. Did he have any idea just how gloriously good he smelled?

'Who?' he asked again.

'Just some people in ski school. Say the visibility's poor and there's debate over whether we put the chairlift on hold—I'm always the first one to say we should do it. Just the thought of a guest going missing in a whiteout, or me being lost with no sense of the horizon, is enough to freak me out.'

'It would freak me out too, and I'm a tough detective.'

She laughed. 'I know, but I don't want to be seen as weak. It's not a good look.'

'I've never met a woman less weak. You asked *me* out, remember, and kissed me first.'

'You should grab your opportunities with both hands,' she said with a smile. 'And what a good cup of coffee it turned out to be.'

He gave a shout of laughter and turned to look at her. 'Definitely my kind of coffee.'

She kissed him, and spoke against his lips. 'Will it happen again, do you think? Would you like it to?'

Vanessa regretted the words immediately. It sounded so needy, and she'd never been that. Sure, she would love to meet that special someone, but she'd been happily single for years. Embarrassed heat flooded her face, and she pulled away. 'Forget I said that. It must be the post-coital glow talking.'

He sat up slowly. She watched from the bed as he stepped into a pair of boxer shorts then turned to face her with a tight smile. 'Let's not get ahead of ourselves. It's not easy being involved with a detective.'

His words chilled her skin, as effectively as a cold shower would have. 'Of course, you're right. I don't know what I was thinking.' She swung her feet onto the floor and looked around for her underwear. Gathering up her clothes, she headed for the bathroom. It was time to get dressed and do the walk of shame back to Long Bay. The least he could do was let her leave gracefully.

'Vanessa. It's not you, it's—'

'Oh, *please*. Really, the whole "It's not you, it's me" thing is totally unnecessary.'

'Wait.' Strong fingers closed around her forearm as she swung away. When she turned to look at him, he laid his other hand over his heart and gazed into her eyes. 'I feel it. I do. For the first time in—' he shook his head, the line between his eyebrows deepening '—I can't tell you how long. But—'

'You don't owe me any explanations, Pierce,' she said softly, aware that she'd never used his first name before. 'Please, just let me get dressed.'

He gave a brief nod and let go of her arm. She hurried into the bathroom, tears stinging her eyes. Pulling on her underwear, she blinked them angrily away. What on earth was wrong with her? It had only been one night, for goodness sake.

Vanessa studied her face in the mirror as she stepped into her jeans then pulled her sweater over her head. She rolled her lips inwards, taking stock of the redness around her mouth and jaw. No big deal. Wind chaff could do worse.

She was running his brush through her hair when he tapped lightly on the door. 'There's something I want to tell you. Something you're going to find . . . shocking.'

Vanessa lowered the brush to her side, her heart beating wildly. 'Okay.'

He didn't open the door, just started speaking. 'Ten years ago, when I was twenty-eight, I was in a relationship with a woman. She fell pregnant, and we had a child. A little girl. Scarlett.' His voice cracked, and Vanessa's hand flew to her mouth.

'In the Force, we get called out any time of the day or night. This day, I was at home when I was called out to a siege. A man had barricaded himself and his two children inside his house. He had a firearm, and was threatening to shoot the kids and himself. I ran to the car.'

He paused, and Vanessa stood stock still, terrified to move or speak lest he stopped talking. Even with the door between them she could hear the heartbreak in his voice.

'When I left the house, Tania had hold of Scarlett's hand, and they were inside. The truth is, I don't know what happened. All I know is that my three-year-old daughter crawled through the doggy door and ran after me. I was already in the car. I didn't see her. I was racing to save someone else's children, when I . . . when I backed over my own daughter in the driveway.'

When Vanessa opened the door, he was standing at the window, one hand propped against the glass, the other on his hip as he gazed out at the shadowy mountain. He glanced at her, a depth of anguish in his eyes she'd only seen once before—in the eyes of her mother as she'd taken Vanessa from the arms of the rescue worker.

'Don't feel bad because you don't know what to say,' he said, his voice raw from the effort of putting his grief into words. 'It's horrific. It will always be horrific. But it's my burden to carry. I'm the one who has to live with the consequences of my actions.'

Vanessa took an unsteady breath, wishing she could do something to help him, but knowing anything she did or said would be unwelcome.

He turned back to the window. 'The accident led to the end of the relationship. Tania couldn't forgive me, and I couldn't forgive myself. I hope you understand that I don't want to subject anyone else to my guilt and grief. It wouldn't be fair on them.'

'I understand perfectly,' she said quietly. 'And I respect your decision.'

A few moments of silence followed before he straightened. 'Thank you. I like you, Vanessa. I know that because I keep thinking about you.' He gave her a sad smile. 'The last thing I wanted to do was to hurt you.'

She shook her head, her heart aching for him. 'You haven't.'

He nodded.

'Can I just say one thing?' she asked.

He turned to look at her, a resigned expression in his eyes as though whatever she was about to say, he'd heard it all before. 'Sure.'

Vanessa took a shaky breath. She'd taken a risk and been honest with him about her feelings—she saw no reason to change that now, especially when he'd opened up and shared his pain the way he just had.

'I just want to say that you're the kind of man I'd make room for in my life. So, don't forget me, in case you decide to make room for someone in yours.'

Don't forget me.

As if he could forget Vanessa Bell.

In the half light, Ryder watched her cross the bridge as she headed home to Long Bay. Her coat was wrapped tightly around her, as if to ward off the icy wind and the chill of his revelation. Ryder swallowed the growing lump in his throat. She wasn't like the other one-night stands he'd had over the years. She was the first woman to have touched his heart since Scarlett's death.

I respect your decision.

She was also the only person who had said that to him. And it meant more than she would ever know. Most people, including his family, had gone to great lengths to reassure him that Scarlett's death wasn't his fault, that it was a tragic accident.

But he would have none of it.

Learning to live with what had happened had been his only choice, other than dying. For months, drinking himself into oblivion and hoping death would claim him on the job had been his preferred option. Until, in a rare moment of sobriety, he'd seen the fear etched into the faces of his family, and realised his behaviour was compounding their grief. His parents had lost a precious grandchild, his sisters a beloved niece. Now, they were living in fear of losing their son and brother.

Ryder had tipped the booze down the sink and applied for a transfer to Sydney.

Away from the pitying looks and the tender care, he'd healed his body in the anonymity of the fast-paced city. And he'd worked under Roman Lewicki, a tough bugger from Cooma whose Polish father was the only member of his family to have survived the Holocaust. He'd set Ryder straight a few times, and they'd been firm friends ever since.

Ryder turned away from the window as Vanessa disappeared inside Long Bay. It was better this way.

So why did he feel so sick in the guts?

He wasn't feeling any better ten minutes later as he stood in the hot shower, nor when he dried off and slung his towel around his waist. In the bedroom, he checked his phone and saw an email from Harriet with the subject line DELANEY. Ryder opened the attachment and saw a photograph of the Tiffany cigarette case found with Celia's body. According to Harriet's notes, it was a slim-line, sterling-silver case with a tiny sapphire set into the clasp. Definitely Tiffany. No identification number found.

Ryder toyed with the idea of calling Celia's parents and asking if they remembered where she had acquired the cigarette case but decided instead to send an email to Newcastle station. He didn't know anyone there now, but one of the detectives could enlarge the photograph and take it over to the house. An image might help prompt their memories.

Ryder stared at the tangle of bed sheets, and closed his eyes against the memory of Vanessa's warmth. He hadn't felt like exercising before his shower, and now the thought of breakfast was enough to churn his stomach.

Three harsh raps on the door made him open his eyes.

'Sarge, are you there?' Flowers' voice held an urgency Ryder hadn't heard before.

He yanked the bed covers up, secured the towel more firmly at his waist and was halfway to the door when Flowers knocked again, louder, his voice more insistent. 'Sarge!'

Ryder flung open the door and looked into Flowers' worried eyes. 'What's up?'

'Someone's been found dead in Long Bay.'

Twenty-one

The scene inside Long Bay was heart-rending. The resort staff, usually so upbeat and happy in their efforts to make sure the guests enjoyed their snow holiday, were congregated in small groups, whispering quietly. Some held each other, and wept openly. Others were half-awake, looking around in stunned confusion.

'This never gets easier,' Ryder said in a low voice as he and Flowers made their way down a hallway towards the kitchen. Three members of staff, still in their pyjamas, were standing around an island bench and speaking in hushed tones. Ryder recognised the surf grommet who'd been dancing with Vanessa last night. A kettle puffed steam into the air, almost at the boil.

Heart beating so hard it was making his legs weak, Ryder scanned every face. *Where was she?* She'd only left his room half an hour ago, so there was no reason for his heart to be going haywire the way it was. Every police instinct told him this was likely to be a drug overdose.

'Police,' he called, holding open his suit coat to display his badge. 'What do we have here?'

'Detective Ryder!'

He spun around to see Terry standing at the end of a passageway that ran at right angles to the one Ryder and Flowers had just walked down. It was narrow, made more so by the ski and snowboard boots lined up against the wall, and the multitude of uniform jackets hanging from hooks.

The bedrooms were on Ryder's left, a darkened TV lounge and bathrooms on his right. Stopping briefly, he kicked aside a stray boot that was lying in his path. A door opened and a young woman wearing flannelette pyjamas, her hair tousled from sleep, leaned out and looked up and down the corridor. Someone inside asked, 'Whose room is it?'

The girl turned and said in a hushed voice. 'Vanessa's.'

A flash cut across Ryder's eyes, and the voices around him receded. Dread seeped into every cell of his being, weighing down his muscles and sending his stomach into a sickening spin. Time slowed down, and he glanced at the jackets lining the left wall. A ski-patrol parka, and the black quilted jacket Vanessa had worn last night, were hanging from the same hook. On the floor, her cherry Doc Martens sat neatly beside her ski boots, the black ones with the bright orange flame on the side.

'Thank God you're here.' Terry's face was chalk white, his hands trembling as he pointed to the door. 'I had to close it. I've sent someone to fetch the doctor, but . . .' He shook his head, and stared hard at the carpet.

Ryder's heart got out of rhythm and his hands felt clammy. Flowers handed him a pair of latex gloves and Ryder worked his shaky fingers inside, all the while bargaining with a God he didn't believe in. Then steeling himself against whatever horror awaited, he snapped the gloves over his wrists and went inside.

A woman was sprawled face down on the floor, her body twisted at an unnatural angle. Too short and fair to be Vanessa; Ryder knew the instant he dropped to his haunches that it was Libby.

Waves of emotion washed over him, swamping him like a close set of breakers. Relief. Guilt. Rage. They pulled him beneath the surface, tossed him into the air then drove him into the sand before he could suck in a breath.

He scanned the room, taking in Vanessa's neatly made bed, testament to the fact she hadn't slept there last night. Shards of glass lay scattered on the floor from the broken moon lamp she'd only just been telling him about.

Bracing himself, Ryder reached out and gently brushed aside Libby's tangled hair. Tinges of blue bracketed her mouth, her sightless eyes fixed on a spot somewhere on the opposite wall. She wasn't lying on the carpet as he'd first thought, but on a trundle that had been pulled out from under the single bed.

He ran a gentle hand down her face to close her eyes, his jaw clenched so tightly his back teeth ached. Fury drove strength into his legs, and he straightened up, his eyes on the angry abrasions circling her throat. This was no OD. This was murder.

Gavin Hutton's face materialised in his mind. Could Libby be the latest victim of the fugitive they suspected of being in the area? Ryder frowned. It didn't fit with Hutton's MO. He was antisocial and slept rough, his kills impulsive, his murder scenes dangerous alleyways and secluded parks. Ryder shook his head. For Hutton to walk into this building would go against everything Ryder had learned about the former soldier. 'Who found her?' he asked.

'I did,' said Terry. 'A couple of staff are down with the flu. I needed Vanessa to work. When she didn't answer my knock, I opened the door and stuck my head in.'

Ryder spun around. 'You did what?'

Terry blinked. 'What?'

'Wasn't the door locked?'

'We don't have locks on the doors. People come and go all night. Some are three to a room. Not the patrollers, though. They get a room to themselves.'

'Is that standard practice? Poking your head inside a woman's room if she doesn't answer?'

Terry's mouth fell open. 'I don't just barge in. I knock and call out a couple of times first. Everyone sleeps pretty soundly. We're all doing physical work.'

'Did you touch anything other than the door handle?'

'I don't think so.' His face turned red with indignation. 'Look, I know our procedures are old-school, but that's how it works around here. We can't rely on the phone reception. And as for locks—have you noticed how old this building is? We're always worried about fire.'

Ryder gave a curt nod to show he understood. 'Round up everyone who lives here. Tell them to assemble in the TV room and kitchen. No one's to come down this way. Oh, and Terry, how many entrances to this place?'

'Five. And those doors don't have locks either. We—'

'What's going on?'

Ryder swung around at the sound of Vanessa's voice. She was dressed in the jeans and jumper she'd worn last night, but it was obvious she'd come from the shower. She stared at him, a hairbrush in her right hand, her freshly washed hair hanging over one shoulder.

Emotion stole Ryder's voice. He couldn't trust himself to speak.

'Terry?' she asked, looking away when he didn't answer. All Ryder could do was watch as Terry reached out and gave her shoulder a comforting squeeze. 'Vee, I'm sorry but, boy, am I pleased to see you.'

She watched him go, then turned to Ryder again, an uncomprehending expression in her eyes.

Flowers came to the rescue. 'We have some distressing news, Vanessa. It's about Libby.'

For a few moments she said nothing. Then she gave a tiny shake of her head, her eyes growing wide and fearful. 'What's happened to Libby? You're scaring me.'

She looked younger than she had last night, and Ryder wished he could protect her from what she was about to learn. She must have hung her coat on the hook outside her room, and left her boots on the floor before going into the bathroom—that decision had spared her the trauma of discovering Libby's body. He cleared his throat and closed the gap between them.

'I'm sorry, Vanessa. Libby has been found dead. She was in your room—'

She shook her head. 'No.'

He nodded.

Her hand flew to her mouth. Stricken, she stared at him for a few moments then dissolved into tears, raising one hand to shield her eyes. Ryder moved closer as her shoulders began to shake, but he didn't touch her. After a while, she sucked in a few uneven breaths and lowered her hand. 'How?'

There was no easy way to say this, no words that would dilute the impact. He stared into her shocked eyes, awash with shattered tears. 'I . . . she was murdered. Strangled.'

Her legs gave way.

Ryder lunged, grasping her under the arms. She swayed, let out a strangled sob as he hauled her against his chest.

He tipped his head at Flowers. 'Get Lewicki. And the crime tape.'

'Yes, sir.'

She raised her hands and pushed him in the chest, but Ryder continued to hold her, fearful her legs would give way again.

'I don't believe you.' She struggled, her hands full of strength and purpose. 'I want to see.'

'Vanessa—'

She twisted in his grip until he let her go. 'She's *my* friend and it's *my* room.'

'All right. We'll look from the door, that's all.' Sometimes, it was better this way. As far as crime scenes went this one was pretty clean. The imagination could be so much worse. Ryder kept hold of her arm and together they walked the few steps along the hallway to her room. Ryder opened the door.

'*Oh*. Libby.' Vanessa began to cry again, calling out to her friend as though she might wake up at any moment. '*Libby*. I'm sorry. I'm so sorry.'

It was enough. Steeling himself against Vanessa's mournful cries, he steered her away, a hum of muted conversation drifting down the hallway where more and more people were gathering.

'I think I'm going to faint.'

Ryder put his arm around her waist. 'It's low blood pressure from the shock.' He scanned the doors along the corridor, searching for somewhere private. 'Hang on.'

She didn't answer, just leaned more heavily on him.

He headed for the women's bathroom, not wanting her to pass out in the corridor.

'Police!' He shouldered his way through the door, scanning the room. Steam swirled in the air, fragrant with the same coconut aroma as Vanessa's hair. Three empty shower cubicles lined one wall, a row of multi-coloured bath towels hanging from wooden pegs were lined along another. A lone wooden chair stood in a corner, and Ryder helped Vanessa towards it, passing the wash basins and the fogged-up mirrors. Whipping off his overcoat, he draped it around her shoulders as she bent her head to her knees. Crouching in front of her, he peeled off his latex gloves and took hold of her clammy hand. He turned it over. Using the tips of his third and index finger, he felt for her pulse. For the next few minutes he counted along, until eventually his own heart rate settled as hers grew stronger.

After some time, she raised her head, her damp hair brushing the skin of his wrist as she looked around the bathroom.

Ryder released her hand. 'Feeling okay?'

She nodded, drawing his overcoat more tightly around her body. Reaction had set in. Keeping a close eye on her, Ryder stood up. Her body would shake for about ten seconds as her system tried to rid itself of the pent-up stress. A period of stillness would follow, before the shaking started up again.

'You'll be okay,' he said gently.

She nodded miserably.

He wished he could make it go away for her, wished that this tragedy wouldn't change her forever, but he knew it would. He checked his watch. Flowers should be back any minute with Lewicki.

'I'm not worried about myself. It's just so sad for Libby, and her family.' Her lips trembled. 'She . . . didn't . . . deserve this.'

'No one deserves this.' Ryder tore a few tissues from a nearby box and handed them to her.

'Vanessa,' he said as she dabbed at her eyes. 'I need you to answer some questions for me. Do you feel up to it?'

She squared her shoulders and nodded.

'Why was Libby in your room?'

'She'd bunked in with me before.' She blew her nose loudly then screwed the tissues into a ball. 'Her roommate . . . enjoys . . . a roll in the . . . snow . . . so, on the nights she brings a guy over, Libby's been sleeping on my trundle.'

It was such a simple explanation, and yet it answered so many questions.

Fresh tears tracked down her cheeks. 'When I chased after you last night, I didn't tell her where I was going. I didn't even say goodnight.'

Regrets.

Always regrets.

'Did Libby have a problem with anyone down here?'

'No.'

'She didn't mention in passing that someone might have been giving her a hard time?'

Vanessa shook her head. 'Libby got on really well with everyone. The guy she followed down here got himself a new girlfriend pretty quickly and, sure, she was a bit embarrassed about being dumped. But she never said he'd been awful or anything.'

'Sarge?'

Ryder swung around at the sound of Flowers' voice ringing out in the corridor. 'In here.'

Flowers came into the bathroom, a roll of crime-scene tape in his hand. Lewicki was right behind him. In all the years he'd worked with Lew, Ryder had often cursed his friend's habit of rising and dressing at the crack of dawn. Not today.

'Lew, take Vanessa to my room and stay there. Don't leave, under any circumstances.'

Vanessa surged to her feet. 'I want to stay here, with the others.'

'You don't have a choice,' Ryder said firmly.

He turned away from her blazing eyes and spoke to Flowers. 'I need to call Homicide. Get the room taped up then chase down the doctor. I want Vanessa checked out, too.'

'Right away, Sarge.'

Ryder stayed, watching as the other three slowly made their way out the swinging door and into the corridor. Lew was already talking quietly to Vanessa as they left.

When the door swung closed behind them, Ryder pulled out his phone and brought up Gray's number. He paced the floor until the Inspector picked up.

'It's Ryder, sir. We have a situation at Charlotte Pass. A childcare worker has been murdered overnight in the staff accommodation. I need as much manpower as you can spare, plus a team of forensic pathologists and the Coroner. I've been using Harriet Ono in Canberra for the forensics on the Delaney case.'

'Jesus. Do you think they're linked?'

Ryder paused. His gut instinct told him yes, but he had nothing concrete to connect the murders. He chose his words carefully. 'My instinct tells me the killer's still in the village.'

'What else do you need?'

'A short-term contract for Roman Lewicki. He's here, eager to help with the case.'

'That's good news. Anything else?'

'Counsellors. There's only one village doctor. And warrants for everything. I can find whoever's responsible, but I need to do it my way.'

'What are you planning?'

Ryder took a deep breath. 'No one enters or leaves Charlotte Pass. All oversnow transport and snowmobile transport is to be suspended. Cleared personnel only, and they have to be choppered in. And I want all the lifts shut down so no one can ski out.'

There was silence at the other end.

'I want a media ban, too,' Ryder went on. 'They're already lodging in Perisher and reporting from there. Let's keep them there.'

Ryder could imagine Gray mulling everything over. He opened the door and left the bathroom. In the corridor, Flowers was securing crime-scene tape in a cross-formation from the top corners of the doorframe to the bottom. Vanessa and Lew were nowhere to be seen.

Ryder paced the hallway and waited for Gray's reply. He checked his watch: 6.40 am. 'Inspector,' he said, running out of patience,

'I've been clear about what I need. If you can't give me authorisation, will you take it up the chain of command?'

Ryder pressed the phone harder against his ear as he waited for Gray's answer. After a few long seconds which felt like forever, the Inspector's gravelly voice came down the line. 'You'll get everything you've asked for.'

'Thank you. The sooner I lock down Charlotte Pass the better.'

Twenty-two

The kids' club had a whiteboard, and the drawings stuck to the windows gave Ryder's investigation team privacy from the curious eyes outside. He and Flowers had put a fine-tooth comb through the place before moving in, looking for anything that might point to a motive for Libby's murder. Their search had turned up nothing.

'Coordinate a search for the murder weapon,' he said to Detective Benson, who had arrived on a chopper with a team of detectives around eight-thirty. 'There are extensive abrasions on her throat and neck. They could be from some kind of cord or rope, perhaps an ocky strap. We'll know more once the forensic pathologist is finished.' Ryder pored over the photocopied map of Charlotte Pass spread out on one of the kid-sized tables. He and Benson perched awkwardly on chairs designed for small people while Ryder drew lines on the map with a pencil. 'Split the resort into four sections. Start with Long Bay. The first responders and forensic teams are already there, so you'll need to work around them. If you turn up nothing, move on to the inn. It's the largest hotel. Then, do the smaller, private lodges. Finally, there are random buildings scattered around the place.' He marked each with a cross on the map. 'This one's the ticket office, which is closed. Same deal goes for these small lifties' huts.' Ryder glanced at Benson. 'I don't like our chances. The murder weapon's probably buried in the snow.'

'It's the most likely place, but you never know. People make rash decisions when they're panicked.' Efficient as always, Benson folded up the map before struggling to his feet. 'I'll get started.'

Ryder stood for a few moments watching him leave before calling Flowers over. 'Made any headway?'

Flowers flipped through his small, spiral-bound notepad. 'I've spoken to Libby's roommate. She hadn't heard of Libby having a problem with anyone. She's shocked and traumatised, and blaming herself for asking Libby to bunk in with someone else. As for the bloke Libby followed down here . . . His new girlfriend is the chef up at Platypus Lodge. She has a room up there, and he was with her all night. They stayed up late talking to some guests, then turned in around half-midnight. According to her he didn't move all night, and was still sound asleep when she rose to start work in the kitchen at five-thirty this morning.'

'What's your gut feeling about them?'

'He has a reasonable alibi and zero motive. If Libby was the target, how would he even know she'd be in Vanessa's room last night?'

Ryder paused before asking, 'Do you think Libby was the target?'

Flowers' eyes bored into his. 'Do you?'

'No. I think Vanessa was.'

A loaded silence hung between them. His junior partner had been watching him all morning, most likely wondering if Ryder sleeping with Vanessa would have an impact on the case. 'Is there anything you want to ask me? Anything you need to get off your chest?'

Flowers held his gaze for several long seconds. 'Not me,' he said with a shake of his head.

'Okay. Did you offer those three young people counselling?'

'Yes. They're over at Long Bay now. The ex-boyfriend wasn't keen, but his girlfriend urged him to go.'

'Anything else?'

Flowers consulted his list. 'Libby's parents have been notified of her death,' he said, his voice shaking a little.

Ryder closed his eyes for a second. Another devastated family.

'Okay, you can go ahead and release her name to the press. And, Flowers, it's okay to be shaken up by this. I sure was.'

Flowers nodded. 'I'd spoken to Libby a couple of times,' he said with difficulty. 'I might have misread things, but I got the feeling she liked me. I was trying to work up the courage to ask her out for a drink.'

Ryder sighed and laid a hand on the younger man's shoulder. There really wasn't anything else he could say.

Flowers swallowed and looked down at his list again. 'Benson has the extra satellite phones you asked for.'

'Did you grab one for yourself?'

'Yep.'

'Get one for Lewicki, too, then pass the rest around,' said Ryder. 'If we don't have enough, let me know. I've spoken to Gray. He's giving Lew an official role. Is that all?'

Flowers looked at his watch. 'Four more police personnel are fifteen minutes from landing, due to set down at ten past nine.'

'Okay. I want you to stay here and take charge of the new team.' Ryder grabbed a file off Libby's desk and handed it to Flowers. 'This is a list of all guests staying at Charlotte Pass, as well as a full inventory of resort staff. I want you to make a spreadsheet—we need a register for people entering and leaving the various buildings. We need to know who comes and goes, and when; they'll have to sign in and out.'

'Too easy, Sarge.'

'Have the new team distribute them to the lodges. It's vital the owners understand the importance of this. I want to be able to look at a register and know at a glance who's inside that particular building. And they can take a roll-call while they're there. I need a starting point.'

Ryder turned at a soft knock on the internal door. Terry was coming towards them. 'Get started right away, Flowers. We can give Terry the one for Long Bay while he's here.'

Terry hooked a thumb over his shoulder. 'Di Gordon's heading up the hill, looking like she's on a rampage.'

Ryder sighed. He'd expected some pushback from her when he'd announced that he was locking down Charlotte Pass, but she'd been too shocked to string a coherent sentence together. He'd left her to digest the news, hoping a little time might help the husband-and-wife team come to terms with the situation. He would need their cooperation and support in managing the guests while they carried out the investigation.

'Sorry to bother you at a bad time,' Terry said, 'but I have staff worried about the hit they're going to take to their working hours. Plus, we're supposed to guarantee the people on visas a certain number of hours per week.'

Ryder listened, pleased Terry didn't seem to be harbouring any ill feeling about their tense exchange earlier.

'Everybody's shaken up,' Terry went on, 'but they're adamant they'd rather be working than hanging around watching the medical teams come and go. What's the chance of opening up the mountain a bit later, maybe with a skeleton staff?'

There was merit to Terry's request, and though it would make Benson's job easier if a whole lot of residents cleared out of Long Bay, Ryder wasn't prepared to take the risk. 'I'm afraid it's non-negotiable. Everyone's confined to the village. If we open the lifts, it's too easy for people to ski into the back country.'

Terry sighed. 'I had a feeling you'd say that. But I told them I'd come up here and ask anyway.'

Ryder nodded. 'Stick around for a minute, will you?' He explained about the entry/exit system they were putting in place. 'Station someone on the door at Long Bay, someone you can trust. Here's a list of everyone who's living there. You might already have a copy of that, but take it anyway. And I need you to do a roll-call for me.'

'Okay. No problem.'

'Detective!'

Ryder swung around to see Di Gordon stride across the room, body puffed up with indignation. Judging by her body language, the cooperation he'd been hoping for wasn't going to be forthcoming.

'You can't do this,' she snapped as she stopped in front of him.

'I've already done it, Mrs Gordon.'

'What about my guests?' she said, looking Terry up and down with unveiled hostility, as if willing him to disappear. To Ryder's amusement, Terry folded his arms and widened his stance, holding the woman's stare until she finally shifted her gaze back to Ryder. 'My guests have jobs to get back to. Others have reservations and are waiting to check in. They're stuck down in Perisher Valley. Where are they going to go?'

'I'm sure they'll work something out.'

'They've paid in advance.'

'They can go home.'

She gaped at him, her mouth opening and closing. 'It's chaos at the Perisher desk. This will do untold damage to our brand.'

Ryder took a deep breath and hung onto his temper, but only just. 'We have a killer in the village, Mrs Gordon,' he said tightly.

'I've never heard of this kind of thing happening before.'

'There are plenty of examples if you'd care to look them up. Martin Place was shut down during a siege. Workers in the surrounding buildings were confined to their offices until the situation was resolved. We have a situation here, and now, if you don't mind, I'm very busy.'

She hesitated for a moment, then when it was obvious Terry wasn't going to move, and she wasn't getting anywhere with Ryder, she said, 'Then you leave me no option but to talk to your superior.'

'Can she make trouble for you?' Terry asked as they watched her leave.

'Nope. She'll be charged with obstructing the police if she keeps going.'

Terry nodded, one corner of his mouth lifting. 'So, how's Vanessa doing?'

Ryder had been wondering the same thing. 'She's asleep at the moment. Well, as of half an hour ago she was.'

'When she wakes up, can you let her know we're all thinking of her?'

'I'll do that.'

'Thanks.'

When Flowers had completed drawing up the register, Ryder gave the sheets for Long Bay to Terry. 'One last thing,' he said, 'make sure everyone knows there's a nine pm curfew. No exceptions. Pub's closed tonight.'

Forty minutes later, just as Ryder had begun to obsessively check his watch, Lewicki sent a message to say Vanessa was awake.

She was in his room, sitting on the side of the bed where only hours earlier they'd made love. When he sat down beside her, she turned bleary eyes on him. He had no words that would make her feel any better. He could only hope that just being there would help.

She clasped her hands tensely in her lap. 'I've seen dead people before today.'

'The ones you pulled out of tree wells?'

She nodded. 'A couple of people had heart attacks and died on the slopes, too. But they were strangers. And they weren't murdered.'

He reached out and took hold of her hands. Cold fingers wrapped around his. 'Do you know who did it?' she asked.

'Not yet.'

'I can hear the helicopters taking off and landing. Lewicki told me you've locked down the resort.'

He nodded. 'It's a drastic move, but it's the most effective way of flushing out the perp. And it's cheaper in the long run than a protracted investigation. What's in that?' he asked, nodding towards the corner where a blue-and-red–striped carry bag sat straining at the seams.

'Oh. The girls in Long Bay had a clothing drive for me, seeing my room's a designated crime scene. They put my toiletry bag in, too. Someone dropped it over while I was asleep.'

'That was thoughtful of them.'

'I haven't had the energy to go through it yet.' She rubbed her hands along her thighs. 'I'll have to get out of these jeans at some point.'

'There's no hurry. You're not going anywhere.'

She glanced at him. 'I don't know whether it's shock, or the medi-cation the doctor gave me, but I have brain fog. And I can't stop going over everything in my mind. Small things. Things that used to seem important but now . . . well, everything's different.'

'I know,' Ryder said quietly. He longed to put his arms around her, but because of what had happened between them, and what'd he'd subsequently said to her, he held back. Instead, he stood up and tugged on her hand. 'Lew's taking a break while I'm here. Come and sit on the couch, it'll be more comfortable. I need to ask you a few questions.'

She stopped when they reached the sitting room. 'Can I use your phone? I need to call home. Lew said the queue for the landline downstairs was a mile long with people calling their families. Apparently, the network's slowed right down.'

'Yeah, absolutely.' Ryder gave himself a mental uppercut. Of course, she wouldn't have had a chance to call her parents, she'd not long woken up. He took the phone from his coat pocket and handed it to her. 'I'll be in the office.'

'Thanks.'

He sat on the typist chair, which had grown wobblier with overuse. He ran a hand over the bare surface of the desk. He couldn't even busy himself looking through the file now everything was up in the investigation area. He pushed back the chair and went to stand at the window. With the exception of a family of four who were building a snowman beside the creek, the resort was eerily quiet. Other than the occasional raven's call, the only sound was the intermittent squeak of an empty chair on the cable as it swung back and forth in the light breeze.

'Hello, Mum.'

Ryder stilled, his eyes on Long Bay where the hem of an orange curtain flapped through a partially open window.

'I'm fine, Mum. Don't freak out. Everything's okay.'

There was a pause, then, 'Oh, there's a hotline? No, I didn't know that, but it makes sense. I'm not surprised you weren't able to get through on it, though.' Another pause. 'One of the detectives gave me his satellite phone to call you. I'm lucky to be able to bypass the queue.' There was a longer pause this time. Ryder slipped his hands into his trouser pockets. The only way he could block out what Vanessa was

saying would be to stick his fingers in his ears. 'Yes, I knew her, Mum.'
Vanessa's voice began to quaver. Ryder held his breath wondering
how the conversation would go. 'Yes, it's tragic. She was a really nice
girl . . . What about you and Dad, are you okay?' It was a good deflec-
tion. 'Oh, that's great. Yes, I can imagine it would be all over the news.
Try not to worry too much, though, we're in good hands. Mum, I'm
going to have to go. I can't tie up the phone too long.'

Ryder slid his hands from his pockets and walked slowly to the
doorway. She was moving restlessly, the phone to her ear, her eyes
on the swirling carpet pattern. She stilled when she caught sight of
him, her gaze tracking upwards to meet his. She held up her free
hand and crossed her fingers. 'I'm perfectly safe, Mum. They've
moved some of the girls out of Long Bay and into the inn. There's a
huge police presence here. I couldn't be safer.' She grimaced, clearly
hating having to lie to her mother.

'You did the right thing,' he said, when she'd hung up. 'You *are*
perfectly safe, if you stay here.'

He sat on the sofa, opposite her, as he'd done with the others he'd
interviewed. 'The fellow Libby followed down here is in the clear.
He has a solid alibi.'

She sat tensely, eyeing him warily.

Ryder rubbed his forehead, reminding himself she was an intelli-
gent woman, and had probably anticipated what he was going to
say next.

'This may come as another shock, but I don't think Libby was
the intended victim. I think someone wanted to harm you, and they
found Libby in your room instead.'

'I already worked that out,' she snapped, before burying her face
in her hands. He waited while she dragged in some deep breaths, her
shoulders rising and falling. After a while, she took her hands away
and looked at him. 'I'm sorry. I'm just so . . . so angry. I want to hit
something.'

'It's not your fault,' he said, uttering the same words people had
said to him time and time again. In Vanessa's case, though, it was
true. She'd only been doing her friend a favour. But knowing it

wasn't your fault didn't help ease the guilt. 'Have you had a problem with anyone down here?'

'Only Bruno.'

Ryder sucked in a breath, the hairs on the back of his neck standing up. 'What happened with Bruno?'

'Everything was fine until the other night.'

'Which night?'

'The night of the flare run. I went to the inn afterwards, but it was so crowded I decided to go home.'

That's the night he'd been in Newcastle, talking to Arnold and Eunice Delaney. 'What happened?'

'He was waiting in the dark, on the other side of the bridge. Scared the hell out of me. He asked what was happening up on Mount Stillwell. He would have known what was going on. It was all around the village.'

'What did you tell him?'

'Nothing. I said he'd have to ask you or Terry. He made a big deal about needing to get the snow out from behind the fences, said if he couldn't do his job then nothing else could happen.'

'I wished you'd told me.'

'I told Terry, the day I saw you in the cafe. He's given Bruno a warning.'

'What did he do, exactly?'

'When I tried to get past him, he grabbed hold of my wrist. I managed to get away, but he followed me inside. He was very intimidating, standing outside my door for a while, clicking his lighter on and off. He even called my name.' Her voice began to shake at the memory. 'There was hardly anyone else in the building at the time. Do you think it's him—Bruno—who killed Libby?'

Ryder moved to sit beside her. Hang protocol. Hang fucking everything. She was at risk, and she wasn't moving from his suite until he'd apprehended the person who'd strangled her friend to death. 'I don't know. But he's my main suspect in the Delaney case. He was the liftie on duty the night Celia disappeared, and he's changed his story from back then. There hasn't been another murder here in over fifty years, and now Libby's been killed the same week the police are back investigating the old crime.'

She stared at him with stricken eyes. 'Oh, my God,' she said quietly, 'that's terrifying.'

He nodded. 'It's very worrying. And I don't believe in coincidences.' He mulled over the facts trying to find a link. 'You and Terry have been involved with certain things up on the mountain. You were there when we found those wire ties but, apart from that, you know little of the specifics of the case.'

'I got a dressing down about spending too much time with the police.'

Ryder frowned. 'From who?'

'The Gordons. Well, Mr Gordon actually. He reminded me who paid my wages, and made a point of telling me that my job should be my first priority. I thought they were going to hand me my notice. Mrs Gordon was firing someone in her office while I was waiting in the hallway.'

'Who did she fire?'

Vanessa shook her head. 'I don't know. I couldn't hear the other person's voice, only her. It could have been one of the band, because she said something like "When the gig's over get the hell out." And then she asked them why they'd admitted to something they'd done when they were young.'

Nigel Miller. 'Oh, Vanessa. Why didn't you tell me?'

'Because it's not my investigation, and I didn't want to be a nuisance running to you with every little thing I overheard. Di was furious, though.'

Ryder had a pretty good idea of why that was. 'Okay. Don't worry about it. I wish Terry had told me about Bruno. Did he back off after he was given a warning?'

'I haven't seen much of him. He made a beeline for me in Long Bay, but I avoided him. And then yesterday, he was up at the snow fences. I saw him for a few seconds when I was chasing some maniac through the trees.'

'Someone was skiing near the burial site?'

'Yes.' The colour was back in her cheeks now, and her voice was growing stronger as though she were better for talking it out. 'This guy was a menace.'

'You're certain it was a man?'

'From his build, yes. I nearly caught him at one point.'

'Did you call out?'

'Several times. He completely defied my authority.'

'You're certain he heard you?'

'Oh, he heard me. He looked around, but I had to let him go in the end. He skied across the tube run. He could have taken out any number of people and injured them. If I'd caught him, I would have been tempted to ban him from the resort.'

'He was that desperate to get away from you?'

She nodded.

'Would you recognise him again?'

'I'm not sure. He was wearing rental gear. That's the olive-green jacket and black pants you see half the people here wearing.' She looked at him, a puzzled expression on her face. 'A couple of things did strike me as odd.'

'Okay. Tell me.'

'Well, good skiers usually have their own gear. The occasional skiers are more likely to rent clothing, and families with children. You can understand them not wanting to buy expensive suits the kids will grow out of in a year. A lot of first-timers rent, too, because they're not sure if they'll like it.'

Ryder nodded. 'Makes sense. What else was unusual?'

'Well, it takes years to become an experienced skier. By then, people know that ski patrol are responsible for keeping the mountain safe, and that the signage is there for a reason. I've only ever been ignored by smart alec kids out for a lark, or a dare, or . . .'

'Or?'

'Or by learners and tentative skiers.'

Tentative skiers. Like Celia Delaney.

'They can be so busy concentrating on staying upright, that they miss a sign and they don't even hear us call out. Sometimes, they get in a situation where they're too frightened to make a tight turn, so they just keep skiing across the mountain. They can end up in the trees between the runs, or in a series of bumps off to one side. Very quickly they can find themselves someplace they're not meant to be. But that's all part and parcel of learning, and usually they're embarrassed and very apologetic.'

'So, it's unusual for a competent skier to do that?'

'It's highly unusual.'

'And you said Bruno was up there?'

She nodded. 'He saw me and pointed after the skier.'

'To show you which way he'd gone?'

'Yes.'

'I don't like it.' Ryder pulled out his phone and called Benson. 'Send someone down to the rental shop. I want a list of all male skiers who have pants and parkas rented out, and details of where they're staying.'

He hung up and looked at Vanessa again. 'How did you know this bloke was up on Mount Stillwell?'

'One of the lifties told me. He saw him duck under the CLOSED sign.'

'And he didn't stop once, just skied straight from the top to the bottom?'

'I think so. I mean, he stopped eventually, down the bottom. I got in traffic and had to pull up. I pointed at him, making it clear I wanted him to stay where he was. But he took off.'

A sense of disquiet unfurled in Ryder's stomach. Why had he been there? To look at the grave? To talk to Bruno? What if Vanessa had interrupted him?

'You're highly visible in your ski-patrol uniform. Even from this window I'm able to pick you out on the hill.'

She flushed a little and glanced at him from beneath her lashes. 'It's not hard. Johan is twice my size.'

'I know. I've seen him.' Ryder linked his fingers together. 'I'm not trying to alarm you, but this menace, he knows which patroller was chasing him.'

A small frown creased her forehead. 'You don't think he'd come after me, just because I was going to confiscate his lift pass, do you? That doesn't make any sense.'

'Nothing ever makes sense. Not until we have all the facts and solve the case. I'm not discounting anyone in this village, especially a person who defies authority, and is brazen enough to ski very close to a police crime scene, especially one where the remains of a murdered woman have recently been dug up.'

Vanessa eyes widened, and she twisted her hands in her lap. 'Now I'm scared.'

'It's natural to be scared. So, no more asking if you can go back to Long Bay, okay?'

'Where do you think I should go?'

Ryder hesitated. 'You have a couple of options. If you'd like to go home to the farm, that's fine. We can access you from there. If you decide to stay on, you'll have to remain in this suite. Lewicki's the perfect one to watch you during the day, and I'll be here at night.' He held up his hands as she went to say something. 'You can take the bedroom. I'll sleep on the lounge, but it mightn't come to that. We're running the investigation from the kids' club now, so we don't need the makeshift office. If Di Gordon settles down and decides to cooperate, she might take out the desk and put the bed back in. Miracles have been known to happen.'

She smiled a little.

'As an aside to that: we tend to hit the ground running at the start of an investigation. I'll be snatching a few hours' sleep here and there.'

She nodded, her eyes flicking around the room. 'I could stay with Eva and Poppy. That's my older sister and my niece. Eva has a lodge in Thredbo.'

Ryder raised his eyebrows.

'What?'

'You have two skiing enthusiasts in the family?'

She smiled a little more brightly. 'Eva's a fair-weather skier. She's a highly trained chef, though. Making gastronomic meals for her guests is more her thing.'

'Well, let me know what you decide,' he said, realising with a jolt that he'd miss her if she decided to go. 'We wouldn't have a problem accessing you in Thredbo.'

'Can I have some time to think about it? I'm not sure I could stay cooped up with nothing to do and only Lewicki for company. No offence to your friend.'

'None taken.' Ryder checked his watch. They were nearly out of time. 'In the meantime, I want you to do everything Lew says. The police presence and being confined will make the perp more desperate. I don't want you in their sights, especially if they think you know something, or could potentially identify them. Do you understand?'

'Yes.'

A knock sounded at the door.

'That'll be Lew.'

They both stood up.

Ryder hesitated, wanting to stay, but at the same time desperate to get on the killer's trail. 'If you remain here, it's on my terms, okay?'

She nodded. 'Okay. But don't expect me to play the useless victim.'

He hesitated again. What the hell was he doing, giving her a choice in all this? Vanessa being located elsewhere was in the best interests of the police, because they couldn't be held accountable for her safety. He should be encouraging her to leave.

Unable to stop himself, he pulled her to him in a gentle hug.

Twenty-three

'Write down your name, please,' the young woman on the front door said in an officious tone, pointing to the column and handing Ryder a pen. 'And the time you entered the building.'

Ryder smiled to himself as he scribbled his name on the sheet. Terry had chosen the right person for the job. 'Keep up the good work,' he said, handing the pen to Flowers.

Long Bay was a hive of activity. Benson was in the hallway, talking to two young blokes about search warrants and their rights, and explaining how it was in their best interest not to obstruct the police, especially if they had nothing to hide.

In the kitchen, a detective Ryder didn't recognise was deep in conversation with a young woman dressed in a university tracksuit and sheepskin boots. Another five girls were waiting in line.

'What's going on here?' Ryder asked, after he'd introduced himself.

'Detective Benson wanted to know if anyone woke during the night and heard anything unusual. These ladies came forward.'

'Right. Let me know if you get anything.'

They found Terry standing in the centre of the TV room, clipboard in hand. Close to a dozen staff members were also in the room. A few were curled sleepily in chairs, while others were stretched out on the floor, their attention riveted to a superhero movie playing on the TV. At a table in the corner, four blokes were engrossed in a serious game of poker.

Terry swung around at Ryder's soft knock. 'I'm halfway through taking the roll-call,' he said. 'I'll catch you up when I'm done.'

A familiar scent of crime-scene chemicals greeted Ryder as he approached Vanessa's room. An emergency-services man came backing out of the doorway and into the corridor holding the end of a stretcher. The man's clothes were covered by plastic overalls, his shoes by plastic booties.

'Sweet Jesus,' Flowers muttered as Libby's covered body came into view. 'She was too young to end up in a body bag like that.'

'Why don't you head back the way we came,' said Ryder. 'Close the door to the TV room and clear those girls out of the kitchen. They don't need to see this.'

'Right, Sarge.'

'Oh, and Flowers, find out which room is Bruno's. I want to question him the minute we've finished here.'

Ryder watched as the two men manoeuvred the stretcher through the doorway. 'How's it going, fellas?' he asked quietly.

'We're ready to take the body to Canberra,' the older of the two men said. 'The helicopter's on standby.'

Ryder glanced into Vanessa's room. Harriet Ono and two members of her forensic team were working inside, their movements quiet, respectful and unhurried.

Five minutes later, Libby's body was taken from the building, and Harriet emerged from Vanessa's room. She pulled down her face mask and raised her eyebrows at Ryder.

'Shutting down the resort, hey? You'll do anything to get your face on telly.'

'Good to see you out of bed at the crack of dawn, Harriet.'

'You thinking about me in bed? I've told you before I'm not interested.'

Ryder smiled a little. It was a way of coping with the horror, of emotionally detaching from the constant exposure to violent death. 'So, what's your take on this one?'

'Well,' Harriet spoke on a sigh. 'From the external examination, she died of asphyxiation.'

'I'm curious about those unusual marks on her neck.'

'Velcro.'

'Velcro?'

'Yep? I've seen the abrasions a few times, not around the neck, but on other body parts.'

Ryder pulled out his phone. 'Flowers, can you ask Terry to come down here, please?'

'Any idea of the time of death?' he asked Harriet.

'Somewhere between four and four-thirty this morning, according to the medical examiner. He's already left for another crime scene, by the way. It's shaping up to be a busy one.'

'Has the luminol shown up anything?'

Harriet glanced over her shoulder. 'A ton of marks have appeared already but, as you know, blood isn't the only activator that glows in the dark. This carpet's been down a long time. A lamp was smashed at some point. Let's hope the perp cut himself.'

'Unlikely. My guess is he was wearing gloves.'

Beyond Harriet's shoulder, Ryder could see a member of the forensics team kneeling on the floor using tweezers to collect fibres from the carpet, while a fingerprint specialist brushed the surfaces for prints.

'I've taken scrapings from under her fingernails. More extensive tests will be done at the morgue.'

'I need you to give this priority, Harriet. I'm relying on you. Without security cameras, it's tough getting a lead here.'

'There's no CCTV footage in the village?'

'Nope. Just a couple of snowcams.'

Harriet rolled her eyes. 'Like they'll be of any use. So, do you think this murder is related to the Delaney cold case?'

'That's at the forefront of my mind.'

When he didn't elaborate, she ducked into the room and came back with her pathology bag. 'I have that cigarette case for you, too.'

Ryder took the small, plastic bag from her and held it up to the light. An officer from Newcastle command had shown a photograph of it to the Delaneys, but neither parent could remember Celia having had the case. He turned the item over, studying it closely. 'Thanks, Harriet. I'll log this into evidence and ask her husband about it.'

Harriet gave a soft chuckle. 'Careful it doesn't give you nicotine withdrawals.'

Ryder snorted and zipped the case into the pocket of his police jacket. 'I'll buy a ticket when you're doing stand-up comedy.' He hadn't thought about lighting up in days. He nodded at the room. 'Have you had a look inside the cupboard?'

'It's mainly clothes. All neatly folded. Whoever's responsible for this, they weren't searching for anything.'

A sudden thought struck Ryder and he leaned around Harriet to speak to the fingerprint specialist. 'Excuse me. Can you do the closet door first?'

Harriet grasped his arm and attempted to drag him backwards. 'Get away from the door, Pierce, you'll contaminate my crime scene. God, you're an impatient bugger.'

Harriet disappeared inside Vanessa's room shaking her head as Flowers reappeared in the corridor with Terry in tow.

Ryder lowered his voice and spoke to both men. 'Harriet said Libby was strangled with a piece of Velcro.' He looked at Terry. 'Where do you find Velcro down here?'

'Velcro? Man, anywhere and everywhere.' Terry turned around and went a little way back up the corridor and lifted a jacket off its hook. 'Mine has Velcro around the neck to attach the hood.' Coming back to Flowers and Ryder, he held the jacket open for them to see, pointing out the pieces of Velcro stitched into the garment. 'There's also a panel down the front covering the zipper, and it's around the cuffs so you can pull the sleeves in tight.'

'He would have needed a piece this long.' Ryder held up his hands a little less than shoulder width.

Flowers pointed to the front of the jacket. 'That piece would be long enough, but who could be bothered unpicking it? Why not use something else?'

Terry snapped his fingers, his eyes lighting up. 'Hang on.' He strode back down the corridor, stopping about halfway along. Squatting, he took something from an open bag.

When he joined them again, a piece of purple Velcro dangled from his fingers. 'This is one of my ski straps.'

'Harriet,' Ryder called, the hairs on the back of his neck standing on end as he took the material from Terry. He wound the ends around his hands then tested the tautness of it. As Harriet appeared in the doorway, he held his fists aloft.

Dragging down her mask, she stared hard at the ski strap. Then her gaze met Ryder's over the strip of purple Velcro. 'That'd do it.'

'We're looking for one of these,' Ryder told Benson a few minutes later. He demonstrated how they worked, winding the piece of Velcro around the top of Terry's skis and showing Benson how it kept the tips together. 'They always come in pairs. The second one goes around the tails,' he said, pointing to the opposite end of the ski. 'It prevents them from coming apart when you carry them.' Ryder propped the skis against the wall. 'Start here in Long Bay, then search the ski rooms at the inn and in the lodges. We'll start with the public areas first then go room to room if we have to. Harriet will wait and take them back with her.'

'Yes, Sarge.'

'Oh, and Benson, you don't have to worry about the hired skis. The rental shop doesn't have straps.'

'Got it.'

'So, what's your take on this?' Flowers asked when Benson had left. 'Do you think the murderer lives in the building?'

'That was my first thought. That why I wanted the hunt for the murder weapon to start here. How would an outsider know which room was Vanessa's?'

'They wouldn't. There aren't any names on the doors.'

'I thought that too, but check out these jackets.' Ryder reached up and touched the sleeve of Vanessa's ski-patrol jacket. 'Here's Vanessa's. And hanging on the same hook are the rimless mirrored goggles she wears.' He pointed further along the hallway. 'Now look down there. There's only one other patroller apart from Vanessa, and his jacket's right there. See how much bigger it is?'

'Yep.'

'And down here,' Ryder nudged Vanessa's boots with his foot. 'These badarse-looking ski boots with the orange flame on the side? They're hers. Any observant person with half a brain could work out that this was her room.'

'And the exterior doors have no locks.'

'Right. The place is wide open.'

Flowers blew out a breath. 'That makes our job a hell of a lot harder.'

Ryder nodded. 'I still think it's more likely that the person who murdered Libby lives in this building, but we can't rule out anyone in the village.'

'Including Libby's former boyfriend?'

'Well, I think he's probably in the clear.'

A whir of helicopter rotors cut through the quiet then steadily grew faster and louder as it rose from the helipad behind the inn. Ryder hoped Vanessa hadn't been standing at the windows when Libby's body was carried out.

'Fucking hell,' Flowers said as the noise receded. 'You just don't know when your number's up, do you? Vanessa was so lucky she was with you last night, Sarge. But . . . not Libby.'

Ryder nodded. 'Libby was in the wrong place at the wrong time. There's nothing more to it than that.'

'I have to admit, Pierce, you're good,' Harriet said, emerging from Vanessa's room again. 'There's a well-defined print on the cupboard door. Looks man-sized, too. We would have got to it, but,' she frowned, 'what made you ask for the closet to be done first?'

'It's a shot in the dark that he might have taken off his gloves, so don't get too excited. There's barely room to put your feet on the floor with the trundle pulled out like that. I nearly overbalanced when I was in there this morning. If the killer did the same, there's a chance he could have thrown out a hand to save himself.'

'Well, we have the best in the business lifting it off with tape right now. And, when we're done, can we please have the room taped up again?'

'You want to keep it as a crime scene?'

'For now. Just in case I have to come back and take bits and pieces of furniture to the lab. Shouldn't be a problem. No one will be in a hurry to move in.' Without another word Harriet disappeared back inside the room.

Ryder looked up at the ceiling, trying to imagine what the building was like when it was bottom station for the old chairlift. 'That print could be anybody's,' he said to Flowers. 'It might be months since that cupboard was wiped over or polished.'

'Why would someone want to hurt Vanessa?' Flowers mused.

Ryder told him about her run-in with Bruno, and the irresponsible skier she chased down the mountain. 'I don't know, but I'm convinced it's linked to the Delaney case.' Ryder unbuttoned the pocket of his jacket and pulled out the Tiffany cigarette case. 'Log this in, then ask Nigel Miller about it. I want to know whether Celia bought it for herself, or if it was a gift from him. Remember, she'd asked Nigel for a divorce. Maybe it was a gift from her new lover.'

'Will do, Sarge.'

'If you don't make any headway, contact Tiffany. A company like that—who knows how far their records go back.'

'Too easy.'

'Detective Ryder.'

Ryder turned at the urgency in Terry's voice. He was hurrying towards them, a two-way radio in his hand. 'What's up?'

'Perisher terminal just called. One of our grooming machines is parked down there.'

'What!' He'd shut down the resort the minute Inspector Gray had given him the go ahead. 'How on earth? Why am I only hearing about this now?'

'They've been flat out at the desk turning people away and explaining why the village is shut down. They only just noticed it.' Terry jiggled the two-way nervously in his hand. 'There's more bad news. I've done the roll-call. Bruno's gone.'

Twenty-four

Vanessa walked into the sitting room, dressed in a pair of track pants and a long-sleeved T-shirt.

'Feeling better?' Lew asked from behind the novel he'd borrowed from the bookcase downstairs.

'Yes. It feels good to be in fresh clothes.' She walked around behind him and peered over his shoulder. 'Good book?'

'Hmm. Pretty good.'

'You're on the same page.'

Lew half-turned to look at her.

'You were on that page when I went to have a shower.'

'Well, I'm a slow reader.'

'You're only pretending to read,' she said, straightening up. 'I know you're watching me, even though the front door's locked.'

Lewicki closed the book and slid it onto the coffee table. 'It's dead boring anyway, pages and pages describing scenery. I looked for a sports magazine in the shop downstairs, but they didn't have any.'

Vanessa chuckled, then quietened as a wave of guilt swamped her. It felt so wrong to be laughing when poor Libby was dead.

'I'll be honest,' he said, his eyes on her as she came around the sofa. 'I'd rather watch you than read that book. I'm curious about you. And I don't mean that in a creepy-old-man kind of way.'

'How *do* you mean it—in a straight-up old-cop kind of way?'

'I'm not getting involved in your personal life, but I know you spent the night with him. And thank God you did, because we would have had two dead women here this morning if you'd gone back to your room.'

Vanessa picked some lint off the sleeve of her borrowed T-shirt. 'I feel like I let her down. I know it doesn't make sense to go back and wish you'd made a different decision, but maybe if there'd been two of us in that room, we both might have stood a chance.'

Lewicki shook his head. 'Look, there will always be the what-ifs. It's part of coming to terms with what's happened. So, I'm going to tell you the same thing I've been trying to tell Ryder for ten years: Things go wrong in life, even when you're trying to do the right thing.'

An image of her mother wrapping gifts for the school's Mother's Day stall came to mind. She'd been busy doing the right thing when her youngest had gone missing for an entire day and night. People had judged her for it. People always judged. And Ryder, rushing to save two innocent children caught up in their father's psychotic episode. Doing the right thing when his own tragedy had struck.

'I'm not sure me chasing after Ryder last night was "trying to do the right thing". It was impulsive and a bit selfish. I didn't even think of Libby.'

'You like him, don't you?'

Heat crept into Vanessa's cheeks at the blunt question. 'Of course I like him.'

'Then it was the right thing, for you, and maybe for Ryder, too, but he doesn't know it yet. And, if he does, he's not admitting it.'

Vanessa studied Ryder's older friend. Perhaps his decades of police work had enabled him to drill down to the crux of the matter, or perhaps he had an innate knack for summing people up. After all, managing people was one of the most challenging parts of any job.

He didn't hold back either.

She cleared her throat. 'You know Ryder a lot better than I do. He did tell me . . . about Scarlett.'

'Did he?' Lewicki's eyebrows shot up. 'I think only a handful of people know the full story. It's not something he can usually talk about.'

When she didn't say anything, he got up off the sofa. 'I tell you what. I could do with a cup of tea. What about you?'

'I'd love one.'

'Stay there,' he said, when she went to follow him. On the other side of the room he switched on the kettle and began sorting through the tea and coffee packets. 'Does a breakfast tea take your fancy?'

'A breakfast tea would be perfect.'

'Good. There'll be hell to pay if we drink Flowers' chamomile.'

When the tea was made, Lewicki joined her at the window and handed her a mug.

'Thank you. I don't know why, but there's something comforting about tea that coffee just can't pull off.'

'My wife would agree. If Annie's sick, or upset, she can't stomach coffee.' Lewicki took a sip of tea, his gaze roaming over the front valley.

Vanessa glanced sideways at him. 'I know you were the original detective on the Delaney case. Wouldn't you be more help to Ryder if you were working on the investigation rather than babysitting me?'

'Yep. You want to tell Ryder that?'

'It's not my place. He'd listen to you, though.'

'I wouldn't bet on it. I had to risk our friendship to convince him to take this case. Now he's here, he'll stop at nothing to get his man.'

'Why would you risk your friendship, if it's so important to both of you?'

'I didn't do it lightly.' Lewicki shook his head and swirled the mug of brown liquid in his hand. 'There are reasons I can't go into, but I needed him on this case. He's a stubborn bastard once he gets the bit between his teeth. That's why he's the best there is.'

A pool of warmth spread throughout Vanessa's body. He was a great lover, too, but she wasn't going to add that to his list of accomplishments. 'Is he really the best?'

One side of Lewicki mouth curved as he brought the mug to his mouth again. 'Well, after me he is.'

There was the sound of a key sliding into the door lock and then the man they'd been talking about came in, a preoccupied expression on his face. He shot them a quick glance and strode towards the main bedroom. 'Bruno drove a grooming machine into Perisher.'

'He's done a runner?' exclaimed Lewicki.

'Looks like it.' There was the sound of drawers being opened and closed, and then Ryder appeared in the doorway, a wallet in his hand. 'He left it parked at the terminal. We've already turned his room upside down—found nothing.'

'Where are you headed?' asked Lewicki.

'Cooma. I got a warrant from the court to search his house. A police car is going to meet us.' His eyes slid to Vanessa then, and his dark eyes softened. 'Do you know where my coat is?'

'Oh. Yes.' She moved towards him. 'I hung it in the cupboard by the door.'

'It's okay. I'll get it.' Everything about his movements showed how impatient he was to get going.

Vanessa hesitated, unsure if she should leave the two men alone, but they didn't seem bothered that she was privy to their conversation. And, even in the bedroom, she'd be able to hear what they were saying. Cradling the mug between her hands, she moved closer to the window, watching as Ryder shrugged on his overcoat. It was crazy, but she wanted to tell him to be careful and to come back safely. Unable to say the words aloud, she bit down on her lip and glanced towards Long Bay.

'Vanessa?'

She swung around. 'Yes.'

He was coming towards her, frowning and patting his pockets like he was checking that he had everything. Wallet, badge, gun—probably.

He stopped an arm's length away, his eyes studying her face. 'Those lights we saw this morning, the ones from the grooming machine that flashed across the windows? What time do you reckon that was?'

'Somewhere around five.'

'That's what I thought.'

'I noticed that the lights were close, but I figured it was because I was here, and not in Long Bay.'

'Do you think it was Bruno on his way into Perisher?' Lewicki asked from the other side of the room.

'I don't know, Lew.'

'What was Libby's time of death?'

'Somewhere between four and four-thirty.'

A fresh wave of outrage slammed into Vanessa's body, the mug almost slipping from her shaking fingers.

Ryder reached out and squeezed her shoulder, his hand warm through the cotton material of her borrowed T-shirt. 'Are you okay?'

She wanted to say no. How could she be okay when some monster had taken Libby's life and left her cold, contorted body sprawled across an old trundle. And it was supposed to have been her lying there. And yet here she was, safe and sound with two concerned detectives watching her every move—alive and well and breathing air into her lungs.

She moved out of Ryder's grasp and sat on the sofa. Outside, the familiar sound of a helicopter grew louder as it approached Charlotte Pass. 'So, it was Bruno?'

'Probably.'

'I don't understand. What do *I* know that would make Bruno think his only option was to get rid of me? I don't get it.'

'I don't either,' agreed Lewicki, 'and my gut tells me Bruno's no serial killer.'

Ryder spun around. 'Sometimes our gut feelings are wrong, Lew. We know serial killers can leave years, even decades, between their victims. Who knows how their screwed-up minds work, or why they suddenly have the urge to kill again?'

Lew sighed. 'He's right. We don't always know why. That's the most frustrating part.'

Vanessa stared at the swirling vines on the carpet. To think that Bruno, a serial killer, had walked among them, slept in the same building, and hovered outside her door. She shivered despite the central heating. It was almost too horrific to comprehend.

'Listen to me.'

She started as Ryder sat on the sofa beside her, his eyes dark with concern. 'We'll get whoever did this. In the meantime, you need to stay here, with Lew. I've arranged for someone in the kitchen to bring your meals and any necessities you both might need. Do not go outside this room, okay?'

Vanessa nodded. 'Of course. But if Bruno's no longer in the village, doesn't that mean he's more of a threat to you? You need to take care as well.'

'Never argue with a woman's logic, Ryder,' came Lewicki's droll response.

Ryder's mouth curved in a smile, and for one heart-stopping moment she thought he was going to kiss her. But right then his phone buzzed from inside his overcoat.

He sighed and fished the device from his pocket. 'Yes, Flowers?' There was a pause as he listened. 'Right, then I guess we're all set.'

The sound of the helicopter was deafening now, as though it were hovering directly over the inn.

Ryder killed the call and stood up, fixing his eyes on hers. 'Okay, I'm out of here.'

Twenty-five

The helicopter rose above Charlotte Pass village, sending the top layer of snow billowing into the air and cutting off the visibility of those on board. Slowly, the chopper cleared the white cloud and the village fell away below them. From this height, the historic Charlotte Mountain Inn sat among the lesser buildings like a proud, bejewelled matriarch.

Ryder sat beside the pilot, Flowers in the rear seat.

'Look over there.' Ryder spoke through the headset and pointed towards Mount Stillwell. 'On the crest of the mountain. You can see one of the pylons from the old chairlift.'

Flowers shifted closer to the window, searching for the spot. He nodded as he caught sight of it. 'I see it. It's like one of those abandoned places you see on the internet, where nature has taken it back.'

'I'll show you a better example of that a bit further along,' said Ryder, his eye on the dark clouds gathering to the south. 'What's the forecast?' he asked, turning to the pilot. The last thing they needed was the weather coming in and cutting off access to the village by air.

'We're expecting snow, but not for a few days yet.'

Ryder leaned back in his seat and stared at the snow-covered road leading into Perisher, the same eight-kilometre stretch Bruno travelled hours earlier. The road twisted and turned, the bright orange poles standing on either side marking the snow depth at intervals.

Normally, at this time, the oversnow transport vehicles would be coming and going, carrying guests and day trippers into Charlotte's. And there were always a few cross-country skiers, chook footers as they were known, travelling the road under their own steam. But, today, it was deserted.

'How's the food situation up there?' the pilot asked.

Flowers' voice came through the headset. 'The lodges have freezer rooms. The owners stock them up at the beginning of the season. The only thing they sometimes need is fresh fruit and vegetables. Right now, food isn't an issue.'

A blur of colour in a highly wooded area caught Ryder's attention. A skier in a bright yellow jacket was streaking through the trees. 'Down there, Flowers. Someone's skiing out of bounds.'

'We're coming into Perisher,' the pilot said. 'There's an old T-bar straight ahead. It's right on the edge of the resort.'

And then the wooded area they'd been flying over gave way to the groomed runs of Perisher Valley, and Ryder could see the skier was heading for the loading area at the bottom of the hill. He sat back, relieved he'd made the decision to close off the lifts at Charlotte Pass. The eight kilometres separating the two resorts was doable in one day. If the perp managed to ski out, they'd soon be lost among the throng of people skiing and boarding at Perisher Valley.

'Check out the carpark,' the pilot said.

They approached a cluster of buildings, a smattering of small chalets, the ski-tube terminal and the day lodge. In the carpark people were huddled in groups, arms folded across their bodies while they stamped their boots on the asphalt to keep warm. Journos, judging by the number of vans with satellite dishes fixed to their roofs. Further along the road, the uniformed boys from Jindabyne had set up a roadblock.

Ryder leaned back in his seat again, certain Bruno was long gone.

They flew on towards Cooma, the pilot giving Flowers a running commentary of the landscape. He pointed out Blue Cow and Smiggin Holes, and further on Sponars Chalet with the fountain shooting freezing water into the air. From there they crossed the National Park until they reached the township of Jindabyne, which hugged the shores of a glistening man-made lake.

'They flooded the old town,' Ryder spoke over his shoulder. 'It's submerged somewhere out there beneath the water.'

'No shit? Why'd they do that?' asked Flowers.

'It was part of the plan when they built the Snowy Hydro. Sometimes, when the water level's low, you can see the steeple of the old Catholic church.'

'Can you dive it?'

'Have you done much diving?' the pilot asked suddenly.

'Yes, in Sydney,' said Flowers.

'You can definitely do it, but altitude diving is a lot different to diving at sea level. You'd need special training.'

'It'd be an awesome thing to do, though.'

Ryder adjusted his headset. 'As long as I don't lose you to the mountains, Flowers,' he said, suddenly realising how much his junior partner had grown on him, despite being a member of the Harry Potter generation.

'Ha-ha. Not a chance, Sarge.'

Ryder smiled. For the past week they'd been eating and sleeping the Delaney case. It felt good to be talking about something normal.

'How do you know all this?' Flowers asked. 'I didn't learn about it in school.'

'Were you even paying attention?'

'Probably not.'

'My father told me. He learned about the Snowy Mountains Scheme in primary school, I think. And Lew's a Cooma local, of course.'

'Bruno, too,' Flowers said with a sudden frown. 'Jesus. I wonder where he is.'

The pilot was speaking into his mouthpiece, relaying their position to someone on the ground. 'We'll be approaching Cooma in approximately fifteen minutes . . . setting down on the local oval rather than the airport. The oval is closer to the house . . .'

Ryder closed his eyes. He'd hardly slept last night, but he wasn't complaining. What sane man would sleep, with a woman like Vanessa in his bed?

You're the kind of man I'd make room for in my life.
Don't forget me.

He'd thought she would run a mile when he told her about Scarlett, but she'd surprised him. No more than he'd surprised himself. He'd seen something different in her, and it had been enough for him to open up. And it worried him that, even with the potential risk to her safety, he hadn't encouraged her to leave Charlotte Pass.

Why?

It's as plain as the nose on your face, his father would have said, but unpacking his feelings for Vanessa would have to wait until after he'd caught Libby's murderer.

'We're coming into Cooma now,' the pilot's voice crackled through the headset.

Ryder opened his eyes. Below them lay a sports oval surrounded by a low, white fence. A squad car was parked in the shadow of a quaint wooden grandstand. The pilot lowered the chopper into the middle of the oval, the airflow from its rotor wash scattering dried leaves in every direction. A couple of bumps later, and the aircraft settled on its landing skids.

Ryder and Flowers removed their headsets.

The pilot turned and gave them a casual salute. 'Watch your heads on the way out, boys.'

Bruno Lombardi lived in a 1950s weatherboard-and-iron house on a quiet suburban street. The low, wrought-iron gate opened with a squeak, and a narrow garden path led to a small front porch. Ryder nodded towards the driveway, then watched as Flowers cut across the front lawn and disappeared down the side of the house.

Ryder gave him a minute to reach the back door, then with a final look up and down the quiet street, he drew his firearm and rapped on the wood-panelled door.

Nothing.

The second time, he knocked louder with the side of his fist. 'Police! Open up!'

Seconds ticked by.

He spun away and went around the back.

A fenced-in yard.

A single carport.

An overgrown vegetable garden.

'Any luck?' he said, joining Flowers at the back door.

'Nope, it's locked. I've checked under the pots and door mat, but I can't find a key.'

'Unlucky. Country people rarely lock their doors.'

'It's inward opening,' Flowers said, stepping back and giving Ryder the space he needed.

Holstering his firearm, Ryder faced the door square on. Aiming at the area beside the lock, he drove the heel of his boot into the door with a forward momentum. A loud crack and the wood splintered. A second kick compounded the damage. A third left a gaping hole big enough for Ryder to slip his hand between the broken shards of wood. He groped around until his fingers closed around a key. One turn and the lock clicked open.

Drawing his firearm again, Ryder stepped into a tidy kitchen boasting seventies décor. Frilly curtains dressed up the lone window while the benchtops were covered in a sunflower yellow Laminex. In the centre of the room, a sturdy wooden dining table was protected by a plastic tablecloth, its red-and-white checked pattern reminiscent of a thousand old-school Italian restaurants.

Leaving Flowers to rifle through the kitchen, he moved into the hallway and did a quick scan of the rooms for signs of life. The home was compact: two bedrooms, a lounge room and bathroom, and at the front a sunroom had been converted into an office. Ryder started with the bedrooms. The first was sparsely furnished with a double bed and a dressing table with a tarnished mirror. Ryder opened the old-fashioned built-in robe. Apart from some lavender sachets, the wardrobe was empty. The dressing-table drawers held nothing but dust bunnies. Lifting a corner of the patchwork quilt, he peered at the mattress covered only by an electric blanket. He heard Burt Crofts' voice in his head. *He's only there between seasons, and the odd holiday maybe.*

Ryder let the quilt fall back in place and went to check the second bedroom. A brown doona with a geometric design covered a bed made up with blankets and sheets. This time, the electric blanket was plugged into a wall socket. In the wardrobe, several items of men's clothing dangled from misshapen wire hangers.

'Bedrooms clear,' he called, crossing the hallway in two strides then standing with his back to the architrave. He scanned the lounge room, grimacing at the mildewy odour. Floral lounge suite. Flat-screen TV. Pine coffee table with a scarred surface. The only other piece of furniture in the room was a squat kerosene heater that looked like it belonged in an antique shop.

'Lounge room clear,' he called, heading for the bathroom. He froze in the doorway, levelling his pistol at an indistinct shadow crouching behind the faded, yellow shower curtain. 'Come out slowly,' he said evenly. 'With your hands up.'

Not a sound.

Not a breath of air.

Only Ryder's blood pulsing through his temples, and the metro-nomic drip of water as it fell from the showerhead and splashed on the tiles.

Conscious of Flowers moving through the house as back-up, Ryder lunged and swept aside the mouldy curtain. A plastic shower chair with wheels, brakes and a footrest sat in the middle of the shower stall. Sturdy steel grab bars had been screwed onto both walls.

'Must have been for Bruno's mother,' Ryder said, holstering his pistol as Flowers appeared in the doorway. 'The house is clear. Keep going with the kitchen. I'll tackle the sunroom.'

He began with a battered two-drawer filing cabinet. It was jammed with faded manila folders full of out-of-date rate notices, land valu-ations and appliance guarantees. Another folder held all of Bruno's group certificates from Charlotte Pass, as well as a stack of taxation returns going back twenty years. Dust irritated Ryder's nose and he sneezed. Obviously, the Lombardis were the kind of people who held onto everything. The bloody place needed a broom put through it.

Further back in the drawer he found two dog-eared folders, their edges torn from the constant opening and closing of the cabinet.

Ryder thumbed through the contents. Report cards and certificates of merit from Cooma Public School. A proud collection of mementos belonging to Bruno and his sister, Angela.

A wash of sorrow choked Ryder up more than the dust. He closed the files and stuffed them back in the drawer, an image of the brightly coloured box he kept in his Sydney apartment coming to mind. Inside was a piece of material with Scarlett's two-year-old handprints on it, funny stick drawings of him and Tania, and pages of colouring-in she hadn't quite managed to keep inside the lines. Precious mementos they split between them, along with everything else they had owned.

'Sarge, take a look at this photo.'

Ryder turned, glad of the distraction. Flowers was holding a photo frame with a picture of Bruno and a woman dressed in a colourful sarong sitting side by side on a beach.

'Didn't he say he went to Thailand occasionally?' asked Flowers. 'I wonder who she is.'

Ryder gazed down at the photograph. 'Maybe someone special. Take a shot with your phone.'

They resumed their search of the property. Ten minutes later, Ryder slid the filing-cabinet door closed and made a start on the desk. Pens, paperclips, sticky notes and rubbers rolled around freely in the top drawer. The second drawer contained larger items, a stapler, a hole punch, a roll of sticky labels and a pencil sharpener. The third drawer held an old-fashioned scrapbook.

Taking a seat at the desk, he opened the cover and blinked in surprise as Aidan Smythe smiled up at him. Goggles pushed into his thick, fair hair, Smythe was holding a silver trophy aloft. Ryder turned the pages, brittle from age and the dried glue that had been used to paste in the clippings. The first part of the book was crammed with action shots of Smythe at the height of his career. Then further on, the articles turned glossy—double-page features of him with his wife at their home north of Vancouver. And, later, business articles analysing the chain of sports-apparel stores he owned in Canada.

'Flowers! Take a look at this.'

Footsteps in the hallway, then Flowers was leaning over his shoulder. He gave a low whistle as Ryder slowly turned the pages. 'Is this Bruno's?'

'There's no name on it. Could belong to his sister.'

'Angela? He said she was a cook in Berridale.'

Ryder nodded. 'Get in touch with Berridale police. I need to know if Angela has seen her brother in the last twenty-four hours. And I want to know who this book belongs to.'

Flowers left to make the calls, and Ryder skimmed through the sports reports from early on in Smythe's career. Many focused on the skier's natural speed and ability. They analysed his times in comparison to his northern-hemisphere rivals. Some doubted he could handle the altitude, the difference in snow quality and the steeper terrain.

'The Berridale boys are on it,' Flowers said, coming back into the room. He peered at the scrapbook again. 'I can't work out if they're a fan, or obsessed.'

'It can be a fine line. And it's not that surprising to find something like this here. Bruno has spent a lifetime involved with the sport.' Ryder leaned back in the chair. 'In Newcastle, where I lived for a while, there are hundreds, maybe thousands of surfers who are fans of Mark Richards. Even now, when he surfs the big break off Merewether he draws hundreds to the beach. He's a local boy—a living legend.'

Flowers nodded. 'Should we take it with us?'

'Yep.' Ryder closed the scrapbook and waved away the dust. 'Write it on the Occupier's Notice so they'll know we've taken it.'

'Should I pin the notice to the front door?'

Ryder shook his head. 'It won't last twenty-four hours out there in this weather. Leave it on the kitchen table.' He followed Flowers out into the hallway. 'Find anything in the kitchen?'

'Zilch. I still have a couple of cupboards to go through.'

In the kitchen, Ryder started on the last two cupboards while Flowers filled out the Occupier's Notice. Grimacing at the accumulated dust and cockroach droppings, he lifted out a collection of

Women's Weekly recipe books and piled them on the bench. 'Burt Crofts said Bruno only gets back here a few times a year. I'd say he's right.' Ryder checked his watch. Almost 2 pm. 'Speaking of Crofts, we need to check if he found anything on the old slides he was going to look at. He was hoping to catch the first oversnow in, but I'd shut down the resort by then.'

'Does he have your number?'

'He has my card but you can ring Benson and ask him to get Crofts' contact details from Di Gordon.'

'Yes, Sarge.'

Ryder began absently flicking through the first three cookbooks. Nothing interesting here except a few handwritten recipes stuck between the pages. Next in the pile were a bunch of operating manuals. One for the stove, the fridge and the microwave. Eager to be on his way, Ryder shook them open then quickly cast them aside. He'd bet no one had touched these since before Mrs Lombardi's death.

He grabbed the next cookbook, and a vice clamped around his heart. Memories flooded back as he stared at *The Women's Weekly Birthday Cookbook*, the one with the famous train on the front.

But I want the train cake, Mummy.

Trains are for boys. Let's make this pretty one with the doll instead.

But I don't want the doll. I want the train. Daddy?

Why can't she have the train, Tania, if that's the one she likes? Does it matter?

Ryder's vision blurred. He would give his life to have one more morning with his little girl. He would make that fucking cake himself. He would make her a hundred cakes to make up for every birthday he'd robbed her of.

He turned the book face down, cruel hands wringing his heart until he could barely breathe.

Flowers, Occupier's Notice in hand, looked up as a gust of frigid air blew through the damaged door. 'Is there anything in the cupboard I can use to weigh this down?' If he noticed a change in Ryder, he didn't comment.

'Hang on.' Ryder gathered the books together and shoved the lot back where they belonged. Moving along to the next cupboard, he yanked open the door. Three baking dishes were stacked on top of one another alongside an old Mixmaster. Behind the baking dishes sat a selection of cake tins of various shapes and sizes. He reached for the baking dishes. 'Use one of these,' he said, lifting the stack out.

Flowers relieved him of them, and Ryder closed the cupboard door on the dust and the cockroach droppings. Turning on the kitchen tap, he looked around for soap so he could wash his hands.

'Sarge?'

He spun around to see Flowers holding something aloft. 'It was in the dish underneath the top one,' he said, his voice shaking with excitement.

Heart hammering, Ryder moved closer, his gaze zeroing in. Sure enough, it was an open packet of coloured wire ties. A few had spilled out into the baking dish.

Ryder took hold of one and held it up to the light. 'Well, what do you know?' He looked back to Flowers. 'We need to find Bruno. Now.'

Twenty-six

They made it to the Cooma pub with five minutes to spare before the end of lunch service. They chose a booth in the corner, away from the locals and the ski crowd in transit. Every so often, two blokes sitting at the bar looked over their shoulders at them, making it clear they stood out in their suits and overcoats.

'I'm glad the chopper's late,' Flowers spoke around a mouthful of hamburger. 'I couldn't have survived without food for much longer.'

Ryder put down his coffee cup. 'Then stop talking and eat.' He cut into his schnitzel, and for the next few minutes they ate in silence. A warrant had been issued for Bruno's arrest. Police units were stationed on the highways, in truck stops, as well as at the airports and bus stations.

Flowers demolished his hamburger in about four bites and seemed to get a second wind. 'Okay,' he said, reaching for their side dish of chips. 'So, Bruno, an obsessed fan of Aidan Smythe, murdered and buried Celia Delaney. For fifty years he's left flowers on her grave. Then, in the early hours of this morning, he attempted to murder Vanessa, but killed Libby instead, because Vanessa wasn't in her room.' Flowers looked pointedly at Ryder and shoved three chips into his mouth at once.

Ryder rolled his eyes. 'Vanessa left my room about thirty-five minutes before you banged on my door. We know what happened after she got to Long Bay. She hung up her coat, took off her boots and went directly into the bathroom.'

'I can't see the connection between the two murders,' said Flowers, brushing the salt off his fingers.

'Okay, let's look at the Delaney case,' said Ryder. 'We'll assume Bruno's guilty of murdering Celia. He's getting old. He's the only one who knows what really happened. So, he digs up the grave and puts some of the bones in a visible place and then asks for workers to be placed in that area. He could have planned this for the race week anniversary, knowing Charlotte's would be swarming with media.' Ryder pushed his plate away, wiped his hands on a paper napkin and dropped it onto his plate. 'We know Bruno asked for fences to be built, but we should ask Terry if he also chose the location for the tube run. If he did, it puts him in close proximity to the grave. He'd have a good reason for being in that area without raising anyone's suspicions.'

'So, if everything panned out the way Bruno wanted, why carry out a second kill?'

Ryder shook his head. 'That's the million-dollar question. Look, all this sounds good if we're going down the track that Bruno's a serial killer. But what commonalities does Vanessa share with Celia Delaney?'

'And Libby. We can't rule out Libby being the intended victim.'

'Absolutely we can't.'

'Celia was tiny with dark hair,' began Flowers. 'Vanessa has dark hair but she's pretty tall.'

'Vanessa's athletic, and a highly skilled skier,' said Ryder, 'but I get the feeling Celia not so much. She had the Priscilla Presley hair. And she was a dental nurse, and a timid skier. Not so outdoorsy.'

'Celia and Libby were more the same height. What about their occupations? Ski patrol, childcare and a dental nurse. All caring occupations.'

Ryder shook his head. 'I'm no profiler, but usually it's something physical that triggers a response in a serial killer, or something in a person's attitude that reminds the killer of someone they hate.

Vanessa stood up to Bruno the night he waited for her outside Long Bay.'

'Maybe he hates strong women, or women who don't cave into his bullying.' Flowers picked up the saltshaker and added another layer of salt to the chips. 'I can't stop thinking about his reaction, though, when we told him Celia had been murdered. I'd swear he was hit for six.'

'I agree. Leaving posies is unusual, too. It shows remorse, something serial killers don't have.'

'So, could he be shining a spotlight on a crime committed by someone else?' asked Flowers.

'He could and, if that's the case, I think it has to be one of the permanent residents.'

'Or Nigel Miller.'

'Right. Don't forget, Bruno changed his original story.' Ryder picked up his cup and drained the last of his coffee. 'He was probably going to piss off before we could charge him with concealing a crime, or aiding and abetting.'

Flowers' eyes widened. 'You think there were two of them involved in Celia's murder?'

'There could have been.'

'So again, why the second kill?'

Ryder paused as the waitress came over to remove their plates. 'I'm not sure. The only thing Vanessa can remember that's out of the ordinary is Henry Gordon chipping her about spending too much time with the police, and not prioritising her job.'

Flowers raised his eyebrows.

'And the bloke who skied beyond the CLOSED sign. It's unusual for people to do that, apparently. They know it's put there for their safety.'

They were silent for a while, each lost in their thoughts as they sifted through the facts of the case. Eventually, Ryder broke the silence. 'I reckon there's only one reason for that skier to disobey that sign.'

'What?'

'He wanted to get to Bruno. Vanessa could have interrupted his plans. She chased him, and he knew exactly who was after him. It's not hard to distinguish between her and the other patroller. Put yourself in the skier's shoes. Do you really think he was afraid of something as trivial as Vanessa confiscating his ski pass? I don't think so. I think he was afraid she'd recognise him. It's only a theory, though.'

Flowers blew out a breath. 'It's a bloody good one though, Sarge.'

Ryder took another look around the room. The men at the bar were buying another round of schooners. The TV on the wall was tuned into a long-running daytime soap opera.

Flowers drummed his fingers on the tabletop. 'Bruno could have bolted because he's afraid of this person.'

Before Ryder could answer, his mobile rang. 'It's Henderson,' he said, taking the call.

'The Australian Federal Police have picked up Bruno Lombardi at Canberra Airport,' Henderson said. 'He was at the gate, about to board a flight to Bangkok. They're bringing him here.'

Ryder reached for his wallet. 'We're on our way, sir.'

'Where are we going?' Flowers asked, as they slid out of the booth.

'Monaro. They have Lombardi.'

'What me to call a squad car?'

'Nope. I can hear the chopper now. The oval's only a block away. It'll be quicker if we run.'

Ryder opened the door to where Bruno Lombardi waited in the sparsely furnished interview room in the Queanbeyan Police Station. Seated at the table, his hands were clasped in front of him, the light from the overhead fluorescent reflecting off his shiny scalp.

Conscious of Flowers and Senior Sergeant Gil Henderson watching through the tinted glass viewing pane, Ryder slipped three CDs into the machine. The first would be kept by the police, the second sent for transcription, and the third given to Bruno.

Once the machine was recording, Ryder read the groomer his rights under Part 9, including his right to legal representation if he so wished.

He didn't.

'Bruno,' Ryder said finally, sitting opposite Lombardi and casually crossing his legs. 'Thailand, hey?'

Lombardi didn't answer, just kept his gaze fixed to a spot on the table.

'What's the weather like over there at this time of year?'

'Go fuck yourself, Ryder.'

Ryder pursed his lips and made like he was offended. 'That's no way to begin our conversation.'

Lombardi didn't look up, just kept his sullen gaze trained on the tabletop.

'I suggest you start cooperating. You see, Bruno, I'm angry, and you won't like me much when I'm angry.' Ryder stared hard at the groomer and let his words hang in the air. 'Where were you in the early hours of the morning?'

'On the mountain, doing my job like I do every morning.'

'When did you decide to take the snowcat into Perisher Valley?'

'About six-thirty. I got all the grooming done so things would be good for today.' Lombardi looked up and met Ryder's eyes for the first time. 'If I'd known you were going to shut the place down, I wouldn't have bothered grooming the slopes.'

'Someone murdered Libby Marken in Long Bay between four and four-thirty.'

'I know. I heard about it the minute I walked into Long Bay.'

Ryder spread his hands. 'So, why did you take off in a grooming machine at six-thirty? Do you know how bad this looks, Bruno?'

'I didn't go anywhere near that girl.'

'Why'd you run, then?'

'I decided to quit.'

'Just like that? The same morning a woman was found murdered in the building where you live?'

'Yeah. I've had enough.'

'Did you hand in your notice?'

Bruno shook his head. 'The Gordons have talked me out of leaving before. I didn't want to give them the chance of doing it this time.'

Ryder frowned. Did the Gordons have another reason for keeping Bruno there? 'Are you frightened of Henry and Di Gordon?'

'I'm not frightened, I just don't like them very much.' Lombardi ran a hand over the scar on his head. 'I've done nothing wrong, other than drive the groomer into Perisher. I didn't want to wait around for the eight o'clock oversnow to leave. I knew someone would be able to drive it back to Charlotte's without too much trouble.'

'We searched your room. You left your clothes there.'

He shrugged. 'Didn't need them where I was going.'

'Did you go into Vanessa Bell's room this morning?'

'No.'

'The night of the flare run, were you waiting for her outside Long Bay?'

Silence.

'Did you harass and touch Vanessa Bell outside Long Bay?'

Silence.

'Vanessa Bell reported you to the mountain manager. You were given an official warning, weren't you?'

Lombardi shifted in his seat, his brow gleaming with sweat. 'Look, I was only trying to talk to her. She got angry and ran off. I called her from out in the hallway, but she wouldn't come out.'

'What was so important?'

Bruno shifted in his seat again. 'I wanted to warn her to be careful.'

Ryder sat back at the unexpected answer. 'That's not what she said. She said you wanted to know what was going on up on the mountain, and when she refused to say anything you got angry and grabbed her wrist.'

Lombardi said nothing.

Ryder forced his jaw to relax so he didn't ask the next question through clenched teeth. 'Why did you feel the need to warn Vanessa Bell? Who are you scared of, Bruno?'

Nothing.

Ryder inhaled deeply and glanced at the window where Flowers and Henderson watched on. 'We searched your house. Sorry for kicking in your back door but you weren't home.' He pulled the packet of wire ties from his suit coat pocket and put them on the table. 'Did you murder Celia Delaney?'

'No, I did not,' he said defensively.

Ryder poked the plastic packet with his index finger. 'These were in a cupboard in your kitchen. We know you've been leaving flowers on Celia Delaney's grave.'

Nothing.

'We found about twenty-five of them near her grave, just like these ones.'

'I'd like to see you prove they're from that packet. Those things are as common as rubber bands.'

Ryder stood up so suddenly his chair almost tipped over. Spreading his hands on the table he leaned forward and got right in Bruno's face. 'Oh, we'll prove it. We'll prove there never was a ski patroller who told you to go inside back in sixty-four. We'll prove that *you* took Celia Delaney up on that chairlift, that it was *you* who murdered and disposed of her body up on Mount Stillwell.'

'I didn't.' Bruno spat out the words. 'I was just a liftie back then.'

'Did you like her?'

Fear flashed in Bruno's eyes. He swallowed, his Adam's apple bobbing in this throat. 'I liked her. She was a nice girl. But not like you're insinuating. She was married, and older.'

'I think you took Celia up on that lift,' Ryder said quietly. 'I think you murdered her just like you murdered Libby Marken at four-thirty this morning when you thought she was Vanessa—'

'I didn't. I didn't even see—'

'Think how *that's* going to sound to a jury,' Ryder circled the table, trying to rattle Lombardi. 'Not that you'll need a jury, Bruno. Oh no, you'll be pleading guilty when they find your DNA in Vanessa Bell's room.'

There was a knock. Flowers opened the door. 'Detective Ryder. Sorry to interrupt. Detective Benson is trying to reach you.'

Ryder looked at Bruno, who'd turned pale during his rant. 'Did you dig up Celia Delaney and put her bones where you knew they'd be found?'

Lombardi froze, his eyes once again fixed on the mark on the table.

'Did you ask for snow fences to be built knowing people would be working around that particular spot?'

Lombardi remained silent.

'Did you leave posies of flowers on Celia's Delaney's grave?'

Silence.

'All right, then. For the benefit of the recording, Detective Ryder is leaving the room. Detective Flowers will continue with the interview.'

'Ask about the skier on Mount Stillwell,' he said quietly as he passed Flowers.

In the corridor, Ryder pulled in a few deep breaths before ringing Benson. When the call went straight to voicemail, he didn't bother to leave a message.

He joined Henderson at the window. 'I want a buccal swab from him,' he said quietly, referring to the forensic procedure. 'If he doesn't agree to it, we'll remove a hair by force.'

Henderson nodded once then checked his watch. 'It's getting close to four o'clock. You're lucky it's Friday.'

'Yep,' murmured Ryder, glancing at the clock in the interview room. 'If he waits much longer to ask for a lawyer, he won't see one until Monday morning.'

Flowers began by showing Lombardi the photo on his phone. 'Who's the pretty lady?'

Ryder smiled, strangely proud of Flowers for trying to throw Lombardi off balance.

'None of your business,' snarled Lombardi.

'At least he didn't tell him to go fuck himself,' Henderson said, with a sideways look at Ryder.

In the interview room, Flowers took another interested look at the picture before pocketing his phone. 'Were you up on Mount Stillwell yesterday afternoon?'

Lombardi frowned, his face a picture of concentration as though Flowers had asked him to explain the theory of relativity. 'Yes, I was up there.'

'Doing what?'

'Clearing snow from behind the fences.'

'Mount Stillwell is closed.'

'Not to me it isn't.'

'Was anyone else up there?'

'The ski patroller, I think, or was that the other day . . .'

'Vanessa Bell?'

'It could have been her. There're two of them.'

'He's bullshitting,' Ryder muttered through clenched teeth.

Beside him, Henderson nodded.

'Vanessa Bell chased a skier down that mountain. She told us she saw you up there. She even said you pointed after the skier, showing her which way they'd gone.'

'I might have,' Lombardi said vaguely. 'I was working. I only looked up for a second.'

'Was the skier who disobeyed the CLOSED sign a man or a woman?'

'No idea.' He broke eye contact with Flowers, his gaze shifting around the room.

'He's lying,' said Ryder.

'I agree.' Henderson folded his arms and transferred his weight to his other foot.

'Can you describe this person's ski clothes?' asked Flowers.

'Nope. Took no notice.'

'Vanessa Bell did. She said he was wearing clothes from the rental shop.'

Lombardi hesitated as though wondering how best to answer the question. 'Maybe. She would have got a better look at him than I did.'

Ryder's phone rang.

He moved away from Henderson. 'Hello, Benson.'

'G'day, Sarge. Sorry, it's taken longer than we thought to collect those ski straps. I had the boys bring the skis in with them. We've cross-referenced them and made a note of where they came from. It seems no one puts their names on skis.'

'Good thinking. Have you given the straps to Harriet?'

'I'm just about to. You know how you said they always come

in pairs, well, we have five orphans here. A few were found lying around the place. Terry said they're easy things to lose.'

Ryder thought for a few moments. Was one of the orphans the murder weapon, and was its twin sitting in somebody's hotel room or ski bag? 'Ask Harriet to test the orphans first before she does the others.'

'Will do, Sarge. There's something else.'

'Go ahead, Benson.'

'We've done the stocktake on the rental gear. Everyone's garments were accounted for, except for one man. He's missing a jacket and pants, size large.'

Ryder's heart thumped, firing adrenaline into his system.

'This bloke came up to me this morning. He said he's been leaving the suit in the downstairs drying room at the inn all week. When he went in there yesterday morning, it was missing.'

'Yesterday?' The day of the chase.

'Yeah. He thought someone had picked it up by mistake. Nothing strange about that, it's easy to do when they all look the same. Anyway, he said he was feeling a bit tired and was happy to have a quiet day. He stayed inside while his wife took the kids out. He was hoping his gear would be back in the drying room this morning.'

'I locked the resort down this morning.' Ryder began pacing. 'Did he even bother to look?'

'Not until he found out we were checking off the rental gear. He went downstairs and had a look. The suit was still missing.'

'Get the guy's height and weight, Benson—'

'Sarge, we found it in the upstairs drying room.'

Ryder stopped pacing and pushed a hand into his hair. 'The *upstairs* room? That's odd. If someone had taken it by mistake, they'd put it back in the same room.'

'Yeah. That's what we think.'

'Bag it immediately and give it to Harriet. I know it's a long shot, but I'm looking for a match with any DNA they might have found in Vanessa Bell's room.'

'Will do, Sarge.'

'And Benson? Tell Harriet to hurry.'

Twenty-seven

'This is quite a good story,' Vanessa said, putting Lew's novel in her lap. 'I'm up to chapter six and it's getting really good. I don't mind reading romance.'

Lew snorted. 'Give me a good western any day.'

'Didn't they have any westerns in the bookcase?'

'No. Whoever chooses them has bad taste in books.'

'Maybe the westerns are so popular they're all out.'

He smiled. 'You're in the wrong job, you know? You would have made a good politician.'

Vanessa smiled. She was seriously considering relocating to Eva's lodge. Not because she felt unsafe, but because she could tell Lew was frustrated at being stuck inside with her all day while the other detectives were searching, patrolling and chasing leads. Ryder hadn't called to let him know what was happening with Bruno either, and with no TV in the room and the wi-fi shut down, they'd had zero interaction with anyone except for Di Gordon. She'd brought up their meals and organised for a couple of the young porters to take the desk out of the second bedroom and return the double bed. Vanessa sighed. At least Ryder wouldn't have to sleep on the couch.

'I was thinking,' Lew said, 'how about we try to get our hands on a pack of cards tomorrow?'

'That's a great idea,' she said, surprised at how the prospect of a simple card game could cheer her up. But that's what happened when death stared you in the face. You began to appreciate every moment.

Her thoughts were interrupted suddenly by the sound of a key sliding into the lock, and then the door opening. Vanessa jumped to her feet, the novel hitting the floor with a thump.

Ryder came in, the collar of his overcoat turned up, his dark hair standing up at the front like he'd been combing his fingers through it. He locked tired eyes on her, and Vanessa couldn't help grinning stupidly, her spirits climbing at the sight of him.

'Here's the man,' said Lew, clearly eager for news. 'Did you find Bruno?'

'He's in custody in Queanbeyan.' Ryder shook off his overcoat and tossed it on the sofa as he always did. 'I thought we were going to have to let him go, but we've pushed the six hours out to twelve. I'll be back there first thing in the morning.'

'It's reasonable you'd hold him until then,' said Lewicki.

'Henderson's okayed it,' Ryder loosened his tie knot, his gaze lingering on Vanessa's face. 'You're still here.'

'Don't look so surprised. I wouldn't leave without telling you.'

One corner of his mouth curved. 'I hope not.'

'Did he ask for a lawyer?' demanded Lewicki, seemingly oblivious to the moment passing between Vanessa and Ryder.

Ryder raised his hands, as if to ward off an onslaught. 'Can we all just sit down for a minute?'

Vanessa moved to sit on the edge of the sofa, and Ryder sat close by, but not too close. Lewicki remained standing, folding his arms and looking down at the two of them. 'I've been sitting all day.'

Ryder gave a sigh. 'Bruno hasn't asked for a lawyer. Flowers has stayed in Queanbeyan. I came back because I got a call from Benson. One of the guests here noticed that his rental gear was missing from the drying room yesterday morning.' He turned and looked at Vanessa, concern deepening the furrow between his eyes. 'I'm guessing it was stolen by the bloke you chased down the mountain.'

Vanessa drew in a breath. 'Why would he do that? To disguise himself?'

He nodded.

'Where's this leading?' asked Lewicki.

Ryder shook his head a little. 'On the surface Bruno looks guilty, but there are some things that don't ring true. One, he's definitely been leaving posies on the grave. We found a packet of wire ties hidden in the kitchen when we searched his house. That shows remorse. Killers rarely, if ever, show remorse. And in the case of Libby's murder, when I asked why he accosted Vanessa the night of the flare run, he said he wanted to warn her to be careful. Even though I pressed him, he wouldn't say who she needed to be careful of.'

'If that's even true,' Vanessa said, 'why didn't he come right out and tell me that?'

'Maybe you didn't give him a chance, which is understandable in light of his approach. Still, my gut feeling is that he's telling the truth, about that part at least. But he clammed up and wouldn't say any more. Now, if Celia and Libby's cases *are* linked, and the same person murdered both women, we have to consider the possibility there is someone else involved besides Bruno.'

'The bloke who flogged the suit?' asked Lewicki.

Ryder nodded. 'It ties in with Libby being mistaken for Vanessa. The motive could have been to stop Vanessa telling Terry, or us, that he'd been up there near the grave, which is a designated crime scene. He'd know it would raise our suspicions, and he'd be doubly nervous if he was someone we've interviewed and he was wearing that rental suit as a disguise. He'd know we'd want to question him about it. As it turns out, Vanessa didn't catch him, and she can't identify him.'

'Do you think he'd take the risk of going into Long Bay with the intent of murdering her on the slim chance she might know who he is?'

Ryder shrugged. 'Normally, I wouldn't be too worried about someone ignoring ski patrol signage, but skiing close to where a body's just been dug up, and with police crawling all over the place, that's something else.'

For a few moments no one spoke, each lost in their own thoughts about the case. Finally, it was Lewicki who broke the silence.

'On the surface, it looks bad for Bruno, running like that, but I have trouble seeing him as a murderer. He came from a nice family. The apple doesn't fall far from the tree—well, not often.'

Ryder shook his head. 'I don't think Bruno murdered Celia, but he might know who did, and maybe he was even involved. With luck, a night in the cells might convince him to talk.' He turned then, shifting his attention away from Lewicki to Vanessa. To her surprise, he took her hands in his, sending ripples of pleasure through her body until a mass of heat settled in her lower belly.

'Can you go over the chase again with me?'

She'd go over the Himalayas if he wanted her to. 'Of course. I'll do anything to help you find the person responsible for murdering Libby . . . and Celia.'

His smile was brief, and he gave her hands another squeeze before releasing them. When she had taken them through her recollection up to the point where she saw Bruno, Ryder stopped her. 'Could the skier have slipped past Bruno without him knowing?'

'The only way Bruno wouldn't have heard us coming is if he had earbuds in. And Bruno's not into music. Coming down through the trees, you're pole planting pretty hard. Your skis are hitting sticks and twigs and scraping over icy patches. I got whacked on the helmet a couple of times by some low branches. We would have been making a fair bit of noise, and that area is quiet.'

Ryder nodded, a distracted expression on his face. 'What happened after that?'

Vanessa drew in a deep breath. 'From the snow fences he cut across the bottom of the cordoned-off area, beneath the gravesite, the same way we went on the snowmobile after we'd looked at the tree well. He got into a skid when he went through that line of trees bordering the tube run. He got out of balance for a couple of seconds. I was hoping he'd fall over.'

'So, there was nothing about this bloke that would make it easy for you to recognise him again?'

'Not really. I thought he was older, and that seemed strange. Usually it's the brash young snowboarders who break the rules.'

'Why did you think he was older?'

'Well, people who ski with that close parallel stance, that is with their feet really close together, like this—' She held her hands out in front of her, palms downwards, with roughly an inch separating them. 'They would have learned at a time when skis were designed with a straight edge.' She lowered her hands. 'The newer, parabolic skis have a curved edge. Because of their shape, they turn with less effort from the skier, so technique needed to change. We began teaching people to have a more open stance, with maybe a foot between the skis. This guy didn't have an open stance. And, when he got out of balance, he used a blocking pole plant.'

Ryder smiled. 'Okay, I'll take your word for all that. It's helpful to know this wasn't a young person out there breaking the rules.'

'Hang on, it's not so cut and dried,' Vanessa said. 'Loads of people who learn to ski nowadays have a naturally close stance. It's not something that's purely a characteristic of older skiers. And lots of older skiers have bought and adapted to the new parabolics. Many of them now ski with an open stance.'

Ryder nodded. 'But, on the whole, people who learned years ago ski with a closer stance?'

'On the whole, yes.'

He rubbed a hand around the back of his neck as though trying to free up taut muscles. 'The rental suit I mentioned was found in the drying room upstairs, so it's likely whoever took it is staying in this building.' He paused, then finished: 'This wasn't a thrill kill. Vanessa was the target.'

There was a long silence and Vanessa's heart ached for her friend who this time yesterday was alive and vibrant and getting ready to enjoy a few drinks and listen to music at the inn.

'Have you eaten anything?' Lewicki asked, breaking the solemn silence.

'We had lunch in Cooma, and I grabbed a sandwich at the station before I left.' Ryder slapped his knees then stood up. 'I need to get up to the investigation room. I have a few questions for Nigel Miller, and if I sit here any longer, I'll nod off.' He looked at Lewicki. 'I don't know what time I'll be back, Lew. I'll be as quick as I can.'

'That's okay. We're all right here, aren't we, Vanessa?'

She nodded, not wanting to add to Ryder's stress, but she'd made up her mind. When he came back tonight, if he came back, she would tell him she would leave and stay with Eva.

'I'm glad everything went okay today.' Ryder's gaze shifted from her to Lewicki and back again. 'Even so, in light of what we know, I'm stationing another officer in the hallway tonight. I'm not taking any chances.'

Twenty-eight

'Anything you want to run by me, Benson?' Ryder asked when he reached the kids' club.

Benson stood up from the adult-sized chair he had commandeered from the office. 'I've given the boys the okay to use the snowmobiles that the mountain operations people normally use. They can get around the village a lot quicker.'

'Good idea. Just make sure they don't leave the keys in the ignition.'

'Not a chance. And Flowers phoned. He's spoken to Angela Lombardi. She's devastated her brother's been taken into custody for questioning. She wasn't aware he'd left Charlotte Pass or that he was planning on going to Thailand again. She also confirmed the scrapbook was his.'

'Good work. Have we heard anything from Burt Crofts?'

'Yep. It took him longer than he expected to find the slides in his shed, and ages to get through on the phone. He can't see them properly. Some of them are damaged and his eyes are bad. He's tracked down a magnifying glass and is going through them as we speak.'

'Good. If you don't hear from him by ten tomorrow chase him up.'

Ryder looked up as Nigel Miller appeared in the doorway. Dressed in black pants and parka, black après boots and a woollen beanie, the musician looked like a cat burglar from an old-fashioned comic book. All he needed was a balaclava.

Ryder waved Miller in. 'Take a seat. Thanks for coming in.'

He took a seat opposite. Miller looked even thinner than he had the other day, if that were possible. 'During the pathologist's examination, an item was discovered on your wife's body.'

Miller frowned. 'What kind of item?'

Ryder took the cigarette case out of the evidence bag and held it up for Miller to see. 'Do you recognise this?'

Miller stared at the piece. For a while he said nothing, just rubbed his jaw thoughtfully. Eventually he nodded. 'Yes. Celia had a case that looked just like that one.'

'It was in her jacket pocket, which helped to protect it. Was it a gift from you?'

Miller's eyebrows shot up. 'Me? Good heavens, no. I couldn't afford Tiffany on the money I made from gigging.'

'You're aware it's Tiffany, then? Where did Celia get it?'

Miller nodded, the strain on his face evident. 'That was a gift— from Aidan.'

Alarm bells buzzed in Ryder's head and he sat up straighter. 'How well did Celia know Aidan Smythe?'

'Pretty well.' Miller's gaze was steady. 'We all knew each other back then. Still do, but it's not the same. People change over the years.'

'Who exactly are you talking about?'

'The old crew. The folks who worked here, like Aidan and the Gordons.' He shrugged. 'This is the last time the band will play here, though.'

Ryder stared at Miller, suspicious of every word the musician uttered. Vanessa had overheard Di Gordon telling someone to get his gear and get out as soon as their gig was over.

'Yes. Someone overheard Di Gordon telling you the band aren't welcome anymore.'

Miller's eyes widened, clearly surprised that Ryder knew about this. 'Yes, she didn't appreciate me telling you about our old arrangement.'

'Why did you? To cast suspicion on her?'

'Maybe.' Miller shook head, his eyes shifting from one side of the room to the other. 'I don't know. As soon as I saw Roman Lewicki,

I knew I'd be in for it.' The musician straightened in his chair, his gaze returning to Ryder. 'Anyway, I couldn't come back now, not after this.'

'What about Bruno Lombardi?' Ryder asked, changing tack 'Was he part of the old crew?'

'The groomer? No, he's mountain staff. They were never part of our circle.'

Ryder turned the cigarette case over in his hand. 'It's an expensive gift.'

Miller shrugged. 'You'll have to ask Aidan about it. I remember Celia being thrilled when he gave it to her. Carmel had one too around the same time. She didn't have it the other night though, when we had a smoke out the back. Me and all the other pariahs who still smoke.'

Ryder would have been one of them, months ago. He stared unwaveringly at Miller. 'Did you and Smythe keep in touch over the years?'

'Oh, no.' He looked at Ryder like he was daft. 'Every now and then I'd spy him on the cover of a ski mag. I'd buy it to see what he was up to. And people down here like to reminisce about the old days, but we didn't phone each other, or write letters.'

'What's your relationship like now?'

'Fine.' Miller raised both hands. 'He's still skiing. I'm still jamming. We're doing our thing, living the dream.'

'Do you get out on the hill much when you're down here?' Ryder asked.

'Sure do. The free lift pass is the best thing about this gig.' Miller stared hard at Ryder, as though expecting a retort about him sleeping with Di Gordon.

Ryder let it go. 'Did you leave your room at all last night, or in the early hours of this morning?'

Miller flushed an indignant red. 'No, I did not.'

'Can anyone vouch for that?'

'No,' he said with a tight smile. 'I was alone in my room all night.'

'I'm sure you've heard that a woman was murdered in Long Bay this morning. There's every possibility the person who murdered your wife is still in the village. It would be advisable to remain in your accommodation.'

Miller nodded, the strain evident in the tight lines around his mouth. 'I did hear the news. It's a terrible thing to have happened.'

'Yes, it is. Oh, one other thing. Did you know that Celia had a relationship with—' Ryder made a show of looking through the file, long enough to make Miller sweat '—Gary Bennett.' He looked up. 'He's your guitarist, right?'

'Yes,' he snapped. 'And, no, I didn't know.'

'I wondered if he might be the man Celia told you about, the one you thought she might have invented to make you jealous?'

Miller raised both hands, exasperation written all over his face. 'I have no idea. You know more about it than me.'

Ryder studied the man's face, which looked to have aged ten years since he walked in the door. 'Okay, I think that's all for now.'

He called Benson over. 'Detective, accompany Mr Miller to the inn, and bring Aidan Smythe back with you.' He spoke to Miller again. 'Please don't mention to Mr Smythe what we've been discussing.'

Shortly after Benson left with Miller, Henry and Di Gordon arrived.

'Detective Ryder,' Di started talking before she'd even reached him. Henry skulked along behind, clearly happy to let her do the talking. 'Have you found Bruno?'

Ryder finished straightening his papers before looking up. 'We have.'

Di's pencilled eyebrows shot up. 'So, that means we can re-open the resort?'

'I'm afraid not, Mrs Gordon. Mr Lombardi hasn't been charged with any offence yet.'

The woman's expression changed from hopeful to crestfallen. 'Detective, we run this place on a very small margin. We can't afford this.'

'You can't afford another murder.'

At this point, Henry emerged from behind his wife's skirts. 'Bruno took off this morning. Doesn't that tell you he's guilty?'

'No. Our investigations are ongoing.'

The husband-and-wife team looked at each other aghast, as though their future lay in the hands of an incompetent police force.

'Before you go, tell me something, Henry,' said Ryder. 'Do you still ski?'

Di blinked.

Henry's eyes bored into his. 'Sometimes, if it's a quiet week. I'm a fair-weather skier. We're here all winter. No need for me to venture outside when the weather's bad.'

It was the first time Henry had volunteered anything without being probed.

'Did either of you leave your quarters last night?'

'Of course we didn't,' snapped Di. 'Heavens above. We came up here to find out if we could open the resort, not to be interrogated.'

Ryder nodded. 'Thank you for answering my questions. Oh, and before I forget, I appreciate you turning my makeshift office back into a second bedroom. We need it at the moment.'

His sudden thanks flustered Di, and she opened her mouth then snapped it shut. In the end, she gave a brief nod and hurried after her husband.

Ryder watched them go, wishing he could dredge up more sympathy for them. He didn't underestimate how difficult their position was, having to deal with demanding guests and the police crawling all over their property, but their pure self-interest and lack of empathy festered beneath his skin. No matter how hard he tried, he was always left with the feeling that they couldn't be trusted.

'Good evening, Detective.' Aidan Smythe folded his elegant frame into the chair opposite Ryder. 'I hope this won't take too long. I have a top-shelf oaky Chardonnay waiting for me in the bar.'

Ryder smiled a little. From the slight slur in Smythe's voice he guessed he was already well on the way. Not that it bothered Ryder. Alcohol loosened the tongue.

'Shouldn't keep you too long,' he said, taking the cigarette case from where it lay under some papers on his desk. 'This was found on Celia Delaney's body,' he said, holding it up for Smythe to see. 'Nigel Miller said it was a gift from you.'

Smythe peered at the silver case then looked up at Ryder. 'Yes, it was.'

Ryder frowned. 'Why would you give another man's wife such an extravagant gift?'

Smythe chuckled. 'I know what you're thinking, Detective, but I didn't *buy* it. Before I went to Europe, I spent some time in the US. I was an up-and-comer, transitioning from juniors to seniors. You might find it hard to believe, but I was young and good-looking back then.'

Ryder smiled. Smythe was likeable, personable, and Ryder could imagine him being very marketable back in the sixties. 'Go on.'

'I wasn't a big name, so I was pretty flattered when Tiffany offered to sponsor me. The exposure in the glossy magazines definitely lifted my profile.' He pointed to the cigarette case. 'I was paid with women's trinkets, to the amusement of my rivals. Most of them were sponsored by the big-name ski brands. I was given about five of those cigarette cases during the course of our business relationship. I gave one to Celia, and I think I gave one to Di as well. I remember handing them out. The girls loved them.'

'Hmm.' Frustrated, Ryder leaned back in the chair, thinking about the glossy magazine advertisements he'd studied in Bruno's scrapbook. So much for his hunch that the cigarette case might point to the identity of Celia Delaney's mystery lover.

Ryder changed tack. 'During the course of our investigations we've learned that at around four-thirty on the day Celia Delaney went missing, a ski patroller instructed the liftie who was working at bottom station to put the chain across and go inside. Can you remember the names of the ski patrollers who were working here back then?'

Smythe gave Ryder a doubtful look. 'That's a difficult one. The ski-patrol industry wasn't formalised in those days.'

The unexpected reply took Ryder by surprise. 'It wasn't?'

'No. Anyone could be added to the ski-patrol roster—anyone who was good enough, that is. I remember the village doctor doing it a lot. Then later on, when the industry became regulated, they got specialised training and uniforms and the like.'

Ryder digested the information with a sinking heart. 'You're sure about that?' he asked. 'The patrollers worked on a voluntary basis?'

'Yes.' Smythe gave him a puzzled look. 'I'm certain.'

Bruno had been adamant it was a ski patroller who had told him to close the lift. It was all there in Lewicki's notes from 1964. And Burt Crofts was supposedly looking through old slides in Jindabyne in the hope of finding out which patroller had been on duty at the time.

Conscious of Aidan Smythe's inquisitive gaze, Ryder put down his pen. 'Tell me about the troubled chairlift.'

Smythe folded his arms. 'We could be here all night talking about that, Detective. The old chairlift,' he mused. 'Well, it was most famous for breaking down, and it was downright dangerous to ride on. To be honest, that whole weekend is a bit of a blur. It was the final weekend in what was a thirty-day blizzard. All season we were rescuing people off that chairlift and, when we weren't doing that, we were repairing it or retrieving luggage that had fallen off and carting the bags into the village. It was a bloody nightmare. I was due to go overseas a few weeks later to compete. The end couldn't come quick enough for me. All I wanted was to finish up and get the hell out of this place.'

So had Celia Delaney.

Ryder smiled and stood up. 'You could be leaving with the same feeling this time.' He held out his hand and Aidan Smythe gripped it in a firm handshake. 'Thanks for coming in.'

'No problem. The sooner you make an arrest, Detective, the better it will be for everyone.'

Twenty-nine

Vanessa stirred and stretched beneath the bedclothes, semi-aware of hushed voices deep in conversation.

A glass pane rattled.

She sat up, her gaze darting from one indistinguishable shadow to the next. She was in Ryder's room at the inn. The voices she could hear were his and Lewicki's, coming from the lounge room. Outside, the wind had picked up. It blew through the pass with a ghostly wail, forcing freezing air through the gaps in the windows and chasing away her fleeting sense of safety.

Vanessa padded across the room, the luminous hands on her watch glowing ten to midnight. She hesitated at the door to pull a hoodie over the top of her flannelette pyjamas.

'There were several Tiffany advertisements in the scrapbook,' Ryder was saying, 'so all that adds up.'

'And Bruno's not talking?'

'Not so far. He's right about those wire ties, too. It'll be hard to prove he was the one who left them on the grave.'

'Might come down to DNA evidence.'

'I'm not hopeful. Long Bay's an old building. God knows what they'll find in there.'

'What about the rental gear?'

'Depends when they were last cleaned. They don't launder

them after every use, apparently. We've got Harriet working around the clock.'

There was a pause in the conversation, and Vanessa shivered, wondering what Tiffany had to do with anything, and who's scrapbook they were talking about. She pulled the hoodie closer around her. The building's central heating was set to low during the night; at this hour, guests were expected to be snuggled up cosy and warm in bed.

'I've got Benson chasing Burt Crofts,' said Ryder.

'You think he's the other person involved?'

Another pause; Vanessa could picture Ryder shrugging or nodding. Then, 'Did you know patrollers were voluntary back in the sixties?'

'No.'

'According to Smythe they were.'

'It's news to me,' said Lewicki.

Another pause.

'I was banking on Crofts.' Vanessa moved closer to the door as Ryder went on. 'I was hoping he'd find the old slides so we could narrow it down to one or two people then put the pressure on Bruno. But if the roster was voluntary, it could be anyone.'

'The village was a lot smaller back then, though, and Crofts might still come through.'

'Or Harriet. We're going into the second day of lockdown. The media frenzy will only build from here.'

'Just ignore that shit.'

'I'm going hard on Bruno tomorrow,' Ryder said on a yawn. 'Whatever part he played, I'm certain he's the key to all this.'

There was the sound of bodies moving as though the men had stood up.

'Get some sleep, Lew. You're too old for this.'

'Fuck off. I'm not going anywhere, not when we have a second chance to solve the Delaney case.'

'And Libby's,' added Ryder.

The suite door opened, and their voices receded as though they'd moved out into the corridor. A minute later, there was a soft click followed by the sound of Ryder turning the bolts.

Vanessa was halfway back to the bed when a knock came at her door. She froze, a pulse fluttering in her neck.

'Vanessa?' he said quietly. 'It's me. Lew's gone back to his room to get some sleep while I'm here.'

'Damn,' she muttered, spinning around. 'How did you know I was awake?' she asked, opening the door. 'You must have the hearing of a—' She caught her breath at the sight of him. He was close, one hand propped against the doorframe, the other resting nonchalantly on his hip. Dark haired, dishevelled and totally distracting. The top button of his white shirt was undone. His tie, the one that had been blown over his shoulder when he'd first walked into the kids' club almost a week ago, was unknotted and hung loosely around his neck—as though he'd been about to slide it out from under his collar.

'You were saying?' he asked.

'Huh?'

He pushed himself off the doorframe and straightened up. 'Something about my hearing . . .'

'Oh, a canine.'

He gave her a lopsided grin. 'I heard the bed creak when you got up. Go ahead if you need to use the bathroom. I can wait to have a shower.'

'Oh, no, I don't need the bathroom,' she said, trying not to think of him naked in the shower. 'I woke up when I heard you talking.'

'Lew said you've decided to go home tomorrow?' he asked, his eyes searching her face.

'Not to the farm. I'm going to Eva's lodge. I can lie low there, and help her with Poppy. When all this is over, I can decide whether or not I want to come back here.'

He turned his head and looked towards the windows, though there was nothing but blackness outside. 'You're doing the right thing.'

'I know,' she said, though her words belied the hollowness in her chest. 'Lew's trying to hide it, but he's desperate to be more involved in the case. And you can better utilise the people you have on the door here, too.'

'Sure.' He brought his gaze back to her face. 'I'm heading to Monaro at first light. Lew will arrange for a chopper to fly you to Thredbo. An unmarked car will take you to your sister's lodge. I can't give you a flight time yet; it depends on the weather. But we'll get you there.'

'Thank you.'

Unsure if this was 'goodbye for now' or 'goodbye forever', Vanessa searched her mind for the right words, but they escaped her. She stared at the carpet.

'Well,' she said eventually, taking a step towards him. 'Take care, Pierce, and thank you for looking after me.' With luck, there would be a prolonged court case sometime, and he'd need her as a witness. Or would he delegate that work to Flowers, while she glimpsed him from afar?

She stood on tiptoe and pressed her lips against his warm cheek, closing her eyes and breathing him in for a few precious seconds. He went to return her kiss, the roughened texture of his jaw scraping her cheek and sending spikes of pleasure rolling through her body. His lips caught the corner of her mouth, lingering there for a long moment.

Vanessa didn't move—didn't open her eyes—didn't dare break the moment.

'Look after yourself,' he murmured, his voice rough with emotion.

She nodded.

Seconds ticked by.

Neither of them pulled away, and from the rise and fall of Ryder's chest she guessed his heart was racing along with hers. Then, ever so slowly, ever so teasingly, he slid warm, firm lips across hers.

'Stay with me,' she whispered, breaking away before he could deepen the kiss. Gripped by a profound longing, she stepped backwards towards the bed, ridding herself of the hoodie in the process. 'I want to leave Charlotte Pass,' she said huskily, watching as he pulled the tie out from under his collar before starting to unbutton his shirt, 'but I don't want this—you and me—I don't want this to end right now.'

He nodded, hungry eyes raking over her body as she flung the borrowed pyjamas onto the floor. 'It doesn't have to. Not yet. Not yet.'

Ryder stroked his thumb across Vanessa's smooth hip, wishing he could slow time down. 'Where are you going to this summer?'

She blinked sleepily at him. 'Deer Valley. It's in Utah, part of the Wasatch Range. They held a lot of events there during the Salt Lake City Winter Olympics.'

'Isn't Utah a dry county?'

'Not in the ski fields,' she said with a chuckle. 'They wouldn't be able to recruit anyone if it were. No, it's amazing there.'

'The skiing?'

'The tips.'

He laughed and pulled her closer. Despite the grimness of their situation, he hadn't felt this good in years.

'I love going over there. I get to work with the avalanche dogs.'

He guessed she would need the dogs, if part of her job was digging people out of tree wells. 'How come you're the rookie here, when you've had all that experience?'

'Well, Johan's worked a few seasons here already, and he's older than me, so he's automatically senior. I haven't been back to Charlotte's since I skied here with Mum and Dad as a teenager.'

Ryder frowned. 'So, where have you been working in the southern hemisphere, then? Victoria?'

'Nope. New Zealand. I went over there to do the back-country avalanche course and, after I finished, they offered me a job.'

'Of course they did.' Ryder curled a long strand of her silky hair around his index finger. 'How long are you going to keep doing . . .'

'The itinerant thing?'

'I was going to say the back-and-forth-between-hemispheres thing.'

She smiled. 'Wondering when you'll get to see me again, Detective Sergeant?'

That's exactly what he'd been wondering, but how could he say that when less than two days ago he'd given her an entirely different message? 'I'm sorry,' he said.

'No offence taken. We get asked all the time when we're going to get a real job.'

He opened his mouth to protest, but she cut him off with a smile. 'I have no problem calling myself an itinerant worker. That's what I am. A seasonal worker who moves around, like a fruit picker, but a lot more glamorous thanks to the God suit.'

'The God suit?'

'The God suit makes the plainest person irresistible, according to the ski instructors. But they're full of it.'

'Irresistible? I'll have to think about re-joining the uniform branch.'

'I don't know if it works for the police.' She stretched her body, unwinding and loosening those long limbs that minutes earlier had been wrapped around him. 'I can't imagine you in uniform. You have the whole serious thing going on—the frown, the white shirt, the dark suit. Hot.'

He frowned.

'See.' She pointed at his forehead. 'There it is.'

'Why are we talking about me, when I asked you a question?'

'If you're questioning me in bed, Detective, can you blame me for forgetting? What was it? Oh, right, how long until I get the snow out of my system? I think Mum and Dad want me to take another couple of years.'

'Your mum and dad do?' he asked, trying hard not to frown.

'They want me to travel and have fun.' She propped herself up, chin resting in her palm as she gazed down at him. 'Believe it or not, I'm the golden child, the responsible one who's going to take over the farm when they retire. That's why I've been living the dream for the last fifteen years, well, not all year. I've been working on the farm in between seasons, you know, learning the ropes. A property like ours—it ties you down. It's not impossible to get away, but it's difficult. Once Mum and Dad join the herd of grey nomads, I'll be tied to the farm.'

It made sense to Ryder now. Her capability. Her practicality. The no-nonsense qualities he'd noticed in her from the beginning. She was natural and outdoorsy, and skied with a graceful athleticism that held him in awe. He had no doubt she would run the family farm with the same efficiency she applied to her job as a ski patroller. 'I can see you on a farm. On a horse.'

'We have horses, and quad bikes and motorbikes.'

She would handle a motorbike the way she'd handled that snowmobile a few days ago. 'One day, when you finally do settle down, I'll take a road trip to the country,' he murmured, the words slipping out before he could stop them.

She raised her eyebrows. 'I think you should wait for an invitation.'

He deserved that. He pulled her to him, consigning his thoughts to the far recesses of his mind. 'You're right, I should wait for you to invite me. No more talking. All we really have is now.'

In the morning, he had a killer to catch.

Thirty

Day 8

Ryder stood at the viewing window and took a gulp from the can of lemonade he'd grabbed from the vending machine. In the interview room, Bruno Lombardi looked drawn and tired, like he'd suffered a sleepless night in the cells. Slumped in the chair, his hands clasped together and resting on the table, he watched while Flowers fiddled with the recording equipment.

Ryder looked around as Senior Sergeant Henderson joined him in the narrow space.

'How was the flight?' Henderson asked, closing the door behind him.

'Bumpy as hell. Stomach feels like a washing machine.' Ryder took another mouthful of lemonade, cringing as the sweet liquid fizzed down his throat. 'God, that's awful.' He put the can down beside Bruno's scrapbook, which lay open on the small table next to him.

'They've cancelled all flights in and out of Charlotte's,' Henderson said.

'I heard.' Vanessa would have to wait until the wind dropped and the clouds lifted before she could safely leave for Thredbo.

Ryder's phone rang. 'Harriet,' he said, his heart rate picking up. 'Any luck?'

'No luck here, Ryder, only pure skill.'

'What have you got?'

'We found Libby's skin cells on one of the orphan straps.' Harriet paused briefly. 'I'm sending you a photo of it now, it's blue.' Another pause. 'It's a perfect match with the DNA we took during her autopsy.'

Relief washed over Ryder's body in waves. They had the murder weapon. 'Great work, Harriet. I'll get in touch with Benson.'

'Hold on, you impatient bugger. There's more good news. We found a hair on that rental suit. It was caught in the Velcro around the neck.'

Ryder began to pace, trying to wear off some of his nervous energy.

Henderson left the room.

'The hair matches DNA we found under Libby's fingernails. Whoever this person is, they have a scratch on them somewhere. And before you ask me, no they don't have a record. We've already checked the database.'

'Fantastic work, Harriet. Thank you.' They had the killer's DNA. Now they needed to find him.

'You gave me the stuff. All I did was test it.'

'You worked through the night on a young woman's body. Go home and get some sleep.'

'I will, Pierce. Good luck.'

Ryder forwarded the photograph to Benson, then called him and relayed Harriet's findings. 'Where did you find this blue strap? It could narrow down the killer's location.'

There was a rustling sound, and Ryder could picture Benson consulting his cross-referenced list and the photographs the officers had taken. 'Okay. This one . . . came from the ski room at the inn,' Benson said.

The inn again. Just like the rental suit. Ryder saw the room in his mind's eye; he'd walked past it numerous times. It was just before the swinging doors that led into the foyer. 'Whereabouts was it?'

'Umm,' said Benson. 'It was on a pair of skis in the back corner, wrapped around the tail end. According to the notes, you couldn't see it until the skis were lifted out of the timber holder.'

Ryder's mind raced, and he peered through the viewing window at Bruno. Was the DNA they had Bruno's? Or was the killer at the inn? He swung away from the window. 'Chances are he's at the inn. Search the rooms. You're looking for a man missing some skin, probably on his face or neck, and the matching blue strap.'

'Yes, Sarge.'

'And take buccal swabs from everyone. Naturally you'll be suspicious of anyone who refuses.'

'Do you want me to send the skis for fingerprint analysis?'

'You can, but I'm not hopeful. I think he would have worn gloves.'

'The skis are pretty old and crappy. It looks like someone left them there years ago.'

'That's why he chose them, Benson.' Ryder looked up as Henderson came back into the room, trying not to think about Vanessa and Lew back at the inn.

'Sir, I need to get Bruno's swab to Canberra.'

With Bruno's mouth swab on its way to forensics, they were finally ready for Flowers to start the interview. Henderson reached up and turned on the speaker. Bruno Lombardi was gazing in their direction as though trying to see through the dark-tinted glass.

'Mr Lombardi, who is Mrs Beverley Roach?' Flowers asked in a conversational manner.

Bruno shifted his gaze to Flowers. 'She's my neighbour.'

'How would you describe your relationship with your neighbour?'

'Our relationship? Like any good neighbourly relationship. Why?'

Flowers nodded. 'I spoke to her this morning. Her garden is her pride and joy.'

'Where's he going with this?' murmured Henderson.

'You'll see.'

'The garden's not at its best now, in the middle of winter,' Flowers was saying, 'but it would be beautiful in spring and summer.'

'Wouldn't have picked you for a green thumb,' Bruno said with a sneer. 'Then again, with a name like *Flowers* . . .'

'She puts some serious hours into it,' Flowers continued, unperturbed. 'Bev told me she'd see you every now and then, leaning over the fence and picking a few of her flowers. She told me she didn't mind. Apparently, she used to give your mother flowers. Thought a lot of your mum, she did.'

Ryder smiled a little. He'd given Flowers the opportunity to open the interview, at least until Ryder's stomach had calmed down a bit. So far, his younger partner was doing a pretty good job. Bruno was already looking harried.

'Who were the flowers for, Bruno?' Flowers asked.

'I . . . I think I gave some to my sister.'

'I spoke to Angela. She said you've been good to her and the kids over the years, but she said you'd never given her flowers.'

He shrugged. 'I gave some to a few people after they'd lost a husband or a wife, I can't remember exactly who. And a couple of young blokes from Cooma died in a car accident a few years back. I left some flowers at their roadside memorial.'

'Did you hold them together with wire ties?'

No answer.

'The wire ties we found hidden in your kitchen cupboard?'

Silence.

'Did you pick flowers from your neighbour's garden and leave them on Celia Delaney's grave up at Charlotte Pass?'

Flowers was silent then, waiting for Bruno to answer.

Bruno shook his head and mumbled a quiet, 'No.'

'No? Could you speak up for the benefit of the recording, Mr Lombardi?'

'No.'

'Thank you. Did you know Libby Marken?' Flowers asked.

'I didn't know her personally.'

'You never spoke to her when she was with Vanessa Bell, in the bar, or elsewhere in the village? You know she ran the kids' club?'

'I know *who* she was, but I never spoke to her.' Bruno unclasped his hands and leaned forward. 'Look, we have different staff at Charlotte's every year. I'm not going to waste my time getting friendly with them when they'll be gone by the end of the season.'

'Libby didn't live in Long Bay,' Ryder murmured. 'It's plausible Bruno had never spoken to her.'

'Then why did he run? Come on, Flowers,' Henderson said in a low voice. 'Go a bit harder.'

'I'm looking for a connection between these three women,' Flowers went on. 'Vanessa found Celia's bones up on the mountain, and then Libby Marken was sleeping in Vanessa's room when she was murdered, so we're pretty sure it was Vanessa Bell who was meant to die in the early hours of yesterday morning.'

Flowers' blunt words sent a chill fizzing down Ryder's spine, and for the first time in days he craved a cigarette. Rubbing a hand around the back of his neck where the tension had gathered, he reached for the lemonade instead and took another swig. 'Jesus Christ!' he grimaced. 'How can anybody drink this stuff?'

'You told us you wanted to warn Vanessa Bell to take care,' Flowers was saying. 'That's why you waited for her in the dark the night of the flare run and called her name out in the hallway. *You* told us that. It seems you were right to try to warn her. Who posed a threat to her and killed Libby Marken instead?'

A blank look from Bruno.

Flowers waited.

Seconds ticked by.

'This is bullshit,' Ryder said. 'He can't remember the name of the patroller, and he can't remember, or won't tell us, who Vanessa needed to be careful of. That DNA test can't come back quick enough.'

Flowers leaned back in his chair and linked his fingers behind his head. 'We found a rental suit. Someone took it from the ground floor drying room at the inn but returned it to the upstairs one.'

Bruno narrowed his eyes.

'Vanessa chased a skier who was wearing a rental suit. You were in the area at the time, clearing the snow fences. Vanessa said you saw the person ski past. Can you identify the person who disobeyed the patroller's signage and her instructions?'

Nothing from Bruno.

'Do you think the skier in the rental suit wanted to talk to you? What other reason would he have for being in that area?'

'Stop!'

Ryder stilled.

Bruno had closed his eyes. His hands came up to cover his ears as though he were trying to shut out Flowers' voice.

'There hasn't been a murder in Charlotte Pass for decades,' Flowers pressed on, his tone turning ominous.

Moments of silence followed.

Beside Ryder, Henderson could have been made of stone. Flowers shot a glance their way then carried on. 'We believe the murders of Celia Delaney and Libby Marken are linked. You live in Long Bay, don't you, Bruno? You're on the floor above Vanessa Bell. You knew exactly which room was hers.'

'Stop it!'

'What the fuck's going on?' Henderson murmured.

Bruno moaned.

Flowers glanced at the window again, then stood up slowly. 'Would you like some water, Mr Lombardi?'

'Bugger,' said Ryder. 'He should have kept going.'

Bruno lowered his hands but didn't open his eyes. 'Yes. I need a break.'

'For the purposes of the recording, Mr Lombardi has indicated that he needs a break and has requested water.' Flowers shut off the recording equipment.

'What do you think?' asked Henderson.

Ryder shook his head and studied Bruno. The groomer's eyes were open now. He was staring at the tabletop, his lips moving like he was talking to himself, or maybe he was praying.

Flowers stuck his head in the door. 'Not sure what's going on but he's as white as a sheet.'

'I have a phone call to make,' Henderson said. 'I'll go now while he's having a break.'

'How's the nausea, Sarge? Are you ready to take over?' asked Flowers.

Ryder told him they had the killer's DNA, and had sent Bruno's sample to forensics for a possible match. 'You're doing a good job, Detective. Stick with it for now.'

'Thanks, Sarge.'

While Flowers went to fetch the water, Ryder sat down and pulled Bruno's scrapbook towards him. They were missing something. He could feel it in his gut, the one he'd left behind in the Polair chopper somewhere between here and Charlotte Pass. While Celia Delaney had plastered her bedroom wall with posters of her favourite bands, Bruno's scrapbook bulged with magazine and newspaper clippings of his sporting hero. Ryder turned the pages, the facts of both cases forming a maze in his head. Right turns. Left turns. Dead ends.

Flowers looked in again on his way back to the interview room. 'I'll give him five minutes.'

Ryder nodded and placed another call to Benson.

'Listen, has Burt Crofts got back to you?'

'Just now. He's looked at the slides. No one's jumped out at him, well no one he remembers being on patrol that day. Apparently, his projector's up here in his room.'

'Yeah, he told me that. He said he's been doing some work on it.' Ryder rubbed a hand down his face and thought for a minute. 'Call him back. See if he can confirm what Aidan Smythe told me last night, that ski patrol were volunteers back when Celia was killed. Tell him the guy we're looking for could be anyone.'

'Will do.'

'What's the weather like now?'

'Better. Trying to clear.'

Ryder wound up the call, and while Bruno sipped his water in the interview room, and Flowers made notes on his pad, Ryder went back to thumbing through the scrapbook.

Smythe hailed from South Cronulla Beach and had shown promise as a surfer from an early age. A black-and-white photograph showed him standing on the Cronulla sand, proudly holding a state-of-the-art fibreglass surfboard. At fifteen, he'd been forced to choose between surfing and skiing. He chose skiing.

Scenic photographs of Charlotte Pass came next, the village huddled at the foot of the mountains, testament to man's victory over the inhospitable landscape. There were yellowed action shots of Smythe winning junior events at Thredbo and Perisher, fledging resorts at the time. Further on were analyses of his natural athleticism and balance.

I'll prove the critics wrong, he told one journalist, *the doubters, who said I'd fail on the continent.*

You don't think you'll have a problem with the vertical and the unfamiliar snow conditions? the journo asked.

There are disadvantages, for sure. We don't have the formalised training that they have in Europe. That's a disadvantage. But conditions in Australia are challenging. We get some good snow, but we get lots of ice and crud as well. That's where I have an advantage. If I can ski that, I can ski anything. If the snow gets chopped up and things get rough on the piste, then I say, watch me.

And your blocking pole plant? What about the criticism that you're weaker on one side?

Ryder's stomach lurched as Vanessa's voice rang in his head. *This guy didn't have an open stance, and when he got out of balance, he used a blocking pole plant.*

Ryder jumped up, his heart a ticking bomb in his chest.

It was Smythe who'd gone beyond the CLOSED sign. Why?

Ryder snatched up his phone, punching in the quick code for Benson. He wrenched open the door and ran straight into Henderson. 'It's Smythe. Get Flowers. I want to talk to Bruno.'

As Henderson jogged towards the interview room, Ryder paced the corridor listening to the repetitive ring of Benson's sat phone. Smythe knew which patroller had chased him, and he was staying at the inn, which gave him easy access to the drying rooms. And it wouldn't have been hard for him to work out which room was Vanessa's.

'Pick up,' he hissed, watching as Flowers and Henderson came running towards him.

'Why do you think it's Smythe?' Flowers asked.

Ryder held up a hand for silence. 'Benson, pick up the god-damn phone.'

Thirty-one

A loud thump came at the door and an unfamiliar voice called, 'Police!'

Lewicki sprang from the sofa with the agility of a man half his age. Vanessa looked up from where she'd been packing her possessions into the blue-and-red striped carry bag.

'Who's there?' Lewicki drew his firearm and stood to one side of the door.

'Detective Benson. I have Terry, er, the mountain manager, with me.'

Lewicki unlocked the door, all the while keeping his firearm at the ready. Vanessa lowered the bag onto the floor, watching as a thick-set detective swept into the room, rain clinging to his shoulders. He was shorter than Ryder, and carrying more kilos. Everything in his urgent movements told her that whatever was happening wasn't good.

'One of our boys got knocked for six off a skidoo while he was parking it,' Benson began. 'He said it was Aidan Smythe.'

'*Smythe?*'

'That's right. He's taken off. We've already put a call in to Thredbo and Perisher.'

'He's gone into the back country,' Terry said, his eyes on Vanessa. Only then did she notice his arms were full of ski gear, including a ski-patrol suit and a pair of fur-lined mountain boots.

'The weather's too bad to get the choppers in,' Benson said. 'We need people who are fast on a skidoo. People like Terry . . . and Vanessa.'

'Vanessa?' Lewicki glanced at her.

'I'm not bad,' Terry said, 'but she's the best.'

Vanessa held out her hands. 'Give me the clothes, Terry.'

'Just a minute.' Lewicki shot out an arm, blocking her way. 'I have strict orders from Detective Ryder that you're to remain here.' He looked at Terry. 'Can't the other patroller go?'

'Vanessa's the quickest of the two, and I need Johan here to cover for me.'

'Terry's right, Lew. I'm the fastest. Let me past.'

'Jesus! I'm calling Ryder.'

'Every second we waste, Smythe's getting further away,' she heard Benson say as she shut the bedroom door. Heart pounding, she pulled the heavily insulated pants and jacket over the top of her tracksuit. Hands trembling, she closed the snaps then raked her hair back into a low ponytail. She emerged from the room in under two minutes, reaching for the boots and beanie Terry was now holding.

Lewicki glowered, the satellite phone moulded to his ear as she slid her feet into the boots. He uttered an expletive, killed the call, and re-dialled.

'If he murdered Libby, I want to go after him,' she said, pulling on the beanie.

Benson nodded. 'Okay, then.'

Terry handed her an avalanche backpack, the kind with room for an extra shovel and a pocket in the strap for a two-way radio.

At the door, she turned and spoke to Lewicki. 'Tell him I'm sorry, Lew, but it's my job.'

Thirty-two

Ryder strode into the interview room, ignoring Lombardi's startled look. He put the scrapbook on the table then switched on the recording equipment. After running through the preliminaries, he dragged out a chair.

'Where's the other detective?' Lombardi asked.

'Making some phone calls.' Benson still wasn't picking up, and Lew's phone was permanently engaged. The fifth time it had gone to voicemail, Ryder had left Flowers with instructions to call the front desk at the inn and have Di Gordon go up to the suite.

'Mr Lombardi, you changed your story from what you told Roman Lewicki back in 1964. Back then, you said a ski patroller ordered you to shut down the lift and go inside. You said prior to shutting it down, you never once left your post to assist anyone, and you never once became distracted. Then,' Ryder consulted his notes from the interview a few days ago, 'after Celia Delaney's remains were discovered, you said you could have been distracted, that there was always something happening around bottom station. You said it was plausible that you'd gone to help someone, or were distracted answering your two-way radio. In addition to that, you said the ski patroller told you to put the chain across and go inside because he was going to do a final sweep, which means the chair was still going. You also said it was a self-loading chair, and someone could have loaded on by themselves without the aid of a liftie.' Ryder pushed the notes away and stared at Bruno.

'You're asking me stuff from decades ago,' Lombardi said with a shrug. 'My memory's not what it used to be.'

'This looks really bad for you, Bruno,' Ryder went on, wondering why the hell it was taking so long for Flowers to get through to Charlotte Pass. Was there a problem with the satellite? 'You changed your story, and then you left Charlotte Pass the morning Libby Marken was found murdered. We discovered wire ties in your kitchen cupboard, the same type as those we collected from around Celia Delaney's grave. Forensic pathologists have matched DNA from a stolen rental suit with skin scrapings from under Libby Marken's fingernails. It's only a matter of time until we know for sure who murdered Libby Marken, and I think at that point, we'll also learn who killed Celia Delaney.'

Lombardi said nothing.

'Where was Aidan Smythe when you were closing the chairlift?'

Lombardi stilled at the mention of Smythe's name.

'You know what I learned last night? That ski patrollers back then were voluntary. They were just people who could ski well. Most of the time it was the village doctor.'

'So?'

'Was Aidan Smythe on the ski-patrol roster?'

'He would have been.'

'So, it's possible he was the ski patroller who told you to go inside?' *Come on you bastard—talk!*

When Lombardi didn't say anything, Ryder pulled the scrapbook towards him then slowly turned the pages over. 'You must have really been looking forward to your idol coming back.'

Ryder turned a few more pages then glanced up to see Lombardi stiffen.

'I can understand why you've been following Smythe's career so closely. He's been a great ambassador for the country, hasn't he, and for Australian skiing.' *Come on, Bruno, set me straight. Tell me how I've got it all wrong, and how bad he really is.* 'He's been an idol for a lot of people, and for you too, obviously.'

'Yeah, I've been looking forward to him comin' back, all right,' Lombardi said with a snarl. 'I've been looking forward to it for fifty years.'

Sensing this was the moment he'd been waiting for, Ryder slowly looked up. The groomer was staring at him in disbelief.

'You know nothing,' Lombardi said, his eyes glistening. 'He's had it easy all his life. The bloke's an arsehole.'

Ryder almost stopped breathing, then spoke quietly, gently. 'Then tell me what happened, Bruno.'

'He destroyed my life, that's what happened!' He stared in disgust at the clippings he'd so carefully pasted in, as though the book itself had betrayed him.

'Tell me.' Ryder glanced at the viewing window. Hopefully Flowers had got through to Charlotte Pass, and Benson was holding Smythe.

Several more seconds passed before Bruno was able to compose himself. 'That afternoon, it was close to shutdown time.'

'Around four-thirty?'

He shook his head. 'Closer to five. There was hardly anyone out. I was waiting for Smythe to come and do his sweep. I was just hanging around when Celia turned up.'

'On foot?'

'Yep. She was in a state, shakin' and cryin' and holdin' one side of her face. She asked where Aidan was. I tried raising him on the two-way, but it had been playing up in the wind. She had this swelling on her cheek. It was starting to bruise. I didn't know what to do. I felt sorry for her, so I told her to wait there while I went outside. I got a handful of snow for her to put on her face.'

'Did she get on the lift?' Ryder asked.

'Not then. A few minutes after, Aidan turned up. He'd been out skiing. She blurted out that she'd asked Nigel for a divorce. And that he'd hit her. She was terrified. She kept cryin' out and saying, "Get me out of here. Get me out. I'm not going back."'

'What did Smythe do?'

'He told her to calm down, that it would be all right. He had his arms around her, but I heard her say, "You're leaving soon. We don't have much time left to be together," or somethin' like that.'

'Did it sound like they'd been together before? That they might have been having an affair?'

'It didn't surprise me. Aidan's a player, always has been, even when he was engaged to Carmel. The prick couldn't keep it in his pants.'

'Where did you think he was going to take her?'

'To his digs in Thredbo. He didn't stay at Charlotte Pass all the time, and Carmel had already gone home to Sydney.' Bruno's voice turned husky. 'Back then, I thought Celia was safer with him than with her husband.'

Ryder's heart contracted. Poor Celia. She'd had no one else to turn to. Di Gordon was sleeping with her husband and, despite the guitarist she'd had a brief fling with, the band remained loyal to Nigel. So she'd gone to Smythe, who'd given her a Tiffany cigarette case. 'What happened then?'

'He told me to put the chain across and to wait for a couple of minutes to make sure no one else got on. Then I could go inside. He was going to shut the lift down at the top.'

'Did you do that?'

Bruno nodded. 'I helped them get on safely. Just before he pulled the cover down, he turned around and winked at me and put a finger to his lips.' He scoffed bitterly. 'As if I'd tell anyone. Smythe outranked me, and it wasn't any of my business.'

Ryder frowned and gave Bruno a few seconds' break. While he was impatient to know the full story, he was wary that if he pushed him too hard, Bruno would clam up again. 'When did you see him next?'

'Not until the next morning. He bailed me up. He had a sprained wrist that was strapped up. People were running everywhere. He told me . . . that Celia was dead.' Lombardi ran a shaky hand over the scar on his head. 'I was shocked. I asked him what happened. He said the fucking chairlift broke down. Those were his exact words. They were stuck in the air between Charlotte's and the restaurant, waiting for the lift to blow over or to freeze to death. The two-way was stuffed. The liftie at the top probably thought we'd shut it down at our end. He said they had no choice in the end but to jump.' Lombardi's voice thickened. 'He told me he survived the jump, but she didn't.'

Ryder heard Harriet's voice. *She was struck in the head first, then thrown from a substantial height.* But she had it the wrong way around. They hadn't gone down with the chairlift. They'd jumped. That would account for Celia's deceleration injury, but . . .

Ryder took a deep breath. 'And Smythe said the fall killed her?'

'He did. And I've always believed that's what happened, until you told me the other day that she'd been murdered.'

'I don't understand. If you thought it was an accident, why didn't you just go to the police?'

'Because he told me that no one could find out that the two of them were together. Carmel's father was loaded. He was bankrolling Smythe's northern-hemisphere campaign. The family were already suspicious that he was playing around. He was shitting himself that if she found out he'd been getting it on with a married woman, she'd dump him.'

'And Daddy would pull his funding?'

'That's right. He said I was the only one who knew they'd gone up there together, and if I went to the police, he'd tell them I was dealing weed.'

'Were you dealing?'

Bruno gave another bitter laugh. 'Yeah, I was his supplier. The bastard knew my situation, so he threatened me. He knew my dad had been killed. He told me to think about what would happen to Mum and Angela if I went to jail. Angela was only in primary school, and Mum couldn't speak English. My money was paying the house mortgage. He said they'd end up homeless. "Who do you think they'll believe," he said, "the golden boy or a dirty dago?"'

'He blackmailed you with all this, the morning after the storm?'

Bruno nodded. 'Before people even knew Celia was missing.'

'Where was her body?'

'He'd thrown her down that tree well. I knew exactly where the spot was when you asked me about it. The snow was deep that year, deeper than it's ever been since. He told me to go up there in the spring thaw and bury her body. I was terrified if I didn't do what he said, he'd implicate me. So, I did it, one day when the Gordons were in Sydney. We didn't open in summer back then. There was no one else around.' Lombardi was staring at a spot on the wall, his eyes glazed, his thoughts in the past. 'I knew she'd still be frozen. She was intact, but her head was caved in on one side.'

The blunt force trauma injury.

Her skull sustained a depressed bone fracture consistent with being kicked in the head or hit with something hard, like a hammer or a rock.

Ryder's scalp crawled. Had Smythe bludgeoned Celia Delaney to death to save his own skin? 'What did you do then?'

'I dug a grave and put her in. It took me most of the day, the ground was so hard. And then I left her up there, with the rabbits, and the pygmy possums.'

'And you took flowers up there, held together with the wire ties we found.'

'Only in the spring and summer, so they'd blend in with the wild-flowers and not be noticed.'

Jesus Christ. Ryder's nausea returned with a vengeance. Lew had been right. Poor Bruno. The scared young man had carried out Smythe's instructions only to keep his mother and sister safe. He looked towards the viewing window and gave the signal to arrest Aidan Smythe.

'He . . . he . . . destroyed my life,' Bruno was saying. 'In the beginning, I lived in fear the police would find her. Roman Lewicki was relentless, but even he gave up in the end. Everyone abandoned her. Everyone except me. As the years went by, I knew if I went to the police, I'd be charged with impeding an investigation or interferin' with a dead body, so I laid low, watching over her, and praying.'

'Praying?'

'For the day Aidan Smythe would come back.'

'Did you recognise the skier in the rental suit the other day?'

Bruno nodded, his eyes glistening 'It was him, all right.' He pulled a crumpled handkerchief from the pocket of his pants and wiped his eyes. 'He was travellin'. He lifted up his goggles so I could see who it was. Then he took off his mitt and shook his fist at me.'

'Threatening you?'

'Yeah . . . the bastard.'

'Did he say anything?'

'"You keep your mouth shut!" Then he dropped his mitt.'

Ryder's heart began to beat faster. 'He dropped a glove?'

'A leather mitten. I'd scooped it up before Vanessa came out of the trees. And then I made another mistake,' Bruno said in a halting voice, the pain evident on his face. 'I hid it, instead of taking it to you and telling you everything then. If I'd done that, you would have questioned him, and maybe Libby wouldn't have died.' He covered his eyes and wept. 'God will never forgive me.'

More that Bruno wouldn't forgive himself.

Ignoring the headache that had begun to lurk behind his eyes, Ryder waited until Bruno had composed himself.

'One thing that's been bothering me, Bruno. When we interviewed you at the inn, you said you tried to warn Vanessa to be careful, the night you waited for her near the bridge.'

Bruno nodded then sniffed loudly. 'I saw her give Detective Flowers a piece of paper the night of the flare run. The spotlights lit up the hill like daytime. There were people everywhere. Smythe wouldn't have seen her because he was leading the flare run. I was going to warn her in a roundabout way not to get too involved.'

But Bruno hadn't wanted to implicate himself either, and he'd gone about it all the wrong way.

Ryder sighed. 'Okay, tell me about this glove.'

'It's leather, brown, from Smythe's shop in Canada. It's got a label on it.' Bruno pushed his handkerchief back in his pocket. 'I was still covering for him then. But no more. Not after he killed that innocent girl.'

'So, that's why you took off, when you heard Libby was dead?'

'I wasn't lying when I said I'd had enough. Plus, I was pretty sure I'd be next.'

Ryder pushed back his chair and stood up. 'Where's the mitt now?'

Bruno gazed up at Ryder, a resigned expression in his weary eyes. 'Underneath my sister's place. Inside the aircon unit. Beside the control panel.'

Thirty-three

Vanessa and Terry rode side by side. Benson and the other detective followed. They roared up the face of the tube run where Smythe had been sighted fleeing the resort, a fresh layer of ungroomed snow making it easy to pick out the snowmobile's tracks.

'This way heads into Thredbo,' Vanessa called as they crested the top of the mountain. Fog surrounded them like spun sugar. 'Do you think he's going to follow the old chairlift route?'

'Who knows?' Terry shouted back over the stutter of the diesel engine. He pointed a gloved finger at the ground. 'The impressions show he's gone towards the old restaurant.'

Vanessa turned, her gaze tracking upwards as a gust of wind thinned out the fog. A crumbling ruin was taking shape in the lowlight, emerging gradually, like a negative in a photographer's darkroom. Stalactites hung from battered eaves, the doors and windows boarded up with a hard-packed layer of ice.

Benson caught up and pulled in beside them. Terry pointed to the tracks leading to the derelict Stillwell Restaurant that stood like a ghostly apparition atop the highest point of the range. 'It's about twenty feet to the verandah. I can't see where the tracks go after that.'

'We'd better check it out,' Benson said, killing the engine and pocketing the key to the snowmobile. 'Come on, O'Day.' Then to Terry and Vanessa: 'You two stay here.'

'They've got their guns out,' Terry said, watching as the detectives waded through thigh-deep snow towards the verandah.

'I don't blame them.' Vanessa tipped back her head and studied the sky as another wind gust tore across the mountains. 'I can see blue up there.'

'That'll make our job easier.'

Terry was right. On a cloudless day, and against a white backdrop, a moving target like Smythe would be easy to track.

'Can you believe this?' Terry asked, staring at her through his plastic lenses. 'I mean, you couldn't dream this stuff up, could you?'

'I know.' Vanessa shook her head. 'It's horrible.'

Suddenly a mechanical roar split the silence and a snowmobile flew out from behind the restaurant.

'What do we do?' Vanessa cried.

'Let's get after him. The others will catch up.'

Vanessa hesitated. 'What if they're injured, or . . .'

'You're right.' Terry switched off the ignition and began to dismount. 'I'll check.'

Benson and the other detective appeared at the side of the building, moving as fast as the deep snow would allow. But their progress was slow. If she had to wait for them, Smythe would get away.

She stood up on the running boards, opened the throttle and took off with a burst of speed that left Terry covered in a shower of snow.

'Fuck!' she heard him yell, before the roar of the two-stroke engine drowned out all other noise. She sank into a semi-squat, knees relaxed so they absorbed the bumpy terrain like shock absorbers. She scanned the white landscape, her gaze locking onto the moving target. Smythe was following the line of the old chairlift all right, flying towards the first of a series of shallow bowls that linked Charlotte Pass with Thredbo.

Using her body weight, and thankful for the years spent riding quads and motorbikes on the farm, Vanessa wrangled the machine through the soft snow. Smythe knew the back country. He'd told her so the day they'd stood admiring the view from up on the back track.

Back in the day, I used to hike out there to Kosciuszko. We used to stop for lunch at the Blue Lake. I loved skiing off-piste.

Then, as she closed the gap between them, she could see him clearly in the blingy gold suit.

I'm afraid my mind might be willing, but the old legs wouldn't stand up to it these days, especially in these boots.

How were his legs now?

He was standing, like her.

How long could he keep going?

Vaguely aware of the distant roar of Terry's snowmobile somewhere behind her, Vanessa checked her instrument panel. She had one choice, and that was to ram Smythe. She might dislodge him, even put the machine on its side, which should give the two detectives time to catch up.

Drawing the angles in her mind, she came at Smythe at forty-five degrees. He turned his head towards her, and the snowmobile fishtailed for a few seconds, but its curved skis stopped it from diving into the snow. He regained control but lost speed in the process. Vanessa eased off on the throttle, and adjusted the angles in her head.

Narrowing her gaze, she locked onto her target, and braced herself for the collision. A calmness came over her. She saw Libby, smiling in the bar; Libby shouting with laughter as she shot downhill in a giant tube; Libby showing such dedication to the children left in her care. They'd had so much fun together, Libby had everything ahead of her, and this bastard stole her life.

A silence descended.

Vanessa took a few deep breaths.

It was just her and Smythe and the vast white landscape.

She could do this.

She would do this.

For Libby.

For Celia.

And for Ryder.

Thirty-four

'Lew!' Ryder stopped pacing and let go of a tense breath. 'We've been trying to get hold of Benson. Smythe's the perp. Bruno's given us the full story.'

'I know.'

Ryder blinked, his fingers tightening on the phone. 'You know?'

'Smythe dragged one of the young detectives off his skidoo, and took off. The young bloke was stunned, but he identified him. Benson and a few of the others are after him now, that's why he's not picking up. Sorry, I've been busy getting as many officers into the area as I can.'

'Christ! Do you have any idea where's he headed?'

'Thredbo, we think, which means he could come out anywhere along the Alpine Way.'

'Let's hope he runs out of fuel. Who's with Benson?'

'O'Day, I think his name is. The mountain manager, Terry . . . and Vanessa.'

'*Vanessa?*'

'Yes, she's with them. Benson asked for the fastest rider and, according to Terry, she's the best. I tried to stop her—'

'You *tried* to stop her?' Fury welled up inside Ryder. He snatched his jacket and caught Flowers' eye. 'Tell the pilot we're on our way. And grab the car keys.'

'Yes, Sarge.'

'Smythe must have known you were closing in on him,' Lew was saying.

'Knew Benson was going door to door more like it.' Ryder told Lew about the DNA they had as he headed for the exit. 'It was Smythe on the mountain, too. He dropped a mitten while gesturing to Bruno. Bruno picked it up, but I think Smythe thought Vanessa had found it, or Bruno had given it to her, and she'd shown us. It's distinctive, leather with Smythe's personal label on it. Flowers has the Jindy boys going over to Angela Lombardi's place now. Bruno stashed it there.'

'Jesus. Well, the only thing I know is that Smythe's bolted.'

'Which means he's desperate.' Ryder bit out the words. 'And if Vanessa's the fastest, she'll reach him first.'

'She said to tell you she was sorry—that she's only doing her job.'

'Bullshit.' Ryder shouldered open the station door and strode towards Flowers, who was backing out one of the patrol cars. 'It's not her job to go chasing after someone who's murdered to save his own skin, twice.' Ryder killed the call and slid into the passenger seat.

'Chopper's on stand-by, Sarge.'

His attention on the weather, Ryder dragged the seatbelt over his shoulder while Flowers gunned the engine. Out on the street, the traffic pulled to the kerb at the first high-pitched shriek of the siren.

Ten minutes to Canberra Airport.

Then they'd be in the air.

Thirty-five

Fog swirled around Vanessa. A man had spoken her name, but she didn't answer. It wasn't a soft voice, a kind voice. This man was demanding. She let the blackness pull her under again.

'Vanessa?' Static distorted the insistent voice. 'Terry to Vanessa.'

She rolled onto all fours, a searing pain coming out of nowhere to shoot through her right cheekbone and into her skull. Teetering on hands and knees like a shocked animal, her stomach heaved, and she retched. Resisting the temptation to roll onto her side and curl up, she spat blood and vomit from her mouth. A headache beat rhythmically on the right side of her skull. A stream of blood dripped from the ends of her hair to turn the snow crimson between her gloved fingers.

Her mind cleared a little and she looked up, only to slam her eyes shut as reflected sunlight blinded her as effectively as a spotlight. She sat down heavily, shading her face in the crook of her arm, her eyes watering from the freezing air. Something rubbed beneath her chin. She raised a hand to her chest, relieved to find her goggles hanging around her neck. Slowly, she untwisted the strap then stretched it out and set the goggles over her eyes. Straightaway, the yellow lenses righted her world a little.

Smythe's snowmobile was lying on its side while hers sat miraculously upright. Her weighty backpack had flown off in the fall and lay ten feet away. The shovel she always carried had speared into the snow.

Smythe groaned from somewhere in the vicinity of his snowmobile.

'Vanessa? Terry to Vanessa. Can you hear me?'

She looked at her backpack again, her neck movement restricted. Terry's anxious voice crackled from the two-way's speaker. Thanks to the Velcro strap, the device was still safely secured in its pocket.

Vanessa surveyed the snow cover around her. The top layer had been wind-blown to an icy crust, and while the frozen base was undoubtedly solid, she had no marker for the snow depth in between. Reluctant to stand, in case she sank to her thighs as the two detectives had done, she reached out and wrapped her gloved hands around the spindly branches of a shrub sticking out of the snow. Eyes fixed on the radio, she hoisted herself forward, using her elbows and knees to slide across the icy surface like a seal.

Another groan, closer this time, pulled her up.

She turned her upper body, unable to rotate her neck without moving her shoulders. Aidan Smythe was on his feet, his left arm hanging uselessly by his side, his right hand reaching for her snowmobile.

Fear drove energy into Vanessa's limbs. Fear he'd get away. Fear the others had gone in a different direction and weren't going to arrive as back-up. Fear he would never pay for what he'd done to Celia and Libby.

Libby.

Finding solid purchase, Vanessa lurched to her feet as he swung one leg over the seat of the snowmobile.

'Stay where you are, or you'll end up like the others,' he said, setting his feet on the running boards.

'You don't have the balls,' Vanessa taunted in a voice she hardly recognised. She bent down and pulled the shovel out of the snow. No use wasting time radioing the others. They wouldn't make it in time to save her.

'Celia trusted you,' she said, unsure if what she was saying was actually true, 'and Libby was asleep. I'd like to see you take on a strong woman for a change, a woman who can fight back.'

He reached for the key, his smile colder than the Antarctic wind. 'No need for something so drastic.'

The snowmobile roared to life. Using his good hand, he turned it in a slow circle, bringing it around so that the nose was pointing straight at her.

He opened the throttle.

Everything turned to slow motion.

Blind fury raced through Vanessa's veins and she took a step sideways, fighting the resistance of the deep snow. Kneecap twisting, her ligaments stretched to snapping point, she took a second step away when he was almost upon her. She swung the shovel like a cricket bat, striking Smythe on his injured shoulder, the machine missing her by a hair's breadth. He howled and let go of the throttle, causing the snowmobile to pull to one side before it lost power. The swing knocked Vanessa off her feet. She fell backwards, knees bent, her boots trapped in the snow.

Prone, she stared at the sky, a cornflower blue now the wind had chased the clouds away. Diesel fumes hung in the air, the back country quiet save for a startled raven's call.

'Vanessa? Terry to Vanessa. Come in.'

She levered herself up onto her elbows, careful not to overextend her knee ligaments further, and managed to drag her right leg free. Fearful Smythe could reappear any second, she worked the shovel, digging out the snow packed around her left boot with short, urgent movements. Sweat tracked a path down her face, mixing with the blood seeping from her head wound.

She dragged her left leg free, then struggled to her feet. Unsteady, her legs shaking, she gulped mouthfuls of freezing air into her burning lungs and wiped her face on the sleeve of her jacket. She could see him now. He was lying on his back—shallow breaths coming from his gaping mouth.

Wincing, Vanessa climbed aboard the idling machine. Twisting the throttle, she drove away from her quarry, her only thought to put a safe distance between them. Twenty metres on, she turned in a wide arc before pulling up. She kept the engine idling and Smythe in her view. There was no way she would risk the possibility of the engine not restarting if she turned it off. She pulled off her goggles and wiped her forehead with her sleeve.

The relief of being out of immediate danger made her limbs weak, and she pushed her hair behind her ears with a shaking hand. She'd have to go back for the radio at some point, but not yet. Right now, this was the only place she felt safe.

She set her goggles over her eyes, and focused on the prone figure in the distance.

Was he dead?

Or close to it?

When Detective Benson had asked her to come out here, she hadn't bargained on getting in a fight to the death with Aidan Smythe. Surely she had done enough. Or had she? She was a ski patroller, after all, her only reason for being on this mountain was to render assistance to whomever needed it. How would she feel later on if she sat here now, a safe distance away, and just waited for the bastard to die?

Swearing ferociously, she twisted the throttle and drove back towards the body lying in the snow beside the upturned snowmobile. She wouldn't put herself in more danger, but she would check on him while she went to fetch the radio.

She circled Smythe's motionless figure time and time again. Eventually, she had no option but to dismount and trudge towards the spot where he lay. She approached him tentatively, heart pounding, half expecting him to rise up, his hands encircling her throat like a scene out of *Fatal Attraction*.

But as she drew closer, she saw that his breaths were growing shallower, and a blue tinge stained his mouth and eyelids.

Vanessa's heart stuttered.

The man didn't deserve to live.

'Vanessa? Terry to Vanessa. Come in.'

She glanced at the two-way radio then back at the criminal who lay badly injured in the place where it had all begun.

Goddamn you, Smythe, for ever coming into my life.

She peeled off her gloves and cast them aside. Falling to her knees, she leaned over and unzipped his ski jacket then spread the sides open. Next, she unzipped the fleecy top he wore underneath, pushing it aside as well until he lay bare to the waist save for his singlet.

Loading her shovel with one heavy pile of snow after another, Vanessa set about burying Aidan Smythe.

Thirty-six

The helicopter stayed low, skimming the treetops as it rose above the summit of Mount Stillwell.

'What happened?' Ryder asked when he had Benson on the sat phone. Seated beside the pilot, he peered through the binoculars at the white landscape, searching for signs of Vanessa, Terry and his men.

'O'Day and I went to check the restaurant. We figured Smythe might be holed up inside. But he took off on us. The other two went after him.'

Ryder pressed the sat phone closer to his ear, struggling to hear over the whir of the rotors without the benefit of his headset.

'I got bogged in soft stuff.' Benson paused. 'You're close, Sarge; I can hear the chopper. Follow the pylons of the old chairlift. We think that was Smythe's intention.'

Ryder relayed the information to the pilot, grateful the terrain below was above the tree line.

'You're behind me,' Benson said a few moments later. 'I'm in the open. You should see me if you're low enough.'

'I see something at ten to twelve,' Flowers shouted from the back seat.

Sure enough, seconds later they flew over a waving Benson.

'Okay, we see you. Where's O'Day?'

'A bit further on. He ran out of fuel.'

Ryder relayed Benson's message to the others then, swearing under his breath, he lowered his binoculars. In what life did Benson imagine that he and O'Day were equipped to take on the treacherous back country—and involve civilians? Right now, Ryder needed to get eyes on everyone, but as sure as hell *that* decision would come out in the debrief.

'Twelve oh five,' the pilot said, pointing through the windscreen.

'We have eyes on O'Day,' Ryder said to Benson. At least they'd had sense enough to stay with the snowmobiles, which were easy to pick out against the white backdrop. 'So, Terry and Vanessa are still in pursuit?' he asked.

'No. A submerged rock damaged one of Terry's runners.'

'Vanessa's on her own?' Ryder's voice came out hoarse, his stomach twisting.

''Fraid so.'

This was all his fault. If he'd insisted on Vanessa leaving Charlotte Pass the morning of Libby's death, she wouldn't be out here. If anything happened to her . . .

'Anyone injured?' he asked, cutting off his negative train of thought.

'Nah. Just a bit cold.'

That meant they were bordering on hyperthermia. Benson was a good cop, but his nature was to downplay everything.

The pilot slowed, hovering over the area they had sighted the stranded detectives.

Ryder peered through his binoculars, searching for the spot where Terry had come undone, though his thoughts kept moving ahead to where Vanessa and Smythe might be. There was no doubt she was good on the snow bike—he had admired her skills the day she'd taken him up to Celia's grave—but he had no idea she was the fastest rider on the mountain, or that Benson would involve her in the chase.

Moments later, they sighted another snowmobile, listed to one side. Unlike the others, there was no sign of its rider, though deep footprints led them in the direction of a nearby granite boulder.

Terry was standing atop the boulder, seemingly undisturbed by his remote location. He gave them a distracted wave like he'd been expecting them, the two-way radio close to his mouth.

'Benson, call the others and tell them to stay put. We'll let the medivac chopper know where to pick everyone up. We'll keep after Vanessa. Have you heard from her?'

'No. Terry's still trying to raise her on the two-way.'

So that's why he'd moved to higher ground. Ryder's anxiety eased a fraction. There could be any number of reasons why Vanessa was out of contact. A poor signal. A dead battery.

Or, she could be flat out chasing Smythe, the same way she'd chased him down the mountain that day.

'I'll get back to you,' he told Benson, killing the call and reaching for the noise-cancelling headset. As he covered his ears with the air-foam seals, a red flash exploded in the sky in front of them.

'Flare!' he yelled into the microphone. 'Take us down. Follow the smoke trail.'

The pilot consulted the instrument panel and began making small precise movements with the joystick. To Ryder, the manoeuvre seemed to take forever. 'Down there,' he said, 'I see two snow-mobiles. One's upright. The other one is on its side.'

'I have one person standing.' Flowers's voice crackled through the headset.

'I can't set the chopper down on the snow, but I can get you close and you'll have to jump. Those circular marks look like they've been made by a snowmobile that's been driven around in circles. The snow looks stable there. Judging from the tracks, it doesn't look too deep.'

'How close can you get me?' Ryder asked, discarding his headset and donning goggles and a beanie.

'Metre. Metre and a half.'

'That'll do.'

They descended closer to the ground, billowing white dust sticking to the windows and obscuring their view. Ordering the pilot to unlock the door, Ryder shoved it open then slid onto the cabin floor. Despite the pilot's protests, he plunged the short distance into the snow.

Smashing through the top layer of ice like a spoon into a crème brûlée, he toppled sideways, the landing softer than he'd expected. After the oppressive humidity of the cabin, the bracing air cleared his head, the snow as welcome as an ice bath after a hard footy game. Once the chopper had risen to a safe altitude, and the snow flurry had begun to settle, Ryder sat up and took his firearm from the inside pocket of his ski jacket. Releasing the safety catch, he stood up with difficulty and trudged in the direction of the snow-mobiles, praying he'd find Vanessa safe.

There were two images that would haunt Ryder for the rest of his days. The first one was of Scarlett lying in the driveway. The second was straight out of a thousand mobster movies he'd seen, when the mafia buried their enemies up to their necks in sand and waited for the tide to come in.

The difference here was that Aidan Smythe was buried to the neck in snow. And while Ryder's heart soared at the first sight of Vanessa standing, his euphoria was short-lived. Streaks of blood tracked into her eyes, only to be smeared across her cheeks when she swiped at it with the back of her hand. Like a Viking shield maiden after a battle to the death, she stood panting, the shovel she'd used to cover Smythe's body clutched in her right hand.

Ryder swallowed the lump in his throat. She was strong and victorious, magnificent and tragic, and he wondered what Smythe had done to drive her to this end. He moistened his lips. This was the last thing he wanted to do, but he had no choice. He raised his Glock.

'Vanessa, drop the shovel, and move away from the body.'

Her eyes widened with shock. Still brandishing the tool, she took two steps towards him. 'Pierce?' she called. 'Pierce?'

He stared at her down the barrel. 'I said, drop the shovel. And move away from the body.'

Thirty-seven

Two days later

Ryder carried his coffee and raspberry muffin to the table where Lew was waiting. 'For a hospital coffee shop, they don't have too many healthy options.'

'At least it's cheerful in here.'

'Yeah, I've been in worse.' Ryder glanced at the other patrons, a mix of staff, volunteer workers and worried relatives doing their best to comfort each other.

Lew leaned forward expectantly as Ryder sat down. 'So, was Smythe awake?'

'Yep.' After waiting all afternoon, the call had finally come through. They'd rushed to the hospital, leaving Flowers at Monaro to finish typing up the extensive case notes.

'Apparently he's had a couple of minor heart procedures in the past, but because he's so fit his recovery's been rapid.'

'Did you charge him?'

'Multiple times. The judge will hear the charges when he's fit enough to attend court.'

'Was he able to talk?'

'I got a bit out of him before the doctor stepped in.'

'Why did he kill Celia?'

Ryder took a sip of coffee and leaned back in his chair. 'He said he couldn't risk Carmel finding out.' Ryder put his cup down and peeled back the paper case on his muffin. 'And we know from what Bruno told us, her father was picking up the bill for what was going to be a stellar career. So, there's his motive.'

'And we know he had the opportunity and the means,' Ryder went on. 'They were isolated up there on the mountain, and he carried all the gear that patrollers carry, torches, shovels and the like. He held all the cards. Only Bruno knew Celia was with him, and Smythe had something on him.'

'Poor bloody Bruno,' Lew said with a sigh. 'He was blackmailed into covering up what he thought was an accident. No wonder he was shocked when you told him Celia had been murdered. It had already ruined his life.'

'Yep. He'll be charged too, but his limited involvement will no doubt come out in the end.'

'If only Bruno had gone to the police and told them where Celia was. All of this would have come out fifty years ago.'

Ryder nodded. 'But Bruno knew there were plenty of others who could attest to him dealing weed in the area, so he did Smythe's bidding.'

'So, did Smythe actually admit to cold-blooded murder?' asked Lew.

'Pretty much.'

'What's his version?' Lew urged, an impatient edge to his voice.

'That Nigel hit Celia and she was adamant she wanted to leave the village. He'd been out skiing when she turned up to bottom station on foot. Apparently, they were involved, and he made a split-second decision to go with her. Then the lift stopped. The radio was on the blink. They were in a bad physical state up there. It was freeze to death or jump. He remembers coming around after the fall. Celia was crying and saying she couldn't feel her legs, that she was numb from the waist down. It didn't cross his mind that her legs could have been numb from the cold—he figured she'd suffered a spinal injury. He panicked. He knew they had to get back to the village, that they wouldn't survive a night on the mountain. Then he says he has a faint recollection of picking up a jagged rock, and then everything became a blur.'

'Do you believe him?'

'I do. Harriet said her injuries were consistent with being hit with a hammer or a rock.'

'So, the murder wasn't premeditated?' asked Lew.

'He didn't intend to kill her when they first went up, but once his future was threatened everything changed.'

'Yes. If he'd got her back down to the village, Celia could have told all.'

For a few moments neither of them spoke, both men lost in their thoughts.

'Harriet was right,' Lew said eventually.

'Yep. She just had it the wrong way around. She thought Celia had been bludgeoned in the head and then thrown from a height, most likely down the tree well. As it turns out, they both jumped from the chairlift, and Smythe did the rest.'

'Do you think he'll plead some kind of mental impairment?'

'Yes—he'll try to play up the stressful conditions and the life-and-death situation up there.' Ryder pushed his coffee cup away. 'Doesn't matter. Libby's murder was premeditated. We have conclusive DNA evidence to prove that. Aidan Smythe is going away for a very long time.'

Lewicki took off his glasses and began cleaning them with a cloth from his case. 'So, how's his wife?'

Ryder looked towards the windows, where streets lights were starting to come on outside. 'Devastated. Their children are on their way.'

'Jesus,' Lewicki said with a sigh, putting his glasses back on. 'What a fall from grace. The sporting hero, the guest of honour and star of Winterfest, charged with double homicide.'

'Yeah, it's pretty bad, certainly not the kind of publicity the Gordons had been hoping for.'

'I felt so sorry for his wife when we went up to their room,' said Lew. 'She was so confused and upset. She didn't know where he'd gone.'

'Thanks again for taking care of that part. I knew I could rely on you.' Ryder reached out and laid a hand on Lew's back for a second.

'Oh, it was all right. I took a couple of the other boys with me. They searched the room while I talked to her. That's when they found the matching ski strap in his bag. She had no idea what was going on at that point. It sank in when we took his shaving gear and other stuff from the bathroom though.'

'She didn't hear him leave the morning he left to murder Libby?'

'She's still jetlagged. Been taking sleeping pills ever since she got here.'

'Well, thanks again.'

'Hey, I owed you. There was so much I missed first time round.'

'You're still the best detective I know, Lew.'

Lewicki was quiet for a few moments. Then he gave a brief smile. 'I wonder if all this has fuelled Daisy's desire to become a police prosecutor.'

Ryder stifled a yawn. 'I hope not. I heard from Inspector Gray this morning. Some people have come forward in the Hutton case. I need Flowers on the job.'

'Then you better get him in here to Canberra. We'll have to shout him one last turmeric latte, or whatever shit it is he drinks, if you're going to be staying on in Monaro for a while.'

Ryder chuckled. He hadn't given Flowers the news yet.

'I've been meaning to ask how he came to be your partner.'

'I gave recruitment my preferences, but they chose Flowers. Saw something special in him, apparently.' Ryder smirked. 'Maybe HR do know what they're talking about.'

Lew stood up with a groan. He looked as bone weary as Ryder felt. 'Probably scored well on one of those bloody psychometric tests. Anyway, I'd better get home to my wife or I won't have one soon. And remember what I told you before.'

'I promise. I won't go back to Sydney without seeing Annie.'

'Not that.'

Ryder frowned. 'What then?'

Lew pressed his lips together and paused, as though weighing up what he was about to say. 'Sometimes bad things happen when people are trying to do the right thing. Take Bruno: he was just doing his job and trying to help Celia; what happened next ruined his entire life. You were trying to save two innocent children when a terrible thing happened to your family.' He pointed a finger at Ryder. 'Let that be a lesson to you. Don't let it ruin your entire life, as hard as it is. Do you get what I'm saying?'

'I get it,' Ryder said around the muscles constricting in his throat. His body was weary, his mind tired, his head aching from trying to piece everything together. And while he hadn't wanted the Delaney case in the beginning, maybe it would be the case that would change his life after all.

'Thanks, Lew. Night.'

Thirty-eight

'You have a visitor.' The nurse with the sunny face and twinkling blue eyes smiled down at Vanessa. 'Are you up to seeing anyone today, possum?'

Vanessa lowered the magazine she'd been trying to read, though the relentless throb behind her eyes made it impossible to concentrate on anything. 'Who is it?'

'A handsome detective,' the nurse said with a wink. 'He called in yesterday too, but we told him it was only family allowed. He's literally cooling his heels out here.'

'I've been waiting all day,' she heard Ryder say, an impatient edge to his voice. 'I really need to speak to her.'

Vanessa nodded. 'It's all right. Send him in.'

He strode into the room before the nurse had finished speaking. He looked exactly the same as the first time she'd set eyes on him at The Rambling Wombat's Kids' Club. Dark hair pushed up at the front, tie awry. Only the vertical frown between his eyebrows had changed. It was deeper than ever. In his hand was a small cane basket wrapped in cellophane and pink ribbon.

He approached the bed slowly, his height making the sterile room with the IVs and beeping machines look even smaller.

'Hi,' he said quietly, putting the basket on her bedside table. His concerned gaze roamed her face then moved to the marks on

289

her wrists where he'd slapped on the handcuffs. 'I tried to see you earlier. Can I . . . sit down?'

She nodded, watching as he brought a chair close. His face was drawn with tired lines, and when he sat down it was with a weary sigh.

'Smythe had emergency surgery for a broken shoulder but he's awake now. He has some kind of heart issue. His surgeon said he'll pull through without a problem though, thanks to you putting him on ice. You saved his life, Vanessa.'

Anger welled up inside her. 'I almost didn't bother. I nearly let him die.'

'But you didn't. You even gave him CPR. You made the right choice.'

'I hate him.' She spat out the words, unable to stop, not caring what Ryder thought of her in that moment. 'He forced me to choose between good and evil, and evil almost won.' She pushed herself up higher in the bed. 'Do you know how I feel, knowing I have it in me to do that? To just let someone die?'

'Everyone has it in them,' he said quietly, 'if they're pushed far enough.'

'Is that what you thought, when you first saw me in the snow?'

He considered her question, his gaze holding hers so intently she couldn't look away even if she wanted to. 'My first thought was that you'd snapped and killed him in self-defence.'

'I didn't snap,' she retorted. Why was she so furious at everybody? At Benson for asking her to go out there. At the others for not keeping up. At Smythe for almost murdering her and for not dying. And at Ryder. Most of all Ryder, for treating her like a criminal.

'I didn't snap,' she said again. 'I made a cognisant decision to line him up and ram him. I was stopping him from getting away. I was doing it for Libby.' *And for you*, she wanted to say, but he'd learn that over her dead body.

He nodded, seemingly unfazed by her anger. 'Tell me what happened.'

Vanessa took a deep breath and tried to stay calm as she took him through the events. When she finished by telling him of her challenge to Smythe to take on 'a strong woman for a change' she saw a rueful smile tug at the corners of his lips, as though he hadn't expected anything less.

'He drove right at me. That should have been enough for me to let him die, but I could see he was breathing. He was cyanosed around the mouth and on the eyelids, which made me think there might be something going on with his heart. It reminded me of something I'd witnessed overseas.' Needing to do something with her hands, Vanessa straightened the edges of the bedsheet. 'A man, in his fifties, had a massive heart attack on the slopes. Turns out he was the luckiest guy in the world—a cardiologist just happened to be skiing behind him. He stopped and gave the man CPR. Then, he ripped his clothing until the man was naked to the waist. He grabbed a shovel off one of the ski patrollers and covered him in snow. Basically, it simulated the man being put on ice until he could be airlifted to the nearest hospital.' She glanced at Ryder. He was leaning forward, elbows resting on the arms of the chair, hands clasped in front of him. And like the first time he'd interviewed her at the inn, he wasn't taking notes.

'Did he live?' he asked.

'He did. I was so happy for his wife and kids who were there with him. They looked like a nice family.' She gazed into Ryder's eyes, sadness sweeping through her and dampening her anger. 'When you save a life, you want it to be someone worth saving, don't you?'

He didn't say anything, but the sympathy in his eyes brought a lump to her throat.

'I mean, what's to be gained from saving someone like Smythe?' she asked. 'So his wife and children can visit him in prison for the rest of his days?'

'No. So Celia's family and Libby's family have a chance to see justice done. You've given them that. You saved a human life, Vanessa, but it's up to others to decide if he's innocent or guilty, not you.'

'I know.' She winced as pain shot through her temples. 'But he killed my friend. He thought he was killing me. You know what she said to me when she asked if she could sleep on the trundle in my room?' Try as she might, Vanessa couldn't stop her lips from trembling. 'She said, "You're a lifesaver." I can't stop thinking about that. Why couldn't he have just died out there?'

Ryder nodded quietly. 'He would have done a lot of people a favour if he had, including his poor wife.'

The thought of Carmel Smythe drained some of the anger out of her. 'Do you think she had any idea?'

'Probably not.' Ryder shifted in the chair. 'Let me tell you something,' he went on. 'Usually when we interview a spouse, or a friend, or a neighbour of someone who's committed a crime, it's like listening to a song on permanent loop. *You couldn't meet a nicer person*, they say. *It's totally out of character*, they say. *I can't imagine them doing such a thing.* If it's shown me anything, it's that you can never really know someone.'

'Is that why you pulled your gun on me?'

'No. I'd already drawn my firearm. I thought . . . It looked like— well, like you'd witnessed Smythe's death at the very least. I couldn't know the circumstances at a glance.' He sighed. 'Look, people can turn on themselves after they've experienced a trauma like you had.' His voice wavered a little. 'I've been there, Vanessa, I know. That's why I put the handcuffs on you. It was for your own safety.'

'You pointed a loaded gun at me,' she whispered, remembering how she'd stared, disbelieving, into the black, threatening hole in the barrel. 'You were terrifying.'

He ran the tips of his fingers over tired eyes then clasped his hands together again. 'I'm sorry,' he said. 'I didn't want to do it. I don't know what else to say.'

'I can't . . . un-see that.'

He nodded. 'I understand. But, like you told Lew to tell me when you went out there, you were just doing your job. I was doing mine.'

Ryder saw a change in her then, as though his words had cut through the trauma and taken the fight out of her. He worried at the effects of her concussion, and the medication she'd been given for shock.

He saw how she winced every time she turned her head, and he could only imagine the nauseating headache the whiplash would have caused.

Now wasn't the time to tell her of his feelings, or of how scared he'd been for her out there. He was desperate to reconnect with her in some way, but this wasn't about him.

'I know you were just doing your job,' Vanessa said, wearily laying her head back on the pillow. 'I can imagine how bizarre that scene must have looked.'

Ryder took a chance then. 'If you ever doubt yourself, remember you were your best self then, not your worst. You were a sight to behold, standing there soaked in blood and clutching your weapon. You'd fought for your life and you'd won, Vanessa. *I* can't un-see that . . . nor do I want to.' He reached out and offered her his hand, resting it on the bed beside her, palm up.

Before she could take it—or not—the door burst open, and a woman rushed in, a small child perched on her hip. 'Oh, my God, Vanessa! I've been out of my mind with worry.'

Ryder retracted his hand as the anxious woman made a beeline for the bed. He stood up as she set the child down on the floor then leaned over the bed to put her arms around Vanessa. 'Are you all right?'

'It's okay, Eva, settle down. I'm fine.'

'Are you sure?' came the woman's muffled reply.

'I'm sure. I have concussion, bruises and sprained muscles. I'll be out of here before you know it.'

'Oh, thank goodness.' The woman brushed Vanessa's hair back from her face and kissed her forehead. 'Everyone knew Charlotte's was shut down but, when I spoke to you, you insisted you were fine.'

Vanessa caught Ryder's eye, and the woman swung around.

'I'm so sorry,' she said, coming around the bed to greet him. 'I'm Eva. Vanessa's sister.'

He could see the resemblance. She was older than Vanessa by a few years, and quite a bit shorter, but she had the same eyes and the same easy smile.

'Detective Pierce Ryder,' he said, shaking Eva's hand.

'Oh.' She looked him up and down. 'Pleased to meet you, Detective. I hope I haven't interrupted anything.'

'We were just finishing up.'

'I would have been here earlier but I had to organise someone to look after the lodge. It took forever. Then, there was an accident at Bredbo. The drive today took nearly four hours.'

'It's okay, Eva. Don't stress, you know Mum and Dad have been here since I was admitted. They only left half an hour ago.'

'I know. We're all staying at the same hotel.'

'Mummy. I want to get up on the bed and kiss Auntie Nessa.'

Ryder would have given anything to kiss Auntie Nessa too. And he would have given anything to have his daughter back. Conscious of Vanessa's gaze on him, he smiled down at the little girl who was tugging at her mother's jeans, the familiar deep yearning so strong it almost robbed him of breath. The child looked about the same age as Scarlett had been when she'd died.

'This is Poppy,' Eva said, blithely unaware of the tension in the room. 'Say hello, sweetheart.'

The little girl gazed at Ryder with clear blue eyes and twisted a strand of blonde hair around her tiny index finger. 'Hello.'

'Hi there.' Ryder turned to Eva. 'Would you like me to lift her up for you?'

'Oh, thank you. She's getting heavier by the day.' Eva slipped Poppy's Wiggles backpack off her shoulders, then dumped it in the corner. Ryder swung the child into the air then settled her on the bed beside her aunt. Vanessa wrapped her arms around Poppy, and for a few heady seconds both of them were holding her, their hands brushing, their eyes focused on the little girl between them.

'Oh, Poppy.' Vanessa hugged the child close, burying her face in her niece's neck. 'I'm so happy to see you both.'

Ryder slid his hands into his pockets, then pulled them out again, remembering from some course or other that it was a sign a man didn't feel like talking. And he did feel like talking to these two women and the sweet little girl.

'I'll go so you can catch up,' he said, stepping away from the bed. Vanessa looked from him to Poppy and back again, her expression showing concern, as if she were worried about how he might be feeling. It gave Ryder hope. 'As far as the investigation goes, I have everything I need for now,' he said.

By this time, Eva had pulled up a chair on the other side of the bed. She smiled at him. 'It was nice to meet you.'

'Get better soon,' he said to Vanessa, feeling strange that he was leaving without touching her. But even a chaste kiss in front of her sister might be as unwelcome as it was inappropriate.

'Wave goodbye to the detective, Poppy,' Eva said.

The little girl gave him a half-hearted wave. 'Goodbye.'

'Goodbye, little one.'

'What's a de-tect? What did you call him, Mummy?' Poppy demanded as he headed for the door.

'Spend time with your family, Vanessa,' Ryder said over his shoulder. 'It's the best medicine of all.'

Thirty-nine

Three months later
Park City, Utah

There were many things Vanessa loved about Park City Mountain Resort, but at the end of a long shift out on the hill being able to ride the town lift all the way into the main street topped her list. It was a shame, though, that every time the chair glided over the tops of the historic main street buildings, as it was doing now, it led to thoughts of another chairlift.

Pushing those thoughts aside, she raised the safety bar and wriggled onto the edge of the seat. The mercury had dropped steadily in the past hour and, despite the heat pads she had put inside her gloves at lunchtime, her fingers were almost numb. So, it was with great anticipation that she looked forward to a glass of mulled wine in the bar on the other side of the street.

Back on solid ground, she clicked out of her skis then hoisted them onto her shoulder, her footsteps muted by a fresh layer of snow. Light spilled onto the sidewalk, the old silver mining town reminding her of a scene from a thousand Christmas cards. She passed a cute little gallery, and The Egyptian Theatre, where every year the Sundance Film Festival was held. According to local lore, when Hollywood came to town, the streets were lined with Range

Rovers parked bumper to bumper while bodyguards prowled the sidewalks like guard dogs.

Leaving her skis in the racks outside, Vanessa unclipped her helmet then pushed open the heavy door. Sighting Terry at the bar, she zigzagged her way through the crowd until she reached him. 'Hey.'

'Hey.' He swept his gear off the stool he'd been saving for her. 'What're you drinking?'

'Glühwein, thanks.' She unzipped her jacket and slipped it off while Terry ordered her drink from the barman.

'How'd you go out there?' he asked.

'Yeah, fine.' She added her jacket to the growing pile of ski paraphernalia on the floor.

'Weather's a bit brutal, hey?'

'I thought it was me, getting old.' She slid onto the stool, relieved to take the weight off her feet.

'Never. You still up for the rodeo tonight?'

She sighed. 'How long's the drive to Ogden?' It had sounded like a great idea this morning but, after working all day, dinner and bed seemed much more inviting.

'Only an hour. Come *on*. This is a real American rodeo with real American cowboys.'

'Okay,' Vanessa said with another sigh, watching as the barman set a fragrant glass of glühwein in front of her. She picked it up and clinked it against Terry's beer bottle, the warm glass bringing the feeling back into her fingers almost straightaway. 'Cheers.'

'I was getting worried.' Terry nodded at the TV mounted on the wall behind the bar. 'It's nine-thirty Sydney time. I thought you were going to miss it.'

'I thought about bailing.' Vanessa stared at the screen where a media scrum had gathered outside the District Court in Sydney. 'I'm not in any hurry to see Smythe's face again.' But she *was* keen to catch a glimpse of a certain detective she hadn't seen in what felt like forever.

Just then, the breakfast-show host switched to a reporter who was part of the scrum. The crowd around them fell silent as the barman turned up the volume.

'In scenes reminiscent of the OJ Simpson and Oscar Pistorius trials,' the reporter was saying, 'this morning, former Australian skiing champion Aidan Smythe makes his second appearance in the District Court here in Phillip Street. Today he is to be formerly charged with the murder of Celia Miller, née Delaney, who disappeared mysteriously from Charlotte Pass back in 1964. Of course, Smythe has been in court before. Back in August, he was formerly charged with the murder of Libby Marken in July of this year.'

The camera switched back to the breakfast-show host. 'Yes, Emma, like those other high-profile sports cases you mentioned, this one is set to grip the nation, and the world. Do we know if Aidan Smythe has arrived at the courthouse yet?'

'Yes,' the reporter confirmed. 'Approximately five minutes ago a prison van transporting the former ski champion pulled up at a side entrance to the court. Smythe was handcuffed and escorted into the building by prison guards.'

Vanessa braced herself for a glimpse of Smythe as the footage showed the van turning into a narrow street. The tail-lights glowed red and the vehicle came to a stop. The camera switched back to the reporter. Vanessa blew out a relieved breath and glanced at the people around her. Most stood, transfixed, their glasses in hand. Some were shaking their head. The story was the talk of the ski industry, no less here in Utah, where Smythe had won a number of events during the height of his career.

'It looks like it's all happening down there in Phillip Street, Emma,' the breakfast host said.

'There's been a steady procession of people entering the court-house, including Aidan Smythe's wife of more than forty years, and his children, who have flown in from their homes in Canada.'

'There's Ryder,' Terry said suddenly.

A white sedan had pulled into the kerb, its rear doors opening simultaneously. Vanessa didn't recognise the man who climbed out on the roadside, but the tall one who stepped onto the kerb was painfully familiar. Dressed in a dark suit and white shirt, Ryder appeared taller, younger and slimmer on camera, or maybe she'd just got used to seeing him in bulky ski gear. He strode towards the entrance, casually buttoning his suit coat and ignoring the media. For once, his tie was perfectly knotted.

And then the camera switched back to the studio.

'Thank you, Emma. Well, as you can see, there's a lot happening outside the courts. Stay tuned throughout the morning, because we'll be bringing you regular updates on the formal charging of Aidan Smythe.'

Vanessa drained her glass then put it on the bar with a thud.

Terry raised an eyebrow. 'Go again?'

Vanessa hesitated for a a bit. 'Maybe a Russian Mule will thaw me out.'

Terry stared at her for a couple of seconds. 'No offence, but I think the guy we just saw on screen has the best chance of doing that.'

Vanessa gaped at her companion.

Terry bumped his shoulder against hers. 'All I'm saying is that you don't seem to be very happy.'

She stared at the colourful label on his beer bottle. 'I didn't realise it was so obvious.'

'Only to me, because I know you.' He began to rotate the beer bottle between his fingertips. 'Anyway, the good news is you've given me hope.'

Vanessa frowned. 'For what?'

'The future,' he said with a grin. 'That love can happen quickly. I mean, you totally fell for the bloke in less than two weeks. I should be so lucky.'

'I did, didn't I?' she said with a rueful smile. 'He brought me strawberries, too.'

Terry frowned. 'When?'

'In the hospital. He brought them in a little basket all wrapped up with a card. I didn't remember until later that he'd put it on the table. Anyway, it was full of strawberries. I'd told him this story, you see, about something that happened on the farm when I was little. He remembered.'

'Hmm. Well, I realise I don't have to like him, but I do . . . if that helps.'

Vanessa's phone vibrated before she could answer Terry. Sliding off the stool, she fished it from the pocket of her ski pants. Lewicki's name was rolling across the screen. 'It's Lew,' she said to Terry. 'Mind my seat. I'd better take this outside.'

Back in the sub-zero temperature, she sheltered from the icy wind in the doorway of an enchanting Christmas shop, and put the phone to her ear. 'Hello, Lew.'

'How's my favourite ski patroller?'

'Freezing my butt off at the moment. It's five-thirty, and dark already.'

'It's bloody beautiful here in Sydney. I'm thinking of going out to the cricket.'

Vanessa smiled. 'Why aren't you in court?'

'No need for me to be there today. They're only formalising the murder charges. The hearing won't be for ages yet. I was calling you because I wasn't sure you'd know.'

'I'm not climbing K2, Lew. We've been watching it in the bar. Congratulations. You've waited a long time for justice to be done.'

'Ryder did an excellent job getting Bruno to confess, but you were the one who put Smythe on his arse in the end.'

'Well, I feel like it was a team effort.'

'It was. I'm glad I lived long enough to see it, and relieved Celia's parents are still alive and capable of understanding what happened all those years ago.' He gave a weary, heartfelt sigh. A few seconds of silence followed, then: 'Who knew that beneath that wholesome, polished exterior lay a dangerous narcissist, motivated by greed and money.'

'A lot of people in positions of power are narcissists, Lew,' she said, sensing Lewicki needed to talk. 'They step over anyone to get what they what.'

'But most of them don't murder. Smythe did. He was desperate for the fame and adulation that his talent was going to bring him. And his rich wife was his back-up plan. He wasn't going to let Celia ruin that for him.'

'It sounds like you know a lot more about him now,' Vanessa said.

'That we do.'

There was a crackle, and for a moment Vanessa thought the line was going to drop out, then Lew's voice came through the speaker again.

'They're having a proper funeral for Celia soon, now her remains have been released,' Lew said, his voice fading in and out. Vanessa pressed her phone harder against her ear. 'Years ago, after the Coroner's findings, the family had a memorial service, but that finding will be overturned now, and Celia can be properly laid to rest.'

'I'm glad, Lew. I really am. And I bet your wife is happy you can close the book on this chapter of your life, too.'

'She sure is. She's lived this case along with me.'

'Well, I guess that's what you sign up for when you get married.'

There was a long pause.

Vanessa bit her lip. Bugger Lew. He was just waiting for her to ask about Ryder.

'How is he?' she asked tentatively. She'd spoken to Ryder a few times on the phone when she'd been staying at Eva's and at her parents' place, mainly to discuss the case and her testimony. He was back in Sydney then, busy gathering evidence for the police brief supporting the charges against Smythe. As the time drew closer for her to leave the country, his calls had grown less frequent. The last few times it had been Flowers who'd called.

'He's really well, Vanessa.'

Vanessa's heart grew a little lighter. 'He is?'

'Yep. It's like he's finally turned a corner. I think a lot of that is due to you.'

Happy tears pricked the backs of Vanessa's eyes, and she smiled. Ryder was a good, decent man, and she wanted him to be happy. 'Oh, I don't know if I had anything to do with it.'

'You did. That's what he told me, and you know what he's like.'

'Yes, he keeps things close to his chest.'

There was a brief pause, then Lew said, 'Well, he found out who his friends were a long time ago. But the other day he said he realised everyone had forgiven him for the accident that had killed Scarlett—but that it was you who made him realise it was time he forgave himself.'

'Oh, really, that's so great,' Vanessa said thickly, tears slipping from her eyes and freezing on her cheeks. 'I'm happy for him.'

'He told Annie that if he wasn't run off his feet with the preparation for these cases, he'd take leave and go after you.'

Vanessa stood stock still, speechless. Why hadn't Ryder told her this himself? And why had he stopped calling her?

Because you couldn't get past him pointing a gun at you.

Because you told him he terrified you.

A shout of laughter from a group of people on the street made her whirl around. She needed to think, and she couldn't concentrate out here with the cold numbing her mind. And she wasn't sure what Ryder would do if he knew Lewicki was telling her this.

She stared at a cute decoration hanging in the Christmas shop window. It was a moose, wearing skis and a joyous expression. How long had it been since she'd felt such joy at the prospect of skiing? 'Lew, I'm really sorry, I have to get going.'

'Oh, okay.'

'Yes, a few of us are heading into Ogden to watch a rodeo.'

'Sounds like fun. Take care of yourself.'

'I will. You too.'

She ended the call without asking him to say hello to Ryder.

Terry was impatient to go when she got back to the bar. 'Come on, we'll be late,' he said, shrugging on his jacket.

Vanessa swallowed, her throat a little raspy from the tears and the freezing air. 'You know what? I think I'll give it a miss. I've decided to go home.'

He gave her a curious look. 'Okay. Maybe an early night will do you good. I'll see you in the morning, bright-eyed and bushy-tailed, hey?'

Vanessa shook her head. She hated doing this but, in her heart, she knew it was the right thing. 'I'm sorry, Terry. What I meant was, I'm going home—to Australia.'

Forty

Two weeks later
Newcastle

Ryder stood up from the table and carried his empty plate into the kitchen. 'That was fantastic, Mum.'

'It was only a hot breakfast. Here, give me the plate so I can put it in the dishwasher.'

'Thanks.'

'Did I tell you how nice you look?' she asked.

Ryder smiled. His mother was thrilled to have him home so she could look after him for the next few days. He was more than capable of looking after himself, but to deny her the pleasure would be mean-spirited. 'Yes, you have, about three times already.'

'Well, you always look good in a suit, and that's a particularly sharp-looking one.'

Ryder leaned against the gleaming countertop and folded his arms. 'Once the funeral's over, it'll be shorts and T-shirts for the rest of my holiday.'

'You deserve some time off after arresting that awful man.' She hit some buttons and switched on the dishwasher. 'Dad and I have been worried about you.'

'I'm okay now. I'm sorry it's taken me so long to come to stay.'

His mother straightened and wiped her hands on a towel. 'You needed to heal, Pierce. Some people were curious, others well-meaning and a lot downright judgemental. Your father and I understood that.'

His mother was right. He had needed time away, because he hadn't been able to stop the bleeding. Ryder pushed himself off the bench and went to hug his mother. 'What I didn't need was time away from you guys, though. That was a mistake. One of a string I think I've made.' And that included not calling Vanessa and telling her how he felt about her. Instead, he'd let her leave for the States, believing she needed time to come to terms with her own trauma, some of which he had caused.

'You're too hard on yourself, Pierce. I don't know who you take after, but you hold yourself to a higher standard than the rest of us. That's why you're so good at your job.'

'He takes after me.' His father appeared in the kitchen doorway with Bentley. When the beagle saw Ryder, he began straining at the leash, his tail rotating in circles.

'How was your walk?' his mother asked, as Ryder bent down to pat the dog.

'It took a while, between saying hello to a dozen other dogs, and the constant sniffing.' His father grinned at Ryder. 'Not much chance of me working up a sweat, that's for sure.'

'I'll take you on in squash, mate,' Ryder said. 'That'll get your heart rate up.'

'He's a beagle, Bill,' his mother pointed out, ignoring Ryder's challenge. 'What do you expect?'

Ryder left them to it and went to wash his hands in the bathroom, the familiar warmth of his family a tonic for his mind and body. 'I'll be back before lunch,' he told them as he picked up his car keys. 'Lewicki knows the Delaneys better than I do, so he'll go to the wake at the bowling club. I'm coming home.'

He'd done everything in his power to bring closure to the Delaney family. Now, he needed to be here, with his family.

Where he belonged.

Normally, Ryder found funerals excruciating, as every single one transported him back to the hardest thing he'd ever done in his life—carry his own child's coffin. And he'd been dreading this one, not because he'd been the investigating detective, but because the Delaneys had endured a similar kind of hell to his.

But, as he stepped up to the table, a different emotion slammed through him. Excitement, and disbelief. *Vanessa Bell* was written in stylish handwriting in the attendance book, three lines above where his pen was poised ready to add his signature. It couldn't be, could it? Vanessa was thousands of miles away working in Utah. And yet he knew it to be true. He recognised her signature from the statement he'd had her sign at the hospital.

He scrawled his name with an unsteady hand then passed the pen to Lew. Organ music drifted from the direction of the altar, and a sombre-looking man in a black suit handed him a booklet. Ryder entered the church, which was close to full, his eyes searching for Vanessa. And then another attendant was beckoning them forward from halfway down the aisle. He ushered them into one of the pews, the people already seated shifting closer together to make room.

Ryder settled himself on the hard, wooden seat and looked to the front of the church. Celia's polished mahogany coffin stood in front of the altar, draped in pink flowers. In the front row, Eunice Delaney was so small, Ryder could just make out her thinning silver hair. Arnold, it seemed, had been wheeled into the church in a special chair, the two layabout children Eunice had talked of so scathingly sitting either side of him.

'These things were built to be uncomfortable,' muttered Lew, looking at Ryder and shifting in his seat. 'It's to make sure you don't nod off.'

Ryder nodded absently, a memory of the religious artefacts displayed in the Delaney household coming to mind. They could be in for a long service.

Nigel Miller passed their pew. Ryder recognised his thin build and manscaped facial hair. He nudged Lew and nodded at the musician who was joining the family in the front row. 'So, he was innocent after all,' he said.

Lew snorted. 'Yeah . . . but he's still a shit bloke.'

Right then the organ music stopped, and someone up the front requested they all stand for the opening hymn. It was then that Ryder found Vanessa. She was in his direct line of sight only four rows in front. Dressed in a stylish suit in muted tones, her lion's mane of hair was wound into a loose bun and held in place with a tortoiseshell clip.

Ryder's heart swelled, along with the voices raised in song all around him, and he pledged that this time he would not let her go without telling her how he felt.

The service seemed to take forever. There were traditional readings, followed by the heartbreaking eulogies read aloud by Arnold's two sons on behalf of him and Eunice. For decades, they said, Celia's parents feared this day would never come. And yet here they were, with their family, their friends and the community of Stockton who knew their tragic story. Even the police who'd carried out the investigations were present, they said, looking in Ryder and Lewicki's direction, as well as the media who'd reported it over the years. But, most importantly, their daughter's precious body was finally back in their care, and able to be properly laid to rest.

Wishing he was sitting beside Vanessa, who was wiping her eyes, Ryder said a personal prayer for Celia, and then, as he always did, spoke silently to Scarlett. Beside him, Lewicki unfolded a cotton handkerchief, and then the aroma of incense filled the church.

The remainder of the service passed in a blur. The final hymn, the throng of people exiting the church, the hearse pulling away from the kerb. Earlier, one of the attendants had made it clear that Arnold and Eunice were too frail to stand outside the church, but that they were looking forward to seeing everybody at the bowling club.

Ryder told Lew he would catch up with him, and went in search of Vanessa. He came to a halt when he found her at the side of the church, standing in the shade of a large liquid amber. He rested his hands on his hips, looked away for a few moments while he gathered himself, then took a deep breath and walked slowly towards her.

She smiled at him. The first genuine smile he'd seen from her since their last night together at Charlotte Pass. 'Hello, Pierce.'

'Hello,' he managed to say. 'I couldn't believe it when I saw you. I thought you were still in Utah.'

'I slipped into the country about a week ago. I saw you going into court on the TV. How's everything going with the investigation?'

'Murder trials are always a long process, but we have a strong case.'

She smiled. 'That's good.'

'Obviously I can't tell you specifics because you're a witness, but I can tell you that it was Bruno who orchestrated the Winterfest celebrations. He convinced the Gordons that it would good for business to bring the former champion back. He even suggested the run under the old chairlift would make a good slope for tubing. His aim was to expose Smythe without implicating himself, but that was never going to happen. He was always going to slip up.'

She shook her head slowly. 'Who would have thought?'

'I know. It's incredible.' Ryder took a step closer and smiled at her. 'What's more incredible is that you're here. I'm so surprised. Surprised and delighted,' he added quickly.

'Really?' Her eyes searched his face, her fingers sliding the silver snowflake she wore around her neck, back and forth on its chain.

'Yes, really. There's so much I want to say to you. So much I should have said before you left. I'm sorry, Vanessa.'

'It's okay,' she said quickly, her eyes soft. 'I wasn't ready to hear it then.'

Hope flared in Ryder's heart. He had to know one way or another if he still had a chance. 'So, I haven't totally blown it, then?'

'No. You were right to give me time. I had a lot to come to terms with. This is hard for me to say, but I started seeing someone over in America.'

The ground seemed to disappear beneath Ryder's feet, disappointment robbing him of breath like a punch in the guts. Of all the things he'd expected her to say, telling him she had a boyfriend was bottom of the list. He swallowed, steeling himself for what was to come.

'I thought I may as well.' A pink colour stained her cheeks and she waved an airy hand. 'You know how big they are on therapy over there? I thought, why not take advantage of it?'

Sudden relief drained Ryder of energy. All he wanted to do was pull her into his arms and never let her go. He knew it now. She was the one. He couldn't believe he'd been so blind.

'I didn't know it at the time,' she was saying, 'but I was suffering survivor's guilt over Libby's death, and I was having trouble coming to terms with the fact that I considered leaving Smythe to die before I actually helped him.'

'But when it came down to it, you didn't cross that line.'

'No. That's exactly what the therapist said.'

'I'm glad you saw someone. It was the smart thing to do.' He stepped closer and lowered his voice, unable to hold the words inside him any longer. 'Look, Vanessa, I know I haven't made this clear, but I've totally fallen for you, fallen in love, probably for the first time ever.' He held up a hand as she went to speak. 'I know this isn't the place, but I need some indication of how you feel, because I'm going nuts here.'

She nodded, her eyes filling with tears.

Ryder didn't know whether that was a good sign or not, so he pressed on. 'Do you remember what you said to me at Charlotte Pass after I told you about Scarlett? You told me that if I ever wanted to make room for someone in my life, not to forget you. Well, here I am, telling you I want to make room.'

She nodded. 'Of course I remember what I said. Why do you think I'm here?'

Before he had a chance to answer, she went on. 'I'm here because it was important for me to farewell Celia properly. I went to Libby's funeral before I left, but she . . . Celia . . . she had such an impact on my life.' Her voice sank to a whisper. 'If it wasn't for her death, you would never have come to Charlotte Pass. I might never have met you.'

Only then did Ryder smile. He stepped closer and took her in his arms, his body humming with the strength of his love for her. She rested her head on his shoulder, and he closed his eyes and inhaled the sweet perfume of her hair. 'Just so you know,' he murmured, 'there's not a chance in this world I'm ever going to forget you.'

'How are we going to do this?' she asked.

'Let's not worry about that now.'

'Well, Mum and Dad don't need me on the farm for a couple of years,' she said, her cheek resting against the lapel of his suit. 'And I'm ready for a warmer climate. I can find a job and thaw out in the big smoke for a while.'

Ryder tightened his arms around her. 'Thank you,' he said, feeling her relax against him as the tension left her body. 'We can work the rest out when the time comes. Who knows, I might go back in uniform, seeing you like them so much, and apply for a transfer out west.'

'You'd do that for me?' she raised her head and looked him in his eyes.

'I'm not making empty promises, Vanessa. I love you.'

'I love you, too,' she whispered, reaching up and caressing his cheek.

In the dappled sunlight shining through the leaves of the liquid amber, Ryder drew her to him again and closed his eyes. He saw Celia in a shift dress and long white gloves, then Libby surrounded by noisy children.

Then finally, like he always did, he saw Scarlett.

She was standing there, looking at them both, and smiling.

Acknowledgements

Thank you to the 'Dream Team' who have been with me throughout the writing of this book. Vanessa Hardy, for lending me your archaeological notes on bones, Nicole Deanne Webb and Kristine Thomas for your invaluable feedback and scintillating company. And to Bernadette Foley, for running the Wednesday workshops, and for having so much faith in my story she agreed to act as my agent.

To my friend, thank you for your time and patience in answering my numerous questions. Your knowledge in helping me understand police procedure and the chain of command was invaluable.

Many thanks go to Annette Barlow and the amazing editors at Allen & Unwin for their hard work and professionalism in making this book the very best it can be.

To the staff at the Thredbo Museum, for their help and assistance during my research visit. I recall my delight in finding one of the cabs from the ill-fated chairlift sitting in the corner.

Endless thanks to my husband, who makes me copious cups of tea and patiently listens while I read out paragraphs of text and ask if it sounds right. To my daughter, a former ski instructor whose knowledge of skiing technique was vital for the character of Vanessa. And to my son, who through his own writing, is a constant source of inspiration to me.

And lastly, to Charlotte Pass, a unique and magical village of historical significance located high in the New South Wales Snowy Mountains. The unszurpassed beauty and magnetic pull of this tiny village provided me with constant inspiration for the creation of this novel.